Praise for *Meetings at the Metaphor Café*

"Oft-quoted American scholar and eternal optimist, William Arthur Ward once said, 'The mediocre teacher tells. The good teacher explains. The superior teacher demonstrates. The great teacher inspires.' We have found in *Meetings at the Metaphor Café* a great teacher, Mr. Buscotti. The descriptions of Mr. B's and Ms. Anderson's curriculum is enough to make anyone want to go back to school, re-read old favorites like *To Kill A Mockingbird* or at the very least, listen to some Bruce Springsteen! Every student deserves at least one teacher like this—a teacher who is passionate about the world we live in and determined to light a fire in each child. This debut novel rings with authenticity. This book is a must for anyone looking for a little meaning and a lot of inspiration, whether you are a new teacher or a lifelong student."

-BaBette Davidson, Vice President, Programming for Public Television, PBS

"If you are an English teacher—particularly American literature—you would want to read this novel right along with your students. *Meetings at the Metaphor Café* will challenge the minds and hearts of teenagers everywhere."

-Bruce Gevirtzman, author of *An Intimate Understanding of America's Teenagers*

"Robert Pacilio's novel works on many levels. The reader meets the main characters and is drawn into their stories, forming a literary friendship he doesn't want to end. It's enlightening—an open window into the teenage soul. Teachers reading it will be educated; it's an entertaining, engaging clinic on curriculum rigor, relevance and relationships. *Meetings at the Metaphor Café* should be required reading for teenagers and their parents."

-Linda Vanderveen, Board of Education Member, Poway Unified School District

"Maddie, Mickey, Rhia, and Pari are so real I actually can *see* them sitting in any classroom. Students will relate to their diverse life experiences and their common bond of needing to make sense of it all. They will see parts of themselves in the characters and feel that the diaries are a true window into the sometimes confusing journey through high school life. Teachers will be challenged and inspired by Mr. Buscotti's brilliant example of one way to be a responsible and caring guide on that journey."

-Linda Englund, Ed.D., A.P. English Teacher

"Meetings at the Metaphor Café reads like an invitation—an invitation to sit down amongst its characters and relive your youth. With the turn of every page, you are transported back to a time when the world was new to you, sitting among friends, sipping a latte, discussing love and the meaning of things, and discovering life all over again like it was the first time. Along with the characters, the readers are sent on a journey towards rediscovering themselves and reconnecting with what really matters at the heart of who they are. All the while, the book reads like a who's who and what's what of the 20th century. As a teacher, I can say that this book is a MUST read for any high school English or history class. *Meetings at the Metaphor Café* should be in the hands of every teenager in America, and those of anyone who once was one!"

-Danielle Galluccio, Trinity Montessori School, Adolescent Academy Director

"I have to tell you how much I wanted to be in Bob Pacilio's class. I wanted to write the assignments; I wanted to sit in on the lessons; I wanted to 'Begin the Beguine' (a personal favorite!). I hope [this] book inspires other teachers to create a dynamic learning environment for their own students that will allow them to think about 'big' ideas."

-Chris Evans, Poway Unified School District's "Teacher of the Year"

"I thoroughly enjoyed this book. Mr. Pacilio inspires the reader to be a better person and gives us faith in our new generation of youth. The take-home messages, however, engage a much wider audience and offer life lessons that build resilience and encourage a positive outlook on life, encouraging both youth and adults to make a difference in our society. This book is a must read for students, educators, and all the people who believe in positive change."

-Michele Einspar, Director, Transformative Inquiry Design for Effective Schools

"Not only did I enjoy *Meetings at the Metaphor Café* very much, but I learned so much about what is possible when it comes to turning a classroom into an experience. My students are captivated by the book and have transformed into more caring people, thoughtful and responsive."

-Kristen Gall, 8th Grade Teacher Tierra Del Sol Middle School, Lakeside, California

"This is a wonderful book and should be required reading for all history and English teachers. I hope that many read it and in some way recognize parts of themselves and once again relive those magical moments."

-Bill Orton, District Director of High School Counseling

"This book was great to read for many reasons. This glimpse into this junior experience is very special. This book made me reflect on my high school English years. I wish I had teachers like Bob Pacilio (aka Mr. Buscotti). I rarely read anything that made a difference in my life or connected to me with any relevance. Thank you for putting the perspective back into the joy of discovering these books. I have never read anything like it, with the mix of music, classic literature, and fiction."

-Victoria Stewart, AP Math Teacher

Letters on the Wall of the Metaphor Café

"I just crushed through the book. It was incredible. I found that I didn't connect so much with just one individual...more of like a blend of all of them. I think that any person who went through high school can discover themselves in some combination of the four...like how you can create any color from red, blue, and yellow."

-Vince Rogers, graduate of the real "Metaphor Café" 1999

"Everyone has a unique lens through which they view life, but Bob Pacilio's is truly special, an insight to which we may never have access. Without a doubt, life-changing!"

-Tony Daher, graduate of the real "Metaphor Café" 2003

"I loved it! It will draw out those sweet memories of our innocent time as young eager minds in that amazing classroom."

-Dylan Cannon, graduate of real "Metaphor Café" 1998

"I really enjoyed it. I was most impressed with how utterly realistic the high school students were, the way Pacilio was able to recreate their thoughts, feelings, and the ways they express themselves. I found myself learning all over again lessons about literature… and life."

-Robert Harkins, graduate of the real "Metaphor Café" 1987

"I see a little bit of myself and the 60 or so other students I shared that year with...it's so universal to what we go through as teenagers, but the experience in the class was one of a kind. I saw faces and got chills. Beautifully written!"

-Hassey Gascar, graduate of the real "Metaphor Café" 2004

"I can say with full honesty that some of the best days of my life were spent in Bob Pacilio's class… *Meetings at the Metaphor Café* reminded me of those vital times in a way far more profound than I had anticipated. I gladly join the choir of happy Metaphor Café patrons singing its praises."

-Ross Cooper, graduate of the real "Metaphor Café" 2004

"Drifting down memory lane while reading Bob Pacilio's *Meetings at the Metaphor Café*. Get it, read it, you'll love it, and will be changed!"

-Shelly Webb, graduate of the real "Metaphor Café" 2008

"The ability to see inside a high school teenager's mind is a rare experience that you may not ever have an opportunity to do. *Meetings at the Metaphor Café* allows you to gain a sense of awareness and understanding of the world around you and the lives of others. A mind opener—a definite page turner!"

-Shabnam Habib, graduate of the real "Metaphor Café" 2010

"If you have a child in high school or middle school, please give your child this book. They will be able to see things from a peer's point of view, and hopefully it will make a huge impression on them."

-Heather Daiss, graduate of the real "Metaphor Café" 1988

"Bob Pacilio has written such an enthralling and just incredible book. So thank you, 'Oh captain, my captain.'"

-Samantha Nothdurft, graduate of the real "Metaphor Café" 2010

"I specifically wanted to mention that had I not read it myself, I would never have believed it possible to convey the power of Mr. Pacilio's 9-11 lecture in text form. Perhaps I have a skewed perspective after having been through his class and being familiar with his style of… whatever it is Pacilio does up there—'teaching,' 'lecturing,' 'presenting,' … somehow every conceivable verb that could describe what Bob Pacilio does falls miles short of the reality of the experience, and I'm loathe to cheapen his talent with an inept description."

-Dan Roach, graduate of the real "Metaphor Café" 2002

Other Works by Robert Pacilio

Meetings at the Metaphor Café

Whitewash, a readers theater

Seventeen, a play

"The Kiss," a short story

"The Secrets of Generation NeXt," published in *Listen* Magazine

"La Petite Café at Midnight New Year's Eve," one of *Creative Communication's* Top Ten Poems by American Teachers

Midnight Comes
to the
Metaphor Café

Robert Pacilio

Dedicated to my loving wife, Pam

Whose patience and selflessness make her

Without question the heroine of my novel.

"Atticus was right. One time he said you never really know a man until you stand in his shoes and walk around in them."

— Jean Louise Finch, otherwise known as Scout

From Harper Lee's *To Kill a Mockingbird*

Prologue: Thanksgiving...again

Madison's Hand

November 20th

We couldn't help ourselves. Okay, I pushed them a little. But after we wrote *Meetings at the Metaphor Café* and Mr. Buscotti and Ms. Anderson loved it so much, we were just so...so...I don't know... We were bursting with pride and, well, we just felt like writers, real writers. Mr. Buscotti then showed us how to self-publish the book so that our friends and families could read it, and now, after the summer and halfway through fall, we have lost track of how many copies we have sold. Anyway, we just got in the habit of writing. We would write about what just happened and send it to each other as the summer blew past. As Mickey started putting it together, so many of our friends (dare I say "fans") wanted to know what we thought about and how we were gonna get through our senior year that, well, like I said, we couldn't help ourselves.

So we begin again...on my 18th birthday. (And now I can vote!)

Okay, here's the deal. You know how Mark Twain began *The Adventures of Huckleberry Finn*? Well, he started by reminding us about what happened in *Tom Sawyer*— about the money they had found and all that. Yeah, well, since Mr. Buscotti taught us that book last year, this year we figured we would—like Twain—remind folks where the journey started.

There are four of us. Rhia, Pari, Mickey, and me. I got us started last year when I was sitting at home depressed about school starting. School starting is still depressing for many reasons. Getting up, as my father says, "at o-dark-thirty" is just one of the many jarring things that happen to all of us. But daughters of former military commanders aren't supposed to complain—yeah right. Anyway, then there is the pressure. Everyone was supposed to have a great summer, and we're all supposed to look tan, thin, and beautiful. And we're supposed to know what we are going to do with our lives. College looms over us like the big ticking clock in Cinderella. It's almost midnight, and if we don't know what we're gonna do, where we're gonna go to college, *if* we're gonna go to college, *how* we're gonna afford college—yikes! It's the shadow that follows us.

Teachers ask us what our plans are for next year—heck, it's still *this year*. Parents keep bugging us, asking if we've filled out this form, applied for that scholarship, figured out when, if, how, why, where we want to "visit" so that we can get a "feel" for our new home away from home. And if we really like it—well, we can't afford it. And if we don't know what we really think because we're so overwhelmed with it all— then we just sit around and have a bowl of ice cream and stare at a movie—like I am now—and wonder how the movies of our lives are gonna turn out.

So, I rented *To Sir, With Love* again. I just get sentimental about that movie. It was the one I saw a year ago when I got the idea to write this book with my friends. I cry at the ending when Lulu sings about all that "Sir" has done for her. Yeah, I know the movie has its corny parts, but when the teacher—Mr. Thackeray—when his eyes fill up with tears because his students mean so much to him—well, it just gets me.

So I am fondly sitting here, wishing I had another year with Mr. Buscotti. I miss him. We all do. He and Ms. Anderson were the inspiration for our book. They co-taught our American Literature and U.S. History classes. We were a "village," they said. We wanted to thank them for all they taught us—about finding our North Star, about how "you don't know where you are going until you know where you have been," about how the Metaphor Café is a state of mind, and if we keep our minds open, then whether the skies are blue or black—we will never be lost.

The four of us would meet at the Metaphor Café, an old coffee house, and we would talk about the class, the books and stories we read, and all the fun things we did—like dancing. It was an escape from everything, you know. But sadly, the owner, Mr. Davidson, told us he had to close down the old place unless he found a buyer. He needed to retire and travel with his wife. It stayed closed until Halloween, when a younger couple re-opened it and decided to continue calling it the Metaphor Café—yes! It is more modern now; on weekends, there is guitar music—if that's what you want to call it. And I hear there are gonna be poetry readings and stuff. It's a great place to chill, and it helped push us to put this novel together. It just seemed like the stars were aligning, you know?

Yeah.

So, it's Thanksgiving and we figured we would get you caught up on last summer first. Mr. Buscotti calls this a *flashback*. Actually, we were separated a lot in the summer, so it took a while for us to write it all and for Mickey to put it together. I guess I should tell you a bit about us first. Mickey is such a sweet guy. We have been dating for a while now. He has long brown hair, and he was named after Mickey Mantle—or so his father tells him. Mickey plays baseball and is a pitcher. We all think he is the best writer of all of us. He had some issues (and still does) with his parents, who are kinda conservative (but I think they are very kind, really), and he just doesn't see eye to eye with his dad, who wants him to be some serious business major. His folks are pretty well off—not rich, though. I don't know what he's gonna do when he has to decide about college. Oh, and he's left handed.

Rhia and I have been close for the longest time. I love her. She's fun and crazy, and she's willing to stand up to anyone and anything. I guess she's tough—but that's on the outside. Inside, she is the kindest, most caring person my age who I know. Her brother, Chris, is—or, *was*—in special education last year, when he graduated. Rhia is very protective of him, and because of him, she was the president of Best Buddies at our school last year. Best Buddies is an organization that links "sped" kids with "regular ed" kids so that they feel like they're a part of the school, too. Rhia's family life is kinda hard—it has been since her father left them—her mom and Chris—and he doesn't help too much with money, I guess. You don't want to be around Rhia when she has just had to deal with her dad. One last thing—Mr. B nailed it when he was kidding her one day. He said something like, "Rhia wins our Stevie Nicks look-alike award." Mr. B cracked himself up, but it was funny because we had no idea who he was talking about. So naturally, we got home and Googled Stevie Nicks and saw the videos from the 80s in which she sings with Fleetwood Mac. I love her version of "Landslide." Well, Mr. B was right—Rhia does dress like her, all gypsy-like. Her big thing is to go bargain hunting at thrift stores. Come to think of it, sometimes her life is like a landslide.

Yeah.

Pari blows me away. You know, I didn't know her at all when last year began, and she told me that she used to be intimidated by me. Me! She said that she thought I was such a leader and spoke up all the time, and she is so quiet and behind the scenes. Well, let me tell you, that girl has changed! She is so smart and so thoughtful. She is Persian—that means her family is from Iran, but she was born in San Francisco. She has gorgeous black hair, and she has danced all her life—she looks like a ballerina. Did I mention she was smart? Yeah, well, she is *scary* smart. She takes math and science classes that I can't even spell. And she had the most amazing summer—she'll tell you about it—because it changed her life. She went back to Iran. Oh, and she started taking French, as a senior, which we all think is very interesting.

And then there's me. Former Navy brat. My dad retired last year after 25 years. He was in Operation Desert Storm and Operation Iraqi Freedom. Now he's dealing with Operation Get Used to Being a Stay at Home Dad. He is still looking for a full-time job—which makes me so angry. He sacrificed so much for our country, and when he gets out of the service, there are no jobs. He has his pension, so we're getting along, but my dad can't stand not having a "mission."

I guess I am my father's daughter. This book is part of my mission. I am the oldest of three, and I have no idea what I "want to be when I grow up"—but I am so happy that I am Mr. Buscotti's TA (teaching assistant). I am with him every day as he teaches what he calls "his little freshman." He inspires me every day.

Maybe the reason I love *To Sir, With Love* so much is because I love what teachers do. Mr. B once said, "I am in the Kid Business." I love children, too. I love that feeling when you *get* something in a class and you suddenly realize *why* a thing has happened or is happening or is likely to happen. My favorite day of all last year was when we gave Mr. B and Ms. Anderson a gift at the end of the year. Mickey made this great speech and all 70 of us burst into applause. Ms. Anderson got all emotional and choked up, but as usual, she said something profound. But Mr. B just could not talk. It wasn't that he was speechless, really— he just could not say anything without completely losing his composure—and that was something he just did not want his students to see, I guess. But his silence spoke to us. I know he has received tons of gifts from his students before, but something about that moment just overcame him and me. All of us, really.

It must have been something we said…or wrote in a corner of the Metaphor Café.

Summer

2008

Chapter 1: An American Girl in a Persian World

Pari's Hand

July 1st

At midnight, our plane touched down on Persian soil. I know that sounds odd to Americans, but to me and the family members I would be visiting—we are Persians. The airplane cruised around the Tehran airport in Iran, but I knew that this beautiful, metropolitan city had its origin in ancient cities like Petropolis when Cyrus the Great created the Persian Empire.

Some of this I knew when I landed—some I came to better understand when I left.

Vacations. How does the expression go? It was the best of times; it was the worst of times. How true. There was a time when I cried because I did not want to come back to Iran. Not because I did not want to see my family, whom I had not seen since eighth grade. Not because I had some American notion that I would be kidnapped by terrorists—no. I simply did not want to come because of the two most important words to any 17-year-old: my friends.

I missed Rhia and Maddie and Mickey so much that I insisted that they *not* come over to my house the night before I left for Iran with my mother. But they came anyway. Do you know that terrible lump you get in your throat when you feel something so much, but you try to hold it in? Well, that is me. I hold things in. But that night, holding it in just did not work so well. I was just so torn and maybe scared, too. I had worked so hard at being one of them—accepted for who I am and what I believe and being part of something bigger than myself. The

Metaphor Café. Mr. Buscotti. How he taught me to love my life. I was afraid my time away would make me feel alone again. Disconnected.

They would be at the beach. The movies. Cafés. Parties. Getting ready for senior year. Getting a summer job. I don't know...they would be hanging out, and I would be worlds away. I would be the outsider again. But this time, I would be an American girl in a Persian world.

And then there was Dan. I had recently started calling him Daniel. He called me Parivesh. After going to the Prom together, we went out several times. And much to my surprise, my father did not make anything of the fact that Daniel was not Persian. Instead, he made it obvious that he liked him. My mother thought he was cute. He is. Really cute. Ironically (Mr. B would love that I am using a literary term here!), Daniel is the one who is foreign. He was born in France and speaks French fluently. I have been trying to learn some French ever since I met him. On our last date before I left for Iran, he took me to dinner at this very cool French restaurant called Le Petite Café downtown. It was so romantic.

So anyway, I was a mess when I was getting ready to leave for Iran. But then again, I cried when I left Iran and all I had come to experience of family, traditions, and, of course, Persian food. I think, for now, I am all cried out.

Naturally, before I left, Rhia set me straight She looked at me and said, "Pari, shut up. You are going on vacation. I am going to work at the friggin' Yummy Yogurt shop. Are you crazy? I would kill to switch places!" Leave it to Rhia to knock some sense into my privileged life.

On the plane, my iPod was my constant companion. Coldplay's "Viva la Vida" was running through my mind. Was it a mere coincidence that the song's theme (again, Mr. B would be proud!) talked about how some king used to rule the world, but now he's dead—how revolutionaries knew that he was a puppet and wanted his head? I could not help but think of the revolution that caused my parents to flee Iran in the 1970s. The Shah of Iran was a corrupt tool of the United States. But the Islamic revolt and the rise of the Ayatollah Khomeini started this insane regime that now controls Iran with a fear that comes from religious extremism and intolerance, which Iran has never seen before. But as I was to discover, there is no way to stereotype Iran—or America, for that matter.

Arab or Persian. Rich or poor. City or country. Soldier or student. Muslim or Christian or Jewish—or, for that matter, not religious at all. There were things I knew before I came here again. But those were the things my parents discussed with me or the slanted view of the media in America, a country that had a President who called Iran "I-RAN," as if it was part of his workout that day. (Okay, just for clarity, it is pronounced *E-ron*). I wanted firsthand knowledge, and the funny thing is that controversy was something I had to force myself to think about during my stay because in truth, I was embraced by my generous, loving, wonderful family, who wanted to know about me and my world far more than I had imagined. They taught me about the word *tarouf.* There is no English translation for the word, but it means to do everything for your guest's pleasure. And I was treated like a princess— a Persian princess, even though I was born in San Francisco.

However, the harsh reality did hit as we went through airport security. I stayed tight to my mother. I felt the harsh gaze of the guards, who had their weapons drawn. They made American TSA personnel look so tame. I went to Iran with only my mother; if my brothers had come, they would have been forced into military service because they were born there. My father had to stay home and work in his business.

We were to attend the wedding of one of my cousins in Isfahan. It's funny, but when I was here four years ago, I was really just a child. I paid little attention to anything but my cousins, aunts, and uncles. We did not travel very much. Everyone came to us—some came great distances to see us. My father was with us that trip, and I remember him discussing politics with other hushed voices downstairs. There is only one thing I remember my father saying to me afterwards about all that: "Pari, we must be very careful. It is not our place to criticize the way things are here; that would make it seem as if we are insulting our family."

There are times when my father reminds me so much of my favorite character in literature: Atticus Finch, who famously claims that you never know someone until you step into their shoes and walk around for a while in them. My father understood this, and I was to walk many miles over many streets in many neighborhoods in a land that once conquered much of the world…but that somehow had been reduced to a third world nation.

July 4th

Independence Day. Right now, my friends are watching fireworks and patriotically celebrating the liberty we take for granted. Here in Tehran, I am almost exactly on the opposite side of the planet, but my cousins, aunts, and uncles are celebrating our arrival with as much joy and as many festivities. Although there are no fireworks, there is so much food being pushed on me that I am likely to explode!

I have turned into an American celeb. My cousins Marjan and Roya want to know about Lady Gaga, rap, Fergie, Eminem, Vans, and shopping! I am blown away by their desire to know everything American or European. It is surprising to me how much English is spoken. My cousins tell me that 70% of the people in Tehran are under age 35, and American culture is all the rage. They bombard me with questions about material things: "What, no expensive Coach purse, Pari? How come? No car? How come?" Marjan, Roya, and my other family members want to see the "riches of America."

Everyone gets gifts from us—aunts, uncles, and cousins. I don't know when or how my mother got all this stuff, but she has something for all the family members. They are very aware of what is made in America—or at least bought there. Roya, who is a year older than me and seems a bit more sure of herself with me than Marjan is, told me an interesting story, which set the tone for what I discovered was something that I have to call *Persian vanity.*

She explained that she once received a beautiful silk blouse with a Pakistani label as a gift. Roya said, "I couldn't throw it away, so I gave it to the poor." I saw in her and so many other Persians I met a very materialistic side. I also noticed that my cousins seemed to view the people of other Arab nations as less than them. But this may have been just their immaturity because I didn't pick up that conceitedness from my uncles and aunts. Strange.

The surprises did not stop with attitudes. The reality of Persian life in Tehran became clear as conversations turned to where I would go to university next year as opposed to where they were heading. Here is where the American media misleads people. My cousins told me that 60% of university students are girls, and they thought that was a conservative estimate. I was shocked. I thought of Iran as a place where women were second class, under a man's thumb (or fist), and clouded in dull garments that covered every inch of their skin. I thought that same oppressive fog spread to their minds because they were prohibited from becoming serious students. I found myself saying to my cousins, *"Really?"*

Of course, that isn't to say that Persian women do not appear to be suppressed. When we were out, we wore a headscarf called a *roo-sari* (which literally translates to *head cover*) with part of our hair showing. Some Persian women wear an overcoat called a *manteau*, but it is the tightest fitting jacket imaginable. No skin showing, no shorts allowed, just hands. We wore jeans (my cousins wore expensive ones), and definitely no capris. As a matter of fact, at the airport, I saw a lady wearing capris; another woman ran up to her and told her to change quickly before she got arrested. The fear in both their eyes was something that I would not soon forget.

Despite all that, Persian women are beautiful; they have to look perfect with dyed hair and polished nails. They live in a very materialistic society, which brings me to the Persian nose story. When

Roya told me that she was considering a nose job, I said, "What?! Why would you do that? Are you nuts? Who wants their nose broken and all that plastic surgery? Roya, your nose is fine—you are gorgeous."

"Pari, everyone gets some work done—especially noses. Mine is too big."

"No, it's not."

"Yes, it is. Nose jobs are no big deal here. It is like getting your teeth straightened. It probably costs less," Roya laughed.

I soon learned what she was talking about. There is a documentary called *My Persian Nose* by Mehrdad Oskouei, who thinks that nose jobs are an epidemic in modern Iran. Did you know that Iran is the *world leader* in cosmetic surgery, with somewhere around 60,000 to 70,000 operations each year?! I was blown away by that statistic. Despite the fact that the so-called "leaders" of Iran hate America and Western culture in general, the young people can't wait to change their noses so that they can look like the models in American and European fashion magazines.

Then Roya said something that, when I think about it, is so idiotic, but so funny: "But you don't have to worry, Pari, because you were born in America and your nose is perfect."

Yeah right. Once my parents came to America, my DNA automatically got better. Right. That gives Independence Day a whole new meaning—at least to Roya. I decided right then that I would not stick my nose into her business.

July 10th

Road trip. My mother wanted me to see the extended family that lived out in the Kermon province, where I discovered a huge difference from the big cities like Tehran. But our "tour" would also take us to breathtaking places that I either had not seen or simply did not appreciate when I was younger. Appreciation would become the theme of this trip.

The road trip's first stop was the Azadi Tower, which is part of the Azadi Square. It is the symbol of Tehran and was built in 1971 in commemoration of the 2,500th anniversary of the Persian Empire. It used to be called the *Shahyad* Tower, meaning *Remembrance of the Shahs (Kings)*, but it was renamed *Azadi*, meaning *freedom*, after the Iranian Revolution of 1979, when my parents fled Iran in what is known as the Iranian *diaspora*, which is a term used when people of one ethnic group are forced out of their homeland. Anyway, the Azadi Tower is considered the "Gateway into Iran," and as a guidebook said, "It is intended to remind coming generations of the achievements of modern Iran." It is 148 feet tall and completely made of marble. It is stunning, and its design seems to be a metaphor for strength—unlike the Eiffel Tower in Paris, which, to me, shows France's elegance. I could have spent hours there, but you know mothers. Off we went from one extreme to the next.

The next stop was Kermon, a province in Iran where some of my relatives lived. They did not live in the city itself, but in the outskirts, where things were, shall I say, a bit more rural. These relatives were my father's family members, who stayed in the country when he went to university. Things were so different in Kermon. Tehran was jammed with people who seemed to feel superior to others. There was an edge to them. Where these relatives lived, the homes were made of wood and outlined in clay. There was a hole in the floor that was essentially the bathroom. The most important rooms were the kitchen and the dining room, where everyone spent their time, eating and talking and laughing. The food was incredible. Fresh. Grown right there or sold at the bazaar, the shopping center in town. I am going to have to work out and diet when I get home!

Although my family in Kermon was well off by rural standards, the poor were visible in ways that shocked me. For example, some people's poverty meant that their children never attended school. The children from families who were better off went to school, but 7-, 8-, and 9-year-olds worked at bazaars for money to pay for their books.

My family in Kermon was more conservative. My female cousins were more…shall I say…modest. All the fashionista attitude that was in Tehran was just not there. Sure, my cousins asked me a million questions about boys in America: were they more like gangstas, like Eminem, or more like the Jonas brothers? (Yuck.) They asked if I was going to a big, fancy college like UCLA, and they told me how difficult the tests were for them to get into university. I asked, "If it's that hard, how do kids get in?"

My cousin Bahar, who was exactly my age and, frankly, the most gorgeous of all my cousins, told me, "The rich go to private schools because they have money to afford it, even if they don't do well on the tests. For us, the hardest part is the tests, Pari. They are so hard that you have to be, like, brilliant to pass them." She looked down when she said this, and I knew what that meant—for her. Her eyelashes and the exotic quality that radiated from her made me jealous in a strange way. She was the personification of Persian beauty—but with little or no makeup at all.

"Honestly, Bahar, it is very much like that in the States," I said. "Really. If you have lots of money, you can go to USC or one of the smaller, private schools, like—"

"Like Duke or Harvard," she insisted. "Will you go there?"

"Bahar, no way. I am not smart enough or rich enough."

"You are too. Parivesh, my father tells me about you. He says, 'Anwar's daughter Parivesh is the smartest in all the families.' So there. And you must have money. Your father has his own business."

I blushed. "No, that is not true. He has business partners. And I am not like that. I just try hard in school."

"And you have a boyfriend?" Bahar seemed confident.

"Okay, well, sort of, but we…"

"What is his name? Is he Persian? Do your parents approve? Do you see him away from your home?" Bahar's questions were a jumble of excitement and curiosity; she was ready to explode. The crazy thing was that in America, Bahar would have had boys fighting over her. One thing that struck me was that my other cousins, Roya and Marjan, had asked me some if not all of these same questions, but Bahar *really wanted to know.* Not because she wanted to compare our lives, but just because. *Just because.* It was a quality I liked about all my family members in Kermon. They were so nice, and they didn't care about what they needed or what they wanted or what might inconvenience them. They just wanted you to be their *guest* and to understand what loving, caring people they were.

The same could be said for other people in Kermon. Like when my mother and I got lost trying to find our family's house. My mother was stopped, and she asked the taxi driver in the car next to ours for directions. He got out and told her to follow his taxi. He said it would be his pleasure to show us where our family lived. And we were, like, really, *really* lost. So, he drove and drove and we followed and followed. And when we got there, my mother insisted that he accept some money for going so far out of his way. But he would not take it. He was so stubborn; he insisted that this was his job—to help visitors to his city. Can you imagine a taxi driver doing that in America?

And that is how people are in Iran. The government is corrupt, but the people are so nice, and they look after you. Dinner for my family was at 10:00 PM. We ate; then the aunts said, "Have more. You eat first." And they were as stubborn as the taxi driver. But at dinner, I noticed that we did not go into politics much; my family members seemed indifferent. My uncle said, "We are ashamed that people think we are terrorists." And with that, he too lowered his head. And I knew what that meant—for him.

July 12th

Wedding bells. The final two stops on my tour were Tabriz, the city of the Azaris, and Isfahan, the most elegant city of all those I had seen, where the wedding was to be held. But I must tell you that Tabriz simply took my breath away. The city is a mixture of ultramodern and stunningly ancient. It was on numerous occasions the political capital of Iran, but now it seems to be the center of learning and artistic culture. Museums are everywhere. Literature and poetry are praised, and art and history are woven into the fabric of the city like the famous Tabriz rugs sold at the Grand Bazaar of Tabriz.

Poetry is critical to Persian society, and Tabriz's poets make it clear that the city is part of their inspiration:

> "As long as I live in Tabriz, two things I need not worry of
> The half loaf of bread and the water of Mehranrud River are
> enough!"
>
> —Khaqani

Tabriz has major universities and schools of medicine, as well as music and 132 parks! It is glorious. I am telling you all of this because, well, in America, these are not the images we see. Iran is not all dust and desert and camels and illiteracy and women with no rights. As a matter of fact, before I left for this trip, I received a gift from Mr. Buscotti and his wife that blew me away and made me understand and appreciate places like Tabriz and the women who live there and in Iran.

After graduation, my family invited Mr. B and his wife to dinner. My parents wanted to thank him and show their appreciation for the special care he took in bringing me out of my shell. But Mr. B did not come empty-handed. Besides a gift of wine for my family, his wife Debra handed me a book that she had been reading (and reading to Mr. B at night, she said). It was called *Lipstick Jihad* by Azadeh Moaveni. I had heard of it but had not read it. It is subtitled *A Memoir of Growing up Iranian in America and American in Iran.* Moaveni is a *Time* magazine reporter who writes about life after the Revolution.

When I started reading the book, I felt a sisterhood with Moaveni from the first page. Like Holden Caulfield in *The Catcher in the Rye*, who always wished he could just talk to the author of his favorite book, I wanted to have Moaveni sitting with me on the plane and in the car when I visited cities like Tabriz so that I could just talk to her and compare my experiences to hers. Her family, like mine, fled Iran before the fall of the Shah; hers left in 1976. She wrote about *everything* I saw in Iran, from religion to politics to the contradictions of Iranian life, like the poverty and the wealth and the secular and the ultra-religious. These things were in many ways *exactly* the same in the States. You know what I mean? I felt like Moaveni was my big sister, explaining to me what my cousins either could not or simply did not understand because Iran was all they had ever known.

Like, for instance, after the Revolution, girls had a better chance of going to college—and they did! But in Iran, it did not matter because they still could not get the jobs that their education qualified them for. So, they had a taste of freedom, but that only made them hunger for more. They had to wait…and wait…and wait.

I don't know. Ms. Anderson taught us about the Women's Rights Movement last year, and what I saw in Tehran was a world that was 30 to 50 years behind America. Yet in Tabriz, I also saw all the potential and possibilities. It made me proud to be Persian.

July 19th

Off to the wedding of Darya and Bahram, my cousin on my mother's side, in Isfahan. To me, Isfahan was a city of fabulous bridges, mosques, and even cathedrals. Because time was short and the wedding was a whole day affair, I didn't see much of the city and craved for more. In many ways, the wedding was much like weddings in America. The DJ, the music, the dancing, the flowers, the ceremony, and the traditions were all versions of a lovely wedding in any culture. Of course, there were a few things that struck me. One was the fragrance of Persian rose. The smell came from several cups of rosewater and a rose extracted from the Mohammedan flower perfuming the air. The bride, Darya, was beautiful. She wore a white veil over her face as she came down the aisle, but she removed it once she and Bahram were face to face. (In the old days, I guess this would have been the first time that the bride and groom would have seen each other face to face…that would have been terrible.) My mother whispered to me that this unveiling used to be called the "Mirror of Fate"—no kidding.

All in all, the wedding was so much fun. I was reminded of the wedding of George and Emily in the play *Our Town*, which we studied in Mr. B's class last year. I remembered how Mr. B—as the stage manager and minister—looked at each of us in class during the wedding vows and said something about marrying thousands of couples, but every so often, one marriage is "very interesting." I hoped that Bahram and Darya's love would be as magical as George and Emily's. I remember Mrs. Soames saying the wedding was lovely and how much she loved weddings—who doesn't? After all, *Our Town* is about the idea that we are all meant to go through life with a companion, two by two. I thought of Daniel, and I found myself daydreaming about what our names would look like on a napkin.

But the funniest and most original part of the wedding by far was the "Knife Dance." It was a riot. Right before the cutting of the cake, the girls in Darya's family and lots of her girlfriends formed a line, and the music started to play. Each girl danced before the wedding couple, holding the knife that would be used to cut the cake. The girls were playful and a bit sexy, I must say. It seemed like the point was to tease the couple. The groom, Bahram, handed each girl money when she went to hand him the knife. But at that moment, each girl pulled the knife back, smiled coyly, and handed it to the next girl in line. Everyone laughed as the groom was tricked again and again. I have been to weddings where guests give the couple money in order to dance with them, but this was the reverse. I hoped Bahram had enough money on him. It was all in good fun. Then my mother explained to me, "All the girls give the money to Darya—or at least they usually do. Who knows, nowadays?"

At times like these, America and my friends seemed worlds away from me. It was strangely wonderful to be in a world like this and at the same time know that I was returning "home" in a few days. Home to SAT tests, college visits, and working for my father in his office. But all that seemed so distant on this night. However, it was the reality of the following Monday.

July 21ˢᵗ

I finished *Lipstick Jihad* on the plane back to America. I was—and still am—so surprised. I loved it all, and I miss Iran and my Persian culture. I know I will return someday.

When it came time to leave Iran, tears streamed down my face as I held my cousins, whom I had hardly known. The terrible lump in my throat was made worse when Uncle Reza, my father's older brother, embraced me.

"You are a Persian rose, Parivesh, but you are also an American beauty," he said to me. "I hope one day to see you in America on your wedding day. You make all of us so proud." That's when I lost it. I just lost it. His face reminded me of the "Mirror of Fate" and of his great hope for my destiny in the free world, where women can be anything and do anything and need not hide behind a veil.

Iranians, particularly the women, *do* want freedom. The people in the cities are not part of a fanatical religious country. But in the rural parts of Iran, there are people—often living in poverty—who are the soldiers who support Muslim power without question. In the people I met, there was no sentiment that Muslims are good people and others are not. Attitudes are changing. My cousins tell me of the provinces of Northern Iran, like Gilan and Mazandaran, which are much more hip and liberal. There is a youth culture in which couples hold hands openly in the streets and gays are much more accepted.

But there is fear, too. Or maybe it's that people complain about the corruption and the tyranny, but to stand up against it now seems unrealistic. The Ayatollah runs everything, and the so-called "President" is just a puppet. Women do not discuss politics in the rural parts of Iran. And perhaps this best sums up the fate of Iranian women: at funerals, men are buried low in the ground, and women are buried above them, and not because they are put on a pedestal. As my mother explained to me, "Pari, in some places in Iran, women are never level with men. Never."

As I looked out the window of the plane and got my first peek of America, I was reminded that Iran's people are not participants in the "Axis of Evil." Iran is not the stereotype we see in the news. It is a place of kindness, history, and beauty.

The famous poet Rumi captured the heart of how I feel about who I am and where I am from and what I was feeling as I flew through the sky back home:

> "This is love: to fly toward a secret sky,
> to cause a hundred veils to fall each moment.
> First to let go of life. Finally, to take a step without feet."

And I touched down—once again, at midnight.

Chapter 2: Rhiaferry

Rhiannon's Hand

I am so happy we are starting again. This whole writing thing just rocks. Listen to me—I sound like some super geek. But it's so interesting to put into words what I feel. I get stuff out, you know? Boy, there are times when I feel like I need to explode, and this summer has been kinda typical. Explode in a good way and in a bad way—if you get what I mean. You'll see.

June 16th

Okay, first day on the job that my mom helped me get at Yummy Yogurt. Yikes. Yuck. Oh well—it's a job, I get to see a lot of my friends, and I work with two girls who I like (plus a guy who is a complete jerk!). Tiffany works with me a lot—she was in our class with Mr. B last year. Remember—she struggled with bulimia, and she told that terrible story about losing her virginity when we were in that group reading *Reviving Ophelia*? I always really liked her...but more on her later. There is also a girl who is a junior now; her name is Leann. She is very nice, but she seems on guard or watchful or something. She acts nicer to me than to Tiffany. More on her later, too.

On the first day, I met the most interesting man—Omar, the security guy for the strip mall. I call him "The Mayor" because he knows everyone by name. He is very protective of the people who work here and the senior citizens who cruise over to Starbucks. What a character! He is like 40 or something, Mexican, hides his tats, and escaped the whole gang scene the hard way. He now speaks to kids around the city about staying clean. He talks about how gangs kill kids' chances for an education. Everyone loves him. He knows my brother

Chris, and he saw him go to the storefront where you enlist in the military. He asked me about it that first week of work.

"Omar, I don't know what he is going to do. He wanted to be a Marine, but I think he is going Navy now. He says he likes the water."

"Miss Rhia, whatever he does, he will try his best. Chris is a good kid. I am sure your family is worried, though."

"Omar, that is, like, a major understatement. But there is no talkin' him out of it."

"Yeah, when I was his age, I was a gangbanger. I wanted to fight; I wanted to prove myself. I wanted to be tough and to belong. But that was then. Heck, my dad split when I was, like, three years old, so I had no one to look up to except gangs. I didn't know anything other than gangs. Your brother was raised right, and what he is doing is for a cause worth fighting for, you know."

I know. But I also don't know. I know there are dangerous people and crazy nations and all that. I know we need to defend our country— but at what cost? And when do we stick our nose in other people's business? And what if my brother comes back without an arm or a leg…or worse? By late July, Chris will be at basic training. And then, he'll be…gone.

My heart aches for him. There is a quiet moment in my conversation with Omar. He senses it and says, "Don't worry, Miss Rhia. Okay?"

Okay.

Meanwhile, life in the Yummy Yogurt world teaches you patience and shows you rudeness at the same time. I mean, people are generally really nice, but, like, they can be a pain, too. They try every flavor— then pick vanilla. They are on their cell phones yelling and trying to figure out what to order. I actually overheard this couple (the guy was in the store; the girl was on the other end of his cell). They got into an argument, and it turned nasty. The guy stormed out of the store, screaming at his cell phone girlfriend. I looked at the two little girls wearing ballet uniforms from the dance studio that is two stores down and said, "Sorry, girls. Don't ever order what he ordered. Now, what can I get you?"

Then there are the "I just can't decide" customers, who just drive me crazy. They stand in line FOREVER, and then when it's their turn to order, they *still* don't know what to do. I wanna say to them, "Dudes, just pick something. Anything!" And after that comes the toppings. They can't decide on those either. One time, a lady had the audacity to say in a nasal tone, "How come you don't have calorie counts on the toppings?" Oh, shut up! I don't know. I don't care. I don't want to know the calorie counts. I just want you to order. If you are so worried about calories, then why are you here at Yummy Yogurt? Why not go to a salad bar—where you probably wouldn't be able to decide what to put on the salad, either? But I don't say any of that. I just smile and say, "No problem. Take your time."

It is at times like these when I remind myself that it's a job and that we need the money. All high school kids have jobs like this. This is my version of basic training, and I gotta make sure that I grow up to have a job where I don't stare at the clock.

Thank God for music and my iPod. It saves me. And I have a new absolutely fave album—*Rockferry* by Duffy. I can't stop listening to it. The sound of it is so old-school, but the lyrics are, like, *exactly how I feel right now.* I wish you could hear each song as my heart beats to the music and to the drama of my summer of melancholy. (Mickey told me that word fits—I love him.) So this is my Rhiaferry world. Let's go song by song:

- **"Warwick Avenue"** – Okay, this song is about a girl who is about to meet with someone from her past who has hurt her bad. She tells him that she is leaving him for the final time. *Fini.* He gets no more than an hour, and she points to the door. And all his lovin' is just crap. She wants to be free.

So this is what happened to me. I get a call from my dad, who left us two years ago (for some younger woman—yuck). He says he is in town, and he wants to see me and talk to me about something "important."

I have been putting this off. I never want to see him again. He drove my mother to attempt to OD on sleeping pills. But I have to confront him on my own Warwick Avenue.

"Hi," he says.
He tries to hug me. I pull away.
He tells me, "I miss you…and Chris."
"I don't wanna talk about the past," I tell him.
"I get it. I understand how you feel."
"No, you don't."
"Let me at least try, okay?"
"You have one hour. No more."
For a split second, the old anger comes over his face. He hates when he doesn't get his way.
"Okay. Look, Rhia. I want to do something nice for you this summer. Give you a trip or something…"
"Try paying for my college."
"I mean for the summer."
"No, thanks. I'm telling you for the last time—I want to be free of you."

He seems like he doesn't know what to do with me.
"Listen, think about it and call me. Or I'll call you. There must be something I can do for you this summer. Call me tomorrow, okay? Give me a chance."
"I'll call. Maybe. Or text. Whatever. I gotta go."
"Where are you going?"
"To work, Dad. To work at Yummy Yogurt."

And I walk down my Warwick Avenue.

But I feel less confident than I act.

- **"Rockferry"** – Duffy's songs keep my footsteps moving forward.

I lied. I was not going to work. I was just going away. I wanted to move to a house in Rockferry, like the song says. She has a decision to make. Me, too. She has had sleepless nights. I have stared at my bed, too—often unable to climb in and find any comfort. She has a bag of sad songs in her head. They give her a heavy heart. My heart is weighing me down so much that I don't know if I can make it home.

But she has the strength in her mind to make this decision and leave. I feel the courage brimming up in my soul. She says she will not write 'cause she is not that kind of girl. Neither will I.

So I make a decision. I will not call. I will meet him one more time…on my terms, in my Rockferry home.

- **"Stepping Stone"** – We meet at the same place. I explode.

"Look, I never want to see your face again. You left us for someone else. So go be with her and leave us…leave me. I will never be your stepping stone. When you call me, it's like a curse. It's like you want to be back in my life—like you can play me, like you are some maestro conducting your little orchestra. Well, I am not playing for you. I am not your stepping stone. I don't want your money. I don't need you. I am gonna stand up on my own. I am gonna step up, and you will not be my foundation anymore. It's too late, Dad. All this 'Delayed Devotion'—it is all love turned to numbness. Your actions mean nothing to me. I don't hate you. I just won't love you."

I turn and walk away.

I never gave him a chance to say anything. He didn't follow me.

You may think I am cruel to him, but I will tell you this—I never used the dagger. I never told him that he almost killed my mother. No, I put that dagger away. It is not mine to use.

I guess there will be no vacations for me as I walk my stepping stones down my Warwick Avenue to my Rhiaferry home.

- **Begging for "Mercy" and being "Serious"** – Okay, enough with all that drama. Wipe away tears. Breathe.

July has been a really great time with Donald. Rewind. He was my date at Winter Formal and Prom. We love to dance. We met in Mr. B's class and danced the swing. As Mr. B said, we "rocked the house." We love to talk. We love to learn about each other. We are from opposite worlds—literally. He has dreadlocks and is dimpled and cute. He is half black and, as he says, "half tropical." His dad is from the island of St. Thomas in the Caribbean—and he says it so cool. *Ca-ribb-e-on.*

Donald is a math guy and a soccer player. When I am with him, Duffy's song "Mercy" plays in my head because he has got me bad. Like Duffy says—yeah, I am under his spell. He is strong. He takes me by the hand. He is so sexy. I gotta control myself. See, that is why I am begging for mercy. God. I even told him I loved him.

"You do?"
"Yeah." I am sure I looked at him like one of those dreamy, dopey girls.
"Cool." He smiled. That was all he said.

Okay, that was not what I wanted to hear. *Cool* is for when you see a nice car. Or when you agree on a topping for pizza. Or when you go somewhere that you think would be cool. Like the fair or something. *Cool* is not what you say to someone as a complete sentence when they tell you they love you. And not just *love you like a BFF* or a soul sister or whatever, but love you like—duh, *falling in love with you.*

Sorry, but *cool* just does not cut it. That is why the song "Serious" is now playing on my iPod. Duffy is the soundtrack of my life! Okay, so "Serious" is about a girl—like me—who doesn't know if she is just an accessory for a guy, or maybe some sorta trophy on his shelf. She feels deep down inside her heart that the guy never gets serious…and that is nerve-wracking.

So, we had this conversation sitting on a park bench:

"Donald, you know when you were hangin' with your friends and you were talking about me? Well, what did you say?"
"I said you were cool."
"Great. Let's talk about cool. Cool *rhymes with* fool. *And I want you to know that you are more than cool to me. And I feel like if that's all we are, then I'm being the fool here."*
"Rhia, I'm sorry. I was not, like, getting where you were coming from. So you want to know how I feel about you?"
"Ding!"
"Well, hmm… How serious is this supposed to get?"
"That is a good question, Donald. Look, I'm not saying that we need to get super serious or anything. But when I told you I loved you, you said, 'Cool.' And that was all you said. Like that was enough. And I was, like, so let down because you never just leave things so…vague. Or whatever."
"I mean, we are going out, Rhia. I do consider you my girlfriend, if that's what you mean."
A long pause.

"Okay. I like that a lot better. We don't have to be, like, attached at the hip, Donald. I just wanted you to know how much I care about you. Okay?"
"Yeah."
I promised myself I would not cry.
"Rhia, if you cry, I'm gonna feel like a total jerk. Okay, maybe I was really stupid. I've never had a girlfriend before, so I'm just kinda lost."

We didn't say much else. We just walked. But he grabbed my hand and squeezed it tight. And then he kissed me. And I don't know how much time passed, but my cell rang. It was my mom, asking where I was. I told her I didn't know exactly.

See, that is why I am begging for "Mercy."

Boys. Seriously.

- **"I'm Scared"** – It is now July 29th. It is time for Chris to go. I don't know if I can even write this. And I want you to know that Maddie helped me with this part. And it's kinda short 'cause I just can't say too much. I have been playing Duffy's song over and over and over. There will be blank pages here in this diary.

My room is dark today, and the picture of Chris smiling at me in uniform sits on my nightstand. You are my big brother.

I go to your room. I see your motorcycle magazines. Your poster of the waves in Hawaii. Your Tony Gwynn bobble-head. You are here, but you are gone.

I'm scared for you. And the fear won't go away.

And I am all alone in my room.

- **"Distant Dreamer"** – Last song on the album, guys—and my favorite. You know, I didn't tell you that my mom loves this Duffy album. She says it reminds her of Dusty Springfield. I don't know who that is, but I will check her out.

If I have given you the impression that my summer was a drag, it wasn't! Me and Maddie and Mickey went to the beach a lot. And when Pari came home from Iran, she was with us all the time, too. She and I double-dated with Donald and Daniel— isn't that, like, so 50s? I also saw the coolest movie—*The Dark Knight*. I cannot believe that Heath Ledger died. He was amazing in the film.

But toward the end of the summer, the four of us—Pari, Mickey, Maddie, and I—went to get pizza. And we talked about music. I told them that Duffy's "Distant Dreamer" was my anthem. See, people think that I can cope with everything. I seem to smile at all my troubles, but the truth is that *I really am filled with hope*. I don't know what I am gonna do with my life— or even what will happen after my senior year—but I am a dreamer. I have a list of all the things that I want to do with my life. I know better things are to come, and when life gets tough, I will do what Mr. B reminded all of us of last year—look for our North Star.

My star is in the distance…in a place I call Rhiaferry.

Chapter 3: "Where We Gonna Go From Here?"

Mickey's Hand

My dad calls me and my brother Marc the "M & M Boys." That is because my dad grew up as a major old school Yankees fan. Mantle and Maris. I got the name *Mickey*, which, BTW, is my legal name. Yeah, I know. Nobody is named Mickey anymore. My brother just thanks God that my dad didn't want to name him Roger. Yikes.

So, it's summer. I remember Mr. B used to say that in high school, the things he loved were baseball, girls, burgers, books, and music—not necessarily in that order. I could not agree more. Except that I would add movies. Movies with Maddie. *The Dark Knight*—very cool. Actually, all four of us saw that. The trouble with this summer was that we were hardly ever all together.

So, where was I all summer? On a fairly constant "road trip"— yeah, we combined a vacation, which my folks said was just not really happening this summer, with baseball tournaments and college visits. And it all began with the M & M Boys on the road again.

June 22nd

Marc decided to hang with me for the only club ball tournament I was going to—I think mostly because it was in Palm Springs and he'd never been. He told me it was very retro there. To me, it looked like the Jetsons in places. Kinda 60s, but pretty cool. No, make that *very hot and windy*. I have no idea why we were there *in the summer of all times!* Our club coach is the one who plans things, but our high school coach is really the one who coaches the team. He's one of those guys who is, like, never, ever hot. It's, like, 95 degrees out *at 10 am,* and Coach is walking around with a windbreaker on, saying, "This is perfect, guys. You can get loose and break a sweat fast." Meanwhile, not a bead of sweat appears on his face.

Anyway, the trip out was me and Marc in the pickup truck. Marc is going into his junior year of college at Santa Clara. He is majoring in all the things my dad loves: business and math stuff. He is going to be a CPA. I asked him why.

"I am a numbers cruncher, dude. It's just what I like to do. The whole tax law scene is very overwhelming 'cause the tax code is, like, legal crap with a math twist. But this past year I decided on a minor."

"Yeah? What?"

"Italian."

"Shut up! Really? That is so cool. I would love to take Italian."

"Yeah, well, I started to talk to Mom and Dad about Italy. I am hoping to study in Rome second semester. You do it through the college, and the University of Rome has the classes in English and all. But I want to start learning the language."

"How much is that gonna cost?" I wondered if he had even considered that. Mr. Numbers Cruncher often infuriated my dad by never knowing what he had in his bank account and calling for last-minute money bailouts.

"Well, it is a program that the university has, so the tuition is the same, and the food is kinda covered if you eat on campus. So, it is mostly just the cost to get there."

"Have you told Mom and Dad all this?"

"Yeah. So far, they are cool with it."

I began to think that my college visits and Marc's Italy plans explained why we were not really going anyplace this summer.

******   *****   *****   *****   *****

The topic changed to girls.

"So you and Maddie are going out, huh? She's pretty cute, dude."

"Yeah."

I really didn't want to talk much to Marc about girls. He is always giving me advice, but he never tells me much about himself. So we always seem to have the "little brother needs help, but big brother is too cool to tell him anything" conversation. But today he surprised me.

"Hey, did I tell you I broke up with Vanessa?"

"Uh, didn't she come down with you on spring break?"

"Yep. She was way too controlling. And besides, I just cannot be so pinned down."

"Oh. Hmm. So you guys just broke up?"

"Well, not exactly. I felt bad when I told her, and she started balling and went totally emo on me. And I guess that is fine and all because, like, she said, 'I never saw it coming.'" I noticed how much faster Marc was driving. He was trying to be all cool about this, but he was getting pretty worked up.

"Hey, Marc? Uh, there are cops around, and you are going, like, 85 all of a sudden."

"Chill. I've been looking. Anyway, with going to Italy and all…and Vanessa may transfer anyway. It's just too complicated." Finally, he slowed down a bit. "Yeah. So, you and Maddie—that is cool. Where is she thinking of going to college? I assume she is going, right? Hey, isn't her dad just back from Iraq? And didn't he just retire or something?"

I decided to take the questions one at a time. "Maddie is great. I asked Dad if she could come with us if we drove to San Francisco to look at schools."

"Is she applying to the same schools as you?"

"I have no idea, but she might. And yeah, her dad is retired. He is trying to find a job, but he's frustrated with the economy and all. Nobody is hiring."

"Tell me about it." Marc was planning on working at Starbucks like he did the summer before, but the summer of 2008 was not looking so good for anyone—including Starbucks. They may only give him a few hours a week.

"Yeah, so money is tight, but he has his military pension and all. He was in the Navy for, like—I dunno—30 years or something."

"Hey, turn it up. I love this song."

It was Mat Kearney's "Where We Gonna Go from Here?" I had just put it on my iPod. The title of the song became the question that dominated my summer and the days to follow. Rhia had her "Rockferry," but me—I was just on a road trip, and I really had no idea where I was going.

As we pulled into the "hotel," we saw that it looked like a piece of crap. We should never let Coach choose hotels. He calls himself the "Chief of Cheap."

This place was one of his favorites—aptly called the Pink Flamingo.

Yikes.

"Love this place," Coach bellowed as we got out of the truck. This was one of those places where you practically parked in the room next to the bed.

"Nice windows," my brother said. "Check out the bullet holes."

"Yeah, it's got character. But you can't beat the price." Coach was in his domain.

"You pay to stay here?" Marc knifed back.

"Well, it's not for the fancy boys from college," he said to Marc, whom Coach knew had never been a baseball player in high school.

Marc looked at me and whispered, "Let's just hope there isn't a drug bust at two in the morning."

"Yep, got great memories of this old place…the Pink Flamingo," Coach said as he grabbed a bag of bats from his trunk. "Oh, you are starting game two tomorrow, Mickey. It will be a tad warm—but you will be loose after five minutes."

"Uh, Coach? I thought I was coming in to be a relief guy," I said.

"Nope. I wanna see you go three or four innings. You're a senior, kid. Time to find out if you've got the stamina. I think you do."

Great. Nothing like testing your stamina in the desert.

***** ***** ***** ***** *****

Okay. I did not die. I lost, like, five pounds of water. I also made it three innings and only gave up one run. But I got hammered in the fourth inning with a double, double—toil and trouble. Three runs later, we were tied 4-4, and Coach mercifully took me out.

"Good job, Mickey. You just got tired. Solid effort," Coach told me as he took the ball from my glove.

"Okay," I mumbled to him. I was walking back to the sort-of dugout, which really seemed more like an oven.

Marc came over to the side, where a short fence was, and handed me two bottles of ice cold water. "One you drink," he said; "one you pour over your head."

I bent over, took off my hat, and poured the whole thing on the back of my skull.

I walked back to the bench, sat down, and put a towel on my head. Coach sat next to me and said, "I think you just earned yourself two things."

"Yeah? What?" I asked him.

"One, you're gonna start games for me, Lefty. And two, you just earned yourself a nickname. The Ice Man."

Great. I just prayed the air conditioner in the Pink Flamingo did not break down—or else the Ice Man would melt.

July 4th

What a weird day. Weird on many levels. The activities included talking with my mom, talking with my dad, talking with my Maddie, and talking with myself. There were a few fireworks in between.

Let's start with Mom. Morning. I read the sports page, eat cereal, and try to ignore her:

Mom: Mickey, how serious are you and Maddie?

Me: Um…I dunno. Kinda serious…why? *(My chewing slows down.)*

Mom: Well, you know what I mean.

Me: No.

Mom: Yes, you do. I am not talking about marriage, Mister.

Me: Um…this is kinda weird, Mom. (*My chewing has stopped.*)

Mom: Mickey, do I need to spell it out? S-E-X, Mickey. I just want to know if you are even thinking about what you are doing…

Me: Mom—

Mom: …and if you have taken any precautions…

Me: Mom!

Mom: …and you two are so young. Is Maddie even 18 yet? (*Mom has built to a crescendo.*)

Me: Oh, my God, Mom. We are dating. Going out. You know? It is not what you are thinking.

Mom: Okay, fine. But, Mickey, are *you* thinking? I know what leads to what…

Me: What?

Mom: Don't be cute with me.

Me: Maddie says I am cute with her.

Mom: That is exactly what I am worried about! Look, this is serious… (*The spoon now permanently rests in the bowl. The sports page has been pushed aside. I am fully engaged, even if I have no idea what I am about to say.*)

Me: I know, Mom. That is where this whole thing started: 'How serious are we?' I don't really know how serious we are. I really, really like Maddie…

Mom: Have you told her you love her?

Me: Jeeze, Mom, we are getting pretty personal here.

Mom: Yes, we are, Mickey. Because when the word *love* gets tossed around and a girl like Maddie hears it, it means more to her than maybe it does to you, and it tells her something that you may not be thinking about…

Me: Like?

Mom: Like…like…well… like she may want to give herself to you…sexually.

Me: Mom, this is, like, way more info than I need—and a little, uh, awkward coming from my mom.

Mom: I don't care if it's hard to hear, Mickey. It is important. Really important. I worry about you and Maddie, and I just want you to know that you need to be aware of how she is feeling and how you are feeling about your relationship. And…

Me: I know, Mom, I know. And I can always talk to you.

Mom: You can. That is all I am saying—asking. Okay?

Me: Okay, Mom.

Mom: Promise me you won't be stupid.

Me: Like Marc?

Mom: Let's not go there. (My mom punches my arm and a burst of laughter floats out of the kitchen as we let the tension go. I grab a red apple. I think of the symbolism. I head to the garage where Dad awaits.)

***** ***** ***** ***** *****

An hour later. Dad has finished cleaning the grill for tonight. He decides to have a beer before lunch. I am his assistant as we "get the backyard ready for company":

Dad: You know, Mickey, I used to be a Democrat.

Me: Yeah, I think you mentioned that before.

Dad: Voted for Kennedy—Bobby—in the California primary. *(He takes a swig of beer.)*

Me: Then he was assassinated, right?

Dad: Yeah. I was with some friends and someone called—I don't remember—it was   late at night—maybe early morning. They said he was shot and killed right after he won. I sometimes wonder how everything would have turned out if that had not happened. *(He takes an even longer swig of beer.)*

Me: Yeah.

Dad: Yeah. Humphrey was a good man, but had no charisma. 'Course, Nixon didn't either…but the damn war just dragged on…and, well, it was crazy.

Me: When did you start being a Republican? *(I bust out the chips Mom places on the table as she gives me the "Don't get into politics with him on the Fourth of July!" look.)*

Dad: Well, I did vote for Carter—and he is still, in my opinion, the best ex-President we ever had—but he just seemed like he could not handle Washington. He couldn't get the hostages out—couldn't save them when the rescue mission failed—the economy was in the pits… *(The beer bottle is metaphorically half full.)*

Me: So then you voted for Reagan, right?

Dad: Yeah. He got things done—first day in office, got the hostages out.

Me: Well, my teacher told us that he traded weapons for hostages, which Carter refused to do.

Dad: Maybe. Yeah, maybe. I dunno for sure. They tried to keep it under wraps because you don't want to be negotiating with terrorists—that is when the whole Middle East went crazy. It still is crazy. Look at Iraq. Iran. *(Beer gauge dropping…fast.)*

Me: Still think the Republicans have all the answers after 8 years of Bush, Dad?

Dad: Hell no. But remember—Bush had to deal with 9.11, and there have been no attacks on America since. *(Beer lower…chips holding steady.)*

Me: Right. But we haven't "smoked out" Bin Laden yet. We have invaded two nations because of all this—and we have gotten a lot of American soldiers killed.

Dad: I know. I know. But Afghanistan was the right thing to do— Iraq was arguable. Hell, even *your* Democrats voted for it—John Kerry, for example.

Me: Ah, but not Obama. And the argument was a lie. Colin Powell's speech to the United Nations about WMD—

Dad: Our best intelligence told us that they had WMD.

Me: It was some jerk named "Curveball," Dad. The Brits fell for it. *(The beer has disappeared in one final chug. The empty bottle taps down on the table.)*

Dad: Yeah, I know. Bush was a disappointment—but who they ran against him was no better. Gore and the whole global warming argument—my God. He would have taxed business to death, and the economy was already starting to fall apart. He was better suited to be a professor—lecturing to us all the time—than a President.

Me: Dad, the economy is toast now.

Dad: Don't remind me. The stock market has already dropped 300 points in, what, two weeks? I dunno, Mickey. Pass the chips over. *(Chip levels are dropping, too.)*

Me: What don't you know, Dad?

Dad: Well, maybe this Obama guy can get things straightened out. It is such a mess. The whole country is a mess.

Me: Hmm...well, he is smart.

Dad: He'd better be—although he may not be *that* smart. After all, he is running for President. *(Dad dramatically poses with a chip before he tosses it into the breach and chomps down.)*

Me: Jeeze, Dad. Let's not get too cynical.

Dad: Cynical, huh? Those SAT vocab words are starting to come out of you. What were you and your mother talking about in the kitchen?

Me: Oh, nothing. Politics.

Dad: Bull. So, are you and Maddie getting serious? I really like that gal...

Me: Oh, no. Not again. *(It starts all over. I roll my eyes and face the inevitable inquisition. What do you do when the chips are down?)*

***** ***** ***** ***** *****

By the time the fireworks started, I was ready to just sit next to Maddie, eat ice cream, and look at the sky.

Naturally, she wanted to talk. I decided to call this one—

Me and Maddie on the 4ᵗʰ of July

"Is it in the stars for us?" she asks
"Or are we star-crossed lovers?" he replies
"Will we reach a fork in the road soon?" she asks
"And choose different paths?" he replies

"How long can fireworks last?" she asks
He knows not what to say
She waits him out
"Until all the fireworks end," he finally replies
"And when will that be?" she asks
"When do you think?" he asks
She knows not what to say
He waits her out

"Maybe never," she replies
She notices the sky is ablaze with color

"How much should we give to each other?" she asks
"As much as we can afford," he replies
"I have so much but so little," she says
"And it is so precious," he replies
"Yeah," she looks down
He knows

The sky is so full of smoke and darkness
That the stars disappear
They kiss
Until the stars shine
And the tears spill over cheeks
To dry
Once more on the 4th of July

July 26th

Where we gonna go from here? Well, another road trip down the highway—the California 101, heading to the Bay Area. You know, we decided to keep the setting of our story an "anyplace in America" type of place. We hoped that Mr. B's idea that an "everyman" approach would appeal to not just us, but also to our friends and kids in America in general because we feel pretty much like them...like "every student." True, we are not dealing with the poverty of the inner city or the fear of being labeled "illegals" who may have crossed the border—but our friends are—and that is part of this novel, too.

Anyway, I guess it is about time folks know that we are California kids. We will just leave it at that.

And now the five of us are headed north. Me and my folks and Maddie and her mom in the van, ready (or not) for college visits. Maddie and her mom came with because it just seemed dumb to deal with the expense of it all when we were checking out some of the same places.

It is so exciting and scary. We checked out USF and UC Davis, but UC Berkeley was the one that I was attracted to. Wow. Huge. The guide was awesome, but when she told us that the average score to get in was around 2000 (out of 2400) and that the average GPA was a 4.0—uh, that was intimidating. And the number of people applying—well, it was really overwhelming. But I also felt like this was big time college with huge lecture halls and famous professors. But more importantly—for me, anyway—I felt that this place had the urban, liberal feel I was looking for. (I wasn't so sure it was what my parents wanted.) Telegraph Road just kinda sent you back to the 60s' protests—the whole Free Speech Movement that is part of the history of Berkeley. I felt challenged there, and all I kept thinking was that if I got in, I was going. If I got in.

All Maddie said was, "I will never get in here." She wanted a smaller school, anyway. She and her mom rented a car and traveled to Sonoma State, USF, and St. Mary's. They also checked out the school my brother Marc was going to: Santa Clara. Maddie liked them all, but she was so freaked out about money. Forty thousand dollars a year for a private school was so impossible. Maddie kept thinking she could get scholarships—and she will—but she told me that the worried look on her mom's face kept peeking through even though she did not want it to show. Sonoma State, which is in Napa Valley—where wine is king— was way more affordable and more suburban. When the trip was done, I knew what I wanted; Maddie knew what she could afford; and neither of us knew if we would get in.

But the highlight of the trip was the night we went to Ghirardelli Square in San Francisco to get the killer chocolate and ice cream. Okay, it is super touristy, but so what? We were tourists. We rode the cable cars (to the stars) and understood why people leave their hearts in San Francisco. I just looked at Maddie as she licked her spoon, which was dripping with dark chocolate, and thought, *"My heart waits there…"*

Sometimes I just can't take my eyes off her.

*****   *****   *****   *****   *****

We made stops at USC and UCLA after the Bay Area trips. My dad loves USC, my mom loves UCLA, and I can see why they do. For me, UCLA was more appealing—it was a lot more like Cal Berkeley, but not as urban or political. It was just as prestigious, just as hard to get into (maybe even harder), and it was in LA. It was just a few hours away, but it was definitely *away from home*. I could tell I could adapt there easier because it was more suburban. USC appealed to my dad's business interests, but he knew that Cal had a great business school, as well. I knew that USC would have to come up with serious scholarship offers because there was no way my folks could afford it—not with Marc finishing up college, too.

I guess I felt like every other soon-to-be senior who was hoping to go to college—planning to go—hoping to afford it. Would I get in? Would I fit in? Would I like the dorm—and my roommates? Could I handle the classes? What would I major in? Why would I choose one school over another? What if I got rejected by all of them? What if I had to go to my "safety school," which I really never wanted to go to in the first place? Could my parents afford it? Would they go in debt— because of me? Would I go in debt? What *was* debt, anyway? Would I miss my friends? Would I make new ones? Would I miss Maddie? Pari? Rhia? Oh, where we gonna go from here?

August 10th

The weeks that followed were fun and tedious (I love that word). Fun because we went to the beach—and once Pari came home, we would all go when we got time off. Rhia worked a lot of hours at the yogurt place, and we went there to see her and talk with her during her breaks. Maddie was working at the hospital—she will fill you in on that in the next chapter—and Pari was working for her dad, and I was working at baseball clinics for Coach at the high school. We worked with the Little League kids for four weeks of camp. It was fun, and it helped raise money for the baseball program. Since I was helping out Coach, my folks did not have to make any contributions to the program or to the club team I was on—so I was saving them money. The week we had the little kids was the most fun. They reminded me of when I was their age and all that mattered were snacks, blowing bubbles, wrestling in the outfield at breaks, and just the joy of getting a hit and standing there at first base, beaming ear to ear. These kids didn't care about being cool—they just wanted to have fun. I told myself to remember this lesson.

***** ***** ***** ***** *****

But the most amazing thing happened today. It is Sunday, and it's my parents' anniversary. They are leaving tomorrow for a week to go to Hawaii, but today they had a barbeque, and they told me weeks ago to make sure that Maddie, Rhia, and Pari could all come over. I had no idea why.

So after dinner, the four of us are sitting around, and my mom and dad come over. My dad says he has something to tell us. He asks us what we are doing on Halloween. We look at him like, *Uh, it's August. How do we know?*

Rhia says, "Well, we aren't trick-or-treating, Mr. Sullivan." And we all laugh.

Then my dad says, "Well, I am treating." We look at him like, *"What are you talking about?"*

My mom says, "Just tell them, honey."

"Okay. We are so proud of you guys and the book and all—and we talked to your folks, and they said it is okay with them—so we are taking you guys to a concert."

"You are? Who?" we all say in one voice.

"Halloween night, you are seeing Bruce Springsteen and the E Street Band!"

"Shut up!" I blasted—which was followed by a series of "No way!", "Seriously?", and "Mr. Buscotti would be so jealous!"

"Actually, guys, Mr. B was the one who called me and told me that Bruce was coming to LA. He is playing at USC. It's his Magic Tour."

We were stunned. My mom said that we were so into Springsteen in Mr. B's class, and we wrote about his music so much—well, we just had to see the real thing.

Pari said, "And my parents said I could go?" She was funny. She could travel across the world to Iran, but she was surprised that her parents would let her go to a rock concert in LA.

"Yes. You guys have four seats together. Mickey's dad and I are meeting friends and sitting far away from you all. Oh, and Mr. Buscotti and his wife will be there—somewhere."

I loved Bruce's new album. His hit song on it was "Radio Nowhere." I did not know where I was going from here—but I knew I was going to LA to see The Boss.

Okay, so my parents proved something to me that summer. Even though we did not agree on everything, they sure had good taste in music.

And come the fall, baby, we would be born to run.

Chapter 4: Make a Wish

Madison's Hand

June 27th

I was just going to surprise my dad. He was working the graveyard shift at the Naval Hospital. He retired the first week of June, but the Navy keeps calling him in as a radiologist "consultant" when things get crazy at the hospital. As he says, "It's always in the middle of the night that they need someone to look at an X-ray of a broken leg."

So off I went. I could not know that on this evening, my senior year would change for the better and that I would understand exactly what Emily Webb meant when she said in the play *Our Town* that people just don't appreciate life very much—until, of course, death confronts them. Death took the form of a fourteen-year-old girl named Jasmine.

The week before, my dad was able to steer me into an internship in the Children's Hospital Volunteen Program. Volunteens work in many areas, including the information desk, the gift shop, the sibling clubhouse, and the clinic waiting rooms. I had put in my first few days and had met so many caring, interesting people. The nurses in particular are, in my dad's words, "God's angels in tennis shoes." And the nurses at Children's Hospital are so wonderful to the kids. I just don't know how they can face these little children whose lives are so painful and not cry all the time. In the coming months, I was to learn how they do it and when they quietly break down.

Yeah.

Okay. But tonight was to be a surprise for my dad—hot chocolate and three fresh baked cookies—his favorite. I was sitting with him in the ER when a family came in with Jasmine—her father was also retired from the Navy. Jasmine and her family are Filipino, and although their skin was that gorgeous, tropical brown that I would kill for (as I bake in the sun and just get redder by the minute), Jasmine's skin was yellowish—as were her eyes.

"Jaundice," my dad told me.

"What is that?" I asked.

"Well, I don't know the cause, but her liver is not operating as it should. That is why her skin yellows."

I could not help but overhear them talking. The family seemed worried, but this Jasmine girl was so funny. She was laughing and acting kinda goofy with her brother. That is when I realized that he looked familiar. He had graduated from my high school last year! His name was Paul, I think. Anyway, I walked up to him and Jasmine and said, "Hi. You guys don't know me. I'm Maddie. I think we go to the same high school."

Immediately, he and Jasmine (I did not know her name then) seemed to embrace me like I was their best friend—I didn't even know them! I was to discover this was the "Jasmine Way." They quickly covered the bases of who we all knew and what college he was attending and that Jasmine was gonna be a freshman this fall. I couldn't help but notice that despite her parents' concern for her and the fact that nurses and a doctor were swirling around, Jasmine acted like this was some drama on TV that she could mute and just ignore. She just kept beaming with joy. *How could someone coming to the ER not be freaked out?* I thought.

I was to find out that she was a veteran of many children's health wars.

Yeah.

So anyway, Jasmine launched into a monologue about "next year:"

"I am so, so, so excited, Maddie! I mean, I am freaking out, too. But so, so excited! I love school…I wish I could go more often. *(She laughs—and her giggle is so cute!)* I get sick and I miss class sometimes, but my eighth grade teacher was so nice to me. I am so excited to make new friends! Is high school scary? I mean, are the teachers nice? I hear that they give a lot of homework. My brother had tons—I mean *tons*— of HW. Yikes. But I don't really care as long as I can go to school." She pauses to take a breath. I try to say something, but it's too late.

Jasmine continues, "Who was your favorite teacher? Mine was my language arts teacher—Ms. Orendall-Smith. Did you have her? *(I try to shake my head no.)* She was so nice to me. She even visited me in the hospital. I missed about a month altogether. My mom wants to put me in an Honors Freshman English class because she says it is my best subject, but I am worried." Then all of a sudden, she just stops. She takes a breath, then lies back and says, "Whew."

I wasn't sure what all that meant, but I took it as a chance to answer some of her questions as her brother was reminding her to chill out.

"Yeah, well, Jasmine, you gotta get Mr. Buscotti as your English teacher. He teaches Freshman English, and he is the best. I just had him for American Lit, and I'm his TA next year. Maybe I could tell him about you and all. He won't freak you out with homework. And he will make you laugh a lot. He is very cool."

Paul, Jasmine's brother, told me he was bummed he never had Mr. Buscotti—but his friends did, and they really liked him. Just then, Jasmine's mom came by and said the doctor wanted Jasmine to stay the night and monitor her. They were finding a room for her. Paul introduced me to her. Jasmine stayed surprisingly quiet. My father came by and introduced himself, shaking hands with Jasmine's dad. Old Navy guys always tell each other their backgrounds, where they were stationed, and stuff like that. My dad has a great bedside manner for a radiologist. He always tells me that radiologists are kind of the nerds of the doctor world—just looking at film all the time. He is the exception.

By now it was 1 AM, and my mom called me to ask what was going on. I told her briefly and said I would get home…and be very careful…and have Dad walk me to the car…and not call Mickey. But before I left, I asked my dad to let me know about Jasmine, and I asked her brother Paul to give me his cell number. I just had this strange feeling that I needed to stay in touch. "At least I can see if Mr. Buscotti can pull some strings and get Jasmine into his class," I told Paul. Jasmine had just dozed off. One minute she was a bundle of energy, and the next she was asleep. Her brother told me, "This is how she is when she is like this." Scary.

I didn't even know half the story.

July 1st

This morning I thought of Pari—she left for Iran today. I will miss her. We started out strangers, really, and now I am just bummed that she is gone for a lot of July. I'm excited for her. I know she will have amazing stories to tell us, and she is posting pictures on Facebook. But she is just…so…well, she just sees things in such a bigger picture—not just because she is so smart, but because she has seen so much more of the world than the three of us combined. Me—I have seen Navy bases. Yeah. And commissaries. Good deals, but not too big on culture.

Rhia is so busy with her job at Yummy Yogurt—isn't that the stupidest name?! But she likes it, I guess. And she has been struggling with her father, and she freaked out about her brother Chris going into the Army, instead of the Navy. She doesn't want to say bad things about the military because of my dad and all, but I told her that I totally get it. I mean, my dad wasn't in the line of fire; he just saw the results of it all, and still we were freaking out.

And then there is Mickey. Okay, I know how dumb this is gonna sound, but I just think of him all the time. I'm not obsessing—I just…just…I wake up and I think of him. I'm not dependent on him. I just feel like he makes everything better. Do people feel this way when they are in love? Does it wear off? Okay, enough mushy love stuff. I have to tell you about this afternoon because Jasmine came back into my world.

It was my shift at Children's Hospital. I had been in touch with her brother Paul, and my dad had told me that Jasmine had been transferred to Children's two days after I met her. Her condition was better, but they were still concerned. Jasmine was a "regular" at Children's, my dad explained.

I found her alone in her room. She didn't have a roommate. She was bopping her head to some song on her iPod with her eyes closed. She was singing away, and the music was so loud that she couldn't possibly hear me. So I just watched her for about five minutes. Jasmine has dark brown hair and huge—I mean really *huge*—round, brown eyes. Her hair is cut pixie-like, and she has puffy cheeks and killer dimples— kind of a baby face, really. She could look as young as 11 or so. And she is tiny. She can't be more than 4'11", and when she is sitting in her hospital bed, it looks like it envelops her. She was all "shake-n-jive"— she was kinda doing the Egyptian thing with her neck as she moved to the groove. It just cracked me up. Finally, she opened her eyes.

"Whoa, I am so, so totally embarrassed!" Jasmine cried. "You must think I am some total weirdo!"

"No, of course not," I said, "although you are the only person I know who says *weirdo.*"

"Yeah, I know. I am a weirdo." Her giggle just melted me. "I love my iPod."

"What were you listening to? You were so into it."

"Oh, well, it is a Christian R&B thing…"

"Oh. Who?"

"Do you know 'God in Me' by Mary Mary? It's like hip hop. It just came out," Jasmine seemed very relieved that it was cool to talk to me about something Christian. I guess sometimes that may turn some people off.

"No, but it sounds cool. Jasmine, do you remember me? I'm Maddie. I saw you the night your family brought you into the Naval Hospital…"

"Duh! Of course I do, you silly." She just cracks me up. She has to be the most uninhibited freshman I have ever met. "You and my brother were hanging out, and I asked you a bunch of questions—and then I kinda passed out…or something. I do that sometimes. It freaks people out. It freaks me out!"

I just laughed. So did she.

"Well, I work here as a Volunteen." I said.

"That is so, so cool. I want to do that someday. Of course, I gotta get better first, huh?"

"Yeah. Jasmine, if you don't mind me asking, what is your condition? My dad is a doctor—okay, a radiologist—but he said you were jaundiced the night you came in—your skin was yellowish."

"I know. Don't I look freaky sometimes? Oh, I don't mind telling you what is up with me. But first, tell me about that teacher you want me to have in English. You said his name, but I am a little fuzzy on stuff that happens right before I pass out."

"Oh, okay. Well, his name is Mr. Buscotti—we call him Mr. B. He is very nice, and he has a way of connecting with kids. And he teaches lots of music…"

"Cool."

"And he just teaches with heart. And he says stuff that is really interesting to kids, and he makes the books and stories come to life. He is also a really good writing teacher, and he is a stickler for teaching grammar."

"Yuck."

"Well, he makes it fun. And it is mostly about using commas and not writing fragments…"

Jasmine was soaking it all in. "I love to write, but I am a mess with grammar stuff."

"Trust me, Jasmine, he will get you so totally organized…and you'd better know who Bruce Springsteen is."

"Who?"

"Well, that is a long, long story. He'll tell you about it when you get him, but Bruce Springsteen's music has some religious points to it, but it isn't Christian music."

"Oh, that's cool. I don't just listen to Christian music, but I am, like, majorly connected to my church and God. That's a long, long story, too. But Mr. B sounds so great."

"I will do my best to let him know about you and see if he can get you into his class. He would be very understanding of your health issues." I was hoping I wasn't promising too much.

"Right. My health. Well, have you ever heard of the Make-a-Wish Foundation?"

"Yes, of course."

"Well, I am a Make-a-Wish kid! See, they 'grant the wishes of children with life-threatening medical conditions to enrich the human experience with hope, strength, and joy.'" She giggled again. "I have that memorized; I had to say it so many times. Okay, my condition is called biliary artresia. It is when my liver doesn't properly filter out the bile in my bloodstream, leading to cirrhosis of the liver. I was born with it, but it isn't genetic. The doctor performed a Kasai procedure on me to buy some time for me as I wait for a transplant. But even though they predicted that I would need a transplant in a year or so, I have lasted for 14 miraculous years! I'm one of the few kids at UCLA Medical Center, where my operation happened, to have survived 14 years with a defective liver. I'm pretty grateful!"

I was blown away. Here was this pretty girl—happy as can be—with a life-threatening condition—and *she* was the one who was grateful. I complain about *everything*—everyone does. Jasmine had the wisdom of someone three times her age.

"I am the grateful one," I told her, "for meeting *you*. How much longer will you be here—in the hospital, I mean?"

"Oh, don't be freaked out about death jokes. I get that all the time. When God wants me—he is The Boss. I just have faith that there is something I was meant to do on this earth, and it is His plan."

We were quiet for a minute. I was trying to take her in. "I admire your courage and your faith, Jasmine. I will check up on you. Let me have your cell number. I will stay in touch, and hopefully, you will be outta here soon."

"Yeah. The food is kinda sucky." She made a scrunched up face.

That was the only time I have ever heard Jasmine complain.

Ever.

July 4th

Mickey wrote a poem about us. It made me cry. (Lots of things do lately.) I am so lost in a whirlpool of questions, and I don't know if the answers are coming soon or at all. And I don't know if I am the person who will answer them or if they will be answered for me by forces and things I can't control.

Is this what growing up is like?

When I kiss him, I melt. I just drop into his arms. Is that good for me? Should I get so attached?

I remember a story I read my sophomore year called "Another of Mike's Girls." It was really the first time I read something in high school that made me think, *Hey, this is about kids like me.* Anyway, I remember that this cute guy named Mike is dating this girl—he has a big crush on her, and she is way into him, too. Mike's dad is the narrator, I think. And he explains that Mike always says he really likes a girl, and then two months later, it's another girl—then another, then another. And he kinda likes the new girl Mike is dating, but he fears for her because he knows what is gonna happen, and he knows she has no clue. Thus the title—you know what I mean?

So anyway, at the end of the story, Mike tells his dad about breaking up with the newest girl and says he feels like a jerk. I remember his dad telling him that he's supposed to feel like a jerk—that he probably really hurt her feelings and that that is the price you pay for being in love—or thinking you are.

Yikes. I just had all that flashing through my mind the last few days. It's not that Mickey is like that character—he's not—I hope he's not. But am I like that girl? Clinging to Mickey like he is my only source of happiness? Oh, and I forgot to tell you how the story ends. Mike's dad runs into the girl at a diner, where she is drowning her sorrow in a monster ice cream sundae. Tears flood her eyes when she asks him the question she promised herself she would never ask: "How's Mike?" She is miserable, and Mike's dad is powerless to help her. Would my dad feel the same way? Would I be that same sappy, sobbing, ice-cream-slurping girl? Am I gonna turn into "Another of Mickey's Girls?"

Get a hold of yourself, Maddie. But you see my point? How much should I give him? How far should I go? Do I depend on him too much? I don't know.

And then he writes that poem—and like Holden Caulfield says, he kills me. He makes me melt.

Oh, I already said that…I'm melting…I'm melting…

July 28th

Forty thousand dollars. It might as well be a million. Multiply that by 4 and I am $160,000 in debt. And that's if the costs stay the same. Mickey's dad says that things are only going to get worse. He figures $200,000. (Maybe people will read this 20 years from now and say, "Wow, what a bargain! Those kids only had to pay $200,000 to go to college. Our generation has to pay half a million!")

College. The other source of my worries. Now that I don't have to worry about my dad being blown up by an RPG in the Middle East, I get to worry about my family's bank account getting blown up just to get me an education. Private schools are so expensive, and even if they give you a scholarship—Mickey and I have friends who still pay at least $40,000 to $60,000 for the 4 years in school, even *with* the scholarships. Sure, there are some people who get free rides—but that is not happening for me. I am not a star athlete—I am not an athlete at all—and I am not brilliant like Pari… So, hmm… Private schools are out.

Public state schools are more affordable—I just have to find one that fits me and that isn't a massive commuter college with parking structures the size of Mt. Olympus surrounding it. I want to go to a school where I live there and feel like it is a college community, you know?

Yeah.

I did like Sonoma State. It's small—maybe 6,000 students—and you can live on campus all 4 years. But it has no football team. Oh, well. I like baseball better, anyway. It is a college that a lot of students go to if they want to be teachers. Hmm… It is in "Wine Country," and it has majors in culinary arts and wine stuff. The apartments on campus seem really nice.

But it is far away from home. But it is close to San Francisco. But it is way less expensive—maybe $10,000 a year. But I might not get in. But I won't know anybody there. But it rains all the time. I seem to start too many sentences in my life with the word *but*. *But* do you think that is a bad sign?

Oh, and one more thing about Sonoma State—did I mention the "Sonoma Aroma?" Cows. Yeah. When the wind blows and it gets warmer and it stops raining, you can smell it for miles. I guess that is why the land is so fertile.

Yeah.

***** ***** ***** ***** *****

Mr. B talked to me the day after last year's graduation when he was cleaning up his room. I came to get him to sign my yearbook.

"So, any colleges in the works to visit this summer, Miss Maddie?" he asked.

I told him my woes. He looked at me thoughtfully, then put his feet up on his desk. It was kinda funny that he did that because he never seemed so relaxed when he taught us. He was in jeans with a hole in the knee, a Bruce Springsteen "Born to Run" T-shirt, and our school's baseball hat, which Mickey had given him last season. Very different from his usual "show attire," as he calls it.

Anyway, he said to me: "Maddie, I think the key to deciding on a college is *how it feels there*. Does it feel like it could be a home away from home? Are the people there cut from the same cloth as you are? Do you feel like it is not going to be too much of a financial burden for you and your family? 'Cause here's the thing—college is what you make it. You can go to Harvard and be miserable—trust me; I have had students tell me exactly that. You can go to a community college and then transfer to a state school and be happy as can be—and not have tons of debt. I have a former student who did exactly that. His dad passed away suddenly, and he had to work while he went to junior college right around here. Then he transferred to UC San Diego to finish his degree. Next thing I knew, he was working at the State Department. Kids want to brag about schools—so do parents. And I am not saying that the great colleges are not great—they are. But *you have to feel at home; you have to feel that this is a place where you can grow and become the Madison I know you will be proud of.*"

He kills me.

So after he gave me a tissue to wipe away my tears, he signed my yearbook. Here is what he wrote next to his faculty picture:

To Miss Maddie-

You gave me the most wonderful gift any teacher could ever dream of:

unconditional love and respect.

Mr. Buscotti

I must have read that dozens of times.

August 11th

Well, Mickey's dad just blew me away last night when he told us about the Bruce Springsteen concert this fall. I have never seen a big time concert. Okay, we saw the *American Idol* tour, and my cousin took me to see Keith Urban, but Bruce Springsteen is, like, a really big rock star.

Of the four of us, Mickey is the major Springsteen fan. Rhia is into Duffy; Pari likes this new singer Adele; me—I like anything. I love music. Taylor Swift. Alicia Keyes. Beyoncé. Coldplay. Kings of Leon. Black Eyed Peas. I just like lots of music. But seeing Bruce—that's, like, big time. My dad has seen a whole bunch of famous old school bands, like Simon and Garfunkel and James Taylor and the Rolling Stones. My mom said she saw Tina Turner and Elton John (at Dodger Stadium!). I mean, when they tell me that, I think, *Wow, how special is that! What if I had seen The Beatles or Elvis? I would be able to say I was there. I saw someone who just changed the world.*

Sometimes I think that music is the thing that connects us all—even if we argue about it and complain that so-and-so is a sellout or a poser or whatever. There are times when my parents and I are so far apart on things—like when they have to explain old stuff like Watergate and Desert Storm and newer things like the Taliban and Osama bin Laden and the "shock and awe" war stuff in Iraq. But when the music starts, we all want to drift into the when and where of the song. Like when women felt that Aretha Franklin was talking about their lives when she sang "RESPECT." Or when all the drug songs came out, like, in the 60s. Or when Neil Young sang "Ohio" after the Kent State shootings. My dad explained a lot of that to me, and I listened to it all. Even though he was too young to go to Vietnam, he still thought about the war—and he still does.

One night many years ago, I wanted to see *Forrest Gump*. The movie came out when I was, like, 5 years old, but I saw it when I was in sixth grade. My mom thought I might be too young for it, but my dad explained a lot of it to me. It is still one of my favorite movies. I think that the film—more than anything I have ever seen—really helped me understand my folks' generation and all they had to deal with when they were growing up. And it helps to understand Bruce Springsteen's music. I got a pretty good introduction to Springsteen last year with Mr.

B, but the new album that is part of his current tour is called *Magic,* and I know Mickey is trying to figure out what the songs are about. That is so Mickey. My favorite song on the album is "Girls in Their Summer Clothes." I don't know what it means…yet, but I love the sound of it—and, after all, me and Pari and Rhia are all dressed for summer, which is fast coming to an end.

Yeah.

August 21st

Well, it is my last day at the hospital before school starts, and Jasmine is finishing up her second stay here. She was here for a week at the beginning of summer—when I last talked with her—and now she has been admitted to check on her condition and discuss her ability to go to high school on a regular basis.

I emailed Mr. B about Jasmine, and he actually had her put into his class—the same class in which I will be his TA. He told me that I can help communicate stuff to Jasmine if she is absent.

"No way! I already love him, and I haven't even met him," Jasmine said to me while she was waiting to be discharged from the hospital.

I asked about her situation and got the latest update.

"Well, here's the scoop. I need a new liver. Eighth grade was quite difficult for me because my liver was starting to fail. But it wasn't so bad that I was in desperate need of a new liver. So I had all the symptoms of liver failure, but I wasn't qualified to receive a transplant because my tests were stable. It's all very complicated."

I said, "Well, Jasmine, whenever you miss class, I will email you, okay? Like, if you are absent, I will type up the notes and send them to you—that was Mr. B's idea. And if there are handouts, we will see if we can get them to you; I can scan them and email them to you. Hopefully, you won't be sick, right?"

"Right."

Just then, the nurses came over, and I could tell that her mom wanted to get going. So we exchanged cell numbers and stuff, and I hugged her. She is so tiny that I could feel her ribs. I know she has a special diet—there are only certain foods that she can digest. She wears poofy dresses because even though she is petite, her stomach is usually bloated.

Jasmine is one of the favorites here at Children's. All the nurses know her, and when I got to wheel her out of the hospital, you would have thought she was a celeb.

"Jasmine, everyone knows you."

"Yeah, I try to cheer up the sick people I see. I think it's the least I can do 'cause the people here do so much for me."

Her sweetness almost hides the fact that she is so strong of heart…and of soul.

***** ***** ***** ***** *****

We drove to the beach later that afternoon—me and Mickey. I told him all about Jasmine. He listened intently.

"Maybe I could write about her for the school newspaper?" he said. He was the Features Editor. "Maybe we could follow her story?"

"I don't know, Mickey. She probably doesn't want all that attention. She just wants to be normal."

"Yeah, I know. Do you think she will hold up?" Mickey asked as we found a parking spot and got our towels out.

"I don't know. Lord knows she has the desire."

As we watched the sunset over the ocean, I realized that the summer was over. Fall would begin the following Monday, when school started. I began to feel sorry for myself. Then I thought of Jasmine.

"I'm making a wish, Mickey. And I know exactly what to wish for."

Just then, the sun set, and we looked for the green flash. And there it was.

Autumn

2008

Chapter 5: Like a Hurricane

Madison's Hand

August 25th

It began like a hurricane: school. You would think that as seniors, we would be cool and used to all the craziness. Yeah, well, just the shock of getting back to five or six classes *bang, bang, bang* and waking up in the dark and all the rules and all the teachers' expectations and all the who did what and who looks different and who broke up with whom and all the where are you going? and the what did you do? and the senioritis that has set in before we have even started…yikes. See what I mean? It's like a hurricane.

So, we decided that we would piece together the first coupla weeks. So, here goes as the wind blows…

Rhiannon's Hand

I gotta tell you—I'm glad summer is over. If I had to deal with 30 hours of Yummy Yogurt for one more week, I would go freakin' nuts. I liked meeting people, and I loved being with Tiffany and Leann, but my legs ache, and I just can't get the smell of all that sugar out of my nose. So going back to school is chill compared to all that. I will still work on Sundays, and my mom told me to not work more than one night and 10 hours max a week.

"You didn't need to work last year, and you don't have to work this year. We can get by. And with Chris gone…" my mom said yesterday.

"Yeah, I know, Mom. But if I do this, I don't have to bug you for money. And I'm banking a lot for college next year."

Mom worries. She has a lot to worry about. Chris is in boot camp in Texas. Army. I am not sure when he will visit us or where he will go after boot camp. He says Iraq, probably. I just close my eyes and pray.

I also know my mom is lonely. You know, she is really very pretty. She hasn't let herself go—know what I mean? She says she was on the "Divorce Diet"—and she has lost, like, 20 pounds. Her hair is highlighted (to cover the gray, she says), and she has let it grow out to her shoulders. Really, she looks fabulous.

I don't need a father—that is for sure—but I think she needs a man in her life. She fights the depression/anxiety/stress stuff. It isn't that she *needs* a man—it is that she *needs to feel love from a man—and she needs to give love to him*. Does that make sense?

I can tell that she is feeling better, though. She went to a wedding the other day for someone from her work, and she had a great time. She loves to dance. She was gorgeous in her new dress.

"What is the color of the dress, Mom? It is so cute."

"It is champagne. You know, I have not bought a new dress in I-don't-know-how-many years." She twirled around and looked at herself in the mirror the way women do, always with their back to the mirror and looking over their shoulder to make sure they don't look fat.

"Mom, you look hot."

"I don't want to look 'hot,' Rhiannon. I am 42 years old, sweetie. I just want to look…nice."

She looked more than nice. When she came home from the wedding and for the next week, her spirits were lifted. It was like she kinda started living again…not just surviving. Hey, I never even told you her name; isn't that funny? Our parents are all just named *Mom* and *Dad.* Like, we only know them by their parent label. Anyway, her name is Patti—with an "i." And I love her so.

Anyway. Tiffany has also gotten things more together. She has so many issues with boys and eating and you name it. But she has calmed down a lot. Surfing helps her. She told me that she is not even dealing with boys right now.

"They are so stupid, Rhia. All they care about is getting into your pants. Some of the surfers are cool, though—the older ones," she told me during the week of our last shift together. I had a feeling that she wasn't being totally honest. I think there is an older surfer guy she likes. But I am glad she has chilled; she was the poster child for "Wild Thing" for a while.

Leann is another story. Quiet. Guarded. It took all summer to get her to talk to me about something other than yogurt. She is a junior, and she just found out that she has Mr. Buscotti for the class I was in last year, American Literature. Of course, I told her tons about the class and how great it was—about dancing, about how Mr. B makes you think, and about how he treats you like an adult. She seemed doubtful.

She did say she *had* a boyfriend, but they broke up in the middle of summer. I remember that in July, she was especially in her own world. Didn't say much to anyone. She did tell me one thing that is typical of a lot of us girls: "When me and Tommy broke up, our friends had to decide who to hang out with. And I just don't even wanna see most of them anymore, anyway."

"So who do you hang out with?" I asked.

"Some girls," she shrugged. "Whatever. It doesn't matter."

That was all I could get out of her until the last week of work. Then she asked me about Donald, who came by the yogurt place at least once a week to flirt with me.

"Do you like him?" Leann said as she swirled chocolate with peanut butter into a cone.

"Yeah. He is very sweet."

"Are your parents cool with him being black?"

"Parent. Singular. Yeah, my mom loves him. His dad is from the Caribbean—I love his dad's accent."

"Oh. He seems older—or more mature."

"Yeah, Tiffany says the same thing. Leann, are you still kinda hurt about the breakup with that guy you were seeing?" The last customer had left, and we had a break in the action.

"No. Well…yes and no. I just try to put it all out of my mind is all. Whatever. He was a jerk."

"Why?"

"Why what?"

"Why was he a jerk?" I looked at her as I cleaned up the Oreo toppings that had spilled on the counter.

"Oh, you know—all into himself and what he wanted and just…" A pause. "I don't wanna talk about it, okay?"

"Okay." Ten minutes passed without a customer or a sound. And then it was closing time. I counted out the money and figured out the tips in the jar.

"Yeah. Well…umm…anyway, Donald seems nice." Leann grabbed a broom as we cleaned up.

"He is. Leann, I wasn't trying to pry or anything."

"No, I know. Maybe I will talk about things more later, okay?" Leann never took her eyes off the crumbs on the floor as she swept them into the trash.

"That's cool. Whenever. Hey, Leann—look at me." It was a demand more than a request. "I like you. You are a good person. If you ever just wanna talk, I will listen. Seriously. Okay?"

Leann stared at me as if she was calculating something in her head that she could not figure out unless she had pencil and paper. "Okay, Rhia. Thanks." She went back to sweeping, and with her eyes focused on the floor, she softly said, "I will."

That's where we left it.

***** ***** ***** ***** *****

Okay, Mr. B is a hard act to follow, but Ms. LaFleur is a really cool English teacher. We are not all in the same class—Pari and Mickey are in AP Literature and me and Maddie are in World Literature, but Ms. LaFleur teaches both classes (and she teaches French 1, too.) So Pari has her twice a day. And we all know why she is taking beginning French. Yep.

Ms. LaFleur is not from France. "I am from Montreal, and I have dual citizenship with Canada and the States," she told us. I guess what I like about her is that she treats us like adults—like Mr. B did—but she is more artsy, and the class is kinda more on us. Let me explain. We sit in a circle, and she sits in it with us. The first day, it was all about getting to know us. She also explained her reason for teaching and told us why world literature matters.

"Look, I know that as seniors, you are the top of the food chain here at school; but very soon, you will be at the bottom. Life is like that. Once you have figured something out, you realize that you have even more to understand. It is accepting life's challenges that makes you wiser.

"And figuring out that there is more to the world than just American culture and its writers and poets is very important. Remember, we Americans are pretty new to the cultural scene. Go to Europe and you see history. Castles from the Middle Ages. The Coliseum in Rome. The mysteries of the Far East. The power of the African savannah. Did you know that Costa Rica essentially has a Xerox of our Constitution? Do you understand Carnival in Brazil?

"Some of you have travelled. Some of you have read the poetry of Shakespeare. But have you read Rumi? Have you read *The Alchemist?* Are you familiar with Amy Tan? Other than 'to be or not to be,' why has Hamlet remained a hit 400 years later? Talk about a revival."

But for the most part, Ms. LaFleur was not "on"—this was her one speech. She closed with these words: "I don't ignore American literature. We will look at some of our finest playwrights, like Arthur Miller. But be warned: once you enter this room, you are not a passive learner. I expect you to read, to write, to listen, to speak, and to think— for yourself. Forget about what all those Web sites say about literature; think about what *you feel about what you read.* I already know what the so-called 'experts' think; they are all old folks commenting on a world when they used typewriters and listened to phonographs. You are Generation Global, and I want to know what you think, even about things like Lady Gaga!"

We all cracked up at that. I texted Mickey, who had her later in the day: **Ms. LaFleur very cool.** He texted back: **Meeting tonight 7 B & N.**

Until the Metaphor Café reopened, Barnes and Noble would have to do.

Pari's Hand

Bonjour!

Well, I am home, but I am missing Iran. I feel a little strange because I have immersed myself in several worlds lately. Of course, being back in Tehran with my family made me appreciate my roots. I feel like I am part of that world, but at the same time, it seems almost surreal to me. I finished reading Azadeh Moaveni's memoir *Lipstick Jihad,* which Mr. Buscotti's wife gave to me at the beginning of the summer. I found the book fascinating because I feel that Moaveni is someone I admire, but not someone who I could really see myself following. She seems more hardcore in her need to become part of the Iranian world. As a *Time* reporter, she has travelled the world, and she saw the Revolution in Iran as it really was—violent, sometimes ignorant, and contradictory. It is just hard to understand how Iran, my homeland, can be so unstable. Can't it pull itself together? I know that sounds juvenile, but I am, as Mr. B used to say, "trying to understand that you don't know where you are going until you know where you've been." I have been to Iran, and I understand more about it now, but in some ways, I am still mystified.

But that is not the only culture I am embracing. *Viva la France!* Yes, I am taking first-year French; I had room in my schedule, and frankly, it is fun! My AP friends think I am really crazy for taking a class that won't help my GPA. They give me all that college admissions garbage, but you know what? I just want to learn more. Is that a crime? And I like trying to talk to Daniel. But I am so bad right now—I am *débile* (translation: totally pathetic). But it is fun, and I love Ms. LaFleur. I totally agree with what Rhia wrote about her. Her class will be challenging for sure. I miss Mr. Buscotti, but as you will find out, we get reports about him from Maddie. And for now, we are meeting at various restaurants and bookstores around town until the Metaphor Café reopens.

There is something else I need to tell you. I hope by the time we publish this I am able to deal with this better, but you know how Daniel and I went out to dinner this summer? Well, my parents were cool with it—and they like Daniel—but they thought we were with other people—like in a group thing. I told Rhia and Donald about this so that they could back up my story. Look, I don't lie to my parents…very often…but I just know they would freak if this were something that they saw as some super serious date thing. I mean, going out alone with a boy—especially one who is not Persian—is not something I think they can handle. They are protective, and I know they still see "American boys" as something to fear—or at least something they don't understand. And they don't think I can handle myself with them. I guess it doesn't matter that Daniel was born France; I can just hear my mother saying that he is simply not "one of us."

Okay. I had to get that off my chest.

So, then there is all the AP pressure this year. Calculus. Physics. English. Government. And there is something else I haven't shared yet. But I just don't feel comfortable dealing with it yet. So I won't. So don't bug me about it, Mickey, okay?

I am getting stressed out just thinking about college and tests and homework and scholarships and... Maddie is right—coming back to school is like a hurricane.

So I need to chill. French is so *détendre*. Daniel just texted me. Oops, I said it wrong. **French is so *détente*.**

Relaxing—sounds great in any language. Now, if I could just turn off my mind and fall asleep before it turns midnight...again...

Madison's Hand

We girls wanted to tell you about our lives *during* the first day of school. Mickey's part is all about the one class we all have together during the same period, and we decided to save that for when we all meet tonight. But I have to tell you what a cool trip it was to be Mr. B's TA and about his first day with his freshmen, Jasmine included.

They pile in. They look scared. But they recognize some familiar faces from eighth grade, and a few smile. There are the lost kids, of course, who say, "Is this the class with Mr. Buu..."

"Yes, it is, Son. Grab a seat before they are all gone. But don't sit there—sit right here, next to this really cute girl. Good. Consider that your first lesson." Mr. Buscotti is already "on" at 7:30 in the morning.

"Hi, gang. I am Mr. Buscotti—yes, like the thing your parents order at Starbucks with their coffee. This is Freshman English. Relaaaxxx. There is no homework, and there are no rules—yet. As a matter of fact, all I want to do today are the three R's: roll, room, and reviews. You know what I mean by reviews? Who goes to a movie without finding out if people who have seen the show before think it's any good? Right, nobody. So, we will have reviews."

I watched Jasmine. She did not know it yet, but her desk in the front row at the center of the horseshoe desk arrangement was a special place—for a special girl. She was all dressed up super cute. Her top was very loose, almost like a sundress—pink with flowers. (I figured the style had to do with her medical condition.) She wore a pair of white capris. She had this little hat—actually, it was a hair clip with a rose on it. All I can say is that the girl has style—and the cutest giggle. She started laughing at Mr. B's wisecracks right away.

"Okay, let's do roll. Hmm... Wow, this class is like the United Nations! My goodness, I've got some names here that are amazing! This first one is *Wocheszniak*. Yeah, I am starting from the bottom—these poor kids always get the short end of the stick. Ah, that is you, huh?" Mr. B looks at a little guy in the back row. "Hmm... Don't tell me your first name—all I have here on this list is your initial: *A*. Hmm... Well, you don't look like an Arthur. Nope. Definitely not an Antonio—as in Banderas. Nope. Hmm... Wow, did you know your last name is worth 34 points in Scrabble? That is, like, a record for my classes. Shut up! Seriously! It must have taken you years to learn how to spell your name. Did you nail it by fourth grade? You must be really smart."

During all this, the class is tittering—some are laughing, some are just blown away that this teacher is having such a good time with this Wocheszniak kid. The kid is a bit shy, but he seems to be taking his celebrity status in stride.

"Alex! I bet it is Alex," Mr. B declares.

To everyone's shock, including mine, the boy says timidly, "Here. Um, how did you know my name is Alex?"

"You just look like an Alex, Alex. Kid, I have been doing this show for 32 years—you get a feel for it." Mr. B spots a girl who does not seem impressed. "You think his name is on this sheet, don't you?" She looks at Mr. B and says in a cynical way, "Yeah."

"Okay, here. Check it out." He hands the girl the roll sheet. Her eyes grow bigger, and then she says to the class, "It's not there. It only says his initial."

"O, ye of little faith."

I really don't know how he did it, but Mr. B got at least 10 kids' names right—or very close. "All these Christinas, Christianas, Kirstins, Christines—they all get jumbled on my radar," Mr. B complained. "Back in the 70s, the parents were hippies, so they named the kids things like Sunshine, Dandelion, Rainbow… Those were so easy to remember! You are laughing, huh? Hey, I taught all those kids—I think two were sisters." He had the kids in the palm of his hand. (After class, he told me, "The first thing they have to feel is that I care. They will all go home and tell their folks what happened today in class—how they laughed at the names. They don't realize that I got two things done today: first, I memorized a lot of their names, and second, I got them to memorize each others' names.")

But Jasmine stumped him. "Hmm… Justine? No. Jackie? No, too presidential. Jade? No, too exotic. Jennifer? No, too boring. Man, you are a tough one!" Then he remembered that Jasmine was the girl I saw at the hospital and spoke to him about so he got her in this class—I could see the wheels turning in his head. "Jasmine!" When she heard him say her name, she burst into applause.

"Mr. Buscotti, you are soooo crazy!" she said in her excited, high-pitched voice.

"I assume that is a compliment, Miss Jasmine." It took him 30 minutes to get through the roll sheet. It was like watching stand-up comedy.

Mr. B then gave the students a tour of his classroom, like he did with us a year ago. It brought back memories. The kids gazed in awe at all the albums strung across the classroom near the ceiling, like a border: Bruce Springsteen, Tina Turner, Stevie Wonder, Madonna, Fleetwood Mac, Jackson Brown, Johnny Cash (at Folsom Prison), Bob Dylan, the Beach Boys, and a new one—although it was an old one, really.

"I know you all know this one," Mr. B said, pointing to the famous Beatles album *Abbey Road*, where the four of them are crossing the street. "But the question is: what are their names?" He looked at the class; almost all of the kids had this look on their faces like they kinda knew one or two of the Beatles, but no one was up to the challenge of naming all four—except the girl who had questioned Mr. B earlier. Her name is Nina.

"John, Paul, George, and Ringo," she said confidently.

"Nice, Miss Nina. How do you know that?"

"My dad is a Beatles fanatic. And I saw the *Love* show in Vegas last summer. It was so cool." This kid was pretty mature for a frosh—and I could tell Mr. B was clued into it, too.

"You rock my world, Miss Nina. This album was a gift from my son. He thought the room needed a British Invasion. None of you get that—except for you, Nina. Never mind, gang. On to reviews."

Mr. B went to the same wall of letters that he went to last year. It was a bulletin board chock full of letters, photos, even CDs that kids had made for him. Some were handwritten, some typed, some so faded that they were hard to decipher. There were dozens of letters attached to graduation photos of the many generations that had passed through Mr. B's "Metaphor Café." He picked one to read to the class.

"Mr. B's English class is not so much a class as it is an experience. It's like being on a raft in the river. We've been floating down Huck Finn's river as we've been listening to Bruce Springsteen's 'Big Muddy.' We've been drifting from love to war to racism, but it seems that the current always leads the four of us to our own corner table at the Metaphor Café."

"Gang, this one was written by that lovely girl sitting behind my desk. Her name is Maddie. She and her three friends wrote a book last year. And they honored me in it. If you ever have a question or a problem and I look busy, just see her. Something tells me she will give you pretty good advice."

I blushed. The kids looked at me like I was a goddess.

Me!

Mr. B's timing was perfect because right then, the bell rang. The kids were as surprised as I was—that was an hour?

Yeah…in Metaphor time.

Mickey's Hand

We are all together tonight. The sign on the closed Metaphor Café says, "Grand Reopening: November 14th!" We can't wait. Until then, we will make do.

We all happen to have Mr. MacQueen for last period AP Government. So we caught each other up on how our classes had been that day. We all agreed that Ms. LaFleur was very cool, that being seniors was great, and that missing Mr. B was inevitable. Maddie's story about his Freshman English class made us all smile. Maddie also got everyone up to speed with Jasmine.

"She is so adorable, Maddie," Pari said. "In my French class tomorrow, I'm going to sit next to her when we get our 'official seats.' And I'm going to tell her that I'm friends with you and that if she misses any class, I will contact her."

Rhia also filled us in on Tiffany and this other girl—Leann—who is in Mr. B's class now. "Leann is very mysterious, guys. I just kinda worry about her." That is typical Rhia—she worries about everyone but herself. I told her so.

"Well, Mickey, someone has to worry about her; she looks lost."

The subject got around to AP Gov and Mr. Mac, as he likes to be called—or just Mac.

I loved the way he started class today. As we were walking in, we heard the Beatles. The song was "We Can Work It Out."

Mac said, "The song is about getting along. Listening. It is also about seeing things 'my way.' So let me tell you what that means in here. Here is what I want you to learn: forget about all the memorization, the dates, the who did what to whom in which city. I will have succeeded as your teacher if I get you to *participate in our democracy*." He emphasized *participate*.

He was sitting on a stool in front of us. We were in straight rows. There was a screen behind him and a remote control in his hand. Mac is in his 40s, I think. His goatee is graying, as is his hair. Nice smile. Big voice. Medium build. His classroom has the "technologically advanced" feel—LCD screen, several computers, speakers connected to an iPod. I could tell he was a little tired since it was the first day of school, and his voice sounded a bit strained. But that wasn't going to stop him.

"Look at the words behind me," Mac said, jerking his thumb toward the PowerPoint slide displayed on the screen.

Everyone is entitled to his own opinion, but not his own facts.
—Daniel Patrick Moynihan, U.S. Senator, New York

"I want you to think—really *think*—about that. You live in a world of Wikipedia, blogs, 24-hour media, liberal and conservative news channels, books that claim to be non-fiction but are as fictional as *Peter Pan*. Whom do you believe?

"Just because you hear it doesn't make it true. I want you to learn to pull out the documentation, dig down to the source of the information, and question it. I want you to confirm sources and become politically aware. Here is why." He advanced to the next slide.

Blind faith in your leaders—or in anything—will get you killed.
—Bruce Springsteen, New Jersey's Rock Star

I immediately looked at the girls. We all smiled. Mr. Buscotti had shown us the video of when Springsteen had said those words; it was when he was singing a song called "War" in concert.

Mr. MacQueen continued: "U.S. intelligence services believed in a man nicknamed Curveball, who told the British that weapons of mass destruction (otherwise known as WMD) were part of Saddam Hussein's arsenal in Iraq. Well, he threw us a curveball, alright. We never found any WMDs, but thousands died in the effort to take down Hussein and his government. Hussein was a ruthless murderer; he gassed thousands of Kurds. Those are the facts—they are not made-up stories. The bodies were piled up. But the WMDs were not facts. You have to know—really *know*—what you are fighting for and what kind of government you want. You can't just make things up to fit your liking.

"Do you know that we had a War on Poverty in the 1960s? Do you know who LBJ was? Do you know that the money allocated to deal with poverty dried up as the war in Vietnam escalated? I grew up hearing the chant, 'Hey, hey, LBJ—how many boys did you kill today?'

"This class is not about Democrats and Republicans, people. This class is about all of us Americans and our collective mission: "to form a more perfect Union." And my mission is to get you guys to see the Big Picture. *I want you to vote.* And you will be able to vote in the most important election—the presidential election—if you are 18 by November 4th. Pretty exciting stuff, huh?

"Oh, and one last thing. Hurricane Gustav will make landfall probably by early tomorrow morning. Watch the news. I want a full report from you. We will talk about it tomorrow. Oh, and Hurricane Hanna is right behind it. I wonder how our government is going to react? Let's follow this together."

*****   *****   *****   *****   *****

"I love Mac's passion," I told the girls after class.

"Yeah, but what do you think about this test we are taking tomorrow?" asked Rhia. She hates tests.

"Chill. It is just some kinda political test to see if you are conservative or liberal," I explained. My brother had told me about it. "You sit in the class based on your answers."

"Really?" Pari said in disbelief. "Are you serious?"

"Yep."

"Man, that is gonna be strange, don't you think?" Maddie wondered.

"Well, I don't know," I shrugged. "I guess the questions will be about, like, what we think of Obama or McCain or, like, who our favorite President of all time is."

"Hey, was George Washington a Republican?" Rhia seemed bewildered. We burst out laughing… I guess you had to be there. It was just funny. Like, who would even wonder such a thing?

"Dude, I don't think they even *had* political parties then. But I am sure Lincoln was a Republican," I said.

Maddie looked at me. "Weren't there Whigs then? I don't mean the white things that bald guys wore to look...I don't know...British. I mean the political party. Didn't we learn about Whigs in, like, seventh grade?"

"Yeah, I think it was spelled *W-h-i-g-s*," Pari said as she reached for her keys. "Guys, I gotta go. Ugh—I have math homework already!"

With that, we left. When I got home, I turned on CNN. The anchor was saying:

> **...It formed this morning about 260 miles southeast of Port-au-Prince, Haiti and rapidly strengthened into a tropical storm. By tomorrow morning it may become a hurricane with winds whipping as high as 150 miles per hour. It is about to make landfall near the Haitian town of Jacmel, we believe. It will likely hit Jamaica and Western Cuba and then move across the Gulf of Mexico. In Louisiana, emergency preparedness officials have met several times to discuss predictions that Gustav will become a major hurricane in 3 to 5 days...**

Little did we know that this was just the beginning of the hurricanes to come. Hurricanes that were more literal than metaphorical.

Chapter 6: Our Secret Gardens

Madison's Hand

August 28th

Oh my God. I am so glad we are writing this *after* it all happened because when it happened, we were so surprised and emotional that I don't know if we could have put it into words. The next 15 days reminded us of why we wrote *Meetings at the Metaphor Café* and why we needed to continue. There are so many lessons to be learned and so many hearts broken and so many people who just don't get it at all— well, it just had to come out. Secrets are hard to hold in…especially when you are 18…or 43.

I remember the first time Mr. B played Springsteen's song "Secret Garden." Mickey had told me it was the theme song to the movie *Jerry McGuire*, which surprised me 'cause it didn't seem to fit. Mr. B taught it to us to get us to understand *theme:*

"It is the point the author is making about human beings—the way we are, why we do the things we do." This was how he began the day with his freshmen. When he taught us last year, he had said the same thing, but the challenge for us was to figure out the theme of the song "Secret Garden"—which Rhia nailed when she said, "It's about the fact that some of us will never, ever let people into the deepest places of our heart and soul—so don't even try." I remember that she was very bitter about her dad then.

But with his freshmen, Mr. B had to go much slower, and he needed to really help them understand what they think an author is saying about characters. The reason I bring this up is that our chapter is all about what we are saying about ourselves—our secrets. Watching Mr. B as his "assistant teacher" made me see the beauty of helping others to understand ideas. How do you even measure or categorize that?

"Let's talk about Harry Potter," he told the students. "I assume you all know a bit about him. Now, why is he a hero? Why is 'He who shall not be named' a villain? Hmm?"

Of course, Jasmine piped up: "'Cause Harry is the good guy."

"Ah, but so are Hermione and Ron and the rest of the gang. What makes Harry special?"

Silence. Freshmen are funny; they are more intimidated by Mr. B than we were. Afraid to be "wrong," I guess. Mr. B pushed "play" on the DVD player, and a clip from the first *Harry Potter* movie (when they were really cute) played. It was the scene when the mean kid with the white hair named Draco grabs a ball from some poor kid—Neville, I think—and whips it away. Harry jumps on a broom and saves the ball, and all the kids applaud 'cause Harry had never flown before. While they all congratulate Harry, I could not help but be brought back to when I first read those books and saw those movies. My mom and dad (when he wasn't deployed) read them out loud to our whole family— but I re-read them myself. The freshmen were all smiling by this time. But I noticed that some of them had never seen this movie before—for shame!

"So why did Harry get the ball for the kid and thwart Draco's overall jerkiness?" Mr. B asked them.

He let them chirp in things like, "He is nice;" "He hates Draco;" "He wants to prove something;" "He is a leader."

"But Hitler was a leader. Voldemort was a leader. Osama bin Laden is a leader. What makes evil…evil? Hmm?"

"They want to kill people…innocent people," said one of the boys whose name I had not yet learned. Of course, Mr. B had.

"Yes, Ronnie, but why?"

"Why what?" Ronnie had used up all he knew.

"Why kill? Why instill fear? Why bully?"

A long pause. Then Mr. B reminded them of this: "What did Harry get for his efforts?"

The answers came: "respect," "cheers," "friendship," "a hero's welcome." *Smart kids,* I thought.

"Right. Listen, team. Harry Potter is a hero for the same reason that the men who stormed the beaches at Normandy in WWII were heroes: he is unselfish. He fights for a cause bigger than himself. He is centered on the feelings of others. He is loyal. What separates him from other characters is that he has a drop or two more of courage. And courage is the knowledge that you are in for trouble when you do something, but you do it anyway because it is the right thing to do. Think those black men and women who went to the lunch counters in the Deep South during the Civil Rights Movement were not brave? They knew they were going to have hot coffee spilled on their heads. Think Rosa Parks didn't know it would be dangerous to not give up her seat on that bus?

"So when I ask you the theme of the *Harry Potter* films, one thing you could say is that some people rise above their selfishness for a cause that makes other people's lives better. Let's try another film. Hmm. *Forrest Gump.*"

Then Mr. B did the funniest thing: he sat down on a chair like Tom Hanks did in the movie and pretended he had a box of chocolates. He said in his best Forrest Gump impersonation, "You know, I like chocolates. In a box like this, you never know what's inside. My Momma, she always reminds me that 'stupid is as stupid does'—but I sure do love Jenny and Bubba and Lieutenant Dan." The class cracked up.

"Now, gang, today I am going to prove that you all can think—and figure out the theme of that film—even if you've never seen it. Guys, is Forrest smart?"

A chorus of "No's" rang out. "Heck, no," said Mr. B. "As a matter of fact, he is so dumb that he loves Jenny even though she is a junkie and a prostitute. Why? Because he told her so. He said, 'I will always love you, Jenny'" (Mr. B again used his best Southern accent). "He is so dumb that when his soldier buddy Bubba is about to die, Forrest promises him that he will go back and run Bubba's shrimp business. Does Forrest know anything about the shrimp business?"

Another chorus of "No's."

"Have any of you eaten at Bubba Gump's Shrimp Company?"

"Yes!" The freshmen were totally with him. One asked him, "Whoa, Mr. Buscotti—so, that was a true story?"

"No, not exactly. One more thing. Was Forrest smart when he ran back to the jungle to save Lieutenant Dan, who had his legs shot off? Remember, that's when Forrest got shot in the 'buttocks.'"

After a brief chuckle, the class was silent. "Why did he do all those things? Do you remember what he told each of those people when they were in great danger?"

One girl in the middle of the room answered as if she wasn't really sure: "He said he would always be there for them?"

Mr. B smiled. "Yep. 'Cause a promise is a promise. You know, lots of girls saw that movie with their boyfriends and elbowed the guys during the movie and said, 'Why can't you be more like him?'

"And the guys sitting next to those girls in the movie theater said, 'But he is so dumb!'

"And the girls turned to those guys, stopped eating their popcorn, and said, 'I don't care. He is so...so...*nice*.' And then those girls turned back to the movie and smiled at Forrest Gump's face on the screen."

Mr. B continued his sermon: "Gang, I was listening to the radio one day, and the author of the book *Forrest Gump* was being interviewed on NPR." (The kids had no idea what that was). "They asked him what the theme of *Forrest Gump* was. The author said it so simply. He said, 'I am so glad you asked. Look, we can't all be smart or rich or pretty. But all people—all people—can treat others with *dignity*.'

"That's the secret, gang. Now, go out there and be like Forrest Gump."

The bell rang as it always does, but for a minute, the students did not move—especially Jasmine.

Pari's Hand

September 2nd

I got into three fights today. Well, not exactly fights...but I hate confrontation, and I don't get angry very often. When I do, it really upsets me. I am just not doing too well right now. I am so upset that the tissue box is empty; I didn't get together with Maddie, Rhia, and Mickey; and it's midnight, and I still have 30 pages of lit reading and another hour of math to do. I am sleepy and weepy. I don't even have time to finish this...

September 3rd

I feel a little better today. I called my friends and got some good advice. It went something like this:

Me: I know you guys were upset with me for bailing on you yesterday.

Them: No worries, Pari. Mickey had to leave early, too.

Me: Well, I'm sorry—I'm just so stressed out. I'm a mess right now, and I feel like I am letting you guys down…

Them: Can we just come over to your house tonight and talk? At least Rhia and Maddie can come?

Me: Yeah.

Them: Just tell us what the topics are…like, did you break up with Daniel?

Me: No, not yet. It has to do with my parents, my time, my stress level, my life…

Them: Yikes! We'll come by at 7:00. Chill, okay?

***** ***** ***** ***** *****

Mickey did make it. After saying hi to my folks, my mom insisted on bringing us some crackers and stuff in my room. I knew that my parents knew that we are not studying that night. I was still upset. I sat on the floor. A small mountain of clothes was piled on the side of the bed where my friends couldn't really see it. Mickey said, "Pari, I like the room. Cool Adele poster."

"Great dance pictures of you, Pari. Look how cute you were when you were in a little ballerina outfit!" Rhia's bracelets jingled as she moved from photo to photo.

"Thanks." I was in knots.

"So what is freaking you out, Pari?" Maddie, always on topic, cut to the chase.

Big breath. Already had a tissue in hand.

"First, my parents got mad at me for staying up so late doing homework. Okay, it is more than that. I have pulled two all-nighters, and I don't go to sleep before 2 AM very often. My parents think I should drop something from my schedule because the pressure is too much."

My friends stared at me.

"I think I can handle it. I think—I don't know. It's only September—I know teachers are harder now and lighten up later on. I know it's gonna get easier. Besides, I don't wanna drop AP Physics or AP Calculus B/C because I am good at those things. And I think I am going into med studies. I don't know."

"What did your parents say when they talked to you?" Maddie again.

"They said, 'Why are you taking French? It is a waste of time.' And my dad says it will lower my GPA even if I get an A. But that is my favorite class! It is the only class I can relax in—right now. And there is the Daniel factor."

That got everyone's attention. Rhia's eyes were glued to me.

I sighed a sigh that would inflate a balloon. "I never told them that Daniel was my boyfriend—I just said he was my friend. I asked Rhia to cover for me if my folks ever ask about the time Dan and I went out to dinner because they think we went as a group. My folks think I should not be serious about a boy...I am not sure they would feel this way if he was Persian...maybe. I don't know.

"I got past the whole brothers/sister stuff last year. My folks told me they totally support me and want me to go to university—and now I feel the pressure of it all. Before, my brothers were just not into school, and they dealt with my parents' disappointment and sometimes their anger. But now they've dropped out of college and have jobs. They are gone, and I am left to, like, fulfill my parents' dream of becoming a doctor, lawyer, whatever. You guys know what I am talking about. We all feel it."

"Not me," Rhia said. "I am in a different world. My mom couldn't afford to send me to a university even if I had a perfect SAT score. But I feel for you, Pari. I really do."

"Then Daniel called one night," I said. "My dad answered the phone. I don't why he didn't text me or call me on my cell—whatever, he just didn't understand. My dad made some lame excuse for why I could not talk to him—homework or something. But Dan got the feeling that my dad didn't like him, or didn't like the fact that he was calling me…at home.

"So my mom and dad asked me point blank about Daniel. This was right after he called Mickey to get my cell number so he could ask me what was up with my dad. I told him to only call me on my cell or text me. He said, "Why?" and I told him that my parents were strict or whatever. Then I had to quickly get off the phone because my folks asked me to come downstairs and talk to them."

"But Pari, your mom and dad are really reasonable," Maddie said.

"I know. I know. But they are also Persian. They have customs and attitudes, and they are so worried that I will end up like some wild American girl. They are also freaked out about my lack of sleep—but that I understand."

There was a pause. My friends all needed time to let everything sink in before I went any further. Mickey had not said a word, but he acted like he was taking this all in and would eventually give some sort of advice. I kinda stared at him. Of my three friends, I knew Mick was the one who was the most like me and felt the same pressures. His quietness was unnerving. I continued:

"Okay, so I go downstairs, and my folks go through the whole 'we're-worried-about-you' speech. We talk about classes I could drop. I tell them I have three more days to drop. We agree that it is my call, but they are very, *very* pushy that I have to drop something. My dad says, 'Why make yourself sick taking too hard of a class load and then get bad grades? That is not going to impress the top universities.' My mom says, 'I care about *you*, Parivesh. I worry that you think you need to push yourself so hard and that we are pushing you, too. We are not.'

"Yes, you are," I told them. "Look, I want you to push me. I know—I sound like a hypocrite. One minute I complain that you don't really care about me because I am a girl, and the next minute, I am getting all emotional on you 'cause of the expectations."

Another pause. "What did they say?" These were Mickey's first words. I felt a bit of relief when he broke his silence.

"We agreed that maybe we had all misunderstood things. We would talk again in a day or two about the class stuff. Then my dad asked whether I was serious about 'this Daniel boy'—that is how he referred to him. Sorta like he was an invader. Up until then, they were cool with him—happy I was not a loner."

"Dad, I don't want to talk about Daniel, okay?" I was getting angry.

"We don't mean to pry," my mom insisted.

"But you are."

"Hmm. You are angry with us, Parivesh." My father said these things when he was trying to decide whether to attack or retreat.

"Yes. No. I don't know. I just don't want to talk about it. Daniel is my friend. I like him. If he calls me, please don't hang up on him, okay?"

"Parivesh, let us agree on two things: first, you need to rethink the pressures on you. You are under so much stress that you are not…your usual self; and second, we will trust you to make wise decisions about classes and boyfriends. But if you keep up this pace—or whatever you call it—*lifestyle*—we will have to make changes. We don't want you to be miserable, okay?" I have to hand it to my dad. He is such the diplomat.

"Okay."

Then my mom added, "We are not against you having a boyfriend. We are just concerned that you may get too involved… Okay, I have said enough. Dry your eyes. I love you, Parivesh. So does your father."

When I told my friends this, Rhia said, "Man, I wish I had folks like yours."

Maddie smiled warmly. "I am glad you had faith in us. Pari, we love you, too."

But Mickey was prepared to drop the hammer. "I just had the same talk with my parents. Look, Pari, you have 4 AP classes; I have 3. If you drop AP Physics and take regular Physics, it will be a *huge* relief, you know? And I can help you in Calculus."

"*You* help *me*?" I laughed for the first time. "You suck in AP Calc!"

"Yeah, I know. But you learn more by teaching it to others—so in the end, I will be helping myself." Mickey took all the tension away with his coy smile.

"I'll think about it—the physics idea," I told them.

When they left, I listened to Adele's debut album *19*. She wrote all the songs on it, and she named it *19* because that's how old she was when she recorded it. I was amazed that she was just a year older than me. The song "Chasing Pavements" is my favorite. It has a line that says something about whether you should give up or just keep chasing the pavement—even if the sidewalk leads nowhere at all.

That question rattled around in my brain until I fell asleep around midnight. By morning, I had to decide how much longer to keep my other secret to myself.

Rhiannon's Hand

September 7th

We all took the test today to see if we were liberal or conservative. I would bet that I am pretty liberal. I don't know about Maddie. Mickey is from a conservative family, but he is, like, a rebel compared to them. Pari—she is a total mystery. The really crazy thing is that when we got the results, we sat in order of our "political-ness"—like, I guess, the Senate with the Democrats and the Republicans. Whatever.

So here is how it went:

What Are You? Liberal or Conservative?

Answer "Yes" if you agree or "No" if you disagree. Do not leave any statement blank.

1. As a world power, the United States should become involved in international conflicts that could lead to widespread war. **I said No—seems like we would turn the conflicts into a widespread war.**
2. Warrantless wiretaps, as provided for in the PATRIOT Act, should be allowed in the arrest of suspected terrorists. **No... Well, Yes. Hmm. Are they unwarranted or what? And what does that even mean? I am still gonna say...Yes...No. No.**
3. All working American families should be guaranteed a living wage. **Duh—of course! Yes!**
4. Due process rights should be guaranteed to all people detained by US authorities. **See above: Yes!**
5. The Electoral College should be abolished so that the President will be elected by popular vote. **Hmm. Not totally sure what the Electoral College is. Sounds like a trick question. I am going No on this one.**

6. The NAFTA agreement should be abolished. **Um. Huh? No clue. So…No.**

7. The US reserves the right to act unilaterally in the internal affairs of other nations if it determines that the actions of these nations threaten US security. **Whoa. Like, if they are gonna shoot a missile at us or something? Yeah, I guess. But not for some dumb reason, like the whole Bush WMD thing, which everyone knows was a bunch of bull. There were no WMDs. Anyway, Yes…but with big reservations.**

8. Upon completion of high school, all legal male residents must serve one year in the military. **No way, José.**

9. Local and state governments rather than the federal government should be primarily responsible for environmental regulation enforcement. **But what if a state is really polluted, and the state downstream gets all toxic? No— somebody has to be in charge.**

10. The Brady Law should be repealed. **Um. Huh? No clue. So, No…again.**

11. Affirmative Action admission policies for public colleges and universities should be enforced. **Ah. Mr. Buscotti would be proud of me—I remember this. But I don't remember which way I used to feel. Hmm. Yes…I think.**

12. A Constitutional amendment requiring a balanced budget should be passed. **But we are in so much debt; how can we just magically balance the budget? I guess it is a good idea. Is being in debt *un*constitutional? Yes…close call.**

13. The federal government should mandate that auto manufacturers only produce hybrid vehicles. **Well, interesting…but too nuts. No. I mean, what if I have to drive to, like, San Francisco? Dude, I will, like, run out of "energy" where the cows are on that long, boring part of the freeway, and then I will so be toast. I mean, I like being "green" and all, but let's be real. No.**

14. Capital punishment (i.e., the death penalty) should be abolished. **Yeah. Well, hmm. Another trick question. Some people deserve to die, but some are innocent; there is all**

that **DNA** stuff we talked about last year. **I am going to say...Yes.**

15. Labor union membership should be voluntary. **Duh—Yes! Like, what are they gonna do—arrest you or beat you up if you don't join a union?**

16. A woman should have the right to an abortion during the first trimester. **Yes. No brainer. Look, I'm not gonna have an abortion. I think it is wrong. I am going to use birth control—if and when I have sex. But just because I think it is wrong doesn't mean I get to tell every other girl what to do, you know? And the "first trimester" part is the important part—after that, maybe they should not allow it? Maybe. But the answer is Yes.**

17. Unemployment is less harmful than inflation. **Dude, where do they come up with these bizarre questions? No! Being jobless sucks. If you don't have a job, what difference does it make if the price of a burger goes up? You have no money, honey. No.**

18. America should increase humanitarian aid to poor nations. **Well, yeah, if they really need it—like when there is a hurricane—like what is happening right now. But we also need to help poor people here. So, Yes.**

19. Voluntary prayer in public schools at the start of each school day should be allowed. **Hmm. How voluntary is voluntary? I pray every day. I don't think it has to be a group thing at school—at church it is different. No.**

20. Private companies should be required to provide benefits to same-sex couples. **Oh, whoa—major trick question. First of all, what kind of benefits? And are these "couples" married? Can they even get married? Maybe that is what we should be asking, you know? 'Cause I am for that. But the way this is worded—this could just be a "couple" that is hooking up. So...No—'cause the question sucks.**

21. Victimless crimes, such as smoking marijuana and prostitution, should be legalized and regulated. **Man. This is a hard test. I am glad there is no right answer 'cause I would fail—I**

think. Okay, let me think. **Driving and weed can kill. Prostitutes are victims—like, the pimps and druggies make a lot of them do it to pay for their addictions. I think I am saying...No.**

22. The United States should place a moratorium on all immigration. **Duh, like that is gonna stop illegal immigration? And what about people who are here legally? The whole question seems very impractical. No.**

23. The federal government should establish a national health care system that would provide basic health care for all Americans. **Yes. I am for that.**

24. Parents should be allowed to send their child to a public or private school with vouchers provided at taxpayer expense. **That is very weird. Are they saying I could go to some nice private school and the taxpayers would have to pay for it? Then who would stay in public schools? This is very confusing. When in doubt...No.**

25. The primary purpose of prison is punishment, not rehabilitation. **Okay, kind of a mean-spirited question, don't ya think? Yeah, of course. But, like, if we turn prisoners into beaten-down monsters and never teach them how to cope better, won't they just get out and do it again? Oh, I guess that is kinda what is happening now, huh? My brain is starting to hurt. I say...a little of both. Wait—I can't say that! Okay, Yes. No. No...final answer...No. Do I win a prize yet?**

26. The United States should adopt a flat tax of 18% for all income levels. **First off, is that a lot? Seems like it isn't too bad. It is almost 20% of your money. But wait—is that all they take out then? My paycheck has federal taxes, state taxes, Social Security—a bunch of stuff taken out. On the other hand, a rich person would pay the same percentage as a poor person? How fair is that? This is a tough one. I say...Yes. No. No. Final answer.**

27. Government subsidies to corporations or corporate welfare to encourage jobs in the private sector should be greatly reduced.

My brain is about to explode. This is my first **AP** class, and it may be my last. This is so complicated! All this to find out if I am conservative or liberal? All this just to figure out where the heck I'm gonna sit in class? Just let me sit in the back, okay? Look, we should encourage jobs, right? Yes...but under protest. I am so confused.

28. Physician-assisted suicide should be an option for terminally ill patients. **Okay, this one I get. Yes—if they are going to die, let them go painlessly and in peace. Yes.**

29. Upon completion of their entire prison sentence, convicted felons should automatically have their voting rights reinstated. **Well, yeah. Why not? I mean, they served their sentence (and they did not get rehabilitated like in the earlier question). Yes.**

30. Social Security and Medicare must be fully funded for all retirees. **Thank God—the end! Yes. I think so. What is a retiree? Is that just an old person? How old? Did they work and then retire from work? Do they have to work for a certain number of years? What if they need, like, a super expensive operation? Or what if they want to live in a nursing home? I mean, they should be able to—and maybe the government should pay a little. You know what? I am so glad I am not in politics. Because this is crazy! No wonder politicians are always screaming and yelling at each other and nothing gets done. It is too damn complicated. Okay, I'll answer the question. Yes. 'Cause they at least deserve their Social Security money.**

I am so confused right now. I have no idea what I am. I am Rhiannon, and I never want to have to take a test like that again. I take things too personally, I guess. We get the results tomorrow. Stay tuned. Whew.

And the next day: September 8th

So, I'm 20-10 Liberal. That means I am on the left side of the room in the second row, fifth seat. There are 11 people more liberal than me. Who would have thought that? And here is the real surprise: Mickey is in the first row, third seat. If his parents only knew! Maddie and Pari are more in the middle. Actually, Pari is a bit more conservative; that's sort of a surprise, too.

Mr. MacQueen revealed a few things that kinda made us realize how much we didn't know about lots of laws, and we talked about class as we drove past the Metaphor Café, which opens up in October, around Halloween.

The remodeling of the Metaphor looks pretty cool—new sign, neon lights here and there, a retro look, lots of stuff still piled in a dumpster in the parking lot. But let's face it—even *I* thought the place needed some serious work. We all looked at the café longingly as we slowly passed the old place. We were all thinking that we couldn't wait to find a new corner table and sip lattes and meet the new owners.

But for now, we headed to a Denny's. The chatter about Mr. Mac's class and the test went something like this:

Mickey summed up Mr. Mac's "revelations" to us:

- When Germany invaded Poland in WWII, we had to get involved internationally to prevent the spread of Nazism
- The PATRIOT Act already allows for *unwarranted* wiretaps
- In 2006, the Military Commission Act decreed that there would be *no habeas corpus* for enemy combatants
- If we had a popular vote for a President instead of having the Electoral College vote, then Gore would have beaten Bush (the "W" would have been an "L")
- America has acted *unilaterally* in North Korea, Iraq, and Iran
- Israel already puts all legal males in the Army after high school (so much for free choice!)

- The EPA makes sure that pollution is regulated because states need oversight
- The Brady Law was about gun control—or at least a five-day waiting period for a gun
- Affirmative Action still applies to some universities
- States have to balance their budgets, but the federal government does not (that's odd)
- The government already makes cars that have cleaner emissions (kinda knew that)
- In 2003, 37 states and the federal prison system held 3,374 prisoners under sentence of death (yikes)
- Most foreign aid goes to Africa
- If a company provides benefits for married couples, then they have to do so for legally married same-sex couples (that was a shocker...but then again, only a few states allow legal marriages between same-sex couples)
- National health care is what Canada and Britain already have—and our taxes would increase to pay for it
- A school voucher would be between $2,000 and $4,000, but fancy private school tuition is around $20,000 (so much for us going there)
- The Death with Dignity Act in Oregon allows for physician-aided suicide (I think the whole state of Oregon would be sitting in front of Mickey on the left side of the room!)
- Twelve states don't let felons vote and
- President Bush (#43) wanted Social Security to be partially privatized—he lost on that one

So we mulled all this over for a while. Politics. Boy, it is so complicated. Mickey is by far the most into this stuff. He loves the show *The West Wing*; he's been into it ever since Mr. B showed us an episode of the show about 9.11. Mickey borrowed all the show's seasons from the library.

Then, as Mickey chomped on his burger (why do all guys eat like it's their last meal on earth?), he spilled the beans." I'm thinking about the whole writing/journalism/reporter thing. I told Ms. Jackson that I wanna do feature stories this year—no more sports stuff. She is figuring out the staff right now with Paul, the main editor of the paper."

"I think Paul is kinda cute," I said.

"Whatever. He has a girlfriend, Rhia, and—wait, why am I even talking about this? Anyway, I am still waiting to hear back from Ms. Jackson."

"I'm surprised I am the most conservative of us," said Pari. "American politics doesn't come up too much with my folks. Except, of course, anything to do with the Middle East—that's different."

Maddie pushed away the fries she had ordered and asked, "Why did Mr. Mac even give us that test? What was the point? To make a seating chart?"

"Don't you wonder where you stand on issues, Maddie?" Mickey asked. "We are so influenced by our folks' views and the news that it is hard to know what *we* think." I was sure Mickey was speaking more for himself than the rest of us.

So I said, "Look, I didn't even know what half of that test was about, so I just kinda guessed on a bunch of stuff."

"That's exactly the point, Rhia," Mickey pushed on. "The test was like a litmus test of some of our values, even if we don't really understand the laws yet."

"Well, all I know is that Gore got screwed," I said as I gathered my hair into a ponytail.

"Yeah, and I'm glad I don't live in Israel. Not that I have anything against the Jews; it's just not what I want to do after I graduate—join the Army, I mean," Mickey clarified.

"Well, we had a draft in Vietnam, Mick," Pari said as she checked her cell for messages—probably from Daniel. "And in WWII, too. Oh, crap—I just remembered something. I gotta go, guys." Pari never seemed as relaxed as she did last year.

"Have you decided what you are doing about your classes?" Maddie asked as Pari tossed in a few bucks.

"Yeah. I dropped AP, and now I'm taking regular Physics. It's a little slow, but…whatever, I have more time now."

"So what's the rush?"

"I totally forgot about my dad's birthday. Crap. My brothers, who are usually so lame, are the ones who are reminding me." She nodded toward her cell, where she had gotten a text. "I gotta at least get him a card."

"I always wait 'til the last minute, Pari," I said. "I am starting to rub off on you."

"It's not the last minute, Rhia. His real birthday is Thursday."

"Huh?" I wasn't following.

"We are celebrating tomorrow—the 9th—because he is leaving on some business trip, and he won't be home until late Thursday night."

"Oh."

"And we don't want to celebrate his birthday on Thursday, anyway."

"Why not?" I asked.

"Because it's 9.11."

Nobody said anything. We just paid the bill.

Mickey's Hand

September 11th ... 9.11

I got the Features Editor position. I knew what my first column would be. I wanted to write about Mr. Buscotti and Ms. Anderson's presentation on 9.11 last year. We were so blown away by how Mr. B used Bruce Springsteen's album *The Rising* to help us understand the meaning of the day and how America faced the tragedy with courage, fortitude, and hope. Regardless of our differences as Americans, politically and culturally, we are a part of "the land of hopes and dreams."

I looked back on the 9.11 chapter we wrote for our first book, and I wondered how the day would be now, with the race for a new President coming up. And I wondered what it would be like for me to see the whole presentation again as a senior, knowing what I learned last year. Would I still be as moved? Would Mr. B's new students be as responsive as we were? Would tears flow down their faces like they did for Maddie and Rhia? Would some of the Persian or Middle Eastern kids feel as Pari did—like all eyes were on her?

I knew this presentation was something that the whole school should experience, not just the 70 kids in this year's "village," as Ms. Anderson calls it. So I asked Mr. MacQueen for permission to miss his class. This became a mysterious exchange between us because when he asked me why I wanted to miss class, I told him about the 9.11 presentation I was writing about.

"Oh, yes. I am very familiar with Mr. Buscotti and Ms. Anderson's memorial to the 9.11 tragedy." Then Mr. Mac stopped—it seemed like he suddenly lost his train of thought. It was as if he just froze—like I needed to snap my fingers to wake him up. At the time, it seemed totally weird. Now it seems understandable.

The pause was so long, I felt I needed to say something. "Mr. Mac? So, is it okay for me to miss class? Do I need to make up anything?"

"No. No. It's fine. If you don't mind, I would like to read the piece you write. Actually, I am not going to be here that day. So we will be taking a short quiz and doing some group work on political parties…" Mr. Mac still seemed distracted.

"Okay. Sure. I will let you read the column first—to see what you think. Thanks."

I glanced back at him as I was leaving the room. He was still shuffling papers on his desk—the same papers he was shuffling when I walked up to him.

*****   *****   *****   *****   *****

I watched intently from the back of the room. I was an observer that day, not a participant, which I found difficult for many reasons. The moment Springsteen's guitar strummed the opening chords to the song "The Rising," I was hypnotized. The rollercoaster of emotions began, and this was the headline I envisioned for my first Features article:

It Takes a "Village" to Understand 9.11 With the Help of Bruce Springsteen and the E Street Band

I tried to capture the emotions of the day: as Mr. B played the song "The Rising," he showed images of the shock when the towers came crashing down; the desperate hope when the first responders raced to the scene in their fire trucks; followed by pictures of the heroism of these people as they saved others' lives while risking their own as they climbed higher "Into the Fire," which was Springsteen's most spiritual song on that album, I thought. Each song told a story, and the pictures Mr. B showed matched Springsteen's lyrics perfectly. The class focused on the total devastation of New York's "Empty Sky"; the prayers of the despondent New Yorkers who were "Countin' on a Miracle"; and the acceptance of loss when people realized that their loved ones were gone for good in Springsteen's haunting melody, "You're Missing."

Somewhere along the way, Maddie slipped into the room. She looked at me with eyes that remembered all too well how this day, more than any other, had cemented our desire to write about this 9.11 presentation in our book last year.

Just as he did in last year's presentation, Mr. B lifted the somber mood in the classroom, asking his students to stand and embrace life like those who met at "Mary's Place" months after the 9.11 tragedy to let the pain, like rain, wash over them—and to make the decision to live again.

And once again, Mr. B and Ms. Anderson showed Springsteen and the E Street Band performing in Madison Square Garden, singing the song that was the anthem for the day. America is a "Land of Hope and Dreams," they sang, and the country, like a train, accepts all riders of all shapes and sizes, all sinners and saints, all poor and downhearted— because we are all part of something bigger. Mr. Buscotti was, as usual, in rare form.

So that is what I wrote about...then. But it was not the story I *really* wanted to write. The real story had to wait until now to tell. Now— when I have permission to tell it. The real story didn't take place in Madison Square Garden. It was part of a different garden—a secret one.

***** ***** ***** ***** *****

When the presentation was over, I went to Mr. B and Ms. Anderson to get a few quotes from them on why they continue to teach something like 9.11—eight years after it occurred. Standard background stuff. Then I noticed that Ms. Anderson was holding a white rose and a small envelope. The same items were on Mr. Buscotti's desk as well.

When I asked about it, Ms. Anderson hesitated and looked at Mr. B before responding, "Come by after school, and we will explain. It is confidential. You cannot use it in your article." I was intrigued, to say the least.

I asked if Rhia, Pari, and Maddie could come, too. She agreed.

When we stopped by later that afternoon, Ms. Anderson cut right to a story that I never imagined I'd hear.

"Mickey, girls, look. The faculty members here know something that we have always kept fairly quiet. You all were not in school here when it happened."

Silence. The four of us exchanged quick glances.

"Mr. MacQueen was not at school on 9.11. There is a reason for that, and that reason needs to remain private. Only he can change that."

My heart was racing so fast that I broke into a sweat. I don't know why, exactly—but I remember it.

Ms. Anderson looked at Mr. B, and he nodded. "This goes no further than these four walls," he said. "Mr. MacQueen's wife died on 9.11—in the second tower."

Only Mr. B's eyes were dry. He was prepared to continue the explanation, but only after Rhia grabbed the tissue box and distributed the little white flags of emotional surrender.

"Mr. MacQueen cannot possibly be here on 9.11. There was a time when he would be gone for the whole week leading up to the date. He would tell his students that he was on jury duty or something. Anyway, last year, when you were in our class, he came in briefly to see the presentation. It was the first time he had stepped on campus on 9.11. You did not know him then. He was quite discreet; he stood silently in the back of the classroom. He only saw us teach the song "You're Missing." Then he left. But later, he left Ms. Anderson and me white roses and a thank you note, as he did today. Naturally, he is visiting his wife's grave today."

Ms. Anderson's voice was shaky. "None of us ever knows what to say…"

"So we just carry on and remember," Mr. B's lips were tight. "But we are telling you this because you deserve to know the truth. We think you will deal with it responsibly and keep it to yourselves."

Of course, we all nodded our heads. We were solemn.

Then I asked Mr. B and Ms. Anderson something that just came from my soul: "Can we ever ask Mr. MacQueen about it? I mean, privately?"

"I don't know, Mickey. Maybe he is ready. But maybe not. He certainly does not want to be pitied. His class is not about him."

"Well, we have to do something, Mr. B," Rhia said as she dabbed her eyes. "Something private, you know?"

"Okay, but if you do, be careful. There is a sign up around him that says NO TRESPASSING," warned Ms. Anderson.

That's when I remembered that last year Mr. B introduced us to another song by Bruce Springsteen. It was called "Secret Garden"—a place where people were not to 'think twice' about entering.

***** ***** ***** ***** *****

We left four white roses on Mr. MacQueen's desk that evening. Mr. B let us into his classroom. We attached a note—handwritten by Rhia—that read:

We love you, Mr. MacQueen.
We know.
Ms. Anderson and Mr. Buscotti told us.
This is the only time we will ever mention 9.11.
It is your "Secret Garden"—and we will always respect that.
And we will always respect you.

Pari, Maddie, Mickey, and Rhia

Chapter 7: "What Will Your Verse Be?"

Mickey's Hand

September 16th

I am still in shock. How could someone keep a secret like that locked in inside? When Mr. B told us of Mr. MacQueen's wife and her death in the second Twin Tower, we froze. Later, I sat up at night and thought of questions that just seemed too inappropriate to ask. Why was she there? How did she die? Was her body found? Did they have kids? What did Mr. Mac do when it all happened?

These were questions I would never broach—to anyone—except Maddie. But the questions always came to the same resolution, and the word *awful* ended every sentence. So we left it there.

I did show Mr. Mac my essay before it went to print for the newspaper. His brow was deeply creased as he read it, and his concentration was immense—so much so that I was afraid he was going to tear it up right in front of me and tell me that I had no idea what I was saying and that we should just leave the dead alone. I don't know. I just stood there for what seemed like a half an hour with my hands in my pocket. I tried to say something like, "If you think it needs…," but he cut me off without so much as saying a word. He merely shook his head, as if he were saying, "Not now."

Finally, he emerged. "Mickey, I want to thank you for this. I have known what Ms. Anderson and Mr. Buscotti have been doing, but I just did not have the—the courage—to step into that place again. But you have helped me to see it all. Wonderful. It's wonderful that the importance of all that happened is not lost on our students." Then he asked me, "How old were you when it happened?"

"Eleven."

"Do you remember much?"

"Not really. My mom freaked out as she was driving me to school that morning."

"You were just going into middle school, right?"

"Yeah. Sixth grade. My brother was a freshman here."

"Hmmm." I think Mr. Mac was deciding how far to go with this conversation. Then he abruptly made up his mind. "It took me a long, long time to get to that song Springsteen sang called 'Mary's Place'—a very long time. There are times when I am still not there. But I know that song by heart, and I play it when…" His voice turned into a whisper, and I felt just horribly out of place. This was sacred ground. I was an interloper.

He finished, "…when I need to move on. You know?"

My lame reply of "Yeah" was so unacceptable.

"But I want to thank you, Mickey. It was well written. Springsteen should hear Mr. Buscotti's 'sermon.' He would be impressed."

"I know," I managed to remember what Maddie had told me. "Buscotti sometimes becomes Springsteen—it is weird."

"Yeah, well, I will try to do my best impersonation of Thomas Jefferson tomorrow." Mr. MacQueen at last broke into a smile.

"Sounds exciting, Mr. Mac."

"You know, he was a radical with long hair, too. Let me tell you— he and Adams did not get along too well. As a matter of fact…"

And he was happily back in time, quoting chapter and verse of the words of our forefathers even before the Constitution was ratified, long before all that we knew about American law and order came crashing down…one deadly morning in September on the island of Manhattan…where once one could marvel at all that American ingenuity had created…in one breathless gaze from the Windows of the World.

Pari's Hand

September 21st—The Last Day of Summer

We met tonight at Rhia's house for a "home cooked, last BBQ of the summer" that Rhia's mom, Patti, insisted upon. We had all agreed to see the movie *500 Days of Summer* that afternoon, and we were just amazed at the way it was written.

"I thought the way it jumped time was so awesome! It kept me totally engaged." Mickey could not stop glowing over the film—so much so that Rhia's mom told him, "Eat, Mickey, before everything gets cold."

"I know. I know. But, you guys, that is what we don't do in our novel—we stay so linear—we never go back and forth in time…"

"Duh—that's because we don't know how our story ends, Mickey," Maddie said, a little defensively. "And besides, we wrote the whole first part as a flashback—in both books. I mean, what more can we do?"

I piped up, "I agree, Mick. Yeah, I love the artsy feel of *500 Days*. But, um, I have no freaking idea where I am gonna be in 150 days. Like, college? Mickey, we can't just write this whole story three years from now, break it into a jigsaw puzzle, and then put it back together in any old way. I mean, it's super clever, but we are just not in that…place." This was my common sense and my anxiety about the future bubbling out of me…and other stuff.

"Well, I do think Ringo was cute." Classic Rhia. "You guys need to stop arguing and remember that this is our last official day of summer. And then, just like in the movie…"

And all four of us said in a chorus of laughter, "It will be 'Autumn!'"

Madison's Hand

September 24th

Just like he had done when our class had watched *Casablanca* a year earlier, Mr. Buscotti dimmed the lights, flicked on the twinkling lights above his students, bunched them into a tight circle with him smack in the middle, and with their notebooks open, he proceeded to be their tour guide as he showed them the film *Dead Poets Society*, which I had heard of but had never seen.

I was supposed to be recording some grades, but that did not happen. I soon found myself nestled next to Jasmine as we were transported into the '50s setting of a private boys' school.

At the beginning of the film, their inspirational teacher, Mr. John Keating, was reminding them to "make their lives extraordinary." And from that moment, the entire class was transported.

There were two storylines here—the one I was watching on the screen and the one I was watching on the faces of the kids watching the movie. Both were fascinating. Even though those kids were freshmen, it was clear that Mr. B was the embodiment of the teacher in the movie. I could see it in their eyes, and I heard it in what they whispered to each other:

Mr. B talks just like that.

He is just as funny as Mr. Keating.

Mr. B made us do that, too.

Doesn't he totally remind you of Mr. Buscotti?

That was not all. Mr. Buscotti was emphasizing the themes of the film, stopping the movie to make sure they understood it. Every time he did, the kids groaned because they did not want him to stop the movie's dramatic flow. But this was a "video textbook," Mr. B had told them. So stop it he did.

"What will you be when you grow up? Why will you be that? What are your dreams for yourself? What are your fears? Will you just settle for what is easy? Will you just do as you are told? When it all comes down to it, 'What will your verse be' in your book of life?"

Watching Jasmine was a trip. She is a girl who has faced the fact that without a new liver, she may not live nearly as long as she is hoping—as any of us hope. She gets the poem read in the film—"To gather ye rosebuds while ye may." *Carpe diem.* Jasmine's eyes never seem to blink while the film is on, and when Mr. B is talking, she is scribbling notes as fast as she can—as if she is thinking, *I gotta know all of this now, before I slip away.* One time, she asked Mr. B a question about what was said in the movie:

"Mr. B, did he say, 'to be a god?' Or was it, 'to be with God?' 'Cause I think that matters a lot."

"Hmmm. Miss Jasmine, he said, 'to indeed be a god.' I think he is saying that he wants to live a life of power and glory and respect. But that doesn't mean that he doesn't want to be 'with God.' You know what I mean?"

"Oh, okay. Duh. I get it, Mr. B." Jasmine was so adorable that the class sometimes just giggled at her spontaneous bursts of joy or curiosity. A lot of the kids knew her from middle school, and, well, she is just one of those people who you just really love. It is hard to explain—but I bet everyone knows someone like Jasmine.

As the movie gets more tense, it becomes apparent that Mr. B wants the kids to understand *metaphor*. He reminds them,

> *"Gang, Mr. Keating makes them walk in the courtyard. And you know why, right? Because in the way you walk, you show a part of you and what you believe in. Do you walk to copy others? Do you walk with a confident stride? Do you walk with a purpose? What is your stride like—what is your voice like? What do you stand up for? What do you speak up for? Mr. Keating tells them to 'find their voice'—why? Because it can hide away, and if you wait too long and are too afraid to clear your throat and sing your own song and speak your own mind—well, then, you may never know 'what your verse will be.'"*

Bang. You could hear a pin drop in the room.

I don't want to spoil the movie for anyone who has never seen it, so I won't give away the ending and all, but there were some tears shed—tears of joy and sorrow. And no one cried more than Miss Jasmine.

When it was over, Mr. B had the kids answer this question as a group: was Mr. Keating successful, or did he fail his students? It was unanimous: "Success!" Mr. B tried to play devil's advocate, but Jasmine said to him, "Come on, Mr. B—the kids all stood on their desks at the end…to thank him for all he did for them."

Once persuaded, Mr. B showed them how to organize a literary analysis in an argument form. Man, it took me back to when he showed us how to do that with our papers on *Huck Finn* last year.

"Which characters prove that Mr. Keating succeeds? List them. Tell me exactly what they did and why that shows that Mr. Keating was a good influence on them," Mr. B demanded. And in colored markers on the whiteboard, he took what they said and chiseled out the paper's form like a sculpture, leaving parts of the statue for them to figure out, but giving enough hints—just enough—to not frustrate them.

As I watched Mr. B work his magic, I knew for the first time.

I knew the answer to the question.

I knew why I was in this room watching this "tour guide."

I knew what "my verse" would be.

Rhiannon's Hand

September 26th

What I am about to tell you is something I kept to myself for several months. I never shared it with anyone, not even my close friends Pari, Mickey, and Maddie. I included this much later, when I knew the answer to the question: what will your verse be?

Today is a day I will never, ever forget. How could I? I think I just need to spill it out of me—here, on paper.

You guys, I don't totally get a lot of things. Like why men beat up girls. Like why girls can be such bitches to each other. Like why people hate homosexuals. Like why people are homosexual? Gay. Lesbian. Whatever. I accept them all—but, like, it's hard to really understand some things, you know?

And the most totally "un-get-able" thing of all is why people want to end it all and kill themselves. I mean, I dealt with that last year, when I found out the truth about my mom and how after my father left us, she tried to overdose on sleeping pills—and then she vomited it all out and went to urgent care and all. I guess I can see how my mom's whole life was wrapped up in my dad. When he left, she just unraveled. Yeah, *that* is something I can get. But what happened tonight is just way beyond my comprehension—and frightening.

So tonight I am working with Leann for the last three hours until closing. It is really slow on account of the rain and the cold and the fact that Yummy Yogurt kinda sucks when it comes down to it. So we've got nothing to do. Leann starts asking me about Donald and how he acts when he is with me. Typical stuff. We had talked about this before. Then she tells me her old boyfriend made her feel terrible when they broke up months ago.

"Why?"

"Cause he called me a bitch." She stopped making eye contact with me.

"What?"

"He wanted to have sex and was so pissed because I was afraid to."

I waited her out.

"So, we were in the car…"

I waited.

"… and it was bad…"

I held my breath.

"…and he kept after me."

That is when she just melts down. Literally. She falls to the floor behind the counter. I yell out, "Leann!" And I look around and grab the store keys. I run to the door and lock the deadbolt. I flip the sign that says, "Closed." I cut one of the lights. I do all this as fast as I can because I have to get back to her.

I dive on top of her. She is in a ball on the floor and sobbing uncontrollably. All I can say is, "Leann, it's okay. Leann, I am here. Leann. Leann."

We lay on the floor together for a good half hour. She cannot talk without crying. I get her water, but she won't drink.

Then she throws up.

"Leann, are you pregnant?"

"No."

"Are you sure?"

"Yes."

Right then, there is a tapping on the window. It is Omar, the security man. Because we are crouched behind the counter, he must have wondered why we have closed early and why the lights are half on and why no one is around.

I peek my head up over the cash register. "It's Omar, Leann. I will be right back."

I talk through the locked door to Omar: "It's cool, Omar. I had to close early. Leann is sick."

"You need help? You want me to call the owners? How sick is she?"

"She just threw up. She'll be okay. I will make sure she gets home. Don't worry."

"Okay," he frowns, "but I know how this can be. You have my cell. Call me if you need anything, Rhia." Omar is a saint.

By the time I get back to Leann, she is sitting up. I guess Omar's presence has kinda shaken her out of her state of mind. I get down on the floor with her, face to face, and take her by the shoulders. "What happened? What did he do to you?"

"He said it was my fault," she whimpers.

"What was…exactly?"

"He said I wanted it as bad as he did…and he did it."

It.

That word.

"He did it to me," she repeats. "I couldn't stop him."

"Leann, do your parents know?"

Before I can even finish that question, she is saying something about how it could have been her fault. Something about how she had teased him. Her words toss and turn into something that comes between gasps for breath and choked back tears. So I repeat my question: "Have you told your folks?"

All she can do is shake her head no.

"Have you told anyone?"

No, again.

"Just me?"

Nodding.

I hug her and hug her and hug her. I find myself drenched in sweat from my own fear of what to do. I want to call my mom. I tell Leann so.

"No, Rhia. No. I can handle it. I can. I just need to get it together. I just needed to get it out." Leann tries to grit her teeth, but they are chattering badly. She clenches her jaw to try to stop the chattering, but that doesn't work.

"Look, Leann. I am calling my mom. Either that or I am calling your mom. I am calling someone—even if it is Omar. You are a mess. I can't let you get in a car—you'll kill yourself." The minute I say it, I regret it.

She looks up at me, and the look scares me. She tries to stop me from grabbing my cell, but I do not let her.

"Mom, come to the store right now. I am okay, but there is an emergency. One of the girls is sick." That is all I can get out because Leann is screaming at me.

I will never, ever regret what I did that night.

It feels like an eternity before my mom shows up even though she got there in ten minutes. Leann makes me feel like I have betrayed her. If she had tried to leave, I don't know if I could have stopped her. But that didn't matter because she threw up again—more of a dry heave. She was sweating all over, and I don't know much about panic attacks, but I have a feeling that I was watching one happen right before my eyes.

You know how moms know what to do when everything falls apart? Yeah, well, that is what my mom does when she arrives. It is magical. She gathers Leann up. Tells her everything is gonna be alright. She makes her drink some water, if for no other reason than to rinse out her mouth. She calms her down enough so that she can at least breathe. I fill her in on the story.

You know how kids feel better when their parents take care of them—how their parents can make fear go away? Well, that works for ghosts and nightmares and stuff, but it takes a lot more when those ghosts and nightmares are real.

My mom calls Leann's folks. Her mom and dad are frightened, but they keep an "everything is going to be fine, honey" look on their faces. But they know better. They knew something was up, I think, for a while, but they could not get Leann to crack.

You know how you hold something in for so long and then it just bursts? I know. I do it all the time. But this explosion is like nothing I have ever seen or felt.

My God.

They take her straight to the hospital. Urgent care never seemed more urgent.

It takes me an hour to stop shaking...

I finally go to bed, but I know I don't fall asleep until

...sometime around midnight.

Chapter 8: The Lehman Brothers and the Loman Brothers

Pari's Hand

October 3rd

"'Lehman Brothers filed for Chapter 11 bankruptcy protection on September 15, 2008. The bankruptcy of Lehman Brothers remains the largest bankruptcy filing in U.S. history, with Lehman holding over $600 billion in assets.'"

Mr. Mac was in full throttle. "'The Dow Jones closed down just over 500 points on September 15, 2008—at the time, the largest drop by points in a single day since the days following the attacks on September 11, 2001.' I ain't making this up, gang. 'This drop was subsequently exceeded by an even larger −7.0% plunge on September 29, 2008.'"

Then Mr. Mac reached his crescendo: "And so today, President Bush decided to act on this global financial crisis in a big way. He signed the Emergency Economic Stabilization Act, which basically allows the U.S. Treasury to buy $700 billion in failing bank assets to bail companies out."

Mickey piped up first. "Um, Mr. Mac, I know things are pretty dramatic, but I have two questions. One, what happens to those people who, like, work for Lehman Brothers? I mean, will the government save their jobs?"

"Nope. As of today, the government has decided to let Lehman either find a buyer—which ain't gonna happen—or get liquidated."

"Meaning...what?" Mickey seemed to channel what we were all thinking—well, at least those of us who were awake. Some of the class had zoned out like zombies because it was Friday and we had a big football game that night; the week was just catching up to everyone. But not my Mick.

"Meaning that 25,000 people will lose their jobs. Look, guys, I know it is Friday, but this is really unprecedented—and it is gonna affect you—fast."

"Why?" I spoke up.

"Well, for one thing, have you seen how the stock market is plunging? People are not hiring, Pari. They are firing, in all sectors. Why? Because everyone is afraid of losing their jobs—lots of folks have already. This could turn into a second Great Depression, which is why the President is acting to protect firms that his administration believes are 'too big to fail.'"

However, Mickey hadn't forgotten the second part of his question: "And, secondly, why did the government bail out some companies and not others? My dad is so ticked off about that. He was telling me that the people in charge have, like, a vested interest. They were CEOs of companies, and it is those companies that are getting the bailout money. Is he right?"

"Right as rain."

Rhia perked up. "That is totally unfair."

"Well, welcome to politics and big business and the power of money." Mr. Mac quickly added, "But some of the banks really are too big to fail. The question is: who to save? Because you can't save them all."

"And my dad says the big wigs are still getting paid bonuses." Mickey had never talked of his dad with such admiration before. It was very interesting.

"Again, people, I remind you of one of my basic tenets: 'Educate yourselves.' So let me explain exactly what happened to Richard Fuld, the CEO of Lehman Brothers, when he was questioned by the U.S. House of Representatives' Committee on Oversight and Government Reform. Rep. Henry Waxman, a democrat from California, asked him directly, *If your company is bankrupt and our economy is in crisis, how fair is it that you get to keep $480 million? Does that seem fair?"*

I guess we got our answer.

Rhiannon's Hand

October 16th

I gotta tell you that I was still a little freaked out about everything that had happened to Leann. My mom and I kept it to ourselves, and I added this 'update' much later (as I said before), when Leann and I finally talked it out. She told me she was cool with me telling her story.

I haven't seen Leann since that night last month. She has not been at work. I know that she has been seen by doctors 'cause her folks called my mom. They also thanked me so much for all I did for her— like I really did all that much. I don't know—it is all so scary. They told me she was "sexually assaulted." I am not sure if that is rape or what, and I don't know what is gonna happen to the guy or whatever, but I know that they want to keep this very quiet.

Leann has been going to classes—or at least some classes, especially Mr. B's. She once told me that he "spoke to her heart." At the time, I did not think too much of it. But I get it—now even more so. If I remember correctly, Mr. B is usually teaching the "love stories" right about now. The one by Ernest Hemingway called "Hills Like White Elephants" would make any girl understand how helpless you can feel when you are in love, but your boyfriend just wants to have sex and party…oh, and you are pregnant, too. Yikes. Like I said, it is all so scary and complicated. Poor Leann.

So tonight, we all got together. It was part class assignment, part curiosity, part missing each other, and part knowing that the Grand Reopening of the new Metaphor Café was coming in the beginning of November. But we all met tonight at Mickey's house to hang out and watch the last debate between Obama and McCain. We were supposed to take notes and whatever, but we were kinda glued to the TV. I have to admit, we were trying to be neutral 'cause Mickey's folks were in and out of the room; they were watching upstairs. Politics is a testy subject in the Sullivan house.

It wasn't the debate itself that made headlines with all of us, though—although it was pretty interesting; it was Mickey's dad who stole the show.

First, the debate. I told Maddie that I had never really cared about all this political junk before now. But Mr. Mac's class, Chris being in the Army, and the Obama "Yes We Can" thing have made me see the "bigger picture." And I really like Obama a lot. He is smart, cool, young, and he seems to speak *to me, to all of us.* He is so much like us, you know. Not from some rich family. Heck, even from a broken one, like mine.

But even though I don't agree with McCain, I do really respect him. I mean, he was a POW in Vietnam; Mr. Mac said he survived the Hanoi Hilton's torture chamber. He is a supporter of the military and very big on helping injured soldiers. I could not help but think of Chris.

Chris had kind of an easier time in boot camp. He is a stud. Just don't ask him to read complicated stuff or do any math past the basic stuff. He was in SPED for the last eight years of school, and asking him to sit still is like torture to him. So being active and physical is his thing. Once my mom and I knew he was committed to the Army, we knew it was inevitable that he would be on a battlefield soon. I just didn't expect it to be this soon. He is somewhere in Iraq. It is all sort of *hush hush.* But he got a few letters to us. He says he is not in danger. Even if bombs were blowing up in his face, he would say that.

"Don't worry," he tells us.

That is his answer to everything.

It doesn't help one bit.

Meanwhile, back at the debate, I think both of the candidates did well. McCain made a point of telling Obama that he isn't running against President Bush, so Obama should stop comparing him to Bush. Good point. But Obama made the point that McCain and the Republicans have been totally behind Bush for the last 8 years, and look where that has gotten us. The economy is in the pits. We are in two wars with no end in sight. Good point.

So I thought it was, like, a tie or something. Then Mr. Sullivan came down. We expected him to totally rip Obama, or else not talk about the debate at all—you know, play the "cool dad" and just pretend that nothing was really going on. I think Mickey was hoping for that. But he surprised us.

"Well, I know you kids are behind Obama, and I have to admit that he is holding his own. But you know who I really like?" He seemed to enjoy teasing us. Mickey was expecting the worst, I think.

"I like Joe Biden. Really. He is a down-to-earth, blue collar guy. I think he will be a huge asset to Obama because he really understands how Washington works. And I'll tell you something else: Obama is going to win. Big." *Big* was the word he seemed most confident about.

"Really? What do you think of Sarah Palin?" Maddie seemed stunned at Mr. Sullivan's prediction.

"Don't get me started, Maddie. That was the worst mistake. She is not nearly ready for the national stage. It is a gimmick—and a pretty risky one, I think. I think it will backfire. There were so many others he could have gone with. Oh, well."

Mickey's dad started to head off in the direction of the kitchen, but Mickey asked him one last question: "Made up your mind on who you're gonna vote for, Dad?"

"Yep." With that, he headed upstairs.

Oh, the drama.

Mickey's Hand

October 27th

The New York Times

"Jobless Rate at 14-Year High After October Losses"

"'So far, about 240,000 jobs were lost in October; add that to a loss of 284,000 jobs in September. America has shed 1.2 million jobs since the beginning of the year. More than half of the job losses have been in the last three months.'" Ms. LaFleur gazed up from the newspaper. She continued: "'The economy is slipping deeper into a recessionary sinkhole that is getting broader,' said Stuart G. Hoffman, Chief Economist at PNC Financial Services Group in Pittsburgh. 'The layoffs are getting larger and coming faster. We're likely to see at least another six months of more jobs reports like this.'"

Ms. LaFleur looked up from her red framed reading classes perched delicately on her nose. She looked like she had just eaten something very sour. Her cheeks puckered inward, and her breath did the same as she took a long inhale through her thin, pointed nose.

Then she exhaled: "Not good. Not good at all. And this is not fiction. It is not a play. It is the hard truth that many of you are already facing at home—or will face soon—very soon. I think it is the tip of the iceberg. I am just a little old English teacher who speaks French fluently, but I can read the writing on the wall."

This was Ms. LaFleur's introduction to the play *Death of a Salesman* by Arthur Miller, the story of the Loman brothers and their pathetic, tragic father, Willy. But her words "*already facing at home*" seemed to be a prophecy of what I would listen to at the dinner table that very night.

My dad was especially quiet during dinner. My mom noticed and asked what was bothering him.

"I think we are—no, I am—going to be delivering some terrible news soon at work," he grumbled.

"Layoffs?" she asked as she put her fork down.

"Yeah."

"Now, right before the holidays?"

"Yeah, the brass upstairs doesn't much give a damn about that. All the 'we are one big family' crap is just tossed out the window when profits don't make the stockholders rich enough. Hey, Mickey, pass the rice."

"Why do you have to be the one who tells them, dad?" I asked, looking down as I handed him the bowl.

"Because I happen to be *management*, Son. None of them wants to deal with the look on people's faces when you tell them they just got 'downsized.'" He snorted the word *downsized*.

"Anyone you are really close to?" my mom asked him.

"Yeah, I'm afraid so." He mumbled this as if he was thinking of what he could do to fend off the inevitable. He suddenly tossed his chair back and said something about losing his appetite—then he rose and turned to me and said, "Sometimes they don't give a damn, Mickey. They just don't give a damn."

And he went into his office. I knew what bothered him. These people were family to him. It took away his authority—his manhood, I guess, when he had to beg his bosses to reconsider. And it just pissed him off that he had to do their dirty work.

I can't explain it exactly, but for some reason, I kinda lost my appetite, too. My dad had taken work home before and complained—but it was about how much people piled on him, or deadlines, or incompetence—but this wasn't about that. It was about something far more upsetting to him.

Greed.

I suppose it was against this "backdrop" (as the novelists would say) that Ms. LaFleur's AP English class took on a new meaning.

My class watched *Death of a Salesman* over three days; each act was followed by discussions. It was the version with Dustin Hoffman. When I asked Mr. B what he thought of the play as I was walking to his classroom to meet Maddie, he said that although the Hoffman version was great, the older one he said he saw on TV with Lee J. Cobb was his favorite. I had no idea who that was. But Mr. B raved about the play, and he was happy to hear that Ms. LaFleur was teaching it, although not in Maddie and Rhia's World Literature class.

Even though the play was set sometime in the late 1940s, I think—maybe the '50s—it seemed to be "ripped from the headlines" today, which was Ms. LaFleur's purpose in reading the current unemployment stats, I guess. But, you know, all that news didn't hit home much—at least, not until I hit home myself.

When I came home tonight, my dad and I started out talking about the World Series between the Phillies and the Rays. But the only reason we had our eyes on the TV was so that we could get to what we really needed to say to each other. The conversation went something like this:

Me: The Rays have no payroll compared to the Phillies. Dad, it's David versus Goliath.

Dad: Don't talk to me about payroll. I had to do something today that made me sick to my stomach.

Me: What?

Dad: I had to lay off six people—two of them kids, but the others I have known for years. Phil Barry, for God's sake—I go back 25 years with him.

Me: Why?

Dad: Downsizing. That and all the damn outsourcing to firms that will do some of our in-house work for a cut rate. It stinks.

[Long pause while we mute a stupid commercial, which ironically talks about a "wonderful nest egg" for the future with some investment firm that is supposedly on the rocks financially. My dad just makes a sound like harrumph.]

Me: We just finished watching *Death of a Salesman* in English…

Dad: Gee, that's not gonna do much to cheer me up.

Me: You remember it much? The play, I mean?

Dad: Yeah. I think Dustin Hoffman was in it—or was it Lee J. Cobb?—wait a minute…that was in the 80's, so it musta been Hoffman. Man, where does the time go? You weren't even born yet. Yeah. Wow. *[He pauses to reminisce, and I cannot help but think of how Willy Loman does the same thing in Salesman.]* Anyway, yeah, it is a great play—very depressing ending, though. But that was how it was back then…

[He has been struck with the same thought as I have.]

Me: The company got rid of Willy because he could not keep up. He was out of touch. He was old. He was all about being popular and having charm and good looks to get ahead.

Dad: Yeah, I know. The corporate world is all about "what have you done for me *now?*" It is dog eat dog. But that is where the money is—and the financial security.

Me: Willy sure wasn't secure. Of course, he blew a lot of money on his useless sons—and women.

Dad: Wait. Didn't he have a rich brother?

Me: Ben? Yeah, but I think he was, like, a ghost or something. It was his "great American dream" to strike it rich. And Willy was so jealous—or so greedy—that he didn't even realize he had it all: wife, kids, house, job. And at that point in the play, he did have respect. But by the end, Dad, he was practically groveling for a job.

Dad: Yeah. I remember.

[Mute button. An even more ironic commercial for Viagra or something to make you "a man."]

Dad: Mickey, they were practically groveling to me today. "Anything part-time?" "Any hope of catching on next month?" "Can't my severance be a bit more?" And all I could say was, "Sorry." Like that was some… *[He is lost in thought.]* Phil was the worst. He didn't see it coming. God, neither did I. When I saw his name on the list of layoffs—and realized that I was the one who had to tell him—I couldn't believe it. Yeah, his numbers are a bit off—but for God's sake, his wife is recovering from breast cancer; he has one kid in college, and one just getting out. At least they gave him a year of severance—6 months full pay, 6 at half—but medical for a year, thank God. *[I wait him out.]* It just stinks. I told him I would see what I could do with other firms—and of course I will recommend him. But after 25 years… heck, he is 50. He is making close to $100,000. He is going to take a huge hit—if he can find something at all. Who wants to hire someone who is 50 or 55 years old, Mickey? Huh?

Me: Are you worried about your job, Dad?

Dad. No. Well...no. I mean, we all worry, but things will turn around. We should bounce back after the election. I think the worst is probably over. But who knows? Oh, for crying out loud, that was a strike! Tampa is getting squeezed here! It's ridiculous— the Phillies have two players who make more than the whole Rays team, huh?

Me: Yeah. That is why I am rooting for Tampa Bay.

[A car commercial comes on touting how Ford will make a comeback—soon.]

Dad: Well, let's hope so. We don't make anything in the USA anymore, Mickey.

Me: But Dad, Willy's problem is he thinks success is all about being popular and funny. He thinks that good looks and charm make the American Dream possible. *[I pause because I think I have suddenly figured something out.]* Do you think Willy Loman is crazy?

Dad: No, Mickey. He is just chasing Fool's Gold. Long ago I learned what matters in life, and it isn't the clothes that make the man, Son. It's the clothes the man makes for his family. Providing for them. Showing them what he stands for. And what he stands for has little to do with what is popular. In life, Son, you work hard. Luck and charm—that stuff is for the movies.

Me: Do you think he deserves what happens to him? Is it his fault that he's 55 or 60? Should he be treated so bad?

Dad: Doesn't his neighbor offer him some money or a job or something?

Me: Yeah, but Willy won't take it—pride, stubbornness, whatever. But isn't he like a lot of Americans? Do we deserve the way we're treated—like your friend Phil?

Dad: I don't know. I really don't. I know that what happened today would drive anyone—man or woman—crazy. *[He turns to me, ignoring the game.]* Lots of people who get "downsized" don't deserve it. The saddest thing is that when these things happen, people in my business say, "It's not personal. It's just business."

[The Rays lose the game and the World Series. The Phillies jump for joy. Dad turns off the TV.]

Dad: Tell the people who we just laid off that it isn't personal.

[My dad wearily leaves the couch, heading for the garage. He mutters something about taking out the trash. His shoulders sag in the same way that Willy Loman's do, as if the weight of his world is tugging him down.]

Me: I'll give you a hand, Dad.

   [Blackout]

Chapter 9: Halloween "Magic"

Madison's Hand

October 30th—Halloween Eve

Best concert.

Ever.

The most amazing three days we have all experienced together. It was no trick and all treat. We actually argued over who would explain what happened in this chapter. As Mickey says, "Maddie, you're our lead-off hitter." So here we go...

On the USC Campus—The Sports Arena

We were all so excited about seeing Bruce Springsteen and the E Street Band that we couldn't control ourselves. Mickey's dad drove up in his monster van. He and his wife promised us that we were sitting far away from them and a lot closer to the stage. They told us that Mr. Buscotti and his wife were going to be there...somewhere. We had Mr. B's cell number to call him. When we got there, Mickey kept looking at the stage. It was long and rectangular with Clarence Clemons' (The Big Man) saxophones on the left and a string of guitars across the stage. A violin stand was on the far right. Drums in the back.

We got there a half hour before the concert started...and strangely, it was kinda quiet. Rhia asked if there was a warm-up band, and the man in front of us—about 40ish—smiled and said, "Guys, this must be your first Springsteen show, huh?"

"Yeah," Rhia told him.

"There is never a warm-up band for Bruce. But by the time this is over, you will be worn out." He smiled as he revealed this to us. He seemed to relish the fact that we were naïve to the ways of the E Street Nation.

Without any warning, it was dark. The lights were blue on the stage, and we could make out the sound of an organ. Then, big figures—I guess stagehands—were carrying a long box. In an instant, we realized it looked like a coffin. They placed it down so it was standing up—about six feet high or so. The lights changed to a maroon color, and then *BOOM!* An arm holding a guitar burst from the top of the coffin, and Bruce Springsteen busted out of the box, yelling, "HAPPY HALLOWEEN! IS THERE ANYBODY ALIVE OUT THERE?"

The place erupted into "Bruuuccce!" His full band came out one by one to thunderous applause. Then The Big Man came out, and the place went wild. The whole stage was blasted in lights as the band roared into "Radio Nowhere."

Everyone was on their feet immediately. It seemed like the entire arena knew all the words and was singing along—and this was just the first song! I had been to concerts before where people sat and maybe sang the chorus—maybe even danced a little—but this was wild. It was as if someone so important had finally dropped into our world—someone rare, someone with a force and a power to just blow us all away.

And it was a real mash-up of ages. I saw grandparents and tons of college students. People my folks' age were kinda the most common, but we saw lots of kids our age, too. It was like a giant wedding.

Yeah.

The amazing thing was that Bruce (we are on a first name basis with him now) was a ball of energy. He finished the first song and yelled out, "One, two, three…"—and *BOOM* we were into "The Ties That Bind," where Bruce sang with Little Steven (the guy who looked like a gypsy). When that ended, he flew (literally) up on the top riser next to the drummer and *BOOM*—they were into "Lonesome Day," where the violinist (a woman) played next to Springsteen's wife, Patti, who sang with Bruce. It was nonstop electricity. The next song they played was one of my favorites from the album *The Rising,* which Mr. B used when he taught us about the 9.11 tragedy.

The four of us were all singing and jumping up and down. I cannot remember smiling more. I was so happy to be there with Mickey and Pari and Rhia. It was the Magic Tour—and it was magic, for sure.

Pari's Hand

After 20 minutes of nonstop music, Bruce finally stopped and talked to us. "Hello, out there!" He talked about how happy he was to be visiting the "left coast." People kept howling, "Bruuuccce!"—and he laughed. He said he was going to "get a little serious, now." Then he attached a harmonica to his neck, changed guitars, and blew life into the song "Gypsy Biker." It was a song, I think, that talked about the death of someone who maybe went to war and didn't come home. The man was to be buried, but what to do with his old motorcycle? What to do with the remnants of his life—his room, his home? All that was left was the love of his family, who looked at the cemetery where he would be buried and knew that soon he would be there and gone…and why did it have to happen?

The crowd slowly sat down while the song hypnotized us. Bruce quietly began the song "Magic." He seemed to play the role of a magician, telling us that it was all just a trick—the words, the promises, the world we are fed in the news media. Don't trust it. Trust only what you feel. The mystery of the song haunted the arena. It was so quiet. I was amazed that this man had turned a rollicking rock concert into a kind of political sermon.

Then Bruce answered the question that his songs seemed to ask each of us: what do we believe? The song was "Reason to Believe." I thought this was a powerful moment where he and his wife, Patti, sang a duet harmonizing about how even in our darkest hour, people of character, of faith, of courage still dig down and find some reason to go on and believe in each other and in the power of faith. When they were finished, a hush fell over the crowd, and I just looked at the others and mouthed *wow*.

All the lights went dark except for those on Clarence Clemons, the sax guy, who was enormous. Dreadlocks, black brimmed hat, black suit—a huge presence who blew life into the song "Night," a tale of a hardworking guy who just busts his butt to make ends meet. And the night is his refuge. The Big Man, as we all call him, is on Bruce's left as he tells the desperate story. And he just explodes at the end, as both men do exactly what the song preaches—that tonight is right, and we are alive, and this night will just set us all free.

And I feel it…something electric. I have goose bumps.

I have a reason to believe.

Rhiannon's Hand

Dude. No sooner than Bruce could change guitars and yell out, "Let's rock it!" than the piano began to play a rhythm that made you know there was thunder coming any minute. Then *BOOM*—Clarence Clemons broke loose with the band in full lights with the song "She's the One." Mickey yelled at me, "This is from the *Born to Run* album!" The whole place jumped to its feet. The "old timers" knew every word of this song, and each time the lights came up on the whole arena, all of us sang, "SHE'S THE ONE!" Clarence was in full command, and I could finally see how he and Bruce were, like, a team. They kinda played off each other, and they just seemed to be having a blast. There was no faking it—you could see pure joy on their faces. It was the same look we all had on our faces—you know what I'm talkin' about? It was killer.

I was amazed how we could go from quiet to, like, freakin' out in one song. Talk about the crowd being with you—this was ridiculous! People here were like family. Bruce played a new song next—"Living in the Future"—and I was glad because this time, I kinda knew a lot of the words. The Big Man started it. I'm not sure I totally get the song, but I think he was saying that we shouldn't worry too much, but that something bad might happen if we don't do something about all the problems in the world. I don't know. Maybe it was ironic?

Then Bruce sang a song I really liked called "The Promised Land." I liked it 'cause it was fun and 'cause everyone all joined in and yelled out, "BLOW AWAY!" But what I liked the most was realizing that I have dreams, too. You know? I want my life to be better than my mom's. I want love; I want magic; I want security. I know nothin' comes easy, and I know people shoot you down all the freakin' time— tellin' you that you can't do this, can't have that, that you're not good enough to get what you want. Dude, I just wanna say, "Screw you!" I *can* do this! I can! I just want to BLOW AWAY all those people who say I can't. I want to find a guy who can handle me—that is what I want, and I am willing to fight for it—so get outta my way!

The rockingest song (is that a word—rockingest? I think Mr. B would frown at that, even if he did think it was the rockingest song) was called "Workin' on the Highway." The place was jumpin', and Bruce was so outta control. He climbed up on a piano, sang to the people behind the stage (really cool!), and leaped back down. Then he came up to the front row, and the people got to touch his hand. Lucky! He danced (if what Bruce does can be called dancing) all the way across the stage. I have no idea what that song was about, but I planned on listening to it on my iPod when I got home.

Mickey's Hand

My turn.

He was dripping in sweat. He changed guitars with each song. During "Workin' on the Highway," he spun his microphone stand around and almost propelled himself into the crowd. He seemed to embody energy.

But then it all stopped.

The lights went black. A trace of blue light began to light his microphone stand. But Bruce disappeared. Then he slid into the faint blue night with his guitar—alone for the first time. Soberly, he sang for us the opening stanza of "The Devil's Arcade," which recounts a tragic tale of war—the dust, the drinking, the prostitutes, the dead bodies—and the bullets and the lieutenants and the beds and the ambulance and the hospital and the blue walls and the hometown and the graves and the faith and sheets of a bed with a body in it and the arcade's final victims. My heart was *beating beating beating*—and the fire burned the whole sports arena as the band rose up from the sad blue night to accompany Springsteen. The tragic fall. The drums. The cymbals. The end.

We didn't know if we should applaud or weep. I thought of the research paper I did last year on the book by Bobby Ann Mason called *In Country*. I remembered the halls of Walter Reed Memorial Hospital, which I had read about, and how many who had suffered in battle were never going to be whole again.

War is the Devil's Arcade.

Bruce spoke then: "I wrote this next song about the men and women who see a disaster and rise up to meet it. I think we all need to do that, you know? But we all ain't brave enough. They were." And then the lights came up on the whole band, and we jumped up as Bruce played "The Rising." I'll never forget the day Mr. B first played that song when he taught us about 9.11—and how he got us to understand "voice." That was the song about the firefighters—when the bell tolls, it tolls for them. They climbed up those buildings for the rising. It was what they did. They saved thousands. And many lost their lives doing it. The arena was so uplifted by the song, by their spirit, and by the knowledge that we as Americans don't give up.

Just as quickly, the band flipped a switch and burst into the song "Last to Die," which is a question that doesn't have an answer: "Who will be the last to die for our mistake?"

Iraq.

"Shock and awe."

America's poverty.

Wall Street.

Greed.

Caskets.

Racism.

Afghanistan.

When does the killing end? The answer appeared in the next song.

It became apparent to me that Bruce had all this planned. This was a rock and roll political high wire act. But he had taken it from the political to the personal. To the human level. To each of us, in each of our seats. How does someone do that? How? We were not here to download a song or two; we were here to listen to a sermon, and its theme flowed into the song "Long Walk Home."

The guitars twanged—Bruce was singing about what had gone wrong with his America. It smelled the same—the town was still there—but things had changed, and it was gonna take time to fix it and even understand it. The stores and such were there, but the people he knew were all gone—or strangers had replaced them. Places were closed. The town seemed broken, but Bruce implied that it was gonna take time. We could handle it.

The Big Man's sax was a call to action. We have friends. We have community. We have a reason to start over. Our fathers remind us of what America is about—sticking together, having freedom, having privacy, what we will do, and what we won't stand for. It may take a while, but we will get there. Our mothers and fathers and their mothers and fathers could all do it. Roll up the sleeves and take that long walk. We may be tired, but we will not give in. I thought of Ms. Anderson's class last year and her admiration for Dr. King's march from Selma to Montgomery. We shall overcome...someday.

Then Bruce stopped, like he was coming up for air, and we all collectively caught our breaths. Then he said something about what a great audience we were. "This was a rock and roll revival—a baptism." I think that's how he put it. One by one, he introduced the band— made a huge production out of all the great players on E Street. But the biggest ovation was for The Big Man—"Do I even have to say his name?"

Bruce, I found out, is famous for the "stories" he tells the audience. He told one that night that I will never forget.

"You know, there are people in this country who need help. That's why when you leave tonight, you'll see folks collecting for the food banks here in Los Angeles. Whatever you can give would be appreciated. I know times are hard. I know that jobs are hard to come by for some people. I know that we've got a lot of work to do. I know there is a presidential election comin' up. I know that you gotta take part in the process. It is our American land, you know.

"But I also know that when I was a kid in Jersey—man, I had nothing. My family just got by, and it was impossible to dream of something like this ever happening—to me. I was lucky—really lucky. But I want everyone out there to know that there are two things ya gotta hold on to. One is that 'nobody wins unless everybody wins.'" There was a huge roar from the crowd. "'And on a personal level, to have just one thing in your whole life that you do that makes you feel proud of yourself—that ain't too much to ask—.'"

Those words were to stay pushpinned to my brain like a girl's phone number tacked up on a bulletin board. That one thing to feel proud of—I want *that* to be my North Star. I know what my folks might want—my teachers, my friends. Is it too much to ask them all to just let me follow my dream?

The second after Bruce uttered those words, he said, "That's why we're playin' this song...ONE...TWO...THREE..." And the blast of sound and fury came pulsing out of the E Street Band as Bruce broke into "Badlands." He was caught in a crossfire—he didn't want the ordinary. He talked about a dream, a fear, a desire to not wait around and not reach that goal—that hope—that desire to be someone who says what they believe. And no amount of badlands is gonna stop him. Ever. Never.

I couldn't believe that the place could go higher, but when the audience started humming along and Bruce played to the entire crowd and said that "it ain't no sin to be glad you're alive"—well, man, the place exploded! We were all chanting "BADLANDS" over and over and over.

And I was more inspired than I have ever been in my entire life.

Rhiannon's Hand

The Encore

When he came back to the stage, everyone went friggin' nuts! And then he played my absolute favoritest song! (I think I made up another dumb word. Oh, well. Mickey said he wouldn't fix it 'cause it was so "me.")

I love "Girls in Their Summer Clothes" 'cause it is brand new and so sweet. Bruce was strumming his guitar by himself, and when he got to the chorus, the whole band joined in. And we were all dancing—me and Pari and Maddie. We hugged each other and swayed back and forth. We sang until our voices were all cracking. The poor guy in the song wants a girl so bad—and I wanna be that girl! I love when Bruce says, "You just saved my life." I love when they dance away in the end. I just think it is so romantic.

Okay, I am a pushover.

Pari's Hand

Bruce then yelled out, "Hey, it's time for my 'big hit!'" He was being sarcastic. I really didn't know he has never had a number one hit (by himself) until Mickey's dad told me later. I find that hard to believe.

Anyway, when he played "Dancing in the Dark," Bruce was beaming. He seemed to know that the party was just jumping. People were bouncing up and down. And so was I. I remember this song being played a lot on the radio, and I loved the beat. As a dancer, I just want to shake things up. I want to break out. I want to move. I want to have a "love reaction"—like Bruce said. Man, you can't start a fire without a spark, you know?

Then a really cool thing happened: Bruce grabbed some totally lucky girl and brought her up onstage to dance with him while Clarence played his solo.

Rhia looked at me and yelled, "Shut up!"

Maddie and I just looked at each other. Bruce whipped his guitar off and made every girl wish she was *that* girl. When she jumped off the stage, we all cheered. But we did not get a minute to catch our breath because almost without warning, the song ended, and all we could hear was Bruce screaming into the microphone, "ONE TIME!"

Mickey's Hand

"Oh, my God—it's 'Born to Run!'" The decibels cranked up so loud that I could hear my ears crackle. Everyone—and I mean *everyone*—was singing at the top of their lungs. This song was his signature. He must have been exhausted—but you would never know it. He was "fuel injected"—we all yelled out "ohhh" on cue. We are all wishing we could "break out and run 'til we drop"—and "ohhh"—and yeah, we are scared, but we gotta know if we can be wild and real and in love. And then The Big Man blew us away with the solo that leads to the dramatic ending. Girls. Guys. Motorcycles. Amusement parks. Kisses. More kisses. Passion. And we all waited in suspense as Bruce held the last notes. He let the audience get so close to him that those down in front of the stage got to play his guitar—strum their fingers on it. It's madness. It is a place where we wanna go—we are all tramps—tramps who were born to run. "Ohhh."

Goosebumps.

Bang.

The crowd erupted as Max hit the final drumbeat.

Madison's Hand

I was pouring sweat. My hair was drenched. My voice was shot. I had no idea how he did it, but right then, Bruce Springsteen brought the whole band to the front of the stage and reintroduced each one. It was like we became a family. And then he bellowed:

"Los Angeles, you have just seen the heart stoppin'—pants droppin'—hard rockin'—booty shakin'—earth quakin'—love makin'—Viagra takin'—history makin'—LEGENDARY E STREET BAND!"

And the violins and accordions (yes, accordions) jumped to life as they broke into a song I had never heard before called "American Land." It was all about coming to this great country and appreciating its beauty and majesty. It was kinda folksy and really old-fashioned. Yeah. It sounded like an Irish jig—and we were all clapping along. It was sort of the song that brought our heartbeats down a notch so we could all come to a finale. When he was done, all we could mouth was *wow*.

When Bruce finally left the stage, I felt like I had been in the presence of someone who doesn't come along very often. Like Michael Jackson or Lady Gaga or something. I just looked at my ticket stub and knew it was something I would keep forever.

It was everything Mr. B had said it would be. It was more than we had ever witnessed at any concert any of us had ever been to. Our ears were ringing. So was my cell phone. It was Mr. B. All he said was, "You have just been to the Promised Land."

I looked at my watch—it was midnight. But I could not be more awake…or alive.

Chapter 10: "Yes We Can!"

Madison's Hand

November 4th –Midnight

"If there is anyone out there who still doubts that America is a place where all things are possible, who still wonders if the dream of our founders is alive in our time, who still questions the power of our democracy, tonight is your answer."

President-Elect Barack Obama in Chicago's Grant Park

I was the only one of the four of us who couldn't vote. I was so jealous of Mickey and Pari and Rhia 'cause I still had 16 days to go before my 18th birthday. But I watched, I listened, and I rejoiced.

Yeah.

I mean, I didn't disrespect Senator McCain. No way. I am Navy, you know. But I just think like a lot of young people that times need to change. All the old ways of discrimination need to end with a bang, not just with some laws that Mr. Mac talks about that passed in 1964 or whatever. But in Mr. Mac's own words, "Laws don't always change men's hearts and minds."

Senator Obama had all the right stuff. He gets it. Even my dad says, "He's going to be one of the smartest Presidents we have had and one of the few who have come from the regular people, like us." (I know my dad voted for McCain, though.)

And how is this for a shocker? Mickey's dad even voted for Obama.

But I don't know much about politics or the economy or all that foreign policy stuff—all I know is that one man can't do it all. And I sure hope people aren't dumb enough to think that change can happen overnight. Like Obama said—it took a long time to get into the mess we are in, and it is not going to be easy to get out of it. Heck, the stock market is still dropping like a rock, Mr. Mac says. He says we have been in this recession since 2007.

Yikes.

It was really cool to see so many people crying when Senator Obama spoke in Chicago tonight. Oprah. Jesse Jackson. So many people said that they never, ever thought they would see the day when a black man would be in the White House—a house built by many black slaves.

Our teachers talk to us about historic moments—you know, like, they remember where they were when JFK was shot, and where they watched the moon landing in '69, and when they went to Woodstock that same year. Victory and tragedy.

Well, I remember where I was on 9.11…and now I know where I was when they announced that Senator Barack Obama was elected the 44th President of the United States of America.

Wow.

November 5th

Of course, everyone was talking about the election today—some really happy, some…not so much. But that all seemed a little less important when I got to Mr. B's class and realized that Jasmine was not there…again. She had been gone since Monday. Mr. B gave me a look, so I walked over to him with his roll book and kinda whispered, "Uh, Mr. B, do you know what is going on with Jasmine?"

"She is back in the hospital, Maddie. Her liver is starting to show signs of failure. Her parents called me last night."

"Oh, my God."

"Yes. She is at the same hospital where you volunteer, right?"

"Well, she was last summer. Is she still going there?"

"I think so... Wait. Yes, that is what her parents told me last night. Could you go over and see her? I mean, are you going over? I don't want to ask you to..."

"Mr. B, of course I will go. I am not scheduled today, but I will go, for sure."

Mr. B looked at me and he did not have to say anything; I had already figured out that he felt the same way I did about Jasmine. How could someone so full of life—so in love with life—be threatened with death? I could not help but think of Holden Caulfield's brother Allie in *The Catcher in the Rye*.

Yeah.

So I talked Mickey into going with me, even though all he wanted to talk about was the election, and we saw Jasmine that afternoon.

Jasmine's room was on the third floor. I wore my uniform so I could maybe get past any "checkpoints," and I told Mickey to just look like he belonged there. I asked the nurse at the nurses' station which room she was in and if she needed anything or was taking visitors. After a few minutes, the nurse said I could go in and see her.

As we got to Jasmine's room, I spotted her brother Paul standing outside with a few others, maybe his friends. I asked if he remembered me from the summer. He said he did, but I didn't really think so. He was being polite, and he seemed worried. I asked if Mickey and I could just say hi to her. He said sure and that only her mom was in there now.

When I peeked in, I noticed she had one of the private rooms. Her mom was knitting something, and the TV was on, but the minute Jasmine saw me, she leaned forward, muted the TV, and in her high-pitched, cute voice exclaimed, "Maddieeee…Hi! What are you doing here? Are you workin' again?"

Before I could say any more than "Jasmine," she was into her monologue: "Here I am again, Little Miss 'Back in the Hospital Girl.' You know, I swear, I practically live here. Seriously. I think I have spent more time in hospital beds than in my own! Oh, and is this *the* Mickey I have heard about from the grapevine?"

Jasmine's mom was already up, getting us chairs and thanking us for visiting.

"Yes, Jasmine, this is Mickey…*the* Mickey. He wanted to meet you. I told him all about you."

"Shut up! You told *him* about *me*? No way. I can't believe you came all this way to see me."

I told her Mr. B was worried about her 'cause she had missed class and all. And I was worried, too. She had the same jaundiced look that she had had in the summer—her eyes and skin were yellowish. So I asked how she was feeling and all.

"Well, *that's* a long story. We don't totally know yet. Remember how I told you I had that operation when I was really little and that someday I would need a liver transplant? Well, I think that day is coming. The doctors say my liver is failing me more and more, and…well, you don't want to know all the yucky stuff, but I guess I am moving up the list of people who need transplants. Yep. That is the short version. Do they have a spare liver around here, Maddie? 'Cause I sure could use one!" And she burst out laughing.

I'm telling you, this girl could be on her deathbed and she would still be filled with joy and laughter. She seemed fearless.

"But I know that God is lookin' out for little ol' me, so I am not worried, you know? I mean, I am worried about missing school and all—especially Mr. B's class. Man, we were doing grammar, and I really need that grammar stuff 'cause I am, like, terrible with commas and all that subcoordinate stuff." She laughed again, and I hoped we were not working her up too much.

"*Subordinate*, Jasmine."

"Oh, yeah. See what I mean? I am so silly."

"Mr. B gave me a small packet of his exact notes and told me to tell you not to worry about anything. You can look it over or not sweat it at all. He just wants you to get better, okay?"

"Well, I will read this stuff because it's gotta be more interesting than all this boring stuff on dumb TV."

"I work tomorrow for two hours, so I will check on you, okay?" Then Mickey asked Jasmine a question.

"Jasmine, I write for the school newspaper. Maddie has told me all about how long this has been going on and all, and I am not saying I would do this—and I would never do anything without your permission—but I thought about maybe doing a story on you and your…" He struggled at how to phrase what he wanted to say.

"Struggle to stay alive?" Jasmine said it like she was answering a question on *Jeopardy* or something.

"Um, yeah. It might be an ongoing piece."

"Yeah, well, let's hope so!" She cracked herself up. "I mean, it better have a happy ending—duh."

It was uncomfortable and strange, Mickey and I said later, how in the face of a breakdown of a vital organ, Jasmine could be so unafraid.

"Mickey, I would be honored if you thought my story would mean so much that you would write about it. So whatever you think. It's coolio with me."

Just then, the nurse came in to take Jasmine's vitals, and we knew this was our time to leave. We said our goodbyes, and as we walked down the hall, Mickey looked at me and said, "Maddie, I don't think I have ever met anyone like her in my life. She is a trip."

What was left unsaid between us was how this trip might end.

Rhiannon's Hand

November 11th

Okay, why is it that everybody has to tell me their troubles? Huh? I mean, I'm the least likely person to have answers, and sometimes I am more messed up than they are, you know?

So in the last week, I have had heart-to-hearts with Pari, Tiffany, and Leann. I am exhausted. Here's the scoop.

It starts with Pari.

She came over to get something that she left at my house. As you know, she is super smart—especially in math. So she asked me if I was taking the SAT in December. I told her no.

"Pari, I am not gonna have the money to go to even a state college—just a junior college. And I'm gonna live at home. Sounds really exciting, huh?"

"Rhia, that is crazy. You have good grades. You could go to a state school and live at home. That would better, don't you think?"

"Why?"

"Well, because you could be working toward a BA, not an AA...I don't know. But you do have to take the SAT to get in."

"Yeah, well, the JC credits transfer..."

"True. But Rhia, don't you want to keep your options open?"

"Yeah, I guess. Hmm. I think I have just been procrastinating on all this stuff," I finally confessed.

"Well, look. I will help you with registering and stuff. I have done it so many times that I am pro."

"Pari, how many times have you taken the SAT?"

"Oh, wow. Between the SAT and the ACT…five, I think."

"God! Why?" I couldn't imagine her not getting a really great score the first time.

"Well, that's what I wanted to ask you about. See, I was taking it over to get a better score in math, and I got a good score…finally. But I feel weird about it."

"Why would you feel weird about doing better? I mean, Pari, you would be a freak if you *didn't* feel great. So I don't get it."

There was a pause, and then she looked down and said, "I got a score that…it was really good…I mean…"

"Pari, for cryin' out loud, what are you saying?"

Then she did the strangest thing. She started to cry. "I got a perfect score on the math section."

"What?" I spat out. "PERFECT! Oh, my God! Pari, that is great! Why are you crying, girl?"

Pari took a while to find a tissue in her purse. "I know, I know. I am so stupid. I am crying over a stupid math score." She finally found the tissue and complained about her mascara running. "I just don't want to tell a bunch of people because I don't want people to think I am some conceited person. I hate it when people put others down— indirectly, of course—by telling them they aced this or that test or whatever. It is just so crass. I don't want to play that game. So I don't want to say anything at all. And I don't want Mickey to know because I know he really didn't do that well in math—he did in English—and I just don't want to rub his nose in it."

I looked at Pari and leveled with her: "Mickey, me, and Maddie— we are all, like, super proud of you. Like, you are gonna be some famous scientist who will discover the cure for cancer or something. And we are gonna say, 'We knew that girl when'. You are gonna be the famous person we will all brag about."

"Get real, Rhia. It was just a math test."

"That's not the point. The point is that you should not be afraid to let people know you are smart—heck, we all know it, anyway. And you of all people are the least conceited person I know. As a matter of fact, you need to get a little bit more *attitude*, girl." That made her laugh. Finally.

As she left, I promised her I would take the SAT—probably bomb it, but take it. And I wondered what it would be like to be so smart. So smart that it makes you cry.

I guess there are some things I'm never gonna know, huh?

Tiffany's troubles

Tiff overcame bulimia and stupid boyfriends. At least, that was how last year ended. And she seemed pretty good during the summer. I always wondered how someone who worried about getting "fat" could work at Yummy Yogurt, but she rarely had any yogurt. Just a little in a "tasting cup."

And you should know that she is a knockout. Like, the girl has no fat. She looks perfect—a little too thin, maybe. But after work, she tells me something:

"Rhia, do you know what AA is?"

"Duh, yeah. Don't tell me you are an alcoholic!"

"No, no. That is one thing I am not. But AA exists 'cause once you are an alcoholic, it is something you have to deal with for the rest of your life. And what I am finding out is that the eating disorder I have had for two years isn't something that goes away. Like, I have to deal with it for a long, long time…maybe forever. I am still too obsessed with my weight and what I eat."

"Well, you aren't throwin' up are you?" I asked.

"No. But I get scared that I will. That is why I brought up AA— 'cause I am in this group with a bunch of other students who have the same problem. We meet once a week after school in the Student Services office."

"Well, that is great, Tiff. That is exactly what a healthy person does, girl. So what is the problem?" I knew there was something she wasn't telling me.

"Yeah, but I am just nervous about it because it makes me think about the fact that something is wrong with me, you know? You know, I try to forget about it and never let it get into my head. The support group gets it out and gives me some people to talk to, but the bad thing is that it makes me remember that I have this problem…"

"Tiff, listen to yourself. You need to know that you are not the only person in the world like this. There are millions of people like you. Remember how we studied this in Mr. B's class? The difference between you and most people is that you have the guts to face it. And you have won the battle."

"But…"

I looked her square in the eyes (again—*me* giving advice!): "Tiff, you are just bummed because this is a problem that you have to face. We all have something we carry. My stupid dad. My brother in SPED. My lonely mom. Us being kinda poor. Me and you workin' at friggin'

Yummy Yogurt! Life is gonna be tough, girl. But you have so much. I mean, guys drool over you. I could use that problem!"

Tiffany smiled. "Yeah, well, guys can be a pain. But I am taking Mr. B's advice for now—he said, 'Boys are nothing but trouble.'"

She smiled at me and then started to cry. "Rhia, you are so sweet to listen to me and my ridiculous issues. I know you're right. I just need to accept some things and move on, right?"

"Right."

"Yeah." She wiped her tears away on a Yummy Yogurt napkin that she had balled up in her work shirt pocket. "You know, Rhia, you are so easy to talk to. I love you for that." She hugged me.

"I know, Tiff. Everyone loves to talk to me."

I drove home from work that night wondering, *So, who do I get to talk to? Huh?*

Leann's letter to me:

> *Dear Rhia,*
>
> *I know I haven't seen you since that night, except when I spotted you at school. But we've never talked. I just wanted to thank you for all you did for me—you may have saved my life that night.*
>
> *Seriously. You have no idea.*
>
> *I saw the doctor, and he referred me to a psychologist. I saw two psychologists, but I really didn't feel that they connected with me. So I am trying another one. But I am starting to feel better about things.*

The one person who has been a constant help is Mr. B. I know he was your teacher last year, and I know about the book you wrote. In his class, every day, for one hour, I forget my problems and listen to him. Really listen. He speaks to me in so many ways. The Hemingway story "Hills Like White Elephants"— you know, the one about a girl who gets pregnant (thank God that isn't me) and then is so angry with herself and the boy that she is with—that's exactly how I feel.

I'm angry at him for what he did to me. Angry at myself for letting him think I wanted him. But I am starting to understand that I need to stop beating myself up.

I scared everyone, I know—my parents, you, myself. I'm still scared.

But you saved me from myself. You are my hero, Rhia. On my iPod, I was listening to a song by Elton John about how "someone saved my life tonight." That someone was you. And I'm a butterfly. Free to fly away.

Love you.

Let's talk. I think I am gonna try to come back to work after the holidays.

Bye,

Leann

I read the letter over, like, four times. I couldn't believe what had happened to the two of us that night. I really didn't deserve all she said about saving her life. I just know that I did what anyone would do, right? I don't know what is going to happen to her—or the guy and stuff—but I do know one thing: I connect to people.

When I showed the letter to my mom, she started to cry. She told me that I was someone who people could trust and that she was so proud of me. That is when we had the final amazing conversation of the week.

My Mom's Secret

Look, I am all about romance. I love happy endings. I wrote in the last book about how much my mom's heart was broken by my father and how my mom tried to take her life two years ago—around Thanksgiving. So when we reach that holiday, I always get a little weird—sad is really a better word (*melancholy*, Mickey told me; I looked it up—yep, that's me). So when my Mom told me she wanted to talk, I kinda freaked.

"Mom, what's the matter? You okay?"

"Yes, Rhia, of course. Relax. This is good news, I think. It certainly isn't bad news. It is just something I want to make sure you understand…and don't feel uncomfortable about."

I was totally unprepared for what she was about to tell me.

"Well, I kinda met someone…nothing that serious…yet. But…"

I immediately interrupted her. "Mom, that is so great! I am so happy…" My sentence stopped short when I heard the second half of her sentence.

"…he is someone you know."

I froze. Who did I know that she knew?

"Who, Mom?" If she had started seeing my dad again, I would have gone *nuts*.

"Okay, well…you know how I went to Back to School Night?"

"Yeah…"

"Well, I had the nicest talk with the AP Government teacher, Mr. MacQueen... (*I think my eyes were bugging out at this point!*)... and then a week later, I was at Starbucks, and he came over to chat. And he told me how proud he was of you and the book that you had written with the other kids. He told me he admired *me* for raising a daughter like *you*.

Well, I think I blushed a bit...I mean, I was so flattered—and you've spoken so highly of him—and, well, the next thing I know, we have been talking for 30 minutes. (*My jaw dropped at this point as I began to realize where this was going.*) And he asked me if I was a regular at this Starbucks. And I told him I usually come here on Saturday mornings after I walk...and, well, the next thing I know, we have met each other twice so far."

All I could get out of my mouth was, "And..."

"And...nothing. But he told me that Mickey's family has invited him to their Thanksgiving dinner. He said that the Buscotti's were invited, too. Sort of a celebration."

That's when I put two and two together. I said, "Mom, we are going there, too. So, like, that is going to be another time you can see him." I felt a little—I don't exactly know the word—*weirded out* because all at the same time, I felt happy for my mom, freaked that she may be dating a man for the first time since my dad, relieved that the man was nice, and *super* freaked that the man was my TEACHER!

Oh, my God. I kept thinking, *what more is gonna happen to me in one week?* I can't exactly remember what was said after that 'cause I was so confused + excited + paranoid + happy all at once. Is that even possible? (I wish Mickey was around to tell me what word all those feelings would = equal.) Anyway, my mom looked at me and asked, "Is all this okay with you?"

"Um...uh, well...sure, Mom."

"Really? You won't feel uncomfortable—I mean, we aren't 'seeing' each other. We are just becoming friends."

I don't know what came over me, but I suddenly had the urge to be a comedian. I said slyly, "Oh, sure, Mom. That's how it always starts, and the next thing you know..."

And we both laughed. One of those nervous laughs—but also relieved and happy and excited.

My mom then asked the one question that always pops into a girl's head: "What should I wear?"

Thanksgiving had taken on a whole new meaning.

Chapter 11: Saba and the Metaphor Café

Pari's Hand

November 14th

The moment I saw her, I felt like I was looking at someone whom I felt deep inside I could be—if I had the nerve…not to mention the talent.

It was Friday night at 7:00, and it was the Grand Reopening of the Metaphor Café. The four of us had been waiting for this day for months. Mickey sensed that without the Metaphor Café, we might never have been able to finish what we had started. There was something about the aroma, the ambiance, the whole indie-coffeehouse-feel that we had all missed.

And it was not just us.

The place was packed. The new owners were former graduates (okay, they are kind of, shall I say, *mature*) from our high school. They had gutted the place, but had somehow kept the feel of a hangout that is not some chain store. They had memorabilia from our school, the town, and a lot of rock and roll. But not all rock and roll because on the walls were posters of bands that were more current. U2. Foo Fighters. Pink. There was a cool poster from the Coachella Music Festival. I didn't go; my parents said no.

The posters were on opposite sides of a triangular stage that had enough room for three or four people, although tonight there was one beautiful singer tuning up. We knew of her, but many in the crowd knew her personally. They had followed her career, which we were to discover made its way through Mr. Buscotti's class, on to UCLA, and on to her own music label. She was simply known as *Saba*.

I was sitting at a small table with Rhia, Mickey, Maddie, and Daniel. Donald, who we think still goes out with Rhia (when she is not working), had to work again. In the far back corner, we spied Mr. B and his wife Deborah. They were sitting with Mr. Mac and another couple we did not know. There was an empty chair, too.

"You guys, my mom is coming tonight," Rhia told us.

"Really?" Mickey raised his eyebrows.

"Um, yeah. There is something I gotta tell you guys, but…" Just then, the new owner jumped onstage and made this introduction:

"Hey, thanks for coming out, folks. I'm Pete. My wife Laura and I—along with Michael and Susan Stimson—are the owners of the Metaphor, and we are so jazzed that the community has come out to see the new Café. Thanks so much."

When the applause died down, I noticed that Rhia's mom had maneuvered over to the table with the teachers, and Mr. Mac had stood up to help her to be seated. I looked at Rhia. She looked at me. I mouthed: *Are you serious?* Rhia just nodded. Mickey and Maddie had not noticed, but Daniel had, and he just smiled. I wanted to say something, but then the owner continued:

"I went to school here with this local star, and we also attended UCLA together. When she heard about what we were doing here at the Metaphor Café, she insisted upon being the opening act. I told her we could not pay her…except with a few cups of coffee. [*Laughter*] But she insisted. She is a singer-songwriter turned indie-rocker. You guys will notice that her 2006 album *Elbo Club* is for sale here. She's been nominated twice for Best Acoustic Performance, and she is one of our own. Please give a warm welcome to Saba."

After seeing Bruce Springsteen, I wondered how anyone could follow him. But in Saba, I saw and heard something so different: feminine, soft, soul searching, and gut wrenching. She was dressed in a black suede dress, black boots, and a red sash tied across her waist. Her hair was jet black and long enough to tie in a ponytail and wrap around her; it lay over her right shoulder, almost touching the top of her acoustic guitar. Her eyes were the most dramatic part of her presence. They were big and full. Black mascara and dark, smoky eyeliner accentuated her features and would have made it hard not to notice her even if she were not the center of attention. She spoke before she started:

"Hello, out there. I have not played a coffeehouse in a while [*strums her guitar once or twice*], and I feel kinda naked without my band, but I would not have missed this for the world. I really wanted to come back and support Pete and his wife and the other owners. I always wanted to come back to the community that raised me and thank folks, you know? I see some of my old teachers here tonight. I hope they don't grade me. [*Laughter*] Especially on my public speaking. [*More strumming*] So I will just let my songs speak for me if that is okay? [*Cheers*] This one is from my new album, which is coming out soon. It's called 'Best Damn Thing.'"

I spent three long, hard years
Moping around in bars, bartenders catching my tears
Filling my drink so high, so I could
Forget about you, stumble home half dead every night

I've got half a mind to leave
Leaving on the next train
Hoping that you'll run alongside
Begging me to stay
You must be a fool to think
Of letting something good just leave
When you sober up you'll see that
The Best Damn thing you had was me
The Best Damn thing you had was me

Sat in the same old hall
Night after night with nothing good to say at all
Watching you sway from side to side
The smoke from your lips was the only sign that we were still alive

I've got half a mind to leave
Leaving on the next train
Hoping that you'll run alongside
Begging me to stay
You must be a fool to think
Of letting something good just leave
When you sober up you'll see that
The Best Damn thing you had was me
Yeah, The Best Damn thing you had was me
Yeah, The Best Damn thing you had was me

She was wonderful. As I listened, I felt her anger at her own poor judgment, her resentment of the time she wasted on this fool. More importantly, she was baring her soul. It took a lot of courage to get up and say to the world what most of us keep locked inside our hearts. I was proud of her; I was glad to know that she went through all that and came to realize that she was the "Best Damn" person he would never have again. Maybe it is the dancer in me, but I just felt something. Something that I fear in myself.

What if I have this desire to perform? What if I want to be a dancer? What are the odds of me making it? What kind of life would I be facing? What if the "Best Damn Thing" I have is this ability, and what if I don't follow that desire?

Saba played another two songs, each melodic and melancholy. After she finished, she spoke: "Thank you. You know, my mother keeps saying, 'Saba, why can't you sing a happy song?' [*She laughs...so do we.*] So here is my newest effort. It isn't *exactly* happy, but it is close. Before I start, though, I want to say something to the students out there. I am looking around, and I see a lot of you. [*She looks directly at our table.*] You know, guys, it is not easy to follow your dreams. It is not a fast ride. It is not always fun and games. You do have to start from the bottom. It is work. But guys, follow your passion. Make sure you don't settle. Don't take the easy way out just because it might be what everyone else thinks you should do. If you have a dream—if you want to do something—and there is risk, well, there is reward, too. I have two degrees from UCLA. My parents wanted me to go into science. But I chose music instead. I do not regret it. Mr. Buscotti is here tonight; he taught me a poem once. Robert Frost. You gotta choose the road you need to travel, no matter how hard the path may be to follow. It will make all the difference. So, to the students: *carpe diem*, and to the teachers: thanks for the inspiration. Here is my newest song, 'New Kind of Love.'

> I could ask myself why
> Every single day to the day I die
> And never have an answer
> And still never have an answer
>
> I could justify every single lie
> And still be lost for all the answers
> And still never have an answer
>
> He may not know what he lost when he let me down
> He may not see the good in me, but I see it now
>
> Go on and find yourself a New Kind of Love
> A New Kind of Love, one that lifts you up
> Get off your knees and find a new kind of love
> A new kind of love, one that lifts you up
>
> I spent so many nights searching for a clue
> For some truth inside of you
> Guess it was lost on you too
> And you run, you run, you run,
> Better than anyone
> In stiff drinks, cheap girls, quick fun
> But you can't outrun the sun
>
> He may not know what he lost when he let me down
> He may not see the good in me, but I see it now
>
> Go on and find yourself a New Kind of Love
> A New Kind of Love, one that lifts you up
> Get off your knees and find a new kind of love
> A new kind of love, one that lifts you up

This is your chance, now is your chance
Go on and find yourself a new kind of love.

So I am gonna find myself that "new kinda love"—yeah. Just then,
I noticed something: Mr. Mac had put his arm around Rhia's mom.

A new kind of love.

Chapter 12: When You Coming Home?

Mickey's Hand

December 1st—The Monday after Thanksgiving

"BAGHDAD, Nov. 27 – On Thursday, the Iraqi parliament approved a security pact that requires the U.S. military to end its presence in Iraq in 2011, eight years after a U.S.-led invasion brought about the fall of Saddam Hussein." —The *Washington Post*

That was how Mr. Mac started the day. He read it in a very neutral tone. Then he added, "Well, it seems clear that the war is over. But winning peace in Iraq will be a different battle."

Iraq had been on our minds these last two weeks—and not just because it was being discussed in our classes. Nope, the war was coming to our homes, too.

*****   *****   *****   *****   *****

Thanksgiving was strange. Thinking back on it now, it was a time when we celebrated some new beginnings, but we worried about some things that seemed to just go on and on.

It was great to have lots of people over. My brother Marc came down from San Francisco along with other relatives. But one highlight was when Mr. Buscotti and his wife arrived with Mr. MacQueen and Rhia's mother Patti. We had learned from Rhia after the Saba concert that, as she put it, they were "just friends." But after watching them, I was not so sure. They joined us for dessert: killer apple pie and awesome pumpkin pie. Maddie came by then, too, with Rhia. Pari was out of town, visiting relatives.

It was a little weird having teachers around, especially for Rhia. But considering what was missing in her life—namely, her big brother Chris, who was still serving in Iraq—she was at least happy that her mom had a "new friend." She kinda played it cool. I mean, how do you relate to a guy who is dating your mom and teaching your AP Government class? So she was quieter than usual. She watched her mom's every move. I noticed that her mom was splitting her time between Mr. Mac and Rhia; it must have been hard on her, too. But I have been around her since Rhia and I were freshmen, and this is the happiest I have seen her in a long while. So that has to count for something, you know? Unfortunately, that all changed the next day.

Friday morning—Black Friday, as they call it—is for shopping, but it was really black at Rhia's house. A bunch of us were going to the mall, and our last stop was to pick up Rhia. I rang the doorbell, and Rhia came to the door. Her eyes were hidden behind her hand; she sobbed something about not going.

"Rhia, what's the matter?"

"I just can't go. You guys go."

"Well, you're crying. What happened? Are you in trouble?"

She kinda let out a sound that told me I had just asked the stupidest thing possible.

"Mickey, just go, okay?" She closed the door an inch.

"Wait, Rhia. Wait. I mean, sorry. Just tell me why you are crying." I surprised myself. Usually, I would run from this kind of thing. Girls crying is just not something I handle well. But just then, Maddie appeared behind me.

Maddie took one look at Rhia and said one word: "Chris?"

Right then, Rhia burst into tears, and Maddie flew past me and into Rhia's arms. All I could hear was a muffled, "Is he hurt badly?"

***** ***** ***** ***** *****

Twenty minutes later, after the others we were with had left, me and Maddie understood what had happened.

"...and we were worried when we didn't hear from him on Thanksgiving. He had said that he and the other guys in his platoon were making videos that would be sent out the next morning at the latest," Rhia's mom explained. She had been crying, but was clearly keeping her composure for Rhia's sake...and ours.

"So this morning, the hospital over there contacted us, and we spoke to his commanding officer, who told us that Chris was in stable condition now, but that there was a explosion that had occurred—a suicide bomber, they think. Chris had been knocked unconscious. He had been out for an hour or so. Thank God he had his helmet on at the time. He wasn't very close to the explosion, but I guess it knocked him off his feet, and a wall smashed down—or a beam—I don't know, whatever—and the next thing they say is that they found him several feet away from where he was standing. Three other American soldiers were injured as well—none too seriously, I hope..."

Maddie asked, "When will you be able to talk to him or have any contact with him?"

"I don't know yet. I don't know. I'm relieved—but we're both so shook up. No one in our family has ever been in the military, Maddie; this is all new to us." Rhia's mom let out a breath that seemed to expel so much tension that I thought her chest would cave in.

All this time, Rhia just kept getting more tissues from the tissue box. There was a pile of tissues so high beside her on the couch that it started to stream down to the floor with each new, wet layer.

But he was alive. Would he come home? Was the concussion really bad? There were no answers that day.

Madison's Hand

Sometimes things happen and you wonder, *Lord, is this all happening for a reason?* Rhia's brother Chris is going to recover; we found out some basic information. He had the usual symptoms, my dad told me, of a concussion—a pretty strong one, he said. Vomiting. Dizziness. Some memory loss about that day. Chris had some cuts and bruises, too, and a pretty good gash over one eye. My dad pulled a few strings with some medical contacts in Iraq. But all in all, it could have been worse—much worse. It was that worry that made all of this so frightening for Rhia.

This will seem unbelievable, but what happened last Monday, just before Thanksgiving, foreshadowed what happened to Chris. That is why I wonder if the Lord had sent me a sign.

$$***** \quad ***** \quad ***** \quad ***** \quad *****$$

Mr. B's Freshman English students were going to be studying a short story called "Where Have You Gone, Charming Billy?" by Tim O'Brien. I had read his novel *The Things They Carried* last year in American Literature. Both stories deal with the effects of the Vietnam War, which O'Brien served in. The main character in the short story is "Private First Class Paul Berlin." It is Paul's first day in battle, and he is fighting the anxiety and fear that war brings. Mr. B decided to read the story out loud to the kids; I think that was smart because it really helped them get the feel (he called it the tone) of the story. When the story begins, one soldier in Paul's platoon has already died from a heart attack. O'Brien explains that he was *literally scared to death*.

As Mr. B read on, I could tell that the class was transforming from a sleepy morning bunch of fidgety 14-year-olds to a serious group of kids who liked the fact that Mr. B was treating them like they were older and capable of understanding something this powerful.

Other soldiers in the platoon tell Paul that he will get used to the fear of jungle warfare, but "Private First Class Paul Berlin"—as the author calls him over and over—is not sure if he will ever get used to all of the fear that this war is causing him—and it is only the first day.

"Will he ever make it home?" Mr. Buscotti asked the kids.

Nobody spoke for a while. Then one boy said, "How would we know?"

"You wouldn't. Couldn't. But if you had to predict, how do you think he will do there in Vietnam?"

Again, silence. As if they were all wondering, *What is the right answer?* Then Jasmine, who had been attending classes pretty regularly lately, said, "I don't know, Mr. B. He is pretty freaked. He may toughen up, but he seems so young and all. I hope he makes it."

"About 58,000 people did not make it, Jasmine. War takes its toll on people. In Vietnam, about 300,000 people were seriously wounded, too."

Silence.

"I guess that is why we should all be very thankful for what the men and women in the Armed Forces do today. It doesn't matter if you or your family agrees with the wars in Iraq and Afghanistan or not. What we all agree upon is that the people who serve the President should be honored for their good service to America. But as your English teacher, I want to ask you about the *theme* of this story. What do you think Mr. O'Brien is saying about human nature? About what war does to someone?"

Mr. B was off and running. He was at his best when he was getting students to think about why? Why do we fight? Why is it so difficult? What lessons can we learn from war? Why do we fear for "Private First Class Paul Berlin?" Mr. B made the students shape their answers into clear sentences about why war leaves scars that are both physical and emotional—scars that may last a lifetime.

There are times when I leave Mr. B's classroom, and I just can't shake what has just happened. How many times did I cry at night worrying about my dad? How many times did my mom lock herself in the bathroom and hide from us so that we would not see her cry? (It did little good, of course—my sisters and I always knew.) How many times did I re-read my dad's letters? How many videos did we watch of him putting on a happy face when he wanted to come home so bad? How many times did I ask him, "When are you coming home, Daddy?"

And now it is Chris and Rhia. It is their home that has been invaded with the fear that war brings. The fear that O'Brien says cannot be shaken. The fear of a mother who cannot do anything to protect her only son.

I glance at the clock. It is almost midnight, and I sit with one of my best friends and listen to her tearful words:

"When is he coming home, Maddie?"

And all I can offer Rhia is another tissue.

Chapter 13: "Just Dance"

Pari's Hand

December 3rd

We met for the first time at the Metaphor Café to talk about stuff. The book. Winter Formal. Our lives. Mr. B's class. Our parents. College.

Just stuff.

I decided if Mickey could write a play as he seems to do in some of our chapters, well, I could give it a try, too. Our meeting sounded like this:

Maddie: I love this place, you guys. I missed it. *[Everyone nods.]*

Pari: I think it is harder to write this new book; do you guys think so?

Rhia: Yeah, well, our lives are so all over the place, you know? Work. Chris. Leann. My mom!

Mickey: Um, yeah. Rhia, your mom is, like, dating *[he has a slight grimace]* Mr. Mac, right? I mean, are they *dating, dating* or just *dating?*

Maddie: Mickey, what are you asking?

Rhia: No, I get it. It is weird, but not bad weird—just different. I don't know. She went to the movies with him. But the awkward part was when he came over for the first time. I mean, they had been meeting at places, you know. But then last weekend, he picked her up.

Mickey: What did you say to him when he came over?

Maddie: Mickey, why do you want to know? *[Mickey never gets to answer.]*

Rhia: It's cool. I didn't say much—neither did he. I think he just felt kinda strange, too. I just said, "Hi, Mr. Mac," and he said, "Hi" back. Then my mom whooshed in and we said, "Bye." But I know my mom is super happy. New clothes. Make-up. She looks good, I must say.

[Mickey's curiosity satisfied, we moved on.]

Pari: Yeah, well, do you guys think the book is harder to write?

Mickey: Parts are. I think it's because it is harder to know what we want to do.

Pari: I never told you guys about my SAT. *[A pause.]* Rhia knows. *[She looks at me with the look that says, "Well, tell them!"]* I'm a little embarrassed, but I just wanted you guys to know that I got...a perfect score on the math section. *[Cheers and versions of "Shut up!", "No way!", and "Awesome, Pari!" followed. I'm sure the relief was evident on my face.]*

Mickey: Well, now it is probably down to Harvard or Stanford, huh?

[He is smiling.]

Pari: Forget that. I cannot afford either one.

Maddie: Scholarships?

Pari: Maybe, but it is still so expensive. I mean, $50,000, you guys—a year!

Mickey: I've heard Harvard doesn't make students pay. They have so much money in endowments...

Rhia: Is that like scholarships?

Pari: Yes and no. They have so many rich people who give to the school that some freshmen pay nothing—or so I hear. But I am not even applying there—and I wouldn't get in, anyway. Besides, I think I want to stay on the West Coast. I have relatives in San Francisco, so Berkeley is where I think I want to go—if I get in.

Rhia: Shut up, Pari. You will get in. Duh.

[General agreement. I frown.]

Maddie: Do you guys miss Mr. B's class? *[Heads nod.]* Well, listen, I have to tell you about what he is doing right now. It is so cool. He is staging *A Midsummer Night's Dream* in his classroom, and he is playing Bottom. Remember—the one who is turned into a donkey?

Mickey: Jackass.

Maddie: Yeah. Anyway, remember how I was telling you about Jasmine? Mickey has been writing a column about her…

Mickey: I'm a little behind on that…

Maddie: Yeah. Anyway, she plays Puck, and she is so cute!

Mickey: Adorable…

Maddie: Will you shut up? You weren't even there. *[She looks back at the girls.]* Anyway, yes, she is adorable. Mr. B's previous classes had painted a backdrop, and they had brought in props like fairy wings and stuff. And the best part is that some art teacher made an ass's head, which Mr. B wears. It is hilarious! But the funniest part—I almost peed in my pants—was when Jasmine—who is pretty religious and very polite, was supposed to call Mr. B an "ass." Her line was, "When in that moment (so it came to pass), Titania waked, and straightaway loved an ass," and she just couldn't do it!

She started to giggle, and then she said, "Mr. B, I can't call you a you-know-what—you're my teacher!" Then she started laughing, and Mr. B—with the ass's head on—looked at the class watching

the play and said in a muffled voice, "Jasmine, will you stop
laughing? I am dying in this heavy ass head. Just say your lines!"
But she couldn't stop laughing. She even fell on the floor! Then the
whole class started in, and before I knew it, I was laughing so hard
I had to find the tissue box. It was so funny! The class was
hysterical. Mr. B finally took off the ass head and looked at Jasmine
and said, "Fine, you can call me a 'big donkey,' okay?" But she
couldn't even look at him. While spazzing out, she just kept
whimpering, "I can't breathe!"

[Rhia, Mickey, and I are all laughing at this point.]

Pari: So what happened?

Maddie: Mr. B had to call it a day and let everyone recover. But every
time it got a little quiet, someone would burst out laughing. Then a
bunch of girls had to go to the bathroom.

Mickey: I guess that's why they call it a comedy.

Rhia: I have to go pee now.

Mickey: Why do girls always say that? Guys never do.

[Rhia leaves.]

Pari: I think it is cool that Winter Formal is before Christmas. I assume
you guys are going?

[Mickey and Maddie nod.]

Maddie: What about you? Did Daniel ask you?

Pari: Yes. My folks are getting a little "concerned." My father asked
me—more like reminded me—to not get serious with Daniel, and
my mom gave me the evil eye from across the room. But do you
think Rhia is still going out with Donald? And is she even going to
the dance?

Mickey: I don't know. Ask her when she comes back.

Maddie: I can't just *ask* her!

Mickey: Seems like the sensible thing to do.

Maddie: No, not while *you* are here!

Mickey: Who, me?

Maddie: Yes, you!

Mickey: Okay, fine. I will go to the bathroom, then.

[He has that smirk on his face. Rhia returns. Mickey exits.]

Rhia: So, what are we talking about?

Pari: Winter Formal.

Rhia: Oh.

[A pause.]

Maddie: Are you...?

Rhia: I don't know, Maddie. Between Chris, Mom, everything... Donald is so worried about retaking the SAT and applying to private schools that he isn't around much. Heck, neither am I. Work takes up so much time, and Pari talked me into taking the SAT, and Mr. Mac's AP Government class is so hard—and I can't screw *that* up! I mean, can you imagine Mr. Mac calling my mom to tell her that I'm getting a D or something? Talk about *embarrassing!* So, I don't know what I'm doing yet. Are you guys going? Duh— why am I even asking? Of course you are.

[Another pause...longer this time. Mickey returns.]

Mickey: Well, I'm back. *[He notices the awkward silence.]* Hey, we are having winter workouts for baseball, and we've got a new guy on the team. His name is Roberto, but we call him RC. He just moved here from Puerto Rico, so the RC stands for Roberto Clemente. *[The girls shoot him a "Why the heck are you bringing this up at a time like this?" look. Mickey picks up on it.]* Yeah, well, he's really good. Plays second. Anyway, I was talking to him, and he was saying that he doesn't really know anyone except the guys on the team. He had to leave his dad and brothers and sisters back in Puerto Rico. He and his mom are living here with relatives until his dad gets transferred—he's in the Navy. I don't understand it all, but he is a really nice guy...

Rhia: Mickey, you are so obvious! Are you trying to set me up with this guy?

Mickey: Me? Set you up? No way. You have way too much of a social life. I just thought you might want to take pity on him.

Rhia: You *are* trying to set me up! I knew it, Mickey!

Maddie: Rhia, Mickey is an idiot, but I have to tell you something. I saw RC when I picked up Mickey after practice. He is *really cute.*

Rhia: Really? *[She pauses, catching her next word mid-syllable.]* Forget it. He has a girlfriend, I'm sure, back in...where did you say he's from?

Mickey: Puerto Rico—3,000 miles away. He's probably lonely. Come on, Rhia. Let me mention it to him. If he is not cool with it, then we'll just forget it.

Rhia: I don't know, Mickey. I need to *see* the guy first, you know!

Mickey: Okay, fine. We can work that out. We will come by Yucky Yogurt tomorrow.

Maddie: Yummy Yogurt.

Mickey: Whatever. If you think he's okay, text me.

Pari: That seems like a good plan.

Rhia: But what will Donald say? I don't know, guys.

Mickey: Dude, Donald had his chance. Besides, maybe nothing will come of it.

Rhia: Yeah, with my luck… Besides, I don't have anything to wear…

[With that, we got up and headed to our cars with Rhia more depressed than ever. She hadn't even really thought about Winter Formal. Or Donald. Or romance. Sigh…]

***** ***** ***** ***** *****

Oh, the drama. You know, being a girl is way way way harder than being a guy. Trust me. And then there is my little dance drama.

I want you to know that although it seems like I am some intellectual snob—which I try really hard not to be—my musical taste runs from Adele to Lady Gaga. It just depends on my mood—and it depends on dance. My studio's Winter Dance Recital is coming up in three days. So my dad picks me up yesterday and watches part of the rehearsal. We are dancing to Lady Gaga's "Just Dance," which opens the show, and "Poker Face," which is the finale. I absolutely love the songs. They are both from her *The Fame* album. They are super high energy. Fun. I don't care what the words are—and yes, I have seen the videos. Okay, she is out there. I get that. Sex. Drugs. Rock. But mostly dance. I think that like all artists, Gaga writes about the world she has to deal with, and that world is pretty wild and sleazy sometimes. But I like her. I think she has tons of talent and her own message. She is a hero to all the "Little Monsters" out there—kids who maybe don't fit in but need a place to be. They are welcome in Gaga's world because that was how she was growing up.

She is a performance artist. In the dance world, her music rocks.

Now, my dad sees the rehearsal and—okay, I admit that what we are doing is a touch raunchy, a little sensual—okay, more than a little. So we have this discussion in the car.

Dad: I don't know about this dance, Parivesh.

Me: What about it? *[I play dumb.]*

Dad: It is, um, how shall I say it? Somewhat provocative. Maybe better suited for adults, not 16- and 17-year-olds.

Me: Dad, first of all, I am 18. Secondly, it is supposed to provoke— that is what dance does. And it is not like we are pole dancers or something.

Dad: Don't exaggerate, Parivesh.

Me: I'm not. You are taking this dance too seriously. We are just dancing.

Dad: Well, what is that "Poker Place" one about? You seem to be taking off your clothes in that one!

Me: It's called "Poker *Face*," Dad. And yes, we are taking off our clothes, but we are not naked. It is part of the message. We are playing poker, and we are not showing our feelings because we are trying to keep our emotions inside.

Dad: Well, why can't you hide your emotions while keeping your clothes on?

Me: Funny one, Dad. Look, it is just dance.

Dad: Just dance. Hmm. *[I take note of the fact that his hands have a death grip on the steering wheel.]* Do you ever wonder what all the songs you listen to mean?

Me: Dad, you are driving me crazy! That is all I do! I mean, I love to listen to music. It is just that Gaga is very pop culture and dance world.

Dad: I have no idea what you just said. Her name is Gaga?

Me: Yes. No. *Lady* Gaga. It is her stage name.

[Dad notices that he is driving too fast. He slows down.]

Dad: There were boys dancing with you girls.

Me: Yes.

Dad: *[Loudly.]* Hmm.

Me: *[Not quite as loudly.]* Hmm. What? It is no big deal. Guys and girls dance together all the time.

Dad: Not like that.

Me: Like what? *[Again, I'm playing dumb—which I'm not very good at.]*

Dad: Do I have to say it, Parivesh? They are doing all this grabbing...and acting like...you know... *[He knows what he wants to say, but without a diplomatic way of putting it, he finally just blurts it out]* ...like they are trying to have sex with their clothes on!

[Dad realizes that he just missed our exit. He mutters to himself. The rain pattering on the roof of the car fills the void where our voices used to be.]

Me: Look, Dad. I get it. I really do. Don't worry. Trust me. It is just a song. That is all it is.

Dad: I certainly hope so. Parivesh, you need to be careful. Boys get stupid ideas. And what you are doing in those dance numbers is, well...I don't know. Let's just say I am concerned.

Me: I know, Dad. I know. It's just dance.

[I try to hide my own poker face as we pull into the driveway. Because I do know what he means. The music is intoxicating...and being a girl is just really complicated.]

***** ***** ***** ***** *:***

Mickey's Hand

December 4th—Two Weeks Before Winter Formal

So, I was in my truck with RC—Roberto. We were heading to the yogurt place. I mentioned to RC that my really good friend Rhia worked there.

"Is she in any of your classes?"

"I don't know. I don't really know very many people yet." RC was one of those scrappy infielders. Short. Strong. Tough. He still had eye black on. He was wearing his Pirates hat. He had already asked Coach if he could wear #21—Clemente's number. He was trying to grow a goatee, but it wasn't happening. I hadn't seen him without a baseball hat on much. But his hair was more black than brown, and unlike my long hair, it was pretty short.

"So, is she cute—this Rhia?"

"Hot."

"Boyfriend, I bet."

"Sometimes. She isn't too serious with this one guy. I think they're just friends." I wasn't so sure about anything I was saying—except that I do think Rhia is really cute.

"She play sports?"

"Nope. Her brother is in Iraq now. She just does school and work. But she likes to dance." I hope the hint stuck.

"Brother's in the Army?"

"Yep."

"My dad's been Navy since he was 19. I've been to more schools than I can count."

We got out of the truck and headed into the yogurt place. No one was there, though. Panic set in for a minute. But then, from the back room, Rhia came around the corner on her cell, saying, "Mom, I don't know how the stupid thing works. The owners are not answering their stupid phones." She looked up. She had chocolate all down her arm and on her apron…and in her hair (I only told her later—I just didn't have the heart to say anything then.)

"Oh, hi!" She grabbed the phone with the only clean part of her other hand. "Mom, I gotta call you back. Customers. Yeah, okay. Bye." She looked down, but then put on a smile and said, "Hi, Mickey." Then she looked at RC and added, "Hi."

RC just nodded.

"What's the matter?" I asked.

"Oh, nothing. The chocolate machine is gunked up or something, and it exploded all over me. I must look like a wreck." She tried to fix her hair, but her hands were so sticky that she decided against it. "It has been a bad day."

"Rhia, this is RC. Remember—I was telling you guys about him? He's the new second baseman. You remember."

"Oh, right. Hi. I'm Rhia. Sorry, I don't know a lot about baseball. I just go to games with Mickey's girlfriend to watch him pitch."

"Oh, so you're friends with Maddie?" RC said. "Well, that's cool."

"Do you guys know what you want?'

I said, "Well, definitely not chocolate." Rhia laughed. She is adorable when she laughs. RC noticed.

As we were ordering, another girl came in. It was Tiffany. I guess her shift was starting soon. Rhia gave us our cones, and RC said he was paying.

"Neither of you guys are paying; this one's on me," Rhia said.

"No way," RC protested. He then put a five-dollar bill in the tip jar. *Smooth*, I thought.

Rhia came around the counter, whispered something to Tiffany, and sat down with us at a white plastic table. I think she wanted to get that ridiculous apron with the slogan "It's Yummy!" off as quickly as possible.

"So, what does RC stand for?" Rhia asked.

"Roberto Clemente…Rivera." My mom is Puerto Rican, and my dad is Navy. My dad and I both love baseball. I know you don't know a lot about baseball, but Roberto Clemente is, like, a national hero in my country. Well, I say 'my country,' but I was born in the USA."

"Springsteen," I said.

"Huh?"

"Bruce Springsteen. You know—'Born in the USA.'"

They both looked at me like I was an idiot, so I decided to shut up.

Rhia rolled her eyes, "Whatever, Mickey. Ever since we had Mr. Buscotti's class, Mickey has been on a Springsteen kick."

"Hey, wait," said RC. "You wrote that book that Mickey was talking about? You and Maddie and him?"

"And another girl named Pari—short for Parivesh."

"What's Rhia short for?"

"Rhiannon."

"I like it."

"Well, I like Roberto better than RC."

"Cool. Nobody calls me Roberto. Except my mom."

"Well, now there are two of us…Roberto. How is the yogurt?"

"Great," we both said.

"RC, a bunch of us are going to see Pari—the other girl who wrote the book with us—dance at school on Saturday night. Wanna come with us?" I asked.

"Well, I don't know much about dance…"

"Well, I don't know who Roberto Clemente is!" said Rhia. "I will explain dance if you tell me about this Clemente guy. Deal?"

RC looked at her. "Okay, deal…Rhiannon."

When we got back in my truck, we didn't say much for a while. Then all of a sudden, RC said to me, "Hey, Mickey, thanks. I know you are trying to make me make friends. I know I am kinda stubborn. It's just hard for me. I moved so much that I hate to make too many friends—I never know how long I am staying, you know. I have been to 7 schools in 12 grades."

"Dude, it's cool. Besides, I am doing this because I need you to turn two when I am pitching." RC laughed. "Besides, Rhia is a really good kid. We are like brother and sister."

"That's great. She is pretty nice. Really. No boyfriend, huh?"

"Not right now."

"Cool." He grabbed his bag and bat.

Later, I got a text from Rhia: "He's CUTE, Mickey! And he called me Rhiannon!"

Ah, young love.

Nothin' better than baseball, girls, cars, burgers......and a good book.

Chapter 14: "And So This Is Christmas"

Rhiannon's Hand

December 25th—Merry Christmas!

Okay, I know it has been a while since you heard from me.

Well, I am still here.

Still working at Yummy Yogurt.

Still scared shitless about my brother. (Oops, sorry about the cursing. It is Christmas, but I couldn't think of a better word, you know?)

So much has happened this month, and things are so completely different from last year at this time. Seriously. Last year was the best and the worst all wrapped into one. My family was just scraping by, and it looked like Christmas was just gonna be totally depressing. Then our family was "adopted" by the Student Services program at school, and Maddie—God, I love her—got me a new cell phone. I was so blown away by it all. The gift cards and the other things that came to us through the school were part of what was to be a tearful and cheerful holiday.

We even went to church—something we had not done since my dad left us. Something we have been doing more of lately, too.

Prayer. Man, have I been praying.

December 6th—The Dance Recital

Pari was fantastic. I loved both of her Lady Gaga numbers. It is obvious that she has great stage presence; she looks out to the audience and her face just glows. Mickey says she "emotes"—I guess that is what it is.

Okay, I know what you wanna know. Me and Roberto, right? So, he was a little out of his element. He sat next to me with Mickey on the other side of him. He is a little different than the other boys I have known. Maybe it is the whole Puerto Rican thing, but the first thing he said to me when we met outside the auditorium was, "Hello, Rhiannon. You look great."

Now, that was a good start! I was wearing my favorite jeans—the super tight ones. And a gold top that was, in my mother's words, "a little too revealing." And my black leather boots. I wore my hair up. Hoop earrings. Not too much make-up.

I told him that I don't always have chocolate all over me.

"Well," he said, "girls don't dress up as much here compared to at my old school. But you look great."

Okay. I think he was nervous. But any girl will take the same compliment repeated, you know? He looked at me like—like he seemed honored to be with me. I know that is kind of strange to say, but it was how I felt.

We made small talk with Maddie and Mickey. Dan showed up with a rose for Pari—how sweet is that? Then we went into the show.

You know that tension you feel the first time you are sitting next to a guy on a first date—like, at the movies or something?—and you are both sneaking sideways glances at each other? Yeah, well, that was going on a lot. I liked what he was wearing. He, too, was a bit dressed up. He had on nice jeans—tight ones—and a white button-down, long-sleeved shirt. But the coolest thing he had on was a black vest that was buttoned. It made him look very mature. In a way, he struck me as someone who had been raised to be polite to girls—or maybe just to people in general. This became more obvious during intermission.

"You may not be dancing," he said to me, smiling, as we stood in the lobby by ourselves for a minute or so, "but you deserve a rose."

"Oh, my," I said. I was really, honestly surprised. I think I even blushed. "Thank you, Roberto."

"You're welcome," he said. "Thank you for getting me to come to the show. I can be a little, um, well—a little hard to get to know. Seven schools. Navy. You know what I mean?"

"Roberto, I can be a little hard to get to know, too. Parents divorced. Brother in Iraq. Know what I mean?"

He nodded.

Then he "escorted" me back to the theater. I held my rose…and when we sat down, I held his gaze a bit longer than either of us expected.

Finally, we both just smiled.

I gotta learn more about this Roberto Clemente guy.

December 20th—(The Same Night as the Winter Formal)—The Movie Date

When Roberto called me a couple of days after the recital, I wasn't sure what to think. I looked for him at school, but didn't find him. So, Maddie and I drove by baseball practice, and I waved at him. He did not come over, but he did the "call you" sign, and I mouthed "okay" back. When he called that night, my mom beat me to the phone. Strangely, she talked to him for about a minute before I could grab the phone away from her.

"Sorry," he said. "I only have your home phone number—not your cell."

"No worries," I said. "This will give my mom something to question me about." Then I felt bad and hoped he didn't think I was mad at him. "I mean, don't worry. You know how moms are."

"Yeah. She seemed nice. Does she know who I am?"

"Well, a little. Umm...not really that much." I paused. "Like, what did you talk to her about?"

"Oh, nothing. I just said who I was and that I was a friend of Mickey's. And that I met you at the dance recital thing. You know, just regular stuff."

"Oh."

"Yeah. Rhia, listen. Mickey has been pushing me to ask you to the dance coming up—"

I nervously cut him off—I don't know why. "Oh, that. You mean Winter Formal. Look, it's no big deal..."

Then he cut *me* off. "Yes, it is, Rhiannon. I mean, like, it's weird 'cause we just met and all, and I don't really know too many people at school. I mean, Winter Formal is so fancy and all. And...look, I think I am sounding really stupid right now, but maybe we could just go to the movies that night or something? I mean, if you aren't already going—I mean, to the dance."

He was being so cute; I figured I needed to put him out of his misery. "Roberto, listen. No, I'm not going to the dance. I went last year. It is not something I *have* to do. If you are asking me if I wanna go to the movies, then I think that would be great. Really." I have to say that I felt a sense of relief. Heck, he was right—I barely knew him.

"Really? Cool. That would be great. One problem: I have to wait until my mom gets off work so I can borrow the car, so..."

"RC, I have a car—it's a piece of crap, but it runs. I can drive. You wanna get something to eat first?"

"Well, yeah. Is that okay? I mean, me not picking you up?"

"Yeah. I think it's fine. What do you wanna see?" I knew *Twilight* had just come out—and I also knew that it was probably *not* going to be his first choice. I had a pretty good idea what was.

"Whatever you want to see. But I am buying the tickets—you already gave me an ice cream." He started to relax. He knew he had just gotten past the hard part.

I said, "Well, I saw the preview for the new James Bond movie, *Quantum of Solace*. It looks good."

"You sure? *Twilight* just came out, I think. Whatever you want."

You know, there was something I really liked about him. He was so—I know this is going to sound super cheesy—but he was so *gentlemanly*. I know, I know. I'm such a cornball!

After some trading off—"What do you want?"—"No, what do you want?"—I finally lied. "Look, I'm not that into all that *Twilight* stuff. I think James Bond will be a lot funner to watch than vampires." I can't believe I said *funner* again. I hate when I sound dumb—I have to work on that. Seriously! (Side note: I haven't read the *Twilight* books—I just don't have time. But the movies are good—and the two guys are so so so cute.)

When I hung up the phone, I just smiled.

Christmas just got a lot less lonely.

*****   *****   *****   *****   *****

We went to this 50s diner called Ruby's near the movie theater. It reminded me of a movie I saw in Mr. B's class called *Pleasantville*. I told Roberto about it. He had not seen it. He then told me that he had ordered a copy of our book off Amazon. I told him that was dumb—I would've just given him a copy!

"No way. I want to support starving writers like you. My mom was a little shocked when I told her I was ordering a book and it wasn't about baseball." He smiled. He had a nice smile. He didn't show it too often, but when he did, it was real. And I liked his dimples.

"So, how long did it take you to write the book? I can't imagine doing that," he said as our burgers arrived.

"Oh, I only wrote part of it—usually the shortest parts. I'm the weak link in the writers' circle."

"That's not what Mickey says."

"Oh? What does he say about me?"

"Well, besides that, he told me that you were cute."

"Yeah, besides that…" Flattery will always make a date great.

"He told me that you wrote some of the most emotional parts of the book."

"Oh, that. Well, my life has been a little crazy sometimes."

"Yeah?"

"Yeah. My dad left me, my mom, and my brother two years ago—at Thanksgiving. Last Christmas would have been really bad if it hadn't been for my friends—especially Maddie."

"Yeah, I like her. I totally get her life, I mean. Her dad finally retired. Mine—he's in it for life. But that's cool 'cause I admire what he has done. He started out as a regular grunt and worked his way up to where he is now. He is a recruiter—actually, he is in charge of, like, a whole region. I just hope he is out here before baseball season starts. He is supposed to be in charge of the southwestern region of the US."

"Did he go to war?" I asked.

"He was in the first Gulf War—Desert Storm—and he was in Afghanistan back in 2002. Or was it 2003? Whatever. But luckily, he has not been deployed oversees since then."

Since the Army isn't the most romantic topic, I decided to ask him just one more question about it: "Do you ever worry about your dad? I worry about my brother Chris all the time."

"Yeah, I know. Mickey told me about your brother being hospitalized. Um, yeah, I worry. I mean, I used to, but I was little back then, and I didn't really understand what was going on. The hardest thing for me is just all the moving from one city to another. My whole family hates it. But I'm the oldest, so I have to suck it up."

It was quiet for a minute—but it seemed much longer.

Then I looked down at his hands. They were light brown. His eyes were big and dark brown, and he had ridiculously long eyelashes. His hand was open, and I said, "Dude. You have some serious calluses."

"Yeah, baseball does it." Then he said the most remarkable thing of the night: "So does the Army."

I reached out and pulled his hand toward me. I looked at him and said, "You sure are tough on the outside. But I'm not so sure about on the inside."

Roberto smiled again. He winked at me—I have never been winked at before—and said, "The inside is the part I don't show much."

"That's what I figured."

We walked to the movie theater, holding hands. Once there, we shared popcorn and a soda.

"So," I said while sipping our Coke, "who is this Roberto Clemente guy?"

So he told me the story. This Clemente baseball guy was, like, a superstar in the 1960's and 1970's, and he played for the Pittsburgh Pirates. They won a bunch of championships, and he did a lot for the people of Puerto Rico, bringing baseball equipment and food to them. He died in a plane crash on New Year's Eve 1972, trying to deliver aid to earthquake victims in Nicaragua. Roberto added, "He was the first Latin American in the Hall of Fame. He was one of the best of all time. The best."

I realized that the whole thing was a metaphor.

It was a great date. And you know what was funny? When I pulled up to his house, he leaned over and kissed me on the cheek.

And he asked if I would go out with him again.

When I kissed him back, he knew my answer.

December 24th—Christmas Eve

Chris is much better. He will be coming home this February. I am so excited. He has been in Iraq for 7 months, and he gets to be home for at least two months before he gets new orders. We think he will be redeployed back there—or maybe to Afghanistan.

You know, before Mr. B's class, I never paid much attention to the news—and definitely not to war stories. But nowadays, I am locked onto what is going on with the Taliban, al-Qaeda, Osama bin Laden, Saddam Hussein's execution—all that stuff. I guess having a brother in war makes you pay attention...

Pay is the right word.

My brother got to make us a video. I have watched it about 15 times already. He seems happy, but he is trying to hide stuff from us—trying to be the big, tough soldier. Here's what he said:

Hey guys. Well, I am still in one piece. You know me—I've got a hard head. [He laughs. We don't.] So I hope you haven't been worryin' too much about me. I was in the hospital for about a week. They treated me good. Took all these tests to see if my brain was workin'. It wasn't. [He laughs again. We don't again.] I think they think I'm some smart guy or something, and so they wanna make sure my brain ain't too messed up. They don't know it has been messed up for a while. [He just smiles. We smile, too.] Anyway. Things here are not really too bad. Really.

I went out on patrol a lot. We try not to be out at night very much—unless it's really important. The people are kinda nice, but also kinda scared of us. Or maybe they're scared of the bad guys who are part of the trouble. Thing is, the people just want to, like, live in peace, but every day there is either some explosion or gunfire or whatever. So everyone is kinda jumpy.

So, how are you guys? [He is funny—not ha-ha funny—because he looks into the camera and seems to wait for an answer from us. That is so my brother!] Rhia, are you still writing that new book like you promised? You better be—or I am gonna kick your you-know-what. You are gonna be famous someday. I just know it. I always like your chapters the best. 'Cause you don't use a bunch of big, fancy words—and they're shorter. [He laughs again. I smile.]

Mom, make sure Rhia doesn't do something stupid with guys. Some of the guys over here saw your picture, Rhia, and they think you're hot. I told them to shut up—you're my freakin' sister! They still think you're hot. Let me tell you, some of them probably get a brain scan and the docs probably see nothin'. [He just shakes his head back and forth with a smirk.] But these guys are awesome. They are. Some of them are never afraid. And some of them are really nice to the locals. I am even learning some Farsi. You just kinda pick up some words, you know?

Anyway, I am kinda babbling right now. It's weird lookin' into the camera. But I hope you guys know how much I love you. I am really fine. And I am gonna be back in February, I think. We are gonna have a Christmas party here. We get a fancier dinner, and supposedly, we get a visit from some high-ups—heck, maybe even the President. Wouldn't that be cool? Man, I gotta get his autograph... Wait, who is the President now, anyways? Is it still Bush? Or Obama? Whatever. I just can't wait to see you. I will give you two a big hug. I will even bring back some gifts, like a bottle of desert sand or some—crap, the camera is gonna die soon; it's running outta power. Shoot.

        Love you, Mom. Love you, Rhia. Bye. Don't worry, okay? Oh, Merry Christmas... Ho-ho-ho!"

I have a lump in my throat. All I can say is that he'd better get home—the big dumbo.

I hear my mom's stereo. She is playing this song that I always listen to around Christmas. I think it is John Lennon; he's singing something like *and so this is Christmas*. The melody is both haunting (Mickey's word) and uplifting. Mickey says that's a paradox. The song reminds me that another year has passed and to embrace the dear ones in my life. God, I wish I could, but my brother is halfway across the world from me. I try to smile as the tears run down my cheeks. Lennon keeps encouraging me to have a Merry Christmas and a Happy New Year. Why does he have to remind me to not have any fear?

And then a chorus of children's voices ring out the anthem of my mom's generation...and now mine, too:

All we are saying is give peace a chance.

Amen to that.

God Bless,

        Rhia, Mickey, Pari, and Maddie

Book Two: 2009

Chapter 15: "Two Roads Diverged in a Wood"

Mickey's Hand

January 15th

"Can you believe they actually landed that plane on the Hudson River—and nobody was killed?" Maddie was leaning forward in an overstuffed chair in the newly designed Metaphor Café. "I mean, someone took a video of it, and you could see the plane splash down. My dad said that the chances of pulling that off and getting everyone out were unreal."

We all nodded. Pari added, "They have pictures on CNN of passengers standing on the wing—I just can't even imagine that."

"I wonder if some of them couldn't swim." This was Classic Rhia. "'Cause I'm sure that the river was freezing and all."

"Well, they didn't have much of a choice, and neither did the pilot," Maddie replied. I couldn't help but think of what we had been talking about in Ms. LaFleur's class recently. We had been arguing about Robert Frost's poem "The Road Not Taken." We couldn't decide what exactly Frost meant. Were the roads exactly the same? Would Frost be okay with either choice? Did he pick one because it was slightly less traveled? Is his point that you should go the way you want and not follow the crowd? You could make a case that both paths might lead to happiness—or not."

I guess that is the beauty of poetry and art. It lies in the eyes of the beholder, as they say.

But for pilot "Sully" Sullenberger, there was no choice. The "Miracle on the Hudson" was an example of a person who was prepared for disaster and who faced it with calmness, coolness, and more concern for others than for himself.

I guess that makes the rest of our questions that night at the Metaphor Café seem trivial. Where are we going to go to college? Will we even get in? How will we afford it? What will our parents say or do? Is college even what we want?

But your choices are parts of the roads you travel, and before you can land a plane safely, you have to know that you want to become a pilot. Which brings all four of us to the real question, which we don't always think about but know we must face sooner or later:

What do we want to be when we "grow up?"

Isn't that such a weird question? Are we really still not grown up? When do you wake up and say, "Hey, today I am a grown up?" Is it some magical moment when we land on the Hudson and save the day? When did Frost know that the road less traveled "made all the difference?" When he was 30 or 40? Or maybe not until he was about to cash in his chips—not until he looked back on some day in his foggy memory? What if we walk up to the crossroads and not even realize that we are *at* the crossroads? What if we don't even have a choice? What about all the people who have choices taken from them?

Okay, I realize this is getting totally depressing. But we are two or three months away from deciding what we will be doing for the next few years. And we are in the last five months of high school. Maybe Rhia was right—what if we can't swim? Maybe growing up and making choices is simply that—making a choice and making the best of it because you can never really predict what the best choice will be. Maybe it is just a gut feeling. Or maybe it is common sense. Is the "right choice" something that makes you feel secure or challenged? I don't know. I guess that is what makes life so…interesting. Huh?

Pari looks over her café mocha while she blows on it to cool it and says, "I know that Berkeley is my dream school, but it is so hard to get into. I applied to UCLA, too. And some East Coast schools that I can't afford. I'm not even sure I would go to those schools, but my parents liked them, and I guess they have great programs."

"Why apply to schools that you don't want to go to?" Rhia asked her.

"I don't know. I mean, there's probably no way I could get into Cal or UCLA, but I think I might be able to get into some others, like the University of San Francisco. We also have relatives in the D.C. area, so Georgetown and American University are possibilities—and so is William and Mary."

"But do you even know what you want to study?" Maddie asked her.

"Well, pre-med, I think. My dad told me not to worry about choosing a major, but schools ask what you're interested in, and that's part of the whole game of getting in."

I told Pari that she has great grades and test scores, so she is in good shape. Like I really know anything.

Me? Well, I am on the same page as Pari, although I wish I had her grades and SAT scores. My dad is pushing USC because of all the business school stuff. (That's University of *Southern California*, for all you non-SoCal peeps out there.) I told him that Cal has a great business school, too. He seems to think that it is just so liberal up there. I was like, "Dad, it is college. It isn't going to be a Republican Convention or something." Then we argued about my major. I don't know—I mean, he is right that it is difficult to be a writer. Journalism jobs are dying, he said. Novelists? Good luck to them. "What are you going to do with an English major?" my dad asked me. I said I didn't know. I don't. Really—I have no idea. I mean, do you go to college to get a job or an education? Does a good education automatically turn into a good job? And for that matter, what *is* a "good" job? What if you do something that enables you to earn a good salary, but the job sucks and you hate it? Or, to follow my dad's point, what if you get a degree in something that nobody thinks is important enough to hire you for?

Of course, this conversation is always followed by a word of warning from both of my folks about drinking, doing drugs, having sex, partying, and generally wasting your time so that you don't graduate in four years.

No pressure there.

"I guess I'm lucky," Maddie tells us as she passes around the Chips Ahoy cookies she has snuck in, "'cause I want to be either a teacher or a nurse." Then she tells us about Jasmine, who got sicker over the course of the holidays and landed back in the hospital again this week. "They say the operation on her liver was never supposed to last this long. It is a miracle that it lasted five years, let alone fourteen. Her doctors say that she is on the liver transplant list, but there are a lot of people ahead of her. The weird thing is that you have to be near death to get a new liver, but if you get too close to death, you can die either before or after the transplant because your body is shutting down."

"That is a Catch-22," Pari said. She was reading that novel in AP English. "It is like you have to be crazy to get out of the Army, but only a sane person wouldn't want to get out of the Army... so then you wouldn't be crazy." We all looked at her puzzled. "See, you have to be almost dead to get a liver, but if you are almost dead, they wouldn't give you a liver 'cause you might die." Oh. We all nodded.

"Yeah, well, Jasmine is bummed because she is missing Mr. B's class, and he just started teaching *To Kill a Mockingbird*. I talked to him about visiting Jasmine and trying to help her with schoolwork, but he told me that school might not be her top priority right now. Jasmine is determined, though. When I saw her at the hospital yesterday, she said, 'You have to tell me what Mr. B said. I read the book, but he makes it so much more interesting and fun. Tell me what he said, Maddie.'

"So I told her that Mr. B got through the first three chapters and that the theme of the book was sort of that part when Atticus Finch tells Scout that you have to step into someone's shoes to really understand them. That is the only way you can have compassion for someone.

"Jasmine was smiling, and she told me that that was her favorite part of the book so far. But then she added, 'But I get so sleepy when I read, Maddie. I don't usually get this way, but I just can't keep my eyes open. I sleep all the time.'

"I felt terrible, guys. So I grabbed her book, and I read Chapter 4 to her. She closed her eyes to listen. I hoped she didn't fall asleep. But sometimes she would poke one eye open and look at me. When I got to the end, she said, 'I love you, Maddie.'"

That's when Maddie started to cry. Rhia got out a well-worn tissue pack from her monster-sized purse. We were all quiet for a while. I hate it when girls cry. I always wanna do something, but there is never anything I can do. Damn.

Rhia then made an announcement. "Well, since things are getting all emo, I may as well tell you that me and Donald officially broke up. Yeah, I know. Big surprise. Well, we are still friends and all; it's just that we are on two different tracks or whatever you want to call it. He is so into soccer and his job, and he has three AP classes. Plus, he is totally freaking out about college. He asked Mr. B to write him a letter to get into some fancy private school—Harry Mud or something. Anyway, he told me that he still really likes me and all, but he just needs to do his own thing."

"Harvey Mudd," Pari chirped.

"Whatever. Anyway. He said he knew that I was going out with someone else and that 'that was cool.' I hate it when he says that! I just wish… I don't know. I told him that I still really like him and that I know he will get into a great college and that he is the best dance partner a girl could ever have. Then, like a dummy, I started to cry."

Maddie gave her back the tissue pack; it was getting down to the last few Kleenex. "I don't really know why I cried—I just did. I don't even know why I am crying now. Crap, my mascara is running."

Girls. I remember when Mr. Davidson, the old—and I mean *old*—owner of the Metaphor Café would come by and see the girls crying last year and ask if everything was okay. For some crazy reason, whenever he asked the girls that question, they always seemed to regroup and brighten up. If I ever say the same thing, they just look at me like, *Dude, you just don't get it.*

Maybe. But I still think Holden Caulfield is right—girls really *can* drive you crazy.

"And I took the SAT test, Pari," Rhia continued. "I'm sure I bombed the math. I probably bombed the whole thing. I dunno. But I tried. We'll see. So…" She trailed off.

"Rhia, that's great! No worries. You underestimate yourself all the time," Pari said with conviction. I know she is right. Rhia has something that lots of people don't have—and it is not something that shows up on tests. She has "people smarts," as my mom says. My mom really likes Rhia, and she told me that she is always pulling for her.

"Rhia didn't have what you and your brother had, Mickey. Rhia had the rug pulled out from under her at fifteen. The scars take a long time to heal." My mom told me this during one of her kitchen sermons; she was subtly trying to help me understand the confusing world of girls and my pushy father, who "just wants you to be happy, Mickey."

Moms. You gotta love 'em.

Rhia regrouped and told us, "I also have the 'Tiffany Factor' to face at work. I mean, she is all about just making money, dating boys, and shopping. I asked her what she wanted to do after she graduated, and she said, 'Get a better job—like maybe in sales at the mall—and just enjoy life.' I thought about that, and I know what she means. That would be great. But, you know, my mom and I were talking, and I just don't want some dead-end job—where all you can make or even do stops at just making a sale and keeping the customer satisfied. I don't know what exactly I want, but I do know one thing: I am a people person. Can you major in *that* in college?" For the first time in a long while, we all laughed a little.

"And then my father called and told my mom that if I went to college, he would help pay for it. Yeah, well, I will believe that when I see it. And even if he does, I don't want his stupid money. And if he gives me any money, I am sure it will have strings attached—you know what I mean?" We all nodded. But I am not sure that any of us *really* knew what she meant. Like Atticus Finch says in *Mockingbird*, you have to "step into someone's skin" to understand what makes them act the way they do. There is no word in the English language that makes Rhia go crazy like the word *dad.*

When the road diverges in the yellow woods, there is supposed to be someone there with a map to guide you through the forest. Otherwise, you could have regrets about the road not taken…

…and find yourself terribly lost.

*****   *****   *****   *****   *****

January 20th

Today we watched President Barack Obama's inauguration on TV in Mr. Mac's class. We caught bits and pieces of it in our earlier classes, but Mr. Mac recorded President Obama's speech, and we watched it and talked about it in class.

This was the first time I had ever really seen something like this. I can't remember President Bush's inauguration, and I've seen a one-minute clip of Kennedy's speech. But this was the first election in which I had voted. And my vote helped put this new person into the role of the "Leader of the Free World," as people call the President. Cool.

The crowds were massive. The day historic. The first black man to serve as President—to live in a white house built by many black slaves. The President's speech reminded people of how far America has come when he said, "This is the meaning of our liberty and our creed—why men and women and children of every race and every faith can join in celebration across this magnificent mall—and why a man whose father less than 60 years ago might not have been served at a local restaurant can now stand before you to take a most sacred oath."

I got goose bumps when he made this challenge: "And for those who seek to advance their aims by inducing terror and slaughtering innocents, we say to you now that 'our spirit is stronger and cannot be broken. You cannot outlast us, and we will defeat you.'" Oh, how I hope he is right.

Last night, I noticed something symbolic as I was reading the text of President Obama's speech, which Mr. Mac had told us to read carefully. The President referred to *roads we travel.* He said, "As we consider the road that unfolds before us, we remember with humble gratitude those brave Americans who, at this very hour, patrol far-off deserts and distant mountains. They have something to tell us, just as the fallen heroes who lie in Arlington whisper through the ages. We honor them not only because they are guardians of our liberty, but because they embody the spirit of service: a willingness to find meaning in something greater than themselves."

It hit me what I need to do when I grow up.

No matter where I go to college, or which major I choose, or what job I find, *there must be meaning greater than myself.*

And that, truly, will make all the difference.

Chapter 16: "To thine own self be true"

Pari's Hand

February 3rd—Hamlet Haunts the Metaphor Café

It has been a crazy few weeks. Seriously. Being a senior is so nerve-racking and stressful that it is hard to take. (Maybe I'm just sleep deprived.) Let's start with *Hamlet,* which all four of us discussed last night at the Metaphor Café. Ms. LaFleur showed us the film after we read the play for a week and discussed each scene. Without the film, I think I would have been lost! I have to admit that I went into the play thinking, *Oh, cool—Hamlet!* Then I thought, *Oh, my God—it is so long…and so depressing!* But by the end, thanks to Ms. LaFleur's explanations and our discussions, I finally figured out: *Oh! Now I know why this is a masterpiece!*

We all had a stake in the play. Rhia, for example, understood why Hamlet hated his stepfather Claudius. She harbors a lot of anger, as you know. All of us girls were angry with Ophelia at first because she appears to be a wimp. I mean, she never really tries to tell her brother that she is *worthy* of Hamlet's affection. Then she bends to her father's will and says she will stop seeing Hamlet (although she obviously loves him) just because he has been acting a little crazy. (Okay, seeing your father's ghost and thinking that he has told you to kill your stepfather because the creep poisoned him might just make you a little loony.) But when she tries to talk to Hamlet about her feelings, nothing really gets said. She just lets him tell her off. I mean, even when he tells her to go to a nunnery, she just takes it!

Honestly, it wasn't until Ms. LaFleur cut into our class discussion that we understood Ophelia's desperation and confusion.

"Look," Ms. *LaFleur explained, "let me point out some things you don't seem to understand. First, she is 14 years old—the same age as Juliet. Imagine the pressures you had at that age. Second, Polonius has told her to do what she is told, and he has the attitude that a woman must play hard to get; she must never reveal her real intentions."*

"Why?" Mickey asked.

"So she is never hurt. It is Polonius' version of reverse psychology." Ms. LaFleur had a wicked smile on her face. "Don't tell me, girls, that that has gone out of fashion."

I looked down at my notes and said to her, "But what about 'to thine own self be true?'"

Ms. LaFleur nodded. "Yes, Pari, I know. But think of the irony behind that statement. 'To thine own self be true.' Polonius is the consummate self-promoter. He is always looking after Number One. Self-interest is his mantra. So, 'to thine own self be true' can be interpreted as 'think about yourself and get what you want.' That is the 'truth' he is pushing."

"Ohhh…" rippled through the class. My mom refers to that as the "ah-ha! moment."

"And remember, folks," Ms. LaFleur said, leaning forward, "Ophelia's father and Claudius are standing behind the partition, listening to every word, when Hamlet is telling Ophelia to go away to a nunnery. She is under so much pressure to do as her father wills her. She knows that Polonius has been feeding her 'lines' in her life's play since she could talk. It is far too much to ask her to rebel at age 14."

When I reminded my group of Ms. LaFleur's analysis, Maddie remarked while munching on a chocolate croissant, "I still think Hamlet was being a jerk."

"Yeah, well, didn't Ophelia's father think that Hamlet was just trying to get in her pants? Wait…did they even wear pants then?" Rhia protested.

Mickey ventured, "Hamlet is so into revenge against Claudius that it causes all this confusion and anger. I mean, he is devastated by Ophelia's death and realizes what he has done to her at the end of the play."

"Yeah, well, too late, Mickey," Maddie said. "Besides, that doesn't explain why Ophelia drowns herself. Suicide or accident—who cares? She was weak." Maddie was firm on this. She may be the strongest of the three of us, really. I sense that when she and Mickey talk things out, she never holds back.

"Fine. I agree," I cut in quickly. "Polonius' 'to thine own self be true' line is cool, but it's such crap. He is just a tool for the King, and he's full of himself, too." But then I remembered what Ms. LaFleur had told us in class: "*Polonius is really voicing Shakespeare's theme that mankind's thirst for power and careless greed eventually destroys innocent bystanders, whose need for revenge creates even more tragedy.*"

Maddie looked at me and conceded, "I guess you're right. The innocent bystander is Ophelia; she doesn't understand herself at all. She is all about what Hamlet thinks of her. Or what her father thinks. When they fail her, she loses hope; she is lost."

Rhia's eyes opened wide. "Dude, when she dies… Okay, wait—oh, I get it. When she dies, she doesn't fight it. Like, she makes no effort to save herself. And when her clothes start to weigh her down, she just lets it all happen to her. Like, all the forces in her life just pull her down. So…she *does* kill herself!" Rhia sat back for a minute, and it occurred to me how much of this was probably crisscrossing back to her mother's suicide attempt when her father abandoned them two years ago…and to Leann's meltdown.

"I know," Maddie said with a sigh. "I just want her to be *stronger*, I guess. I want her to fight, you know? The more I think about her, the sadder I get." Maddie's face tightened; she was clearly angry that this is the way life plays out for so many girls.

Of course, it also occurred to me that all of this "girls should be independent warriors" chatter is in itself my own ironic issue. I mean, the whole chastity/sex thing is a big deal in my house. My dad already flipped out over the Lady Gaga dance numbers, and lately, the Daniel-as-my-boyfriend issue has been discussed—sort of. It was summed up by my dad when he said at dinner, "I hope you know where this is going, Parivesh?"

I hope I do, too.

We talk about…things—Daniel and I. He knows he is going back to France next year. He applied to the University of Paris at Sorbonne, and he thinks he will get in. And I do like him…very much. It is so warm—so fulfilling—to know that I am not alone. That he and I can go out to a movie. That I can have his company. I love his accent. I love kissing him. I do.

But when Ms. LaFleur was lecturing about the whole dating scene back in Hamlet's day, her words struck a chord in me:

"Look, everyone. Let's be clear. The wealth of a family back then was in the ovaries of the daughters. So parents were very protective of their daughters. It was about money—dowries. And one thing is for sure: the noble classes did not want stray dogs invading their families' DNA. You married whom you were supposed to marry. In Romeo and Juliet, do you remember how furious Juliet's father was when she refused to marry Paris? He would have tossed her out into the street for disobeying him."

Ouch. I'm not being totally honest with my parents. They still think Daniel and I date *with other couples*. I know I am pushing the envelope—and I am not always sure I am in control. Could I lose myself? "To thine own self be true?" Yeah, that is the question.

The four of us argued about other stuff in the play. Was Hamlet crazy? Was the ghost real? What was the meaning of the "to be or not to be" line? Could it all have been avoided if Hamlet had just taken his revenge on his jerk stepfather Polonius right from the start, saving a lot of misery and about three hours of the play? In the end, we agreed that all of those questions were what made the play so intriguing. However, Shakespeare's warning "to thine own self be true" would haunt all four of us for a while.

Rhiannon's Hand

February 5th —Hamlet Haunts Yummy Yogurt

Revenge.

"I'm Not Your Steppingstone" by Duffy is still playing in my head (and on my iPod) as I drive home from work. Two things are bugging me a lot. One is what happened when I was sitting at the café the other day talking about *Hamlet*. I didn't like the play as much as the others did—too depressing. But I got all the Hamlet anger stuff in a big way. See, my dad talked to my mom recently and told her that he was offering to pay a lot of my college expenses. My mom was way more okay with that than me, and she told me so. She said, "Look, Rhia, I know how you feel about your father. I do. Believe me, okay? But this is your chance to get an education, to move out, to do all the things I never got to do. You know?"

"Yeah, I know, Mom. But it would be Dad's money that I would be doing it with. Money he wouldn't give you (at least, not much of it) when he left us."

"Honey, that is a long story, and it is between me and your father. It is old news. This is about your future. Don't be *so* angry at him that you don't see that he is trying to make things up to you."

I am still so angry with him. Damn it. I get so pissed because I know—I just *know*—that this is gonna cost me. I will have to be nice to him. I will have to say, "Thanks, Dad." I will have to wonder if his promise to pay my tuition is for real. I mean, maybe it will just be a one-time thing? Maybe he will flake out and I will have to quit school the very next year?

I told my mom this.

My mom is so strong. She looked me in the eye and said, "Rhiannon, I will do whatever it takes for you to have a better life than I did. If your father bails on you, I will make college happen. I will. If he makes demands on you, I will stick up for you. You don't need to do anything but do well in school, okay?"

I swallowed. I let out a breath of air. I wiped the tears from my eyes as soon as they started to fall. My desire to make my dad pay up for abandoning our family was biting me. Biting down hard.

"Okay, mom. Okay. But *you* have to tell him. I don't wanna talk to him."

"I will, honey. But you can't not talk to him at all. You realize that, right?"

"Yeah." The word was like poison on the tip of a sword. I only hoped I could avoid my heart being pierced. I kept thinking, *"to thine own self be true."* A conscience can be a pain in the butt, you know.

*****   *****   *****   *****   *****

So as I started my shift at the dumb yogurt place, I was hoping for a slow, chill night. But you know me—I am a bull's-eye for other people's problems. Leann was working with me that night, and when it was quiet (it was freezing out, so who would want friggin' yogurt?), she asked me a loaded question.

"Rhia, when does a person know if they are gay or straight?"

Bang. That both got my attention and freaked me out a little. "Um...gee...I don't know, Leann. I mean, I think some kids figure it out, like, really early, and some, I guess, later on, after they have been with people?" I had no idea what I was saying; I was still wondering if Leann thought she was a lesbian.

"Oh."

Silence.

Then she said, "Don't you think it is weird that guys think two girls together is sexy, but they freak out about two guys being together?"

"Yeah. I guess. I've never really thought about it much."

"I think it is stupid. Who cares about other people's sex lives? Why do people freak about it so much?"

"I dunno. Straight guys get all weird because they think gay guys are going to hit on them, I guess." I said this because it was all I could think to say. I wondered when Leann would get to the point. Finally, I asked her what was up with all this gay talk. "Leann, do you think you are gay?"

"I don't know, Rhia. I mean, I'm...I'm scared of guys, you know? After Tommy and all. And I think maybe that..."

"That what?"

"I don't know...that it might be safer with girls." Leann looked down, wiping the counter in the same way that that guy did in the movie *Pleasantville*—over and over in the same spot.

I felt I had to say something. "Well, um, are you, like, attracted to girls more than guys?"

"I don't know if that is it, exactly. I mean, maybe I am, but I am too afraid to think it. Or maybe I am just interested in girls because I am afraid that other guys will be like Tommy. I mean, can a person be both straight and gay?"

"Um, I'm not sure. Why?"

"Well, my doctor says that some people are in the middle. You know, like, there is a line with heterosexual on one side and homosexual on the other, and some people are in the middle."

"Oh," I replied. She had obviously been thinking about this for a long time. I think that what her boyfriend did to her has shaken her up so much that she doesn't know who she is—sexually, that is. But, of course, I couldn't say that to her.

So instead I said, "Look, Leann. I think it is really important that you are talking to your doctor about this. I think that you are still feeling some trauma, you know? I mean, what happened to you is gonna take a while to deal with. But—and I am definitely no expert here—but you just need to get stronger. And maybe not worry so much. I mean, I think all this will be clearer for you when you are not hurting so bad...or being angry...or feeling afraid of being intimate with guys or whatever..." I felt like I was just babbling. The whole time, Leann was looking at me like I had the answer. But I was not even sure I understood the question.

I don't remember when I woke up dreaming of boys. I just know I did. I don't understand being a lesbian, but I definitely don't think that I should judge them. I certainly don't think I am prejudiced, and I don't think that gay-bashing is right. I hate it when people call my brother a "retard," and I hate it when people call each other "gay." I mean, I understand that most people don't mean it in a hateful way, but the thing is that *they don't mean it in a good way, either.* Let's face it—it's complicated. I say, live and let live.

That is when it hit me: "to thine own self be true." But for Leann, knowing herself and what is true is the heart of the matter. Is she just so frightened because she has been raped that she doesn't know *what is true* anymore?

And what about all the kids who are gay? What happens to them when they come out and tell the truth, huh? Just look at all the gay kids out there who have committed suicide because of what people have said to them. It makes me sick.

As I drove home after my shift, I thought about all that had happened to Leann. That night when she collapsed in fear and panic—

what would she have done if I had not been there for her? I thought about *Hamlet's* Ophelia. If only Ophelia had had someone to talk to, maybe she wouldn't have collapsed in the river and drowned in her sorrow. I wonder why Hamlet never told her sooner that he loved her so much. Why do people wait until it is too late to tell each other what is in their hearts?

Then I thought about my father.

Mickey's Hand

February 11th —12 Angry Men

I could hear some people moaning about how Mr. Mac was showing another old black-and-white movie called *12 Angry Men*; they made the usual protests: "No action!", "Boring!", and "Do we have to take notes?" What morons! I don't understand how they can be in an AP Government class and not be totally fascinated with this "film," as Mr. Buscotti would say.

I won't spoil the movie for those of you who haven't seen it, but let me just say that this one juror, played by Henry Fonda (I recognized him from a film Mr. B showed us last year called *The Grapes of Wrath*) absolutely captures what it would be like to be in a jury deliberation room, wondering if someone is truly guilty of murder. The movie makes its audience think about what responsibility a citizen has when they step into a jury box and try to be fair, impartial, and willing to really listen carefully to the facts that are presented in a courtroom.

Henry Fonda's character is stacked against great odds: 11 jurors vote to convict; the boy seems to have little defense (which is typical for poor people, I think, unless an attorney has the integrity and the time to really fight for them); and the jury has little patience to sit and deliberate like they are supposed to. Anyway, Fonda, known only as juror #8, just isn't sure that the 18-year-old Latino kid really killed his father, and if he is found guilty of first degree murder, he is going to the electric chair. Fonda pushes the concept of "innocent until proven guilty beyond a reasonable doubt," while all the other jurors believe their preconceptions of the boy—or they just want to get the heck out of the room and catch a ball game or whatever.

The film is just amazing. It is over 50 years old, and the justice system is still dealing with all the flaws that human prejudice brings into the courtroom. During our discussion of the film, Mr. Mac remarked, "William Blackstone, a British law scholar, wrote in the eighteenth century that 'the law holds that it is better that ten guilty persons escape than that one innocent suffer.'" He then asked, "Do you think that is fair?"

"But Mr. Mac," Maddie piped up, "we don't really know if the boy is innocent."

"Yeah, but it is not reasonable to believe that he did kill his father," I answered.

"Okay, but what if the jury lets him off and he kills again? Then that person's blood would be on their hands," a guy named Brad who we knew from last year, protested.

Pari came to my defense. "Yes, that's true, but you can't assume that he will commit *another* murder when you can't even prove without a shadow of a doubt that he committed *this* one."

I followed this with, "And there is a big shadow there." Okay, it wasn't the smartest thing I said that day.

When I left class, I asked Mr. Mac if I could take the film home and watch it again. He handed it over with a look like, *If you lose this, you are dead.* He wasn't kidding. So when I got home, I watched it with my mom, who plopped down on the couch next to me with some popcorn. She was as happy as a clam, watching Henry Fonda in action. As we watched the film, I thought about the fact that Fonda *really didn't know* if the boy had killed his father. I mean, it sure seemed like an open-and-shut case. But Fonda knew one very important thing. He thought, *Before I send a boy to his death (or even to a life behind bars), I have to know that I am doing the right thing. I have a life in my hands.*

I mean, how many times in our lives can we actually say that to ourselves? *I have a life in my hands.* I'm not just talking about the results of a ball game or the score on a test or a college acceptance letter or a girlfriend's love. I'm talking about when the future of a *living, breathing human being* is in our hands.

In class that day, Mr. Mac had spoken about the Innocence Project, which is a program that is "dedicated to proving the innocence of wrongly convicted people through the use of DNA testing and reforming the criminal justice system to prevent future injustice." Of course, back then in the 1960's, they didn't have a clue what DNA testing was. But they knew skin color. They knew poverty.

So Fonda stood up to the ridicule of the others and made his case that there was a "reasonable doubt" that the teenage defendant may not have killed his father. What he said made me realize something that I figure Mr. Mac was trying to get through to us:

You *can* make a difference if "to thine own self be true."

Madison's Hand

February 14th —Valentine's Day

Oh, my God. Do you ever feel like things are just happening for a reason? This whole month has been just like that. I never thought that working as Mr. B's Teaching Assistant would be so important and life changing. It is almost scary. As a matter of fact, I've heard that sometimes life imitates art—you know, like how the stuff in books and music and paintings inspires people? But I am wondering if it might be the other way around—maybe art imitates life. Maybe people's lives inspire artists, who create great works of art. It may be the chicken or the egg. All I know is that something important and maybe frightening is happening, and I am a witness.

So, you know how I have been visiting Jasmine at the hospital? Just to give her stuff from Mr. Buscotti…and, well, just because I really have grown to love her.

Yeah.

So yesterday, I am sitting in Mr. B's class, listening to him discuss a chapter of *Mockingbird*. It's the chapter when Atticus has to explain to his kids why he is taking a case that he is sure to lose. His daughter Scout can't understand why he is putting them through all of this if it is a lost cause.

Atticus tells Scout that your conscience is something that you can't let others decide for you. That you have to be able to look at yourself in the mirror and know you did the right thing—not what the majority believes, but what you believe in your heart.

Yeah.

So later that day, I tell Mickey that I want to stop by the hospital before we go to the movies.

"Really?" he looks at me. This is not on his agenda.

"Really. I have stuff for Jasmine…and a Valentine's Day card, Mickey. I mean, come on, she has been in the hospital for a month! She must be lonely. We won't be long." I am determined, but I know what Mickey is thinking: *The hospital is not the setting for a romantic night out.*

Anyway, we go up to Jasmine's hospital room and knock on the door.

"Jasmine? It's me, Maddie. Can I come in? Mickey is with me."

"Maddie, is that you? Come in. Wow. I can't believe you are visiting little ol' me—and it is Valentine's Day! You should be out partying with Mr. Baseball." (Jasmine has been calling Mickey that for the last few weeks—it's cute.)

Mickey laughs and says, "Hey Jas, I heard you were hosting a huge party in here."

"Oh, you are so silly, Mickey," Jasmine giggles. "Yeah, I am having everyone over to check out my new drugs and my cool 12-station TV—not to mention the fancy hospital food they serve here."

"I brought you a card, Jasmine. I wasn't sure if you could have chocolate, but I snuck some in, just in case—and Mr. B's notes," I tell her this as I rummage though my purse for the pink, heart-shaped box of candy.

"Oh, yum!" Jasmine says. "I can eat chocolate—just not a whole box at once." Then she bursts out laughing. "I have to watch my petite waistline, like Mr. B always says. He cracks me up!"

Just then, her mom and dad come in, and introductions are made. Jasmine's dad makes a point of saying how nice it is that we came by on February 14th—and he winks at Mickey.

"Oh, my dad is such a cornball," Jasmine explains. "He is always teasing me about boys…not that I have a boyfriend." Her giggle makes Mickey laugh; he is just not used to her humor.

Jasmine's parents then leave the room so that Jasmine can visit with us, which I think is pretty thoughtful. Mickey and I grab a couple of chairs, and after a brief "What's going on at school?" chat, I ask Jasmine about her condition. Mickey remembers that he wants to write a story on her for the school newspaper, so he asks me if I have a pen. He jots down what Jasmine tells us on a napkin.

"Well, since you asked," Jasmine begins, "you might notice that my eyes are kinda yellow right now…"

"Jaundice," I whisper to Mickey.

"Yeah. And lately, I have been sleeping a lot. I mean, like, for *hours* during the day, which is unusual for me. My stomach is really bloated. So I'd better be careful with the chocolate, I guess…"

"It's just four pieces," I say, worried that I have done something dumb.

"And, um, the doctors are really nice, but they seem to be getting more concerned because I have all the symptoms of liver failure. And for the first time, my sodium is really low—and that is dangerous, I guess. And other tests are not showing me as stable as they had hoped. Sometimes I feel sick…*really* sick. But I am not yet at the point where I can move up to the top of the liver transplant list."

"You gotta get sicker?" Mickey was incredulous (he told me to use that word). "Man, Pari was right—it *is* a Catch 22."

"Huh?"

"Never mind, Jasmine. It is a book that someone is reading about things being sorta crazy."

"Yep, well, welcome to my world. I'm going crazy here!"

I don't know how she can laugh when her life is on the line. I changed the subject and told her about Mr. B's *Mockingbird* lectures.

"So, the first part of the book ended with the Mrs. Dubose scene…"

"Where she dies? Oh, that was sad."

"Yeah. Mr. B talked about how Atticus wanted his kids to see what courage was."

"Oh, that was my favorite part," Jasmine says, leaning forward. "Atticus knew he was beat, but he did it anyway because it was the right thing to do!"

I nodded.

"Well, I have faith that God is with me and that I will get better, you guys," she says, apparently sensing our mood. "So please don't be sad on my account, okay?"

We try to smile.

"Besides, you two have some lovey-dovey Valentine's Day stuff planned, I'm sure, so you two need to get out of here and get your party started," Jasmine says, doing the "raise the roof" sign with her hands.

We laugh, say our goodbyes, and walk down the hall. Mickey looks at me and his eyes say it all:

This girl is all about courage.

Rhiannon's Hand

February 21st —Chris Comes Home!

I have never hugged someone as hard as I hugged Chris today. He told me I almost broke his ribs!

"Man, Rhia, I just got outta the hospital! Don't put me back in there, girl."

We laughed. I cried. Mom balled. Then she laughed. Then we ate. Then we laughed. It went like that for a while.

He didn't want to talk a whole lot about the war, except to say that he believed in what they were doing. He had total respect for his "brothers," as he called them. He had faith in his commanding officers. And he was glad to be home. *Really* glad.

Glad doesn't begin to explain how I feel.

Relieved. Blessed. Grateful.

And I can't tell you how proud I am of my brother.

So I won't.

Besides, it's midnight, and I'm all cried out…for one night.

Chapter 17: "Gotta Be Somebody"

Mickey's Hand

March 2nd—Reporter's Notebook

It's been two weeks since I visited Jasmine with Maddie on Valentine's Day, and things have only gotten worse. Her liver is sucking all of the life out of her. I've already written a column on her, and each edition of the school newspaper now has a "Jasmine Watch" update. No matter how perky and upbeat she acts, you know she is hurting. It's like she is one of those wind-up dolls that is just winding down. Time is running out, dwindling into a danger zone. Her family is filled with a mixture of hope and dread.

I feel like an intruder when I go into her hospital room, but Maddie insists that Jasmine wants the company. Besides, Jasmine's family needs us to treat her as normally as possible so that she can feel as upbeat as…as, well, as a person in desperate need of a new liver can feel.

I did some research. (Actually, Mr. Mac has been helping me and is allowing part of my work to count toward my research paper for AP Gov.) Apparently, liver transplants are in very high demand. In 2008, just in California alone, there were 3,400 patients who needed a liver, but only 671 actually got them. Basically, you have to have a near-death experience to move up on the waiting list.

Steve Jobs, the CEO of Apple, needs a liver transplant, and even *he* can't get it—and he is a billionaire! I read an article online that said he is looking to have a transplant in another state because certain states make it easier for people to donate their organs; you just okay being a donor on your driver's license, I think. California is trying to pass a law like that, and if that happens, then the donor rate could go way up from the 30% we have now. But all this doesn't matter to Jasmine because time is working against her...fast.

If Jobs can invent an iPod, maybe he can also invent an iDonor?

So anyway, Jasmine sits and waits. She is bloated, sleepy, frustrated, and weak. She told me something I can't forget: "God is with me. I know it, Mickey. And I just know there's gotta be somebody for me." I told her that is the title of a Nickelback song, and she said, "See, Mickey, I am on the radio. That is so crazy!"

So I went and got her the CD. She's been playing the song over and over.

So have I.

So has Maddie...and Rhia...and Pari.

Rhia and Pari also visited today. Rhia told Jasmine about her new "friend" RC, and Jasmine laughed. "Silly girl, he's not just a friend—I think he is a new *boy*friend."

It was one of the few times that I have seen Rhia blush.

Jasmine then fluttered her eyes. "*Roberto.* Doesn't it sound so romantic?"

Then she giggled. As Holden Caulfield would say, she kills me.

Pari told her not to worry about Mr. B's class. We would all catch her up in the summer if we had to.

Summer.

She has to make it that long.

Jasmine's brother Paul talked to us outside her room when we all realized that she needed to sleep. "Well, we pray for her to get better, but we pray for her to get worse, too. It is the only way that the doctors can push her up the transplant list."

Then Paul looked at Maddie and said, "I can't believe you all have been here so often. She's a freshman and you're seniors—you must have a million things to do. I appreciate you caring for my baby sister."

Of course, we told him that we were very worried about Jasmine and that we had all the time in the world for her.

But the truth is that time is our nemesis right now. We are studying for AP tests and waiting for college admission letters; we are bogged down with homework, and in my world, the new baseball season starts next week. The stress is making all of us sleepless and on edge.

But inside room 208, Jasmine sleeps confident that God will keep her alive.

So what are we worried about?

Pari's Hand

March 3rd—The Ides of March

Look, Mickey is right. What are we worried about?

Yes, when it comes to life and death, Jasmine puts everything into perspective. But that doesn't change the fact that by March 15—supposedly when Julius Caesar got stabbed (a bad omen, don't you think?)—I will find out if I've been admitted to Berkeley.

I told everyone at the Metaphor Café this afternoon that I got into some schools back east. But I didn't make a big deal about it because first, I don't think I really want to go to those schools, and second, even if they give me $10,000 or $15,000 in scholarships, my parents can't afford the rest. I mean, the cost is at least $45,000 per year. We can't afford that over 4 years.

Berkeley is $18,000 a year. I can probably get some scholarships, and it is rated the best public college in America. (I know, I know—UCLA folks don't agree. If I get into UCLA, I will be totally happy, too. It's just a little too close to home for my taste.)

But the scary part is what I hear: "You need a near perfect SAT score to get into Berkeley;" "They're limiting acceptances 'cause of budget cuts;" "They had a *bazillion* applications this year!" Oh, March 15th—you could be a disaster.

Of course, Daniel is calm. He already knows that he has been accepted to the University of Paris. Correction: *l'Université de Paris*. He was so casual about it—like it was a foregone conclusion. I guess he has "connections." Okay, I am just really jealous. He has the grades; he is bilingual; his older sisters went there; and his family is well educated.

I love all that about him.

It is just that right now, I hate him.

Oh, and one more thing. He is getting on my nerves, too. Typical conversation:

"Why can't you go out?"

"I just can't."

"Why?"

"Um, because it is a school night, and my parents will freak, and I have a ton of homework."

"What about tomorrow night?"

"Daniel, tomorrow night will be the same as tonight."

"But you have to have some fun."

"I know. I know. I can have fun after March 15th."

I can hear the disappointment in his voice—and in mine. But it isn't just that I don't have time to go out. It is something else, too.

I talked to Maddie about it when Mickey left the hospital with Rhia. I told her I would wait to take her home, since she needed to do something for her dad, who was working that night. I needed Maddie's advice.

"Maddie, can I ask you something personal about you and Mickey?"

Maddie looked at me like, *Duh, of course you can.* I am always so in awe of her. She does so many things for so many people; she is so organized; she is so unselfish.

"Um, does Mickey pressure you? You know, I mean, sexually? God, I can't believe I am asking you this…" I stammered.

"Well, I don't think so. I mean, we had this talk about it, and I told him that I hoped I didn't frustrate him or lead him on too much. I just told him that I'm not ready—yet—and he seemed to understand. Why are you asking? Is this about Daniel?"

"Yeah. See… Oh, God, this is hard to explain. Okay. He is European, and they just don't have the same kind of *attitude* we have— um, I have—or so he tells me. I mean, sex is more out in the open there. And all the birth control things are more…you know, available. Maybe *expected* is a better word. So, he thinks it is silly that we just, well, stop 'over here in the States.'"

"Oh. Do you want him to stop?"

"Yes…and no. Mostly, yes. I mean, I am dealing with so much right now, and there is no way I am ready. Besides, my parents would kill me. My brothers would kill him. I mean, when I get to college, things will be different. I think. Oh, Maddie—do you know what I mean?"

"Totally. Totally. Pari, you aren't wrong. It is just who you are right now. I completely relate. I love Mickey. I really do. I just don't want to mess things up and get *that serious* right now. I know the gossipy talk—everyone is apparently hooking up. But I don't want a hook-up thing—not with Mickey. You know what I mean?"

I just stared at her. The girl read my mind.

I don't care how smart my SAT test tells me that I am—

I am a complete fool compared to Maddie.

Rhiannon's Hand

March 7th—In-N-Out Burgers with Chris

"Rhia, I can't tell you how killer these Double-Double burgers are. Man, I was sitting in the freakin' desert eating the mess hall crap, and I was just wishing I could have one of these. Man, the fries, the shake. Dude, so awesome!"

Chris is on his second Double-Double burger (that is code for twice the meat and cheese). He's eating like he hasn't had a meal in months, even though Mom made him his favorite meals all week. Something about In-N-Out triggered "the surge," I guess. I'm just nibbling on fries. I'm trying to lose five pounds. Yummy Yogurt can be a pain in more ways than one.

"So, Rhia, tell me about Mom and this Mr. Mac guy. Like, what is Mom thinking? Does she *really* like this guy?"

Why am I always the person people go to for info, huh? Why me? I take a breath and *wade* (Mickey's word) into the drama of "Mom, ex-Dad, Mr. Mac, and Me."

"Well, first off, Chris, Mom was really lonely. And you remember all the suicide stuff, right? So, she got right and saw the doctor. She has probably been taking antidepressants, and—"

"You mean like Prozac?"

"Yeah. I think. She won't talk about it. She is worried that I will think she is…I dunno…weak or something. She has a problem with the whole 'taking medicine' thing. I think it is so stupid. Anyway. Where was I?"

"She was getting better."

"Right. So then she meets Mr. Mac at my school and then at Starbucks. And they kinda hit it off. Very low key, but I can tell she thinks he is very nice."

"He's single, right? Or, like, is he divorced, too?"

"Oh, that's a very long story. I don't wanna go into the details, but his wife died in the Twin Towers on 9.11."

"What?!" Chris stops chewing, and his eyes zoom out at me like in one of those goofy 3-D movies.

"Yeah, I know. Mr. B told us about it, and Mickey talked to Mr. Mac about it…a little. He doesn't ever talk about his wife—like, ever."

"Do you think he tells Mom about her?"

"I don't know. Anyway. Where was I?"

"Uh, he is single."

"Right. Okay. So then, like, we go to the Metaphor Café for the "Grand Reopening," and we watch Saba play a concert…"

"Wait. Saba? You mean the same Saba that graduated from our school and is, like, a famous singer now?"

"Yes, Chris. Who do you think? Who else has a name like *Saba*?"

"She's hot."

"Will you stop interrupting me? I am trying to tell you about Mr. Mac and Mom."

"Sorry." Chris begins eating again, chomping the last of a burger in one enormous mouthful.

"Wait. Dang it! Where was I?" I ask—again.

"They went to the Metaphor Café."

"Oh, right. Then they went to Mickey's house for Thanksgiving…"

"Yeah, yeah—that I knew."

"And they usually go out on Saturday nights—or sometimes on Sundays for lunch."

"Does Dad know?"

"About what?"

"*Duh!* About Mom and Mr. Mac!" Chris is sucking down the chocolate shake, which is kinda funny because it is so thick that you have to suck so hard that you practically implode (Mickey's word) your friggin' cheeks. So I start to laugh.

"Rhia, what's so funny?"

I can't help it—I get the giggles. "You are dumbo, with your suck-down-the-entire-shake-until-you-pass-out thing." (Mickey says this is the goofiest wording that I have ever put into the book, but it's the only way I can explain it, you know? So shut up, Mickey—Mr. Synonym!)

When we finally stop laughing and I wipe the tears away, I feel that awful feeling that brings on other kinds of tears. "Chris, I don't give a damn about Dad. As a matter of fact, to me he is *ex-Dad*. He tried to talk to me this summer—I never told you this because I was so upset—but he tried to 'patch things up' with me."

"Yeah?"

"Yeah, but it is all bullshit. He feels guilty. Whatever. I wish I could just forget about him totally, but lately, Mom has been on my case about college. Dad wants to pay for most of it."

"What?! Really? Wait. Dad is gonna pay for your college? Wow. That is great. I mean, is he serious?"

"Probably. But he has flaked out on us so often that I don't even know what he is thinking—and I don't care. Anyway, no. He doesn't know about Mom and Mr. Mac, and he probably could care less. He has his new girlfriend or whatever up there in Oregon."

We are quiet for a while. Nothing left to eat. I clean up the table.

"He's a jerk, Chris."

Then Chris pulls my hands toward him. "He wrote to me, you know. I got about five letters from him."

I'm taken off guard. "Letters?"

"Yeah. He was worried about me. And he asked about you and Mom."

"What did you—did you write back?"

"Yeah, I did. What else is there to do unless you have duty at night? I told him I was fine. Chill out. Don't worry. You know. But I didn't say much about you and Mom—heck, I didn't even know all of this was going on."

"Good."

"Rhia, Mom looks happier than I have seen her in years. This Mr. Mac guy—he must be nice to her. He must be special, 'cause I just feel it coming from Mom. You know I ain't too smart, Rhia. But I know what I know—and I know that whatever is between them is real. I mean, there's gotta be *somebody* for her, you know? She's the greatest." He pauses for a moment to let all of that sink in. "I wanted to know all of this 'cause isn't he gonna see Mom tonight?"

"Yeah, they are going to the movies."

"Well, when I meet him, I wanna thank him."

"Huh?"

"I wanna thank him for making me less worried about Mom. And for helping you have more confidence to go to college. And I wanna thank him for making Mom happy." Chris looks off into the distance. "Doesn't she look pretty now?"

"She always looks pretty, you dumbo."

"Yeah, well, so does Miss AP Girl."

I slug him on the shoulder, but for the first time ever, my fist crumples as I hit him. "Ow!"

"Don't go messing with the Arm of the Army, girl," he laughs.

We walk out into the afternoon sunshine. He hugs me, and for the first time in my life, I feel like he's stronger than I am.

Mickey's Hand

March 14th—Me and Coach in the Dugout

It's Saturday. Tryouts. Day one. Coach called me yesterday and asked if I could come early—at 6:00 AM (yikes!)—'cause he wants to talk to me. Alone. He told me it's not anything serious; he just wants to ask me about the team. Hmm.

Now, I have to tell you a few things about Coach that I might not have mentioned in the summer. First off, I think he is pushing 60. He had a hip replaced five years ago, and he calls the whole thing "a damn pain in the ass—literally." He winces when he gets up off the bench, and lately, the assistant coach has been hitting more fungos to the infield.

Coach has managed the team since the school opened—going on 37 years, I think. He has won lots of league titles, but he has not won the championship in a long time. He talks about a team in '91 that was his best ever; he is still in touch with those guys. I hope we win the championship, but this year will probably be a tough one. We graduated a lot of seniors. Lost our best pitcher and first baseman, who crushed the ball, and we are looking for some freshmen and sophomores to step up. Thanks to RC, we have some new blood. RC is a rock in the field but mostly a singles guy; he will probably bat lead off.

Most of this was the topic of the first 15 minutes of conversation in the dugout this morning. Mostly business and a "thanks for getting up so early." Coach was already in uniform—which was a topic that we would get to later.

"So, Coach, why'd you wanna see me so early?"

"Well, first off, Mickey, I don't want you writin' a tell-all book about this season," he said with a chuckle. Then Coach surprised me. "Hell, I don't read much, Mickey, but that book you four wrote—well, it was pretty damn good. I wish I could write like that. Never had the patience, though."

"Yeah, well, we are working on another one right now."

"Well, if I'm in it, you'd better be careful. I might just punch you out after graduation if you print something I don't much like, Son." He had a wry smile on his face that said, *I'm kidding—but only a little.*

"Don't worry, Coach. I won't write anything that you don't agree with. Besides, I was gonna make you into this young, handsome coach who goes on to the Major League."

"Now *that* is total bullshit, Mickey." This time, he laughed for real. "Mickey, I want you to start this season, and I want you at first. Don't tell me you are a lightweight with the bat. I've seen you. You've got a nice stroke, Son. I ain't lookin' for power; I'm lookin' at the two hole, and I need someone to move RC along and get on base—and you do that. Besides, I like the way you pick 'em at first. You ain't afraid of the damn ball."

I just sat there. A toothpick somehow appeared out of nowhere as he looked out to the well-manicured infield. Coach still rides the lawnmower from time to time and touches up the mound until it is just right. He is old school. Heck, when he first got here, he built these dugouts with his bare hands. Brick by brick.

Coach turned to me for a nanosecond. "But none of this is why I asked you here. Mickey, you are not a typical ballplayer. You are smart as a whip—and not just baseball smart. People smart. You are a leader, Son. Leaders don't just hit homers or clock in at some ridiculous speed on a jugs gun. It ain't always about what you are born with. *It's about what you do with what you've got.* You make the most of what the Good Lord gave you, Mickey."

Then Coach looked out at the pitcher's mound and tossed the toothpick out on the grass.. Finally, he turned to me. "I want you to be the captain, Mickey. I ain't takin' no for an answer."

"But Coach, I was just a relief pitcher and a bench guy last year."

"Well, you ain't no more. Look, I'm not lookin' for a superstar. I'm lookin' for someone to help me get these new kids to believe in themselves. I see how people look up to you. All I'm asking is for you to speak up, play the game the right way, and help me understand these young punks who think they know everything just because their club coach tells them they are God's gift to shortstop. Times are changing,

Mickey. I gotta figure out a way to reach these guys. You with me, Son?"

This had to be the most surprising conversation that I had ever had with any coach in my entire life. Not that I'm that old, but you know what I mean. It told me something about the man. Something about why he does what he does. Something about his priorities. How could I say no?

"Okay, Coach. I am on board." Then I looked down at his socks. This is gonna seem weird, but I just blurted out what I had always pondered. "But Coach, you gotta tell me something. What's up with your socks? Why do you wear them like that—you know, with the stirrups? Is it just because it is old school?"

Dumbstruck, he looked down at the red stirrups. "Oh, my socks? Well. Um. I like them this way. This is how players wore 'em when I played—the way our heroes wore 'em. Al Kaline, Willie Mays, Koufax, Aaron—they all wore the sanitary white and the stirrups over the top. Knee high, so that the umpire wouldn't call the low strike. It was just— well, it is just my way."

I listened to his voice as he rattled off the heroes of his youth. Then I said, "Coach, you know what? We've got a new look this year. A new-old look. We're going old school."

"No, we ain't, Son."

"Yes, we are, Coach. It's my first decision as *captain*."

Coach just shook his head and muttered, "Good luck with that. Players these days wear their pants so low that they practically trip on 'em. Heck, they chew up the bottoms with their spikes, the knuckleheads."

"It's a new season, Coach."

Now, all I have to do is convince my teammates.

And that may be my first pitch of the spring.

Pari's Hand

March 15th

We all got an email that said that the University of California and Cal State systems had so many applications that they would not announce admissions until April 1st. That has to be a bad sign, you know.

April Fools.

Madison's Hand

March 18th

Jasmine has taken a turn for the worst. I know—how can it get any worse? But the good news is that they have moved her up on the transplant list. Some of the folks at the Make-a-Wish Foundation have been contributing money to her family, and rumor has it that there may be a liver for her at UCLA's Medical Center. I guess there is someone on life support…for now.

Jasmine is in such bad shape that they may have to Life Flight her there. My dad says that will cost around a $1,000, but it will be worth it. He says the liver has to be removed and transplanted in a certain amount of time, and the ambulance ride will probably take too long in LA traffic. Jeeze, LA freeways are such a nightmare!

Fingers crossed.

Mickey is updating things on the school's Web site, and there have been donations coming in. Jasmine's church has been the most supportive of all. They are so confident that she will recover.

This all reminds me of something Mr. Buscotti said when he was explaining the symbolism of *To Kill a Mockingbird*. He said that Atticus Finch believed that killing a mockingbird was a sin because mockingbirds never did any harm; they just added the joy of music to everyone's world. But their music was a signal for hunters to shoot them—like they did Tom Robinson. "Another character named after a bird," Mr. B had said.

I couldn't shake the thought that Jasmine was a sweet bird, too—singing out to others, loving everyone she met. What reason was there for the Good Lord to have her be born with a defective liver? Why?

I think of this often, but whenever I am with Jasmine, she is so filled with hope and so sure that Jesus will not let her fade away. "But even if I die, Maddie, I will be with Him. So that's not so bad," she tells me. Then she adds, "But I just know that God has plans for me and that I am going to get better. So no sad faces, Maddie. I am going to be super-duper. So don't be a party pooper." And then she giggles.

One time, a nurse was with me when Jasmine said something to this effect. Once we were outside Jasmine's door, the nurse grabbed me by the arm and said, "She is so sick, Maddie. I just don't know. But I will tell you this: I just wish I believed in her God as much as she does."

Yeah.

Me too.

Chapter 18: "Waitlist Song: (How I Get into College)"

Pari's Hand

April 1st—12:02 PM

I want to call Mick, but I am so afraid—what if he didn't get into the colleges he applied to? If I call him before he calls me, is that a sign? What would I say? Did he ditch class like me to check his email for the noon "announcements of admissions?" I didn't see him all morning, and our calculus class meets after lunch, and then we have AP Gov… Where is he? And where is Maddie? She must be freaking out, too. At least they can be miserable together.

I saw Rhia at break, and she was sort of semi-worried. She told me her SAT math score sucks, but I told her that her overall score is pretty good and that she has a really good chance of getting into the state schools. I honestly think so, but I think she doesn't want to get her hopes up. And then, of course, there is her "dad factor."

But I have to call Mickey! My folks aren't home. I have to tell somebody. But what if I get shut out? Then I'll want to lock myself in my room, bury myself under the covers, and chuck my cell out the window. Oh, my God—I am a nervous wreck!

I am staring at my computer. There are two separate email notifications. The first one is from UCLA. The second one is from Berkeley. Which do I open first? I click Berkeley, and I just jump up out of my seat as I watch it open up. I hold my breath.

The first word is *Congratulations.*

YESSSSS!

I skim through the email quickly, just to make sure it is the real deal. Yes. I am admitted to UC Berkeley. I am a Golden Bear!

I minimize the letter.

I stare at the UCLA email. I hold my breath…again.

The first word my eyes focus on is somewhere in the first line: *unfortunately.*

Ugh.

I sit down.

Oh, well. So what?

I let out a sigh that seems to hold all the nervous tension that has been cooped up in my lungs for the past three years. Then I stand up, and without a soul in the house, I yell out, "I GOT IN!"

Then I call Mick.

Mickey's Hand

April 1st—8:45 AM: Reporter's Notebook

I am riding in my truck. I only went to Ms. LaFleur's class first period, which isn't my regular class period, but I didn't want to miss the class 'cause she was going to pass out our papers on *Hamlet.*

I have been texting Maddie all morning about Jasmine. Her status has moved her up to the top of the transplant list. Maddie went directly to the hospital early this morning because her dad told her that things are getting really bad. They say she may be Life Flighted to UCLA Medical Center today.

I'm worried about Maddie, too, because she is so attached to Jasmine. I mean, it's hard not to be. It's just in Maddie's DNA to be...I don't know how to explain it...to just be so committed to someone. And I worry what will happen if this all turns really bad.

I look down at my backpack, which is lying on the empty passenger's seat. Sticking out of the top is my *Hamlet* paper, which has Ms. LaFleur's distinctive handwriting scrawled across the top in green ink: *Mickey, this is a wonderful paper. You have the heart of a writer. You are an old soul, young man. Bravo. 97/A*

Her note means a lot, I guess, but I'm just not smiling as I pull into my driveway.

On top of the whole Jasmine situation, today is the day we find out about college admissions. Pari must be freaking. I just didn't see her because I raced home to tell my mom my plan for the next few hours.

"Mom, I'm going to the hospital to meet Maddie, but I will probably be back by noon to check my email. But if I don't make it back in time for some reason, I will call you and have you find out about the acceptances."

"Mickey, are you sure you need to go to the hospital?"

"Mom, I have been writing stories about Jasmine for two months! You just gotta trust me on this—I just gotta be there, okay?"

"Okay, but do you really want me to open your emails?"

"Yes."

"Are you sure?"

"Yes."

"But...what if it is bad news?"

"Then it is bad news. Mom, how bad can it be? I'm not the one who is dying of a shredded liver."

"Okay. Okay. Don't worry, Mickey—and drive safely. You drive way too fast."

"Right. Love you, Mom."

Maddie is standing in the hallway outside Jasmine's room. She's on her cell, talking to her mom.

"I know, Mom. Yes, I know. Dad is gonna check for me. Yes, I know. No, we don't have any idea about when she can be transported. She is in and out of consciousness this morning. Yes, I will call when I know more. Yes. Dad and I are texting. Remind him that Sonoma State is the one I want him to check first, okay? It's the most important. Right. Okay. Love you, Mom. Okay. *Okay*, Mom, I will. Right now—I will. Mickey is here, and I promise I will eat breakfast. Okay. Love you too. Bye." Click.

Maddie gets up and hugs me. Tight. Then she bursts into tears.

"I've been holding it in, Mickey. All morning. I am just so afraid she will die before they can get a donor."

Maddie is someone who cries from deep inside. It isn't that kind of crying you see on those stupid reality TV shows, where someone weeps and then makes some grand speech while the music builds and makes it all seem heroic. With Maddie, it's like her knees go weak. Her body just falls into me. She can't talk. Her eyes are red, and there is a sadness that shapes her face and makes you wish you could save her day. But you can't. Nobody can.

I tell her we should eat breakfast, but food is the last thing she wants.

"I can't eat, Mickey. You get something."

"But you promised your mom."

"Tell her I ate if she bugs you about it. I just can't."

As we walk to the caféteria, I ask her for the latest.

"Well, they thought they had a donor, but he was a very old man who died in a car crash, and he must have been an alcoholic or something because his liver was shot."

"So he was no use to anyone—even himself."

"Yep. When Jasmine was admitted to the hospital, it was because her sodium level was way too low and her kidneys were failing. She was put on dialysis and moved to the ICU because she was unconscious last night. That bumped her up to be second on the donor list because she is so critical. While she is on dialysis here, we wait."

It takes a while for all that to sink in. Then Maddie asks me, "Have you seen Pari? She must be freaking out."

"No, I haven't, but she texted me—I just haven't answered yet. She is in class now, anyway."

"Rhia?"

"Pari says she saw her at break. Are you sure you don't want anything to eat?"

But Maddie was looking down at her cell. "Mickey, you're not gonna believe this, but Mr. Buscotti just texted me. It's his prep period. He told me he never texts—ever. Hmm. He wants me to call him when I have news about Jasmine."

"I thought he didn't know how to text?"

"Well, I guess he figured it out. He's so funny—he spelled out every single word and even punctuated the sentence!"

We laughed. It felt good to smile. It's funny what makes you smile.

I finish my breakfast burrito and look at my cell. **10:17.** Time moves so slowly in hospitals. Maddie says an hour in hospital time is actually three hours in normal time. We walk by Jasmine's room. Her family is all gathered there. We feel like intruders. "No change," someone says.

We decide to walk outside. **10:34.** Maddie asks me about my *Hamlet* paper.

"I did okay."

"I know you, Mickey. You got an A, right?"

"Whatever."

"Don't 'whatever' me! I bet you got a perfect score."

"Nope. 97%. I always mess up my tenses."

"Big deal. Congratulations. Did Ms. LaFleur say, 'You have the heart of a writer?'"

"How did you know that?" I look at her suspiciously, like, *What have you been saying about me to Ms. LaFleur?*

"She talked to me last week. She thinks you are one of the best writers she has ever taught. She told me about how you guys talked about UC Davis's Writing Program and how it's, like, one of only 12 public colleges that are in the top 25 best writing programs—or something like that. How come you didn't tell me you talked to her? Just curious."

"Well, my dad was all pumped that USC accepted me, but he knows I don't really want to go there. I've told you how I want to go to UCLA or Cal, but lately, the whole 'big school' thing is just feeling kinda strange to me. But it won't matter 'cause I'm not going to get into either one of them…"

"Oh, that's not true…"

"It's not gonna happen, Maddie. My SAT is too low—for them. But UC Davis is way smaller, and I have been following the whole writing program there. And there is one more thing."

"What?"

"They have a good baseball program—okay, well, it's not *great*— but it's a program that I may be able to actually play for. I could probably walk on. Coach told me that he would talk to their coach up there. I don't know…it's a possibility. And if you get into Sonoma, we won't be too far away from each other."

Maddie looks at me for more than a minute without saying anything. Some days, I get her and some days, she is a mystery. Today is Mystery Maddie. She asks, "How big is Davis?"

"4,000 freshmen. About 20,000 total."

"That is still big, don't you think?"

"It's not 35,000 like UCLA. And besides, I think my dad will kill me if I turn down USC for UCLA."

11:22. Now I am getting jumpy. I tell Maddie I have to go pretty soon. I ask her how long she is going to stay at the hospital.

"I just want to know if she gets a transplant today. I promised my mom this would be the only day I would miss school. My dad understands more." Right then, her cell rings.

"Hello? Paul? Really? When? Is that—I mean, does that mean she has a donor?"

Maddie frowns. I try to read her face. She hangs up in a hurry. She turns to me and explains. "They are flying Jasmine out in the next hour or so to UCLA. They think they have a donor, but it is touch and go. If she is there, then there's a way better chance for her, even if this one doesn't work out."

"That sounds promising."

"Yeah. I am gonna head up there and say…" Maddie chokes up.

"Yeah, I know. I'll go with you. We'll say goodbye together."

Maddie just looks down, holds her hands over her mouth, and nods.

We just quickly dart in to kiss Jasmine. She smiles and tells us she loves us. We are quick. We don't want to get in the way or anything. **11:49.** It's crazy how hospital time moves so slowly, but then all of a sudden, it's a fanatical rush with people flying in and out, checking and re-checking everything, unhooking and hooking back up a million different monitors.

Amidst all this chaos, Jasmine looks peaceful. Maddie tells me that she knows Jasmine is praying.

I don't go to church all that often—not like Maddie—but I still remember how to pray.

Rhiannon's Hand

April 1st—Mr. Mac's Last Period Class

"Well, Rhia, it was just a few of us here today," Mr. Mac says to me. It is **2:45**, and the bell has rung. I am one of only 12 seniors who showed up to class today. Everyone else is checking on college admissions and either partying or getting depressed. I got a text from Pari. I'm so happy for her. Berkeley was always her first choice. I text back that we will all meet up later to celebrate.

Mickey and Maddie are still at the hospital, I think. I don't know what is happening, but Jasmine must be doing really bad. It's so sad.

"I guess everyone didn't think my lesson on judicial activism was all that exciting. I'm just kidding. I know everyone is excited about college," Mr. Mac says to me as he shoves stuff into his briefcase—papers he has to grade, I guess. "Hey, I don't mean to pry, but you seem pretty down, Rhia. Are you okay?"

"Yeah," I say to him. "It's just the whole Jasmine thing, you know, and…" I drift off.

"How come you're not finding out about schools? Your mom tells me you applied to some."

I let out a sigh. "I know. I should be checking my email somewhere. But I will probably get rejected, and—I don't know—I mean, I just don't feel like facing it right now."

"I have an idea," he said. "How about we meet at that place you guys like—the Metaphor Café? I'll treat you to something. They have Wi-Fi now. I'll bring my laptop, and we can see what's happening."

"Oh, Mr. Mac, that's real nice and all, but when I get rejected in front of my teacher—I mean, that is, like, the bummer of all bummers. Seriously."

"Rhia, I'll tell you what. We go. I get you a caffè mocha, which I know you love, and maybe—just maybe—we check one email from one school. Maybe the one you don't even want to go to. Come on." He is charming, I have to admit. I can see why my mom is always smiling around him. In many ways, he is the opposite of my ex-dad.

"Okay, Mr. Mac, but only one school."

"Deal."

"Deal."

So we sit at the same table the four of us usually sit at. It is kinda crazy sitting here with my teacher, but he is being so nice.

"You know, I have never gotten one of these caffè mochas before—with all the whipped cream. It sure is more fun than a straight black coffee," Mr. Mac tells me as he sets up his laptop.

"I used to say it was 'yummy,' but then when I started working at Yummy Yogurt, the word 'yummy' turned up on my list of banned words."

He laughs. "I worked at a peanut butter factory in the summer when I was going to college. I can't eat the stuff now. And I used to love it."

"Yeah, I *so* get that," I nod.

We sip away until his computer is ready. I tell him my Gmail address, which I gave to the colleges. All of a sudden, I feel a knot in my stomach and perspiration on my forehead. Why am I so worried?

"Gosh, Rhia, what did you do—apply to *all* the state colleges? There are about 12 emails here." He looks up at me smiling.

"I just checked the boxes where the common apps can be sent. I really have no idea where I want to go, sooo…I just checked all of them." I say this like, *Duh, doesn't everyone do that?*

Mr. Mac busts out laughing and then quickly realizes that he may be insulting me. He says, "Rhia, you crack me up. You are the most honest, unpretentious student I have ever taught."

"Is that good?" I think he figures I don't really know what *unpretentious* means.

"You are down to earth, Rhia. You don't act…phony." He smiles. Pauses. "My wife was the same way. Midwesterner. Blue-collar girl. Took her coffee black and was honest to a fault." He stops abruptly. I wonder if he just realized who he was talking to and who he was talking about. He quickly looks down at his laptop. "Well, which school sounds the *least* appealing? We can just check that one."

I don't know exactly what made me say the next four words:

"You still miss her?"

Silence. Then his fingers tap ever so lightly on the keys.

"You never stop missing someone you love that much." His eyes are glued to the screen.

"I guess it depends on *why* they leave you," I tell him.

He finally looks up. "I guess so."

Then, after hesitating a moment, I ask him something I've wondered for months: "Can you love someone that much...again?"

Mr. Mac closes his eyes and seems to go someplace else. Now my palms are sweating for an entirely different reason, and the stuff on that computer screen seems pretty unimportant right now.

He opens his eyes and looks at me. "I wasn't sure, Rhia. I wasn't sure for a long time. When those towers fell, my life, my heart, everything I had come to believe in that was true and good just burnt right down to my core. I thought the hole could never be filled. I didn't even want to try. At first, I couldn't talk to your mom much because...well, I just don't let my feelings out. Now it's different—with her. I can't believe I am telling you all this. I guess I owe it to you. You have let me share your mom. So all I will say is that she and I are kindred souls. We have seen the dark side, and we both know that when we're together, we are in the light." He looks up above my head and softly says, "So yes, I think I can love again."

The intensity of our gaze is so tight that I don't even notice that my dumb cell is buzzing away with messages.

"Mr. Mac, I feel special that you told me all that. I think you are a great man. I'm glad my mom met you. Whatever happens between you guys—well, I just think she deserves someone like you."

"Thanks." That is all he says. His eyes tell me all I need to know.

After a minute, I say as I raise my mug, "Hey, do you think I got into any colleges?"

"Which one do you want to check on first?"

He raises his mug and we toast: "To new beginnings."

Mickey's Hand

April 1st—12:30 PM: Reporter's Notebook

My cell rings. It's Pari.

"Mickey, where are you?"

"I'm with Maddie at the hospital."

"Oh." Pari seems to stop dead in her tracks. "Oh, my God. Is it Jasmine? Did she have the transplant?"

"No. She is really bad, though, Pari. It is a long story. She is on dialysis, and she lost consciousness for a while last night. They are putting her on a helicopter to LA. They think they may have a donor."

"Oh, my God, Mickey. Could she...could she die?"

"Yeah, she could. They are on, like, super high alert. It's crazy. The nurses and doctors are great, but they seem worried—not in front of her, but outside in the halls, you can hear them talking."

All of a sudden, I realize what time it is and why Pari is calling. "Pari, what's going on? Did you get into Cal or UCLA? What?"

Silence. I guess Jasmine's situation has put a damper on things for Pari.

"Yes and no."

"What? Pari, look, I know this whole Jasmine thing is terrible, but I gotta know what has happened!"

"Mickey, I got into Cal. But UCLA said no."

I know Pari; she is trying to downplay her joy 'cause she is worried about whether me and the girls will get in—not to mention Jasmine's situation. I ain't playing that game.

"Shut up! Parivesh—YOU *ROCK*, GIRL! I am so psyched for you! I gotta tell Maddie." I move the cell away from my ear. "Maddie, Maddie—Pari got into Cal Berkeley!" For the first time all day, Maddie beams and tosses her arms into the air.

"Yes! Gimme the cell, Mickey. Pari, Pari—I am so happy for you! You did it! I wish I could hug you right now. Okay. Yes. Okay, I will. Love you." Maddie hands me the cell, still smiling ear to ear.

Pari asks, "Mickey, what happened with you?" Her voice is full of the tension that I have tried to ignore all day.

"I don't know yet. Pari, I just can't leave right now. I'm gonna call my mom and have her check."

"What?!" Pari seems blown away.

"Pari, we have cable, so I cannot check my email here. I told her I would call her. I'm gonna do it now. I promise I will tell you as soon as I know."

"Look, Mickey, I am coming over to the hospital, okay? I am going to call my dad and tell him the news—then I'll tell my mom. But I am coming over. Where are you?"

"ICU corridor. 4th floor. I will look for you."

"Okay, bye," she tells me.

I decide I have to call my mom.

It's **12:45.**

Madison's Hand

April 1st—1:00 PM

My dad turns the corner and sees me. "Maddie, there you are." He is moving quickly towards me.

"Hi, Dad. What's up?"

He looks at me like he can't believe that I don't seem to get it. "Maddie, *what's up* is that I just got off the computer."

All of a sudden, it hits me. With all this crazy stuff going on, I've lost track of *my* life. "Dad, did you check on Sonoma State?" My voice cracks; it does that when I get really freaky.

"You are going to Sonoma, Maddie. You got in!" He just grabs me and picks me up off my feet. I had forgotten how strong he is. When he puts me down—like I am a doll or something—he looks at me and then at Mickey. "I called your mom. Wait, that is not all. They know about the book you guys wrote, and Sonoma offered you a scholarship, Maddie. It's $1,000 per year for four years, and because I'm military, you are getting a housing allowance of another thousand, too."

"Oh my God, Dad!" My hands are on my cheeks, and I can feel the heat coming off them. I'm sure I am beet red. Then I look at Mickey in disbelief. All he can say is his favorite expression for this kind of moment:

"Shut up!"

I hug him.

My dad is still smiling when he turns to Mickey and asks him, "What about you, Mickey? Do you know anything yet?" Dad sort of looks a little worried, too.

Mickey's face drops a little. "No, dang it. I gotta call my mom. She is probably freaking out. Crap." He looks down at his cell. "She's called me three times already."

I tell him, "Maybe you should just go home and check?"

Mickey is so stubborn. It's **1:30**. "No, I'm staying. I'm calling her right now."

"You said that an hour ago."

"I know," he smiles at me, "but there has been too much excitement."

I guess you can tell why I really, really love him.

Mickey's Hand

April 1st—1:35 PM: Reporter's Notebook

"Mom, it's me."

"Mickey! I've been calling and calling and you haven't answered. Are you still at the hospital?"

"Yeah. Sorry about that. It's been kinda crazy."

"Yes, tell me about it, Mickey. I am staring at the emails, and I want to open them up, but I've been waiting for you to call. Your father just got off the phone with me and told me I should just read them—but I can't. He is meeting with a client until 3:30, and he wanted to know what was going on. I had to fight him off. You owe me, Mister!"

"You're right, Mom. I owe you big time. I'll buy you a BMW when I'm rich."

"Yeah, well, by then, I might be so old that they'll take away my license."

"Good one, Mom. Okay. Mom. Pay attention. Are you at the computer now?"

"Where do you think I am?! I have been hovering over it since noon!"

"Okay. Look for the UC Davis letter."

"UC Davis?"

"Yes."

"Don't you want to know about UCLA first?"

"No, Mom. Too depressing. Besides, I just want to know about Davis first."

"Okay. Here it is. Should I open it?"

"Yes, Mom!"

"Okay. Here goes. I am clicking on it now."

Silence. More silence.

"Mom? Mom?! Did you double click? Did you right click? Mom, what does it say?!"

"Wait. I am still reading, Mickey."

"Mom, it isn't a novel! Does the first sentence have the word *congratulations* in it?"

"Yes. Yes."

"Oh, thank God!" My heart is racing. I can't believe me and my mom are doing this.

"Yes, honey, you are accepted! It took me a while to read the first paragraph and make sure."

"Okay, Mom. GREAT. That's all I really need to know."

"What? Are you serious, Mickey? What do you mean?"

"Okay, Mom, listen. Don't get emotional here. We *are* going to open the other emails, but I'm telling you it probably isn't gonna be too great."

"Don't be such a pessimist, honey."

"I'm a realist, Mom. Trust me. Okay, let's do UCLA."

"Okay."

Silence. More silence.

"Mom? What's happening?"

"Nope, Mickey. I'm sorry, honey. They said that you are qualified but that there are so many other applicants…"

"Okay, fine. Never mind, Mom. They say that to everyone. Let's try UC Santa Cruz."

"Okay, but do you even want to go there?"

"Mom, just open it! I don't totally know what I want, but I think I will get in, so I don't wanna be depressed."

"Right. Okay."

Silence. More silence.

"You're right! You're in!"

"Great. Okay, try…"

"Mickey, Santa Cruz says you are a 'Banana Slug.' What is that?"

"Never mind, Mom. Stay focused. It's just their mascot."

"A Banana Slug? That is the most ridiculous thing I've ever—"

"It doesn't matter, Mom."

"If you go there, I am *not* wearing any sweatshirt that says, 'Banana Slug' on it, Mickey. I'm just telling you that right now."

"Mom, *that* is not gonna happen. Okay. There should only be Berkeley left?"

"Right. Isn't this the one you want the most?"

"No. Well, yes. I don't know, Mom. UC Davis is the one I had to have. Berkeley isn't gonna take me if UCLA doesn't. Go ahead, Mom. Open it."

Silence. More silence. Even more silence.

"Mom, for crying out loud, what does it say?!"

"Mickey, this is strange. It says you are on the 'waitlist' and that you could be admitted… Wait… No, you might be admitted the *second* semester. Wait, I'm gonna read this part again: 'If the number of students originally admitted declines admission, you will be notified, and you may also be considered for the Fall semester—'"

"Mom. Stop. I get it. Cool. Well, that is interesting. So I am on the waitlist."

"Right. Mickey, I am so proud of you—whatever you do. You have lots of choices: USC, Davis, maybe Berkeley—and that Banana Slug school."

"Santa Cruz."

"Do you want to leave a message on your dad's cell? Or do you want me to?"

"Let's keep him in suspense, Mom. I'll call him at, what, 3:30, right?"

"Right. If he gets out of his meeting early, I'll tell him to call you. I love you, honey."

"I love you, too, Mom. That was fun, wasn't it?"

"Yes, it was. I think we'll always remember this crazy day, huh?"

I just hope that this crazy day has a happy ending.

Compared to Jasmine's, my waitlist seems pretty trivial.

Rhiannon's Hand

April 1st—4:00 PM

I come flying in the door and yell for my mom and Chris. I have just spent an amazing hour with Mr. Mac at the Metaphor Café.

"Rhia, hi. Where have you been?" my mom says to me as she dries her hands on a dishtowel.

"Mom, where is Chris?" I say, breathless.

"Why? What's the matter?" She has completely forgotten that today is the day I hear back from colleges.

"Absolutely nothing is wrong, Mom. Actually, absolutely everything is right…well, almost everything. Where is my brother when I need him?"

"CHRIS!" For a petite woman, my mom can really bark out his name. She's had a lot of practice.

Chris pokes his head out from his room upstairs, holding his videogame player stick-thingy or whatever you call it. "What's up? Hey, Rhia."

I tell him to get down here right now, and he drops the stuff and practically leaps down the entire staircase. I tell them to both sit down on the couch. Then I begin:

"Okay. This is about college—"

Chris immediately interrupts, "Did you get in somewhere?!"

I give him a look that says, *If you interrupt me one more time, I am going to scream.* He shuts up.

"Okay. I have been sitting with Mr. Mac for the last hour at the Metaphor Café—"

My mom interrupts, "With Andrew? What? Why?" She seems totally taken off guard.

"Long story, Mom. But after school, he asks me about college. And remember, Mom, today is the day they send admittance emails to people who applied."

"Oh. Of course. Go on, Rhia," Mom says, realizing that she too is interrupting.

"So, he asks me which colleges I have heard from, and I tell him that I haven't checked yet. But Mac knows that half the senior class is ditching school 'cause the letters come out at noon today, and it's, like, 3:00. So, he asks me why I don't want to know. And I tell him that I am scared to find out that I am Miss Rejection. And he says that that is silly. And he tells me—*asks* me, really—to meet him at the Metaphor Café so we can go online and check it out. He wants to get me a coffee—he is just being nice. So I tell him, *No way am I getting humiliated in front of my teacher.* And he says that we will only check one school— like, the one I don't even wanna go to anyway—and just see what happens."

I catch my breath. My mom is sitting straight up on the couch, and my brother is looking at me like, *Girl, get to the point!*

"So I tell him *okay*. We get there, and we are talking about stuff— I'll tell you about that later, Mom, 'cause I know you don't really care about all the emo stuff, Chris." Chris smiles and nods. "And so we check the first school. But when you send the common application out, you can check as many schools as you want to—free. So I did. I checked almost ALL OF THEM. Mr. Mac kinda freaks when he sees all the emails. And he cracks up when I tell him why there are so many."

My mom can't stand the suspense. "Rhia, tell me what happened! You can give me all the details later. I'm having a heart attack!"

"Right. Sorry. Okay. So we check Cal State Dominguez Hills. Believe me, I have no friggin' idea where the heck that is. But I got in! So then we checked Cal State Fullerton, which I have heard of, and—I got in! Then we checked Cal State Northridge, which Mr. Mac says is kinda above LA—and I got in! Mom, this is, like, so crazy. We check San Jose State and San Francisco State—I GOT IN! I am, like, freaking out. We check Long Beach State—and I didn't get in. But that's okay. Then we check San Diego State—nope. Rejected. The last one was Fresno State—and I GOT IN! You guys, I got into six of the eight schools that I checked. SIX SCHOOLS!"

My brother leaps off the couch and shouts out, "YEAH, MY LITTLE SISTER IS GONNA BE A COLLEGE GIRL!"

My mom has the biggest smile I have seen on her face in a long, long time. Then, as I thought she would, she starts crying. Which makes me cry. Chris just looks at the two of us and says, "Dang it, why do women always start balling when it's good news? I'd hate to see you two if you had gotten rejected from all those schools. You would probably go looney tunes."

Leave it to Chris to sum up the whole afternoon.

Looney tunes.

Pari's Hand

April 1st—7:00 PM: Back at the Same Table at the Metaphor Café

So here we sit. Exhausted. Caffeine crazy. Sharing all the bits and pieces of a day that never seems to end. I tell them about my mom and dad and how they called all the relatives and how proud they are of me and how they are having a giant Persian party—of course, Maddie's and Rhia's and Mickey's families are all invited. My parents were a little over the top, but as my father said to his brother in Iran, "Pari isn't just going to university; she is going to BERKELEY!" My brothers are all super happy. I think they feel relieved 'cause now the pressure to carry on the family's college tradition is off of them. Brothers!

Rhia's story is amazing. "I told you, Rhia!" I feel that pride that maybe a teacher feels when she encourages a student and they realize that they really have what it takes. "What are you going to do now that six colleges want you?"

Rhia is sitting like she always does, with one leg tucked under her long, gypsy-like skirt. "I really have no idea, you guys. I think the first thing I need to do is find out where the heck these places are!"

We all laugh.

Maddie is satisfied but more somber. She keeps glancing at her cell. Jasmine has been at the UCLA Medical Center for at least four hours—and no word. Maddie tells us about her mom's reaction to Sonoma and the scholarship money. She says her mom just fell into the recliner like a giant weight had been knocked off her tiny shoulders. The whole family, she says, went out for ribs to celebrate. But I don't think she ate a whole lot.

Then there is Mick. He is the Master of Ceremonies tonight, moving from me to Rhia to Maddie. But finally, I pose the question to him: "What did *your* father say?"

"He was surprised. He's stoked, though. I had to explain the whole Davis thing to him again. I said something about the Writing Program to him two weeks ago, but he seemed distracted with work. I just didn't think he knew a lot about Davis.

"The funny thing is that he actually *was* listening—'cause the first thing he said was that they have a great law school. He kidded me about UCLA; he told me that he'd kick me out of the house this summer if I went there instead of USC. He is still on the business school trip. He asked me what the whole 'waitlist' thing meant, and he studied the letter for, like, *eons*. I told him that I wasn't too jazzed about the idea of sitting out a semester. But if Cal accepted me 'cause there were some openings—well, then, I would have to think about it.

"To be honest, I think Cal is too liberal for my dad. But he says that the Hass Business School there is the best on the West Coast. Whatever. I'm just glad it's all over."

We all nod. A song is playing that none of us has ever heard before. Something about being on a waitlist. Mickey quickly Googles it. It is called "Waitlist Song...(How I Get into College)" by Genna Matthew. Her soft, pleading voice bounces off all four of us:

> **"Won't you please listen
> 'cause I've been waitlisted
> and I know
> I got more to show.
> Don't you see
> I can't take this
> Won't you take me off your
> waitlist?"**

What a coincidence, we all think.

A few minutes later, Maddie's cell goes off.

Jasmine's brother tells her that the donor's liver is too big.

She will have to wait.

It is **8:15 PM.**

And the life has gone out of the party.

Chapter 19: "Soul of the World"

Pari's Hand

May 1st

No, that is not a typo. It is May 1st. We have had another extraordinary month, and we all got so busy with AP tests (which we don't want to write about because they are too headache-packed to share with anyone!). But in all the craziness, we decided that the best way to explain this month was for me to be your narrator and take you back in time to April, when, as they say, we reached a fork in the road.

This part of the story begins with Ms. LaFleur introducing us to Paulo Coelho's *The Alchemist,* and it ends at the hospital with the "Soul of the World."

Rhiannon's Hand

April 4th—Me and Roberto

It's three days after Jasmine's trip to the UCLA Medical Center was supposed to happen. Maddie has been getting texts from Jasmine and calls from her brother Paul.

Nothing has happened. Her family waits and prays. So do we.

I've been on my computer and talking to my mom about college, trying to decide what to do. All the schools look good—great, actually. I just don't know. I have narrowed it down to San Jose State and San Francisco State. My mom says we can drive up and see them in the next few weeks. I can't believe this is happening. I hope I am ready for all of this college stuff. But I wonder if I really am, you know?

My brother is excited for me. It is all a little scary. I mean, leaving home and all. Maybe it was just in the stars that we started reading *The Alchemist* two days ago, because I am like that Santiago kid, who is just minding his own business with the sheep when all of a sudden, these dreams that he needs to follow his heart hit him. I've been dreaming, too. One night, I woke up in a sweat about college. I dreamed that I was majoring in sheep herding at San Francisco State and that I had to get all the sheep across the Golden Gate Bridge. But then THEY STARTED TO FALL OFF THE BRIDGE! And then I was arrested for sheep murder, and I was in a courtroom sitting next to some freaky Oakland Raider fan.

That's when I woke up!

I told my mom, and she said I am just a little nervous.

"It's a big change," she said, smiling. She must have thought that I've lost it.

"But, honey, whatever you do, just remember: I am just a few hours away, and the phone is right by your side."

That made me feel better. I guess all this "follow your own Personal Legend" stuff can be harder than it seems, huh?

Me and Roberto have been hanging out a lot more lately. Sometimes he meets me at the yogurt place after I'm done working. He's usually in his baseball uniform. I've promised him that I will get to as many games as possible. The season is just about to start. He's excited—and nervous, too. The funny thing is that he tells me that sometimes *he* wakes up in the middle of the night all sweaty—like me.

"Dude," I tell him, "I think this dream thing from *The Alchemist* is, like, getting to us."

"I'm just a little nervous—new team, people think I'm good. I don't wanna let anyone down, especially Mickey."

"You'll do great, Roberto."

"Thanks. So, um, you figure out college, yet?"

"No. You?" I ask.

"Well, I'm gonna go to one of the junior colleges, like I'd planned, you know? Get my AA degree. Maybe play ball. Maybe transfer to a four-year, or maybe just go and get my EMT training, or maybe even become a firefighter. I can't really think about any of that stuff right now, though. It seems so far away…"

"Yeah. Well, not really. I have to decide soon on college. And then I gotta talk to my ex-dad about all the money stuff."

"Why do you call him your 'ex-dad?'"

"You *know* why." I say this like he should know better.

"Yeah, but he is still your father. I mean, it's none of my business, but you're so sweet to everyone I know, and…well, you are just so *angry* with him. It just isn't *you.*" Roberto looks at me with those dark brown eyes that have seen his own father less than he would like. His eyes express what it means to have to move to follow the military's path.

I let out a sigh. "I don't look as cute when I am angry, huh?"

"Well, not as cute as when you smile." He says this with his own little grin. Then he adds, "Um, Rhiannon, I hear the Prom is at a really nice place, and I was wondering if—well, if you might wanna go—with me. You know, to the Prom. We have a game that day, but I can still go, and I wondered if you might wanna go—with me, I mean. To the Prom."

I smile and let him suffer a bit. Then I say, "Well, I don't know, Mr. Roberto Clemente Rivera. I can't be seen at the Prom with a guy wearing his #21 uniform, you know."

Then I grab him by the brim of his cap and for the first time, kiss him…really kiss him, ya know what I mean?

Madison's Hand

April 6th—Five Days Since Jasmine Left…

I just got a text from Jasmine's brother Paul. It reads:

> **Jas is getting transplant in two hours.**
> **God is looking out for her.**
> **We pray it works. Jas is hanging in there. Needs it NOW.**
> **I'll text when she's out.**

I call Mickey. He's on the bus for the start of the first game of the season. When I tell him the news, he tells his coach, and I hear some cheers in the background.

I tell Rhia and Pari. They yell, "YES!" into their cell phones. Rhia has to work. Pari has to study. I wish one of them could be with me now. I tell my dad, and he explains all the medical stuff that has to happen for the liver to take with the new body. As he talks, I think he senses that all this scares me, so he wraps it all up with, "But the doctors—they really know what they are doing, Maddie."

Then I ask him what he is doing for the next two hours.

"Not much. Why?"

"Can you and I drive down to Mickey's game? It is only 30 minutes from here." My eyes must reveal something about how I am feeling.

"Sure, let's go," he says without hesitation. "Hey, how come you want to go with your old dad?"

I look down. "I just don't want to be alone right now."

He just nods. Then he goes into the kitchen.

"I've got the peanuts. Let's roll."

I hug him—tight.

We don't need words.

Mickey's Hand

April 6th—Opening Day

Coach has no idea. This has been on the down-low for weeks. I met with every guy on the team, and they're all in on it. We learned it is Coach's 61st birthday in a month, and we figured out how to give him a season-long gift—win or lose.

My dad is a key player in our scheme. He loves the idea, and he and a few other dads chipped in and found what we were looking for.

We open the season at a high school that isn't in our league— literally. They are a new school, and this is their first year varsity. Their coach is one of our school's alumni, and he should be cool with our plan. It is their first ever home baseball game, so they'll have a lot of people there—us, not so much. Maddie texts me that she and *her dad* are coming. So we will have the usual dozen fans and one extra dad. He hasn't seen me play in a while.

No pressure.

The season gets way tougher later this week, and we have a tournament this weekend. We are still figuring out who is doing what. I am starting in two days, but today, I am at first base. Coach dropped me to the bottom of the batting order—maybe 'cause the other team is starting a lefty. Or maybe I just suck when it comes to hitting. I'm probably the only first baseman in the history of high school baseball who will bat ninth.

Kinda embarrassing.

But like Coach says, "Mickey, you are there to pick 'em. We ain't payin' you to hit, Son. We're payin' you to pitch and pick 'em."

"But Coach," I add in my usual wise-ass way, "if you recall, 'you ain't paying' me at all."

"Who says anything about money, Son? What I'm payin' is somethin' you can't cash at a bank."

"Yeah, I figured *that*."

"Let's see if you figure *it* out." With that, he turns away to bark at our catcher. "Hey, why aren't you two playing long toss yet? Do I have to write it in the sky, Yogi?"

Coach always calls our catchers *Yogi*. Some guys are so dim that they think he is calling them a bear instead of *Berra*—as in Yogi Berra, catcher for the Yankees, whom my father once explained to me is the "winningest" player in baseball history.

"Won 10 World Series, Mickey. Appeared in 14. Yogi was the best bad ball hitter I ever saw," my dad would remind me…over and over.

So anyway, we are up first, and their pitcher is pretty pumped—so much so that he walks the first two guys and hits the third. We get a sacrifice fly to right and score the first run of the season. Then a wild pitch and we are on third and second base. Then a whiff from our catcher, Yogi—aka Tom. The sixth guy up hits a high chopper to third; the third baseman has to charge in, and with all his weight going towards home, he decides to toss it to the catcher, who has to tag the runner. But our guy, Terrance, kicks the ball out of his glove, and it is

2-0. The next guy up whiffs, too. Inning over. That was sort of how most of the game went. We hit okay, but they played like a team that had never been varsity before.

But really, this isn't the story.

The bottom of the first is when it happens.

As we take the field and our starter, Matt, warms up, Coach gets out his sunflower seeds and starts his usual routine of putting a wad of them in his cheek. He does this to break his tobacco habit, which he kicked 20 years ago. Coach likes calling our starting pitcher, Matt, "The Big Train"—and even *I'm* not sure why. So he barks out something as Yogi tosses the ball to RC at second. RC whips it to me, me to Terrance at shortstop, and then to Sammy at third.

But instead of flipping the ball to Matt, Sammy looks at me and tips his hat. Our entire team, including the guys on the bench, then reach down to our shoes…and at the same time, we all pull the bottom of our pants up to our knees.

We are all wearing white sanitary socks and red stirrups.

Coach looks at us and spits out the entire wad of sunflower seeds.

The other team looks amazed, but their manager—who, like I said, played for our school under Coach—is just smiling ear to ear.

The parents start applauding—even the parents of the other team.

Coach just looks down and shakes his head as if to say, *Man, these kids are too much.*

But the best thing is that when we get into the dugout, we all agree to not say anything about it—just go about our business like nothing happened.

Coach just stares at us as we chirp at Matt about his two strikeouts.

Coach wears an expression that says, *So that is what you knuckleheads were up to?* But there is a noticeable lack of bite to his bark as he stuffs a new batch of seeds into his cheek, claps his hands together, and spits out, "RC, you're up. You *look* like Clemente; let's see if you can hit anything like him. Mickey, you're on deck."

RC doubles. I bunt him to third. RC scores on a routine grounder. 3-0.

And that is how it goes, inning by inning. We win 11-2. I get a single and go 1-3. RC is 2-4 and all smiles. He tells me, "Bro, it's the socks. I got the 'Clemente Magic Socks.'"

But the best smile comes from the stands, where this pretty girl and her dad are sittin' there crackin' peanuts.

Madison's Hand

April 7th—The Phone Call

The strangest thing is that with so much going on in my life—in all of our lives—it takes a great book to *make us pay attention.*

The Alchemist is a great book. I just read the part where Santiago learns about the "Soul of the World" and how we are all connected to each other. He knows he must follow his heart's true desires, and that is what his Personal Legend is all about.

I can tell you, for sure, that I feel this connection. Whether it is Jasmine or my family or my great friends or my wonderful teachers, it just seems like everyone is linked. I read where we are all within "six degrees of separation"—and maybe that's true. I can't completely explain why, but in the same way that *The Catcher in the Rye* made me feel for Holden Caulfield, Santiago makes me wonder where my path will take me and what it is I really believe in.

In *The Catcher in the Rye,* I remember how shattered Holden is when his innocent brother Allie dies of leukemia. I can't help but think about all that when I check my cell for the latest update on Jasmine. I refuse to let her escape my mind. I am on pins and needles waiting to hear how her liver transplant went. Why is it that certain people hold your heart in their hands? Why do they dominate your thoughts? What will I do if I hear that she isn't going to recover? And who am I to her, anyway? I'm just a friend. What about her family?

But I remember. Waiting with my mom, watching the news of this week's dead on TV, wondering if the uniformed officers will come to our door and say, "I am so sorry…" That fear dominated our house for years. Fear can do that. I look back down at my cell.

It is dinnertime. I am about to bite into some corn on the cob when my phone rings. I am so jumpy that the corn goes flying out of my hands as I reach for my cell. My heart is racing. I pause for a second. Look at my parents. They have that look of concern that only parents can transmit with their eyes. Neither one moves a muscle as I say, "It's Jasmine's brother, Paul."

"Hello?"

"Maddie? It's Paul. Maddie, Jasmine is awake. She has been up for several hours."

I let out a guarded sigh of relief. "How is she?"

"Well, we don't know for sure yet. She took a long time to come out of recovery, and she has been in the ICU since then. They are monitoring her vitals, and it *seems* like she is slowly regaining her senses. She smiles. And she has talked to me and our mom and dad, but her voice is so faint—like a whisper."

"Oh, my God," I say to him.

"Funny you should say that—'cause that was exactly what *she said to me.*"

I thank Paul for calling. I don't want to overstay my welcome. I put down the cell, and my mom does something she has never done before with us at the dinner table.

We all put down our forks, hold hands, bow our heads, and say a prayer.

Naturally, I start to cry.

Yeah.

Pari's Hand

May 1st

So, that was the night we all heard the news about Jasmine. Later, we met up at the Metaphor Café, toasted her, hoped she was not going to have any more complications—knowing she was still far from being out of the woods—and then moved on to baseball, AP tests, the Prom, and college pros and cons.

For me, it is a done deal. My father has already ordered a Cal hat. He's too much. When my brothers decided not to go to college, he was so disappointed. But now he is all up into Cal. He and my mom and I are heading up to "Cal Days" tomorrow. There will be tours, dorm info, speakers, and lots of other stuff. I'm excited.

Maddie is set on Sonoma State, which excels at the two majors she wants: teaching and nursing. Her problem is that she has no idea which one to pursue. I can see her as either. Both are just in her DNA. I tell her not to worry about any of that. "Just be a freshman!" I tell her. She nods. I think there has been so much in her life lately that it is just hard for her to breathe. Her dad retiring. Mickey. College. Jasmine. Mickey. Money for college. Mickey.

I know that high school sweethearts are so cliché, but with Mickey and Maddie—well, who knows?

Then there is Rhia. Now, this is my favorite part of the whole college choice thing. Here is a girl who didn't even think she had a chance of going to college. She doesn't give herself any credit. She thinks she is so ordinary, but we all know—all three of us—that she is the person who steps up and deals with the *hardest, messiest* problems. I mean, seriously. Leann. Chris. Her mom. The whole dating situation with Mr. Mac. Her ex-dad. Boyfriend issues. And the Yummy Yogurt job.

I feel so lucky that my life is protected from all that crap. Well, most of it—boyfriends are an issue I will get to next. But my point is that Rhia is a rock. And she doesn't know it. So we talked to her about college, and Mickey made a good point.

"Rhia, the whole San Francisco State scene may be perfect for you. You gotta check it out. You got some city girl attitude in you."

She smiled. Her signature look, which Mr. Buscotti used to tease her about—the Stevie Nicks gypsy look—is in full swing. The bangles. The hoop earrings. Tonight she even has a bandanna in her hair. She is adorable.

Mickey ends the coffee talk with his announcement that he is going to accept UC Davis. He's not waiting on Cal Berkeley. I am a little disappointed...more than a little. But I understand. Who wants to sit out a semester? And what if nothing happens? And besides, *Davis suits him,* he says.

I ask how his dad took the news.

"Well, he is doing okay with it. I mean, he knows he will be saving a boat-load of friggin' money compared to USC, but he is bummed 'cause he was hoping that the whole big-school-football-scene-in-LA thing would happen. I think the business major stuff is still what he sees me doing, but he also thinks that maybe I will get more attention at a smaller school. He also talked to Coach about the baseball connection with the UC Davis coaches. I dunno. But he's pretty cool with things. I think my mom has really helped 'cause I think she likes Davis a lot. She has a sister in Sacramento—my Aunt Laura—and she wants to visit her—and me—more often."

I guess talking about college always means talking about parents, too. Maybe that is the way it should be. At least we all have parents who care. What about all our friends who are just *out there* after graduation—just floating around, trying to get a job or a car or an apartment? We all know lots of kids who are so frustrated with the way things turned out. We have so much to be grateful for.

So maybe the Personal Legend we are searching for is simply the fact that we have been given the good fortune of having the opportunity to *look and seek*. Maybe the fact that we *can* choose our path is the real hidden treasure that Santiago seeks in *The Alchemist*.

Knowledge is power, as the saying goes.

Then there is me and Daniel. It was two weeks ago…

April 14th—The Pizza *Monsieur*

I have been studying almost 24-7 for an entire month. I have ignored Daniel most of that time. We even had a "fight" about sex and how uptight American girls like me are. The funny thing is that to him, I'm an *American* girl, but in my own mind, I've always been a *Persian* girl—in an American world.

Okay, I will also admit that I am a little uptight. But in my culture, to do some of the things I have done (like bend the truth about when I see Daniel and with whom) makes me a bit of a rebel.

So anyway, it is around dinnertime the day before the AP test for my Government class, and I am cramming my brain with everything that Mr. Mac has tried to shove into it, when the doorbell rings, and yep, there he is—pizza in hand.

"Bonjour!" he announces to all.

My parents think he's cute, and he is. I'm flattered that he likes me. He's very charming.

So much for studying.

We put some pizza on plates and eat in the kitchen. My folks decide to "give us some privacy." But, like, what are we gonna do with Katie Couric in the background, reporting on the latest car bombing in the Middle East?

"So, are you ready for the AP Gov exam?" Daniel asks.

"I'm never ready."

"Well, do you think all this cramming helps?"

Why is it that whenever I eat pizza, a long string of cheese always forms a bridge between the bite I have taken and the origin of the slice I have pulled it from? After I indelicately break the strand of cheese and stuff it in my mouth, I smile at him and say, "Look, you are probably right. But I would feel so guilty if I didn't study. It is an obsession with me. Aren't you still looking over the study guide Mac handed out?"

"No. I did for a while. I read it over. Let's face it, Pari—I'm French. I will never really understand American laws all that well. In France, *tout est beaucoup plus simple.*" I get his drift.

"Yeah, but aren't you thinking of dual citizenship?" I ask with purpose that I hope is not blatantly obvious. But I guess it is.

"No, Pari. I love the States. I do. But America is not my home. I will always like to travel here on holiday, but I miss my country, my family. It is just another world in France. Everything moves at a different pace there. The people *live life*—everything isn't so rushed. Just look at how you Americans eat—we take our time and enjoy each other's company. Things are old there, but more alive." He stops. He does not want to deliberately insult me and my country. Then he adds, "You must understand. You were in Iran this summer. You told me how much you loved it there, too. It's hard to leave, you know?"

I do know.

I also know how much I am going to miss him. He is my first real boyfriend. In many ways, he is so much more mature than I am—wiser, I guess. I know that the light is fading for us, and I don't want it to turn off so soon.

"Daniel, let's go to the Prom and promise not to talk about when you leave, okay? Let's just enjoy the time we have. Let me keep messing up French and keep being patient with me... *d'accord?*"

"*Tu es très belle,*" Daniel says, taking my hand.

Only the French can make you swoon while eating pizza in your parents' kitchen.

Mickey's Hand

April 23rd—"Baseball was my whole life. Nothing's ever been as fun as baseball."
—Mickey Mantle

That's the *Mickey* I was named after. *The Mick,* my dad calls him. I never came close to seeing him, except on ESPN Classic. Here is one big difference between us: Mantle could hit great from either side of the plate. I can't hit the plate. At least not today.

Background. I won my first start of the season at home. It was really cool. I went 5 innings, and the final score was 6-3. But baseball is humbling. We lost the next 2, won the first 2 in a tournament, and then got eliminated. So we were 4-3 going into this week. We won a nail-biter 2 days ago, when the other team came back from 5 runs in the last inning, but thank God our centerfielder, Jeremy, hit his first ever homer in extra innings to win it. Coach was not too happy with all the errors, walks, and, in his words, "bonehead plays." Coach says that "winning ain't always about the scoreboard, boys; it's about the way the game is played."

I guess he is right because today I just sucked. I walked 6 guys. *Six!* Yeah, we won, but despite me, not because of me.

"Mickey," Coach said to me in a post-game talk, "you see that plate over there? It is 17 inches wide. A baseball is 2.8 inches in diameter. Son, you can fit about 6 of them balls over that plate. Now, do you know what Ted Williams once said?" (He knew I knew who the heck Ted Williams was.) "Ted said, 'The hardest thing to do in baseball is to hit a round baseball with a round bat, squarely.' Now, look, Mickey. None of those guys in that other dugout are Ted Williams. Most of 'em can't hit a lick. They hate lefthanders like you. But you let 'em off the hook. Why? 'Cause you're afraid to challenge 'em. You nibble around and forget that you got 8 guys behind you. And look, if they hit you, make sure that you gave them your best pitch, and then tip your hat."

Then he added with a nasty wink, "And the next time they come up, remind them who owns that plate, Son." That was something I knew, but it was something I needed to hear.

Fear. Man, it can mess up your head.

I picked up a baseball and grabbed our back-up catcher, Brad, and said, "Come on. I gotta work something out, dude."

I threw hard. I was mad. I needed to stay that way. It didn't matter a damn that we had won that game. I knew we would lose if I didn't learn my lesson.

Madison's Hand

April 30th—UCLA Medical Center

Road trip with Dad. Last week, I finally got a chance to actually talk to Jasmine on the phone. She sounded weak but very happy. She made me promise to visit her. I asked if she was sure, and she told me that her parents insisted. I told her that my dad and I would visit when she felt well enough.

Today she felt well enough.

On the way up, my dad and I talked about college, about the fact that the beaches were totally clouded over during this Spring Break, about what I wanted for graduation (which freaked me out because it was the first time I had even thought about all that stuff), and about Mickey.

He knows how I feel about him. He knows we will be at schools somewhat close to one another. But he also knows that college is a new phase of my life—and Mickey's.

"You are gonna meet a lot of kids from up north, you know."

"Yeah, I know."

"You know UC Davis is pretty far away from Sonoma State."

"Dad, I get what you are trying to say. Mickey and I will deal with it, okay?"

"I know you will, Maddie." He snapped his head around, and you could hear all the crackling in his neck. He carries a lot of tension in his neck, and my mom is constantly giving him massages. I wished I wasn't the one causing *more* tension. He switched lanes and admitted, "I hate talking about this stuff."

"I know, Dad. Just leave it." I sounded like I was mad at him. I was. And I was mad at myself, too.

So we drove in silence for a while. To his credit, he didn't bring up anything about Mickey again. But I did.

"Dad, I just want to enjoy the last month of school—and the summer. I just want to chill. I know all the things you and mom are worried about—like how I am going to be all heartbroken when Mickey and I split up and how I am going to be totally homesick at college…"

"Yes, those are two things that have crossed our minds…" My dad snuck into the conversation as he clicked off the radio.

"…and how I will probably be a mess. But you told me once that life's messy, and you have to buck up. Well, I've been bucking up for 18 years now, and I just gotta do this. I'm tougher than you think, Dad."

He looked at the road while I was pouring out my soul to him. He only glanced at me when he said the words that ended our conversation:

"No, honey, I think you are *a lot* tougher."

My dad is in his element at the hospital. He guides us like radar to Jasmine's room. Outside her room, Paul is discussing something with the RN. My dad stops and introduces us to the nurse. Paul hugs me and tells me that he is so happy to see us. Before I go in to see Jasmine, Paul warns me that she is hooked up to "all this medical equipment" and that she looks worse than she feels. He tells me that she will put on a happy face but that she gets really tired really fast.

"Of course. I understand," I tell him. Meanwhile, my dad starts nosing around, talking to the medical personnel about Jasmine's condition. Naturally, he sees people he knows from who knows where. So I go into her room.

She is asleep. I hear the pinging of monitors. Her mother sits quietly reading next to her. As soon as I come in, she rises and whispers in the most jubilant way possible, "Hello, sweetheart!" She grabs my hand, but then realizes that a handshake is inadequate. She pulls me towards her and hugs me.

She says, "Jasmine knows you're coming. She tried to stay awake. But she can't keep her eyes open. Let's let her rest for a while, and then we will wake her."

I insist that she sleep as long as she needs—I'm in no hurry. "My dad is here with me. He is getting some coffee. You know doctors, Mrs. De Andres; they can't exist without coffee." She nods knowingly. Before I can say anything else, Jasmine's mom guides me to a chair and tells me the story of the last few days.

"Maddie, we are so lucky. God has given Jasmine a gift. But it is also so sad." There is an ever-present tissue rolled up in her fist, and she uses it to dab her eyes. "Jasmine was dying, Maddie. Her vitals were down, but—you know Jasmine—her spirits were up. The doctors warned us that something had to happen soon. They were hopeful, but they were also very concerned.

"Then all of a sudden, everything just happened. Around midnight, there was a terrible traffic accident. A high school girl was killed only a few miles from the hospital. Preparations were made. And the Good Lord saw fit to give a part of a young girl's life to help Jasmine's life continue. It was terrible and wonderful all at once. I cannot imagine the mother of the girl who was killed, and she probably cannot imagine my joy when I saw Jasmine's eyes open after surgery."

Her eyes are red. I pull out tissues from my purse and replace her old balled-up ones. I look at Jasmine sleeping so peacefully there—even with tubes and wires all surrounding her. She looks like a doll—one of those dolls whose eyes close when you lay her down and open when you sit her up.

Mrs. De Andres regroups. "Maddie, all of you kids at school—and the teachers—have been so wonderful. So wonderful. Mickey and his articles in the school newspaper. All the prayers…"

I make a rare interruption. "Mrs. De Andres, Jasmine is so special. She just bursts into a room and lights it up. There's a spirit about her. I can't explain it, but it is why so many people love her."

"I know, Maddie. She has been like that from the moment she was born. It is almost as if God didn't give her a liver that would work, but He made up for it in other ways."

"She's all about soul," I say, just as my dad quietly walks in.

Again, whispered introductions are made. Paul and Jasmine's father are there, too. They tell me that her cousins and extended family will be there tomorrow. They are trying to slowly reintroduce Jasmine to everyone who wants to see her. I feel so honored to be there now. Just then, the nurse comes in to check on Jasmine, and as if on cue, Jasmine's eyes flutter. She turns her head to us and focuses for a second. Then she says in that adorable, high-pitched voice I have come to love, "Hey, Maddie."

I don't even notice how all the adults slowly disappear from the room as the nurse finishes up.

"Maddie, I must look like a wreck with all these wires and gismos and weirdo machines hooked up to me."

"You look fantastic, cutie," I tell her.

"Where is that handsome boyfriend of yours?"

"He wanted to come, but he had a baseball game today. He told me to kiss you for him."

"Well, how about that! I get a kiss from a star pitcher."

"Well, I don't know if he's a *star* pitcher… Rhia and Pari send their love, too."

"I bet Mr. B misses me, too."

"He can hardly teach without you. The class gave me this card for you. They all signed it, including Mr. B. Everyone is so happy for you."

"Oh, this is so cool! Oh, look! They drew a picture of me. You know that guy Andre in my class—the one who sits two seats behind me?"

"Yeah."

"Well, one of my girlfriends says that he has a crush on little ol' me."

"Really?! He's kinda cute, Jas!"

"Kinda? He's *super* cute! But think about it, Maddie. I can't marry a guy named *Andre*."

"Huh? Why not?"

"Can you even imagine me being known as *Mrs. Andre De Andres?* That is, like, *so* wacko." Then comes that Jasmine giggle.

"Jasmine, you wouldn't be known as that. You're such a silly girl."

A pause.

I ask, "How do you feel?"

"Well, I feel good, but I keep falling asleep. Sometimes I am just talking to my mom or dad, and the next thing I know, it is, like, hours later. It is so weird. But so far, the doctors say that my body has shown no signs of rejecting the liver—and that is the most important thing."

"How long will you be here? Do you have any idea?"

"Nope. But I'm gonna get moved to a regular room maybe in a week. Can you help me sit up a little, Maddie?"

As I fluff up her pillows, I think about what it would be like to be a nurse and help people like Jasmine. Am I cut out for that? I don't know. Really. I only know one thing—that as I reposition her, I can't help but feel the warmth and love that the human touch creates.

We talk some more. Her folks come in. Jasmine insists on kissing my dad. She tells him that she wants to be like me when she grows up.

I blush.

Then like a fog, sleep just seems to envelop her (Mickey's word), and we watch as she slips down into the pillows. We know that we must go. I kiss her cheek. I touch her hand. She squeezes my fingers. She lets go.

As my father and I drive home on the crowded freeway, my worries seem to melt away. I don't know exactly where I am destined to go, but the ride is an adventure, and I look forward to meeting all the people who I will be fortunate enough to meet along the road. All of us make up the "Soul of the World."

Chapter 20: "Glory Days"

Mickey's Hand

May 6th—Field of Dreams

You know, of course, that there is no *I* in the word *team*. So I don't want to bore you with a lot of play-by-play details of the season. But today was a special day for me.

We have been winning a couple and then losing one pretty regularly, so we're in second place in the league and in a good position for the playoffs later this month. I've been throwing better and even hitting better, too.

I started today. We were facing a pretty good team. Lots of lefty hitters, but that was to my advantage.

First inning: three up, three down.

Second inning: three up, three down.

Third inning: error, walk, double play. No hits, no runs.

There is a tradition in baseball that says you don't talk to the starting pitcher if he is tossing a no hitter. Coach is big on traditions, as you know. He gives the entire bench the evil eye. We also haven't scored. Pitchers' duel, as they say.

Fourth inning: Terrance makes a great catch of a blooper over his head at short. Long fly to Andre in center. No hits, no runs—not a word said on the bench. We score three runs on a three-run homer by Matt, who plays first when I am pitching. Now we *all* call him "The Big Train," and he comes into the station in a big way. (One should note that our games only go seven innings—and it gets dark, too.)

Fifth inning: RC grabs a liner. Foul pop-up to Yogi. Walk. Walk. Coach comes out to talk to me. "Remember our discussion, Son?" I nod. "You tired?" I tell him no way. "Is he tired?" Coach asks Yogi, who also says no. "Okay, then this guy can't touch you if you keep it down. Let's go with fastballs low and then finish him with the curve. Jump ahead. I know the kid will be takin' strike one." As he walks away, Coach looks back at me and says, "Hey, how many inches?" I tell him 17. He says, "Yep, that right. It's also your number."

First pitch: He takes strike one.

Second pitch: Low fastball. Ball one.

Third Pitch: Foul ball. He is late on the swing.

Before I throw the fourth pitch, I notice that everything has suddenly slowed down. I know people are yelling, but I just don't hear anything but muffled signs. The next pitch is supposed to be a curve low and away. I shake off Yogi. He stands up and walks out to me.

"Coach wants the curve. You got this guy," Yogi says.

"He's looking outside. He wants to slap it to left field. Let's straighten him up with a fastball high and tight. Then the curve," I tell him.

Yogi looks nervous. "Okay, but don't hit the dude." He glances at the dugout, but I stay focused on home plate.

Fourth pitch: Up and in—high heat. The guy falls back, loses his balance, and gets dusted. He looks pissed. I think, *Good. I want you pissed. I need you to swing.*

Fifth pitch: I start the curve inside at his head. He hesitates and starts to bail. In the next instant, he realizes that it isn't a fastball—it's a curve, and it is breaking over the plate. Too late for him to do anything but try to foul it off. He ticks the ball. Yogi hangs on to the tip.

Fifth inning over. No hits, no runs.

Coach won't break tradition, even though he probably wants to chew me out for not doing exactly what he said. I wasn't being cocky—I just had a feeling, you know? I am also on a pitch count—I know I am over 80—and I never go much past that. But that is another thing Coach isn't talking to me about. He calls Yogi over and talks to him. Yogi doesn't react much. Just nods his head. Then Coach says loud and clear to the bench, "Boys, can we get some runs this inning so we can enjoy this game, huh?" More than a few smiles break out. No one even looks at me.

Bottom of the fifth: We single. Steal. Sacrifice. Get hit by a pitch. We have runners on first and third. Then RC hits what looks like it might be an inning-ending double play. But he busts it out of the box, his head down, and I have never seen any player on our team go harder up the line to first than "Clemente" did just then. He's...safe! He jumps up in the air like he just won the World Series or something. Run scores. 4-0.

I come to the plate. RC gets the sign for a hit and run. I'm left-handed, so the shortstop is covering second. I try to hit the hole with a sharp grounder, but I hit it too hard and too high. RC slows at second base to get back when the left fielder catches it. I round first and watch.

Then I realize...it went *over the fence*... it's gone! I hit my first ever high school homer...and I was just trying to hit a single! Crazy game. RC jumps up and claps his hands. I try to round the bases like it is no big deal. I touch the plate, and RC bounces on me. 6-0. We head to the dugout, and finally, everybody talks to me. Lots of high fives and stuff. And then suddenly, I sit down and realize that everyone has moved away from me...again. Tradition.

Funny thing about baseball is that it doesn't really attract big crowds. Today the word spread as the game continued. I knew that Maddie and my folks were going nuts when I hit the homer, but once I got back on the mound for the sixth inning, it all got quiet again. And the crowd swelled.

Sixth inning: Hot shot to third. One out. Liner to left…coming in…coming in…snags it and slides on his belly. Clearly ESPN Top Ten material. I look at Rob in left and realize that it isn't Rob. Coach had replaced him with one of our best defensive guys, a sophomore named Juan. He gives me a look like, *No big deal, Mickey. Had it all the way.* Two out. Next guy up—pop-up to first. Matt has it. No hits, no runs.

I can tell that everyone wants to get to the seventh inning—myself included. By now, there are more people in the stands than I can ever remember. I just try to calm myself down and remember, *17 inches. Eight guys behind you. Trust your stuff.*

Last inning: Heart of their order. I know I have thrown close to 100 pitches—or maybe even more. Coach is warming up Chris, our other lefty. But I don't look anywhere but at Yogi. First guy up, and I am three balls and no strikes. I don't want to groove one, but I don't want to walk him either. I know Coach is worried that I am way over my limit with pitches, but he is not gonna take me out…yet. Let's go fastball, up and in. He hits a towering shot down the left field. Juan keeps drifting…drifting…but he pulls it foul. It would've been gone.

No problem. Strike one.

I decide to throw a change. Up and in again. This time he rips it *way* foul. Next pitch, a curve. He swings and tops it back to me. I bobble it. Fire my best fastball to Matt at first. One out. I can hear the cheers and then the quiet. Next guy up. I hit him in the back with a curve that breaks way too much—and he doesn't even try to move much, either. Oh, well. It only took one pitch. Next guy up is their usual starter—a huge guy. Bigger than anyone on our team. He has hit every ball I have pitched him earlier in the game—hard. I decide to go with low fastballs. Coach chooses not to hold the guy on first—he is playing back to cut off a single. Smart. First pitch. Guy takes off for second. Lined to Terrance at short. Fires to Matt at first. Double play.

Game over.

I turn to Yogi, who comes running out to me, and before I know it, we are all in a dog pile on the mound. It takes a while to calm down and shake hands with the other team. Then we all run to the dugout. Lots of parents and friends had come inside the gate, and we all hug. My dad bear hugs me so hard that I think he is gonna hurt his back. I hug my mom…then Maddie…then Rhia (who had rushed over from work wearing her silly Yummy Yogurt uniform)…then Pari. *Whew!* It's wild.

About then, I realized that there was one person I hadn't said anything to—Coach. I looked around. He was sitting in the dugout, believe it or not, on his *cell phone!* (Until then, I didn't think he even knew that cell phones existed.) I went over to him. He stood up and shook my hand.

I said, "Well, Coach, I guess I finally earned my pay today."

"Yes, you did, Mickey. I don't say this more than once a decade, but I will say it now. That was some of the gutsiest pitching I've ever seen from one of my kids."

I didn't know how to react. It was the way he said it—like he felt I had done something that he had never seen before—and he's seen so much. I was speechless.

It was then that I realized how I got paid.

Coach paid me with the highest compliment he knew.

Pari's Hand

May 9th—The Prom: Second Time Around

Some things are timeless. The ritual of asking. The thrill of being courted. The fun of shopping for a dress. The chatter about who is part of which group. The hair. The corsage. The tux. The pictures with the parents. The romantic (but still affordable!) restaurant. The holding of hands. The girls all running off to the restroom together for a final touch-up. The hotel. The ballroom. The music. The dancing. The songs.

LMFAO –"Party Rock Anthem"

We The Kings – "Check Yes Juliet"

Chris Brown – "With You"

Lady Gaga –"Just Dance"

The Veronicas – "Untouched"

Boys Like Girls – "(Bring on the) Thunder"

Akon – "(You're So) Beautiful"

The Plain White T's – "1,2,3,4 (I Love You)"

Oasis –"Wonderwall"

Taylor Swift – "Love Story"

Lifehouse – "You and Me"

Adele – "Make Me Feel My Love"

In between the songs, other rituals play out. Seeing the teachers and showing off (a bit). Having Ms. LaFleur compliment us on our dresses. Noticing (again) that the mysterious Mr. Buscotti is not there. (Rhia explained that he and his wife went on a double date with Mr. MacQueen and her mother.) Realizing that the punch is never really spiked, despite all the rumors. All the talk of after parties.

This year, Mickey's folks hosted a sleepover/after party event. The people in our limo and some of our other friends stayed overnight at his house—it was fun. We changed clothes. Laughed. Slept in different parts of the house. ("Guys here, girls there"—yeah, whatever.) Talked. Played games. Flirted. Woke up.

It was all so much fun just being with everyone. We danced in Mickey's living room, and Mick insisted that we listen to at least one Bruce Springsteen song. So we all got up and turned out the lights and found ourselves "Dancing in the Dark." That was fun, too.

But there were three moments from the Prom itself that stood out to me.

Rhia's face tucked under Roberto's chin as they danced to "1,2,3,4 (I Love You)"—two souls needing company and finding out that being worlds apart at the start of a year makes no difference when it all comes down to the end of a year.

Mickey and Maddie. Inseparable. Laughing. Filled with spirit and drive and confidence as they swept each other away to Taylor Swift's "Love Story."

And Daniel and I. Knowing that this will be one of the last times that we will be this close—for the oceans will divide us, as will the old European world and the urban beat of Berkeley. As I held him on the ballroom dance floor during a slow song, I remembered Mr. Buscotti's fox trot dance lessons from last year, when he cautioned all the girls: "Float, girls—soft in his arms." I felt the power of Adele's "Make You Feel My Love" run through the both of us. I looked up to him— Daniel, so quiet, so understated—and I whispered:

"What would my senior year have been like if I didn't have you?"

He smiled and said, "Maybe someday we'll have Paris."

I closed my eyes and swayed to the music; the warm rocking of our bodies gave off a heat that melted us together. He kissed my neck and then my lips and murmured, *"Tu vas me manqué."*

He will miss me. But he has no idea how much I will miss him.

I looked up into his eyes and asked, "I wonder if I will ever find someone like you?" Then I whispered to myself...*don't forget me.*

Oh, how bittersweet.

Rhiannon's Hand

May 14th—Chris's Orders

He is being deployed on June 1—just ten days before my graduation. It sucks on so many levels. But he is eager to go and "be a warrior." I'm petrified for him. I admire him. I'm learning firsthand what Maddie's life has been like all these years. There is a knot in my stomach when I think about June 1st. So I am gonna do two things: I'm gonna appreciate every day I have with him and do something nice and kind for the sweetest brother ever. And I'm not gonna write another word about it 'cause I will start balling my eyes out...like I am starting to right now.

Shit.

(Ten minutes later.) Okay. I can't end with that word. So I will tell you that he is first going to Virginia for some kinda training, and then in a couple of weeks, he is off. Probably to Afghanistan. He says it is gonna be hotter than hell there—but not to worry 'cause when it is so damn hot, nobody wants to do anything bad and people just try to survive the heat. So I guess that is a good thing.

He says he will be deployed for seven months. So the good news is that he will be back before Christmas. (Probably. "You never know for sure with the military," Chris tells me.) The bad thing is that he will miss my graduation, and then I won't even see him when I move to San Francisco for college. I'm scared enough, and missing my big brother is just another thing I have to deal with.

I've been going to church more. I know I will say a prayer for him every day.

He tells me that he will do the same for me.

God, I love him.

Please, please, please don't take him...please.

Madison's Hand

May 20th—Jasmine's Video

My dad is my hero for so many reasons. But yesterday, it was because he was up at the UCLA Medical Center visiting Jasmine. He made a video of her talking to all of us about how she is doing. Mr. B showed it to his first period class; then the whole school saw it during homeroom later in the day.

While watching the video, I noticed something in Mr. B's face that I had not seen since the last day of school last year, when we had given him a gift, the old sign from the Metaphor Café. Muscles in his face twitched involuntarily. He covered his mouth with his hand. His ever-present baseball cap was pulled down low so that the kids could not see him struggling against the surge of emotion. He was so choked up that he didn't speak for a while.

I was a mess before it even started, so I was no help.

Here is what Jasmine said:

"Thank you, everyone. I am so lucky. God has blessed me with something so precious—and I will be forever grateful." (Then she looked above the camera—presumably at my dad—and said, "Am I doing okay with this video thing?" Then she giggled. At that point, all of Mr. B's class started to laugh because it was so Jasmine. A man's voice could be heard saying, "You're doing great. Keep going.")

"Okay. Well, hi everyone! I love you all. So, I got this liver transplant. You don't wanna know all the yucky stuff—and trust me, it is very yucky—but I feel great. I know I don't look so hot; I must look like a weirdo with this hospital stuff all around me, and I know my hair is a total mess. But I feel so much better, and the doctors think I will be shipped out to another hospital closer to home pretty soon. And that will be nice 'cause then I will be able to see some of you guys.

"I want to say that I love you all and that everyone—all my friends and teachers and doctors—have been so great to me. I'm just so overwhelmed with everyone's love and support. I will hopefully be back in school next semester, but when I get home, please come and visit. I love all you guys in Mr. B's first period class. (The class erupts in cheers, but tissues are coming out of purses, and even some of the guys are wiping their eyes on their sleeves.) And Mr. B, I want you to know that I read almost all of the *Mockingbird* book—and what I couldn't read, Maddie read to me. Oh, I love you, Maddie! And Mr. B, I loved that book so much. I miss you. Can I take your class again? (The class cracks up again—but the lump in my throat grows bigger.) And I appreciate all those newspaper articles that Mickey Sullivan wrote about me. I love you too, Mickey.

"Anyway, have a great summer, everyone! I hope to see you soon.

"God Bless... Bye for now."

Jasmine ended up being Mr. Buscotti's lesson plan that day. There was no way he could teach anything else.

Mickey's Hand

May 30th—The Playoffs

The Clemente Magic Socks have taken us to the semifinals again. I was the starting pitcher in the quarterfinal game. I threw pretty well, we hit up a storm, and we played awesome in the field—so we found ourselves facing the top seed today. Coach told me I was not pitching under any circumstances; he said I had thrown a lot lately and he needed me for the finals…if we got there.

Matt, aka "The Big Train," was our starter, and despite his best effort, we were down 4-0 after the first inning.

Yeah, I know. Bad sign.

But there is something to those magic socks 'cause we fought back, got a break on a throwing error, and found ourselves down 5-3 in the fifth inning.

We were the road team, and by the time the sixth inning started, a lot of our fans (and parents) had gotten off work; it was the biggest crowd of the year. I got a kick out of watching the girls: Maddie, Rhia, and Pari with their pom-poms. Every time Roberto got up, Rhia waved around a small Puerto Rican flag and yelled, "Go Clemente!"

I swear, Rhia thinks baseball is the most boring sport ever—except when *her guy* is playing.

So in the sixth, our catcher, Yogi (aka Tom), hits a solo homer. He really is a good player—maybe our best all-around. So the score is 5-4. We hold them in the bottom of the sixth.

Last inning. I gotta admit, it's white knuckle time. We need a run to tie, or the season is over. They have this guy who is their best pitcher coming in—sort of a closer, I guess. They are probably gonna use him for just this inning because I'm sure he is gonna start in the finals if they win. And he is a lefty.

The good news is that I ain't coming up this inning. Whew.

The bad news is that this guy is nasty, but he is wild. He hits Terrance with a 2-2 pitch. Man, I can tell Terrance is hurt—and pissed. Coach has already told him not to steal 'cause the guy has a good move to first. That was obvious when he almost picked Terrance off when he was only a few feet from the bag. But Terrance is kinda angry, and he and the pitcher are giving each other a look that says, *This ain't over yet.*

Andre bunts Terrance to second. One out. Sammy hits a ball off the plate that bounces up high—so high that the pitcher decides to bare hand it as it is coming down.

Really dumb.

He bobbles and then short-hops the first baseman, who can't scoop it out cleanly. Sammy is safe. We've got runners on first and third. One out. We need a sacrifice fly or a slow roller to tie the game.

They decide to play in on the corners and back for the double play. The outfield comes in a few steps, but they know they can't let anything go over their heads or in the gap. On the other hand, they need to be close enough to throw Terrance out at the plate—and Terrance is a madman on the bases. He's even angrier than usual; his back (where the fastball plunked him) must be reminding him of how much he wants to score on this jerk.

Matt, the pitcher, is up with a chance, as they say to redeem himself. He fouls one off. He misses the next. Fouls off another. Takes a ball way outside.

Then he is late on a fastball, but manages to hit it in the air to shallow right field. But the ball is slicing into foul ground. The second baseman is chasing it; so is the first baseman. The right fielder is coming in...he crosses the line and, moving to his right, he backhands it.

As fate would have it, the right fielder is left handed, so he has to try to stop and throw across his body. I'm thinking the whole time, *Why didn't someone tell him to let it drop? It's gonna be a tough throw to home to get Terrance.*

Then I realize why.

The guy has a cannon for an arm.

Terrance is coming home, and the ball, the catcher, and Terrance are all on a collision course. Everyone is up on their feet. I'm not on my feet—since I'm jumping two feet in the air.

Terrance goes in head first because the catcher is blocking the plate. The ball barely beats him, and the catcher has it. Terrance hits him, and everything goes flying: catcher's mask, batting helmet, dust...

...and the ball.

He is safe.

Oh, my God.

It's 5-5.

And that is how we go to extra innings.

Bottom of the ninth. This will be the last inning because it is getting dark and we have no lights. If we hold them, the game will continue tomorrow.

If...

They have a runner on second. Two outs. I'm playing first. Roberto is next to me at second base. We play back, trying to make sure nothing goes through the infield. If it does, there is no tomorrow. Their runner on second is the lead-off guy, and he's fast—very fast.

When I see the ball come off the bat, I think it is at me. Then I realize it is moving too fast and is too wide right of me. At the instant that I dive for the ball coming off its second hop, my peripheral vision spots Roberto, who is full out diving, too. He must have it, I think. I hope our pitcher's covering first. Even if he isn't, we just gotta knock it down. It can't get through. We come up with the same thing...

Dirt.

Our right fielder, Matt, charges, but with two outs, it is pointless. He grabs, fires, and one hops Yogi. But when Yogi catches it, their guy has already slid past him and is leaping into the arms of the team that is going to the finals.

And I'm on my knees, staring at my empty glove filled with dirt.

Roberto slams his glove into the outfield grass.

Baseball can be as glorious as it is brutal.

Our "glory days" are over. The Clemente Magic Socks took us far—farther than anyone expected.

Except for me.

We shook hands with the other team. I admit they were a classy bunch—except their jerk lefty, who I thought Terrance was gonna punch out. Their manager surprised me when he came up to me and said, "Mickey, I voted for you 'First Team' for the Section. You're the craftiest southpaw I have seen this year." I was flattered, but too deflated to really appreciate it then. (Later, I came to realize that he voted me the left-handed pitcher over his own left-hander. He probably knew that guy was a jerk, too.)

Coach gave us another great talk. He was all rumpled and tired looking, but he said, "Guys, you know there is no cryin' in baseball, but it is a cryin' shame you had to lose that game. Neither team deserved to lose. But that's baseball.

"We're going to dinner together—like last year—over to In-N-Out. Parents' treat—thank you, parents," Coach said. This time, there were no cheers. We smiled a little. But when you get this close, and it is a heartbreaker like this, you kinda lose your appetite. Leave it to Coach to know how to pull us together.

"I gotta tell you guys two things that I hope will make you all feel better. 'Cause I know it hurts. It's supposed to hurt. If it didn't, we would never have pushed ourselves to get this far. You ain't the most talented bunch I've ever managed. Matter of fact, you guys play way over your heads—why? 'Cause you got each other's back. It shows. Nobody is more important than the next guy, and it took all of you to get us here.

"So here's the deal. There were some college coaches in the stands today, and I know you five seniors were part of who they came to see. I had contacted a few of 'em. One of them is a little disappointed I didn't pitch Mickey. But that's okay. He knew why. And you guys know why I made Mickey the captain—him and those crazy socks." Coach paused for a second. "You guys made my year. Really, you did. I felt like I was watching a ball game from when I was a kid. It was great. It took me back a few decades." He kinda laughed at that.

"One more thing. So, I went into the attic of my house the other day, looking for something. You know this kid here—RC—came to us from Puerto Rico." Coach tipped his hat at Roberto, who would have done the same, but his hat was on backwards (a fashion statement that Coach hates, by the way.) "And I just thought he was a gift to this team. And gifts need to be repaid. So I dug around and found what I was looking for. Roberto, I don't know if you have ever owned one of these, but this is a 1966 Topps Roberto Clemente baseball card. Yeah, it's worth something, I bet. But so are you, Son."

"Coach—whoa—that's the year he was the National League MVP." Roberto obviously knew *everything* Clemente.

"Yep. It is." Coach isn't one to get all slobbery on us, so he says, "Shoot. I am hungry, and there are some folks waiting to talk to you— coaches, family, and a few pretty girls, I think." Coach smiled wide. I can't explain it, but his smile was like the Magic Socks—it just slid some of the disappointment right off my shoulders.

I looked up and caught my dad's eye. We might disagree on a lot of things; however, there is one thing we both know: *God, we love baseball.* I am sure glad he taught me how to play the game.

As I sat in the booth eating my Double-Double with Maddie, RC, Rhia, and Pari, I was thinking, *It just doesn't get much better than this.*

And Roberto couldn't stop staring at Clemente, photographed in his prime on a baseball card.

Chapter 21: "Pomp and Circumstance"

Mickey's Hand

June 1st—The Announcement at the Metaphor Café

How do we begin the last chapter of a journey that started two years ago in Mr. Buscotti's class and will end right where it began? In that little corner table of the Metaphor Café, of course.

However, today there sits a fifth chair, and it belongs to Mr. Buscotti himself. He has asked us to meet with him here because he wants to answer our request to have him edit this book, as his teaching partner Ms. Anderson did with our first book, *Meetings at the Metaphor Café*.

But that was all a ruse, as Mr. B would say.

We sat huddled together with Pari peppering Mr. B with her ideas for the speech she will be delivering at our graduation at the end of next week. Pari was so excited that she was chosen to speak. Unlike most schools, our school has an audition for the speaker rather than just having the valedictorian speak. None of us were surprised when Pari was selected; the shocker was that she tried out in the first place. Oh, whatever happened to that shy, demure girl? I guess she has come out of her shell, huh?

Anyway, after jotting down some words of wisdom from Mr. B, Pari seemed satisfied and then officially asked him if he would be our editor. "The manuscript is almost done, except for the last chapter," she added.

"Ah," Mr. Buscotti nodded, slowly sipping his black coffee. He looked particularly casual in his jeans, turtleneck, and baseball cap.

"Well, I would be honored to be your editor; however, that is not what I came here to tell you."

Silence. Everyone froze.

"I am retiring on the day you graduate. I started teaching at our school in 1977. It has been quite a run, but it is time for me to move on—just like all of you."

Our jaws just dropped. None of us knew what to say. We were all just shocked.

It took hours for me to formulate what I am about to write.

Mr. B was still in his prime. He had given no hint of tiring. Sure, he looked exhausted at the end of the day, when we would visit his classroom—but all teachers look like that. Perhaps that happy face was just part of the show he did five times a day?

No. He really was filled with joy. That was no act. He loved what he did. He loved kids. He loved what he taught and how it affected us—and we loved him. So all we could ask was *"Why?"*

"Well, gang, have you ever seen the movie *The Godfather?* 'They made me an offer I couldn't refuse.' The district calls it a 'Golden Handshake'—a pretty nice offer to retire. The school can hire a couple of younger teachers with what they are paying me."

Rhia frowned. "Yeah, but do you wanna retire?"

He paused. "Rhia, there are a lot of things I want to do. You guys don't know this, but I started this teaching gig at 22. I had friends who could not figure out what they wanted to do. Not me. I didn't know how to be a teacher, but I knew that this was what I wanted to do—at least for a while. Well, 'a while' turned into 33 years…and it has gone by faster than I ever thought it could.

"So now I want to travel. I want to read. I want to bike and hike and enjoy the fresh air—not the stale air and florescent lights of a classroom with too few windows and way too many kids packed in. I realized a few years ago that no matter how often I 'reinvented' myself—teaching new classes or new stories or even new songs—I needed a change. And right now, I'm awfully tired."

We sat in front of him, mesmerized. No one sipped their coffee. No one said a word. We let his soliloquy roll on.

"So I want to leave while I still love it. I've seen too many bitter teachers push themselves and get angry with the system, the kids, the work—everything. I just can't go there. Too dark for me. Too far from my North Star."

We smiled. The North Star. How many times had he referred to that guidepost last year when he taught us that "you don't know where you're going unless you know where you've been?" How many times had we walked under the banner that read, "Your I WILL is more important than your IQ?" How many "sermons" had he delivered to us on Holden Caulfield, Huck Finn, Emily Webb, Jay Gatsby, and a cast of characters that had helped us understand what our hopes and dreams might be and when to look up to the "silver pepper" of the night stars, which would guide us when we would navigate the dark waters of the "Big Muddy?" How many times would Springsteen's guitar resonate with us, and how many times would Mr. B surprise us with a revelation about the music of our generation?

Maddie broke our silence. "But wouldn't you miss teaching?"

"Maddie, I have been thinking about that a lot. I hope to still be involved with teaching somehow. I can do workshops, tutor, or volunteer. Heck, you four have practically made me famous with the book you wrote!" He laughed, breaking the tension. "I can always come back and help out Ms. Anderson from time to time…but it is time…it's just time."

With that, we picked up our coffees, took a few sips, and wondered.

We weren't going to be the only ones marching to "Pomp and Circumstance."

Rhiannon's Hand

June 6th—My Mom's Announcement

Andrew. That's his name. Mr. Andrew McQueen. Isn't it funny how teachers are really not "first name people?" I mean, it's almost like they exist as characters on TV or something—you never really know them.

But now I know Mr. Mac. He is Andrew. Not Andy. Not Drew. Just Andrew—straight up. I learned this on the night my mom told me that we were gonna go out to dinner—just me and her—a rare occurrence. I figured it was a graduation thing.

Uh, nope—not my graduation. More like hers.

"Honey, I have to ask you about something very important to me. I really want to know what you think. I haven't made up my mind about this yet," my mom began after she had taken a few sips of her red wine. "First, you know that your father and I agree that we can afford to send you to San Francisco State, and we know that is your first choice." She watched my reaction. I was looking at her intensely, sensing that something bigger was coming.

"So that is your decision to make. You can go to a closer school if you want. But if you do that, your father and I agree that you should live on campus." She took another sip of her wine.

"Okay," I said. "That's great. You think that Dad is committed for the four years, for sure?"

"Yes. Definitely." One more sip. I could see she was nervous.

"So." Long pause. "I need to ask you about Mr. Mac and our relationship…"

"Oh."

"Well, he and I have been getting very close, and it has been a little awkward, you know, with you being in his class and all that. And, you know, with your father being gone these last three years. And with the divorce and all that." Another sip. The wine was almost gone. The salad arrived. The waiter asked Mom if she cared for another glass. She hesitated—she *never* has a second glass. When she told him yes, my heart started beating faster.

"Where was I?" she said, turning her attention back to me.

"Something about you and Mr. Mac…"

"Oh, yes. Right. Well, Andrew and I—"

"Andrew?"

"Oh, sorry. Mr. Mac. No, wait. I can't call him that. Honey, his name is Andrew." She let out a sigh, determined to just say whatever it was that she was gonna say to me. "We think we want to live together—for a while. To see—to see if this thing between us really works. You will be gone soon, and Chris is gone… And I won't sell the house or anything… But we—I mean I—would move in with him and see if what we have is real."

That is when my mom's eyes could no longer contain all the tears that were making them glossy. I will never forget how at the same time, two tears chased two paths down her red cheeks, down the creases that outlined her mouth, and down to her chin before her napkin could swipe them away.

It took me less than a minute to respond. "Mom, I think that is great. Mom, I am really happy for you. Why are you crying?"

She fought to regain her composure, especially when the second glass of wine swooped in.

"Rhia, I am just so nervous. I have never been alone. I have always had you two kids. I worry that I'm afraid of being lonely. And I'm afraid of everything I am feeling for Andrew. He is just so wonderful. He's the opposite of your father—"

"*Ex*-father."

"—and we understand each other perfectly. He was hurt so badly—literally crushed—as if those towers in New York fell on him *and* his wife. He never thought he would recover. He was used to being alone. I am so afraid of being alone. I don't know if this will work out. I just know that we both want to try—and I *really* know that he cares for me."

I had not touched my salad. Neither had my mom.

"Mom, do you love him?"

She lowered her head and nodded. I know her. She had reached the point of not being able to talk any more. So she picked up her salad fork and took the tiniest bite imaginable.

Now I was the one with the tears racing down my cheeks.

Boy, could I have used a glass of red wine, too.

Madison's Hand

June 10th—The Last Day of Classes

The school year is just flying by. We had a senior breakfast this morning, and we got our yearbooks. I promised Mr. Buscotti that I would come by his freshman class this afternoon to help him record some grades and take care of all the little things he needed to do.

The word was out on his retirement, and he was very casual about it. Some kids were shocked. Some teachers were, too. People kept coming by to wish him well. He was kinda flustered with so much to do. How do you wrap up 33 years of teaching?

Yeah.

I know he particularly loved his "little freshman class"—the one Jasmine was in before the transplant had moved her from hospital to hospital. Right now, she is being transported to a local hospital for recovery. I had visited her twice, and I know Mr. B had gone to see her, too.

I think teachers like Mr. B know that they need to be fair and treat everyone with respect, but it is impossible for some students to not get under their skin—good or bad. Jasmine was so important to Mr. B because, I guess, he could not face her passing away and then leaving teaching. She just had a special place in his heart.

He gave me the nicest card when I walked in, thanking me for being his "secretary and intern." He also told me that what I did for Jasmine was the mark of a "mature, loving soul." I will always cherish that card. Always.

Yeah.

Mr. B had finished giving the kids a test and was wrapping up with a story called "The Point." He said it was an allegory about individualism. It was based on an album recorded many years ago by Harry Nilsson. He told the kids, "It is the story of Oblio, a boy born in the land of Point, where everything and everyone has a point—even the people, who have a point on the top of their heads. All of them except Oblio, who is born round-headed," he told the class.

Well, by the end of the story, the class—and Oblio—discovered that nobody is "pointless" and that Oblio's difference is his "point." He learns that being unique is what makes each of us special.

When Mr. B finished, the class applauded. He tipped his cap.

He told the kids that they could sign yearbooks for the next 15 minutes or so. At that moment, I realized that it was the last lecture of his career.

But it wasn't over.

In the first row of seats, a petite Asian girl named Jessica stood up, holding a big, handmade card. Just as she was about to say something, I saw Nina, the girl who knew who the four Beatles were, take out her iPod and some music started playing, which I faintly recognized.

Jessica said, "Mr. Buscotti, we aren't done yet."

He replied smartly, "Well, I am." Still with a smile on his face.

Jessica handed him the card; in big, bold letters, it read, "OH, CAPTAIN, MY CAPTAIN!"

That's when it started. One by one, each of Mr. B's freshmen got up on top of their desk and said, "Oh, Captain, my Captain." That's when I realized that the music was the theme song to *Dead Poets Society*.

My eyes darted over to Mr. B. He got it instantly. His face crumbled; the illusion that he could just not let all this affect him had imploded (Mickey's word). He simply could not look up as he tipped the brim of his cap down so that the kids could not fully see his face. Tears were streaming down. He was in anguish, trying to keep his emotions in check, knowing that these 14-year-olds had just paid him the highest compliment that students could ever pay a teacher.

I looked up at the faces of the kids standing atop their desks; they were so proud of themselves. One of them held a picture of Jasmine, whose desk was the only empty one in the room. I then noticed that Mr. Jim Reifeiss had slipped into the room, wearing a suit; he was obviously dropping by from work. I recalled that he was the speaker on 9.11 who had told us about the fires that had destroyed so many homes in our city. But more importantly, I remembered that he was part of one of the first classes that Mr. B had ever taught. His face told me all I needed to know: *I just want to be here on the last day of Mr. B's career.*

It took a while for Mr. B to force out a "Thank you all—very much." His head was still tilted down. His students were asking him to sign their yearbooks.

He smiled and said something like, "As long as you don't mind if I get all these teardrops on them..."

They didn't mind.

And they stayed for what seemed like eons, waiting patiently in line for his signature. Outside, the bell had rung and school was over, and kids were running around screaming that they were free from school for the summer. But not these kids in this room with this teacher.

They just didn't want to leave.

And neither did I.

I was the last to say goodbye to Mr. B. We couldn't even make eye contact before we hugged each other. It was the most special moment I have ever had with Mr. Buscotti. He is the reason that I will become a teacher. I can only hope to one day have his magic.

I knew *my* "point."

Pari's Hand

June 11th—Graduation Day

To say I was nervous would be an understatement of monumental proportions. Petrified was more like it. I had practiced my speech a gazillion times, including earlier today, when Ms. LaFleur had listened patiently to it. She gave me lots of good advice—the most important: "Smile, breathe, and know that all 532 graduates are pulling for you."

Merci, Madame.

So I walked to the podium and looked out over the sea of smiling faces wrapped in red graduation gowns. I took a deep breath, relaxed my shoulders, and began my last high school "assignment."

Class of 2009—we made it! [Cheers from the students, sighs of relief from the parents.]

I am honored to speak to you and for you today. I hope that what I have to say captures what we all feel.

Hope.

In my bedroom, there is a poster of President Barack Obama. Beneath his picture, there is only one word: HOPE. The word comes from the title of his book and the theme of my speech: The Audacity of Hope.

I believe that we all need a sense of optimism right now. My classmates and I are flooded with messages that are so negative: we'll never have what our parents have; college is too expensive; we'll struggle to get good jobs. Even when we were little, we were told to never trust strangers because the world is a dangerous place.

But if there is one thing I know for sure, it is this: you can't find your North Star if your eyes are closed, if your mind is made up, and if all you can focus on is darkness.

So I say to my fellow classmates: let there be light.

I hold a candle to the world, and "I Hope"...and here is what I hope for:

I hope that the older generations believe in us.

I hope we continue to believe in ourselves.

I hope "my g-g-generation" learns from the mistakes of the past.

I hope we learn new languages.

Learn forgiveness.

Learn compassion.

Learn dedication.

And learn determination.

I hope we understand the difference between what we want and what we need.

I hope we don't let our fear get in the way.

I hope we "gather ye rosebuds while ye may."

I hope we give back what we take.

Give much to those in need.

Give as often as we can.

And give love...because we must.

I hope we can laugh at ourselves.

I hope we dream big and never be afraid to "go for it" when the opportunity arises.

But most importantly,

I hope we fall in love.

Because our journey was not meant to be traveled alone.

I have been a dancer for much of my eighteen years. And in dance, you learn a great many things: balance, posture, timing, teamwork, focus. But the heart of dance is what I want to leave you with today.

Our heroes in school have been our teachers. They have pushed us to do what we couldn't or wouldn't do. Each of us knows at least one teacher who made a difference in our lives. They inspired us to read or write or calculate or demonstrate or punctuate or postulate or articulate—and ultimately, to create. This was the dance we learned from them. They were fearless when we were fearful. They pushed us out there on the dance floor and said, "Listen to the music; let go of your fear; don't worry about making a mistake; you can do it."

Our teachers embodied the audacity of hope—for us.

And so I say to you, the class of 2009—

"I Hope You Dance."
I sincerely hope you dance.

Congratulations and bon voyage!

And the next thing I knew, names were being read, caps were being tossed in the air, and pure joy was filling the stadium. Mickey was the first to reach me, and all I remember him saying was, "Pari, that was the most awesome speech I have ever heard! Did you even realize that we were all standing—*all* of us?"

I nodded. I was in another world. I knew that my senior classmates had stood up to applaud, but I found it hard to look up. I was just overwhelmed. It was so emotional. I didn't want to cry and have my mascara run. I don't know if I will ever forget that moment. Ever.

Maddie and Rhia ran to me next, and the four of us hugged each other. Then pictures were taken—kids were laughing; groups were hugging; parents were posing proudly with their arms around us.

And *whoosh,* the time flew by.

Finally, I saw Daniel. I got a lump in my throat. Our embrace only ended when my father touched me and said, "Pari, let me take a picture of you two."

I know that picture will be on my wall in my dorm room at Berkeley…

…and in my heart forever.

The Afterword

Mickey's Hand

June 12th—Mr. Buscotti's Room

We were up all night. Grad Night was in the gym, and the parents who organized and worked on the whole event threw us a party that was unbelievable. We danced, signed yearbooks, and played card games (like in Vegas). Simply put, it was awesome.

At 6:00 this morning, the administration let us out of the gym, and the six of us, including Daniel and Roberto, went to breakfast. We were exhausted but still on an adrenaline high. Food helped perk us up. Before we went home to crash, I told everyone that I was heading back to school to see Mr. Buscotti. I had something to tell him.

Just as I was about to drive away from Denny's, the three girls walked up to my car window.

Rhia said, "We are coming too, okay?"

Of course it was.

It was 7:30 AM when we got to Mr. B's classroom. He was sitting at his desk, reading a letter. He had taken some of his room apart; some albums were down off the walls—and some photos and posters, too. The letters and memorabilia were still up. When we came in, he immediately jumped up, put the letter down, and greeted us. He praised Pari's speech, telling her it was the finest one he had heard in a long while, and he quickly hugged each of us. We asked if there was anything we could do to help.

"Are you crazy?" he said. "You all must be exhausted! How was Grad Night?"

We told him all about it. He smiled the whole time. Then he said, "Well, you all deserved it."

I finally admitted my reason for coming to his classroom. "We came here to help you, Mr. B—and to take one last look at *your* Metaphor Café before it closes." I looked toward the sign that we had given him a year ago; it was from the original Metaphor Café, and it was still hanging near his door. Back then, I had no idea that it would only be one year until Mr. Buscotti would close up shop, too.

Mr. B smiled. "Oh. Well, you guys, that sign is a keeper."

We nodded.

"Rhia, I want you to know that I got a letter—I just read it for the second time—from a friend of yours: my student Leann."

Rhia looked surprised.

"You know, you saved her life, Rhia. She told me in her letter what you did for her that night. And then she told me that my class changed her, too." Mr. B stopped to see the affect this had on Rhia, who was astonished. "I say you saved her life because she told me in her letter that she was going to commit suicide soon. But what you did for her *that night*—and when you later encouraged her to get help—that made a huge difference."

He held the letter out to Rhia. She began reading it. We all were quiet.

Then Rhia said, "You're being very kind, Mr. B, but she writes here that 'you and your class made a huge difference.' She writes, 'You were (and still are) so encouraging, and you inspired me to think that maybe I was good enough or smart enough—and that I could follow my North Star.'"

Mr. B looked at Rhia. "Yes, well, if you hadn't acted the way you did *when* you did, I wouldn't have had the chance to reach her."

It was quiet for a minute. Then Maddie, ever the taskmaster, looked around the room and said, "Mr. B, this room is a hot mess. We gotta start helping out, or you'll be here for a week, trying to clean up."

"Well, thanks, guys, but I am sure you are wiped out..."

"Forget it, Mr. B." Maddie was already taking stuff off the walls. "You've got us for at least a few hours, so put us to work!"

Mr. B smiled. "Okay. Mickey, you are tall enough to reach the albums up there—along the top of the wall. Let's take them down. Oh, and if you guys want any, please take them. I know you want the *Born to Run* album, Mickey," he said with a laugh.

Rhia and Pari went over to all the letters and pictures on the wall. Mr. B kept these to remind him of the fact that he had made at least a small difference in his students' lives—and that they had made a huge difference in his. A letter from each of us was tacked to the wall, and there were senior pictures of Pari and Rhia. There was also a picture of Maddie and I at last year's Prom. Man, we looked so young back then!

Pari turned to Mr. B and said, "Mr. B, these letters are amazing! I don't think I've ever noticed how far they go back. This one's from 15 years ago! Just look at all these kids! I'm sure you want to save them. Maybe you could even write a book about all of these students—and about how you made a difference in their lives."

Mr. Buscotti was staring at a picture on his desk of his wife Deborah. He looked up and said, "I don't have to. You four have already written it."

One time, Maddie wrote that she wished to find her *To Sir, With Love*. Well, she got her wish...we all did.

Mr. Buscotti would be in his classroom for days, sifting through the memories that he had created for us and for the generations that had come before.

Acknowledgements and the Backstory of the *Metaphor Café*

Samia Salem, an English teacher at Southwest High School in El Centro, California, wrote me a letter after she read my first novel, *Meetings at the Metaphor Café*. She wrote, "Please tell me that the parts of your novel that refer to the lessons of Mr. Buscotti are true. If not, you will break my heart." I told Ms. Salem that Mr. Buscotti's lessons were based on my own classroom lessons, which spanned 32 years, and that I would be happy to recreate them at her school and introduce her students to *Meetings at the Metaphor Café*. With the support of Southwest High School's administration, I found myself speaking to a wonderful group of 800 students. That was "the beginning of the beautiful relationship" that I have had with the teachers and students who have "patronized" the *Metaphor Café* since its publication in 2009.

The most rewarding aspect of writing *Meetings at the Metaphor Café* and its sequel, *Midnight Comes to the Metaphor Café*, is that I have been allowed to remain a teacher and, at the same time, live every English teacher's dream—to become an author. To all the teachers who have shown faith in me by opening up their classrooms and allowing me to reach the minds of the many, many teenagers whom they have already inspired, I cannot thank you enough. Let me take a minute to thank the following teachers, who were, as they say, the early adopters of *Meetings at the Metaphor Café*: Robin Blalock and Monique Lampshire-Tamayoshi at Mt. Carmel High School in San Diego, California; Kristen Will at Tierra del Sol Middle School in Lakeside, California; and Faye Visconti and her wonderful English Department at Los Osos High School in Rancho Cucamonga, California. I must also thank my first editor, Kathy McWilliams, and my two teaching partners, Christiana Jenny and Karen Harkins-Slocomb.

As for the sequel, *Midnight Comes to the Metaphor Café* was brilliantly edited by Christa Tiernan, who sensed early on that encouraging me was part of her job description. She kept me in touch with the Millennial Generation, and it was such a joy to work with her. She is currently teaching at the University of Wisconsin-Madison, and her knowledge of English literature surpasses mine by leaps and bounds.

When writing *Midnight Comes to the Metaphor Café,* I accepted the advice of many former students and teaching colleagues who made sure, as Anderson Cooper often says, that I was "keeping it real." Asal Mirzahossein, a wonderful young English teacher, and Shayon Said, one of my finest former students, were invaluable to me in understanding the people and culture of Iran. Dr. Linda Englund made sure that I captured the depth of the tragedy that befalls Ophelia in Shakespeare's *Hamlet* and Willy Loman in Arthur Miller's *Death of a Salesman.* Kris Hizal gave me insight into his own state-of-the-art lessons for his Advanced Placement Government course. Lori Brickley, the San Diego County Teacher of the Year in 1996, helped me understand the complex and often confusing issues of sexuality that teenagers face. Sandra Gonnerman, the library and media guru for San Diego County Schools, gave me a platform on which to present to a fantastic group of librarians, which included Erica Turner at Mount Carmel High School. Barbara Charlebois is my lifelong friend, and her dedication to Student Services and her insight into the hearts and minds of troubled teenagers has given me much inspiration over the years. Thank you all.

I must also credit the photography and artistry of Robert Bjorkquist, who designed the covers of both of my novels. Bob is a Renaissance man whom I have always admired. Tony Loton and his design agency in London do a remarkable job working on my manuscripts. I would be lost without his expertise. Jim Reifeiss, who appears in both novels, and David Rosenberg have contributed to the success of the *Metaphor Café* books and the 9.11 presentations that I deliver. But more importantly, they are positive role models to the young people in our community. Dave founded The Storefront, a center for homeless teenagers in San Diego, and his efforts are a tribute to his desire to help children who are alone and on the street. Dave knows how these kids feel because he was once a seventeen-year-old boy whose teacher took him in when he was homeless. I tip my cap to all three of these gentlemen.

In *Midnight Comes to the Metaphor Café*, three women who have touched my life fictionally impact my quartet of protagonists. Jasmine de Andres came as close to death as one can until a liver transplant saved her life in the last possible hour. It is challenging to capture the many facets of her personality. Suffice it to say that Jasmine never needs to be reminded that life is precious and that each day is to be celebrated. Saba, more formally known as Saba Berenji, is a wonderful singer/songwriter whom I had the pleasure of teaching oh-so-long-ago. She is an artist who follows her dreams and puts it all on the line. I commend her and am envious of her, for I do not have the talent to sing my songs as she sings hers. The character of Leann is based on a former student who experienced much of the turmoil that her fictional counterpart faces. This student's letter to me at the time of her graduation is perhaps the single most important slip of paper that a student has ever handed me.

Finally, my wife Pam and my adult children Nicholas and Anna have always kept me aligned to my own "True North." Their advice and love made both of these novels possible.

Many of my readers ask me if Maddie, Mickey, Rhia, and Pari are real. My answer is simple. They are bits and pieces of the teenagers I met during my teaching journey. My hope is that teenagers and parents as well as teachers see portions of their lives within the pages of the *Metaphor Café*.

After all, isn't that the point of a metaphor?

Songs and Notes from

Midnight Comes to the Metaphor Café

Chapter 1: An American Girl in a Persian World

- Michal Lumsden. "Lipstick Jihad: An Interview with Azadeh Moaveni." *Mother Jones magazine.*
- Kelly Hartog. "Mullahs, Mini Skirts and Carson Daly" California Literary Review. 2007
- Azadeh Moaveni. *Lipstick Jihad : A Memoir of Growing Up Iranian in America and American in Iran.* PublicAffairs Publishing. 2005.
- The 2006 film, "Nose, Iranian Style," about the prevalence of nose jobs in Iran, a world leader, per capita, with 60,000 to 70,000 operations a year.

Chapter 2: Rhiaferry

- Duffy. "Warwick Avenue" from *Rockferry.* 2008
- Duffy. "Rockferry" from *Rockferry.* 2008
- Duffy. "Stepping Stone" from *Rockferry.* 2008
- Duffy. "Mercy" from *Rockferry.* 2008
- Duffy. "Serious" from *Rockferry.* 2008
- Duffy. "I'm Scared" from *Rockferry.* 2008
- Duffy. "Distant Dreamer" from *Rockferry.* 2008

Chapter 3: "Where We Gonna Go from Here?"

- Matt Kearney. "Where We Gonna Go from Here" from *Nothing Left to Lose.* 2006

Chapter 4: Make a Wish

- "Teen Volunteens" is a Nationwide Children's Hospital Volunteen Program
- Mary Mary featuring Kierra Sheard. "God in Me" from the album *The Sound.* 2008
- The Make-A-Wish Foundation® of San Diego was chartered in 1983 has granted more than 2,700 wishes to children in San Diego and Imperial Counties. In fiscal year 2010, it granted 187 wishes. The Make-A-Wish Foundation has spread throughout the country and abroad to become the largest wish granting organization in the world, with 64 chapters and over 200,000 wishes granted to date. Wikipedia. 2011. Jasmine was a Make-A-Wish child.
- Robert Cormier's short story "Another of Mike's Girls" is in his collection *8 plus one.*

Chapter 5: Like a Hurricane

- "Maddie's letter" *Meetings at the Metaphor Café.* 2009
- The Beatles. "We Can Work It Out" released as a single in 1965.
- Daniel Patrick Moyihan. BrainyQuote.
- Bruce Springsteen and the E Street Band. Introduction to the song "War" from *Live/1975–85*
- Hurricane Gustav. Wikipedia. 2008.

Chapter 6: Our Secret Gardens

- Bruce Springsteen. "Secret Garden" from the album *Greatest Hits.* 1995.
- *Harry Potter and the Sorcerer's Stone.* 2001
- *Forrest Gump.* 1994. The film is based on the 1986 novel of by Winston Groom, who was interviewed by National Public Radio (NPR) for PBS.
- Adele. "Chasing Pavements" from the album *19.* 2008.
- CNN Report: No WMD stockpiles in Iraq. NUCLEAR WEAPONS. Saddam Hussein did not possess stockpiles of

illicit weapons at the time of the U.S. invasion in March 2003 and had not begun any program to produce them, a CIA report concludes. October 07, 2004.

Chapter 7: "What Will Your Verse Be?"

- Bruce Springsteen and the E Street Band. "Mary's Place" from *The Rising*. 2002.
- "Windows of the World." The restaurant atop the Twin Towers in NYC.
- *500 Days of Summer. 2008*
- *Dead Poets Society*. 1989.
- "Gather ye rosebuds while ye may…" from the poem "To the Virgins, to Make Much of Time" by Robert Harrick.

Chapter 8: The Lehman Brothers and the Loman Brothers

- "Lehman folds with record $613 billion debt". *Marketwatch*. 2005-09-15. Wikipedia: Retrieved 2008-09-15.
- Michael Grynbaum. "Wall St.'s Turmoil Sends Stocks Reeling". *The New York Times*. Wikipedia. Retrieved 2008-09-15.
- Andrew Ross Sorkins. "Lehman Files for Bankruptcy; Merrill Is Sold." *The New York Times*. Business Section. September 14, 2008.
- Jon Swaine. (2008-10-07). "Richard Fuld punched in face in Lehman Brothers gym". *The Daily Telegraph* (London). Wikipedia. Retrieved 2010-04-26.
- Peter Goodman. "Jobless Rate at 14-Year High After October Losses". *The New York Times*. November 7, 2008.
- Arthur Miller. *Death of a Salesman.*1949.

Chapter 9: Halloween "Magic"

- Bruce Springsteen and the E Street Band. "Radio Nowhere" from the album *Magic.*2007
- Bruce Springsteen and the E Street Band. "The Ties That Bind," from the album *The River*. 1980

- Bruce Springsteen and the E Street Band. "Lonesome Day" from the album *The Rising*. 2002
- Bruce Springsteen and the E Street Band. "Gypsy Biker" from the album *Magic*. 2007
- Bruce Springsteen and the E Street Band. "Magic" title song from the album *Magic*. 2007
- Bruce Springsteen and the E Street Band. "Reason to Believe" from the album *Nebraska*. 1982
- Bruce Springsteen and the E Street Band. "She's the One" from the album *Born to Run*. 1975
- Bruce Springsteen and the E Street Band. "Livin in the Future" from the album *Magic*. 2007
- Bruce Springsteen and the E Street Band. "The Promised Land" from the album *Darkness on the Edge of Town*. 1978
- Bruce Springsteen and the E Street Band. "Workin' on the Highway" from the album *Born in the USA*. 1984
- Bruce Springsteen and the E Street Band. "Devil's Arcade" from the album *Magic*. 2007
- Bobbie Ann Mason. *In Country*. 1985.
- Bruce Springsteen and the E Street Band. "The Rising" from the album *The Rising*. 2002
- Bruce Springsteen and the E Street Band. "Last to Die" from the album *Magic*. 2007
- Bruce Springsteen and the E Street Band. "Long Walk Home" from the album *Magic*. 2007
- Bruce Springsteen and the E Street Band. "Badlands" from the album *Darkness on the Edge of Town*. 1978
- Bruce Springsteen and the E Street Band. "Girls in their Summer Clothes" from the album *Magic*. 2007
- Bruce Springsteen and the E Street Band. "Dancing in the Dark" from the album *Born in the USA*. 1984
- Bruce Springsteen and the E Street Band. "Born to Run" from the album *Born to Run*.1975
- Bruce Springsteen. "We Shall Overcome" The Seeger Sessions. "American Land" from the *American Land Edition* of the album by the same name. 2006

Chapter 10: "Yes We Can!"

- Andrew Romano. *Newsweek.* "Now, before 240,000 supporters in Chicago's Grant Park, our new president takes his turn. Here's Barack Obama's 2008 presidential acceptance speech…" November 5, 2008
- Ernest Hemingway. "Hills like White Elephants."Short Story.
- Elton John and Bernie Taupin. "Someone Saved My Life Tonight." From the album *Captain Fantastic and the Brown Dirt Cowboy.* 1975.

Chapter 11: Saba and the Metaphor Café

- Saba. *Elbo Club.* Spinster Recordings. 2006.
- Saba. *Best Damn Thing.* Spinster Recordings. 2009.

Chapter 12: When You Coming Home?

- Sudarsan Raghavan. "Iraq's Parliament Approves Security Agreement with United States." *Washington Post* Foreign Service.Friday, November 28, 2008.
- Tim O'Brien. "Where Have You Gone, Charming Billy." Short Story.

Chapter 13: "Just Dance"

- William Shakespeare. *A Midsummer Night's Dream.* Puck says: "When in that moment (so it came to pass); Titania waked, and straightway loved an ass."
- Lady Gaga. "Just Dance" *The Fame.* 2008.
- Lady Gaga. "Poker Face" *The Fame.* 2008.

Chapter 14: "And So This Is Christmas"

- John Lennon and Yoko Ono. "Happy Xmas (War Is Over)/ Give Peace a Chance," from the album *Shaved Fish. 1975.*
- Roberto Clemente. Wikipedia.

Chapter 15: "Two Roads Diverged in a Wood"

- Robert Frost. "The Road Not Taken." 1915.
- "US Airways Flight 1549, an Airbus A320 carrying 155 people, ditches into New York City's Hudson River." CNN. January 15, 2009.
- President Barack Obama's Inaugural Speech. January 20, 2009.

Chapter 16: "To thine own self be true"

- William Shakespeare's *Hamlet.* Polonius to Laertes: "to thine own self be true." (I.iii.55 ff.)
- *12 Angry Men.* Directed by Sidney Lumet. 1957.

Chapter 17: "Gotta Be Somebody"

- Nickelback. "Gotta Be Somebody" from the album *Dark Horse.* 2009.
- "The Last, and Lasting, Legacy of Steve Jobs." *San Diego Union Tribune* Editorial. October 24, 2011. B-5. Note: Steve Jobs eventually received a liver transplant in Tennessee "where the supply/ demand ratio was in his favor"; Jobs helped back legislation that "would require Californians applying for a driver's license or ID to answer yes or no to one of the most important moral questions of our time: *Do you want to be an organ donor?"* Nearly 9 million answered yes. Jobs' lobbying efforts has helped create the first statewide *living donor* registry under the management of Donate Life California. This may have been Steve Jobs' most important and lasting invention.

Chapter 18: "Waitlist Song: (How I Get into College)"

- Genna Mathew. "Waitlist Song...(How I Get into College). My Space. 2009.
- According to *US NEWS and World Report,* U C DAVIS is one of the top rated Public Universities for its Writing Program.

Chapter 19: "Soul of the World"

- Paulo Coelho. *The Alchemist.* 1988.
- Yogi Berra. www.MLB.com

Chapter 20: "Glory Days"

- Bruce Springsteen."Glory Days." From the album *Born in the USA.* 1984.
- LMFAO. "Party Rock Anthem." From the album of the same title. 2009.
- We the Kings. "Check Yes Juliet." From the album *We the Kings.* 2009.
- Lifehouse. "You and Me." From the album *Lifehouse.* 2005.
- The Veronicas. "Untouched." From the album of the same title.2007.
- Boys Like Girls. "(Bring on the) Thunder." From the album of the same title. 2008.
- Akon. "(You're so) Beautiful." From the album *Freedom.* 2008.
- The Plain White T's. "1,2,3,4 (I Love You)." From the album *Big, Bad World.* 2008.
- Oasis. "Wonderwall." From the album *[What's the Story] Morning Glory.* 2008.
- Taylor Swift. "Love Story." From the album *Fearless.* 2008.
- Chris Brown. "With You." From the album *Exclusive.* 2007.
- Adele. "Make You Feel My Love" From the album *19.* 2008. Originally written by Bob Dylan from the album *Time Out of My Mind.* 1997.
- Bruce Springsteen."Dancing in the Dark." From the album *Born in the USA.* 1984.
- "Jasmine's Story." You Tube video. *JCATIZZLE.* Song playing is Jared Anderson. "He Loves Us" and "Come and Listen to What He Has Done." http://www.youtube.com/watch?v=F2n0vjktGQ4

Chapter 21: "Pomp and Circumstance"

- "...silver pepper of the stars" is a reference to *The Great Gatsby*.
- "...the 'Big Muddy' is a Bruce Springsteen song we learned last year.
- Harry Nilsson. *The Point.* Album . *1971*
- Lee Ann Womack. "I Hope You Dance." From the album of the same title. 2000.

Robert Pacilio was born to teach. He taught high school English for 32 years and was awarded San Diego County's "Teacher of the Year." He is a regular presenter at educational conferences, including the California Teachers Association Conferences, and in various school districts. *Midnight Comes to the Metaphor Café* is the sequel to his debut novel, *Meetings at the Metaphor Café*, which has been adopted in school districts as part of the English curriculum. Recently retired, he lives in San Diego with his wife, Pam. He enjoys visiting schools, where he reads portions of his novels with classes, answers questions, and turns classrooms into the Metaphor Café as the fictional Mr. Buscotti.

He can be reached at **robertpacilio@gmail.com**

Made in the USA
Charleston, SC
13 January 2012